DARK SECRETS

AZHANA FALLS BOOK TWO

WILLIAM J. SEYMOUR

DARK SECRETS is a work of fiction. Names, places, and incidents either are a product of the author's imagination or are used fictitiously.

A Book Furnace Publications Book

Published in English by Book Furnace Publications, York, Pennsylvania

ISBN: 978-1-943266-12-8

Cover Images: © Wisconsinart | Dreamstime.com

© Oleg Zabielin | Dreamstime.com

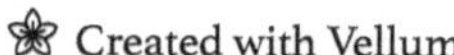 Created with Vellum

DARK SECRETS

1

———

Gun fire and smoke.

Explosions of thunder and fire laced with lightning that burns its way across the sky.

The world of chaos and survival, dark shadows and horrid deaths. The monsters continue to come, their hunger for destruction unquenchable and the holes dug in for trenches and last stands not deep enough to get the job done.

The smell of cooling rock in the air. Laced with sulfur and living poison. Spent gunpowder and drying blood coat everything. The screams of the dying and the injured. The anger of combatants locked in mortal combat is real and can be felt on the skin. Each side refuses to give up ground no matter how many bodies fall.

An explosive detonates too close. Dirt rains from the sky. Little drops of crumbled rock and pebbles sprinkle on black army uniforms filled with sweat and blood. Starched collars and creased lines fade beneath a layer of gore or are torn completely away to die as wispy pieces of fabric. Coleena rams another magazine into her rifle and fires a round across the smoke blurred field. Dried husks of dead plants. Hot sand that blurs with heat and chips of broken rocks lay scattered like confetti. What trees remain are nothing more than brittle skeletons of what they once were. Sad reminders of the world they lost and will never get back.

Bright orange blood spurts as lead tears through solid skin and the molten rock inside fountains into the air, cools, and hits the ground as brittle rock. The beast falls. All hardened muscles and razor-sharp talons. Blood made of magma cools and eyes of flame go dark. A final growl of breath and a new target takes its place.

"Incoming!" a hoarse voice yells.

Coleena and the other soldiers of the Desert Spear cover their heads and duck onto their knees as the recognizable whistling draws closer and ends with a rupture of earth and sky.

The ground quakes. Soot and super-heated ash lift into the air burning them where they stand and crawl. There isn't enough cover to shield soldiers from enemy. Pain and death find them all. There are no innocents on this field of battle.

Blood and the thick syrup of mud sticks to the inside of their mouths as they recover their senses and jump back into the fight.

"Keep pushing them back!" Lieutenant Arkens calls, his voice hoarse and broken.

The man is a machine. Broad shouldered, shaved head, and arms like tree trunks as he squeezes more rounds out his rifle. Black rivers of mud run across his arms as they flex with the recoil of the weapon, brass jingling as they pile at his feet.

Coleena does not hesitate. Back on her feet, she sights down the barrel and sends more projectiles into the bodies of the monsters now horribly too close. Glowing liquid rock flies into the air with chips that rattle as they hit the ground. Howls cry into the late afternoon hour. Growls of triumph come before the screams as more men and women lose their lives.

She can smell the burning magma. Sulfuric and bitter. The life blood pumping through the bodies of the enemy mixes with the shit left behind by the corpses of their victims. The heat of their anger cooks the perspiration across her flesh, bubbling and popping with the desert heat. Hot acid drops from their fanged teeth, sizzling across the ground as the monsters try to clear the distance.

A thunderous boom of another rocket rings her ears into a temporary silence. Dark streaks flash across the sky and the first two rows are obliterated in an inferno of earth and fire.

Shadows move in the collecting dust. Coleena squeezes the trigger and more glowing blood spills, the sound of angry demonic wailing biting at the chaotic sound of war and death.

"Desert, advance to the next trench!" Arkens orders.

The team does as it is told.

Keeping her rifle trained at the wall of smoke and shadows, Coleena watches for movement and fires with her comrades as the monsters fade in and out of her sight. Black silhouettes pass before her, disappearing from vision like ghosts. The crunch of boots over dry gravel a distant memory against the raging of the war machine keeping their enemy at bay.

A man screams. He could be ten feet away or one hundred.

The death cries are followed by the crunch of bones and the bubbling gurgles of a final breath. Coleena holds within the cloud of dust, and her knees flex with anticipation. The rifle sits solid in her grip.

She is alone.

The shadows thicken, a swirling cloud of forgetfulness and imagination. Images flash before her eyes. Men, demons, everything fights around her, but nothing approaches.

She sees long piercing claws rip into the bowels of a shadow that appears right beside her. Their guts spill on the ground, a wet sound full of heavy hopes and wasted dreams. The monster roars with a satisfactory rage born only by the pits of Hell.

Three more rounds exit the end of her rifle. The darkness fades and the monster and its victim or gone. A silent world swirls around her. In the distance she can hear the chattering pop of machine gun fire and explosions as armored T-89 tanks rake the approaching lines of Banshees and Gorgoths. But that is somewhere else. Not here. Not with her. She is alone as she moves forward. A one-woman army.

A shriek rips through the air, and she spins on her heels. Talons sharpened to dangerous points rake through the air, slicing the mist and dream state with a fine edge. The tips cut a gash through the shoulder of her uniform. Releasing the rifle with one arm, the stock locks into place beneath her shoulder, the muzzle swinging free, and she squeezes down hard on the trigger.

Red angry fire erupts from the glowing red barrel and the world is a drumming base of death as the bullets shatter the face of the Banshee less than a hand's length away. She screams words that even she cannot hear. Orange magma melts through rock hardened skin and turns to black as its head disintegrates beneath the onslaught.

Falling into a heap beside her, she has little time as the next monster jumps from the chaos and barrels into her like a drunken asshole, all hands and hot breath clawing to expose whatever skin it can find.

The weight of three men cracks the bones of her back, and she finds herself flattened to the ground. Rifle spinning away, her hand drops as she kicks and rolls. Releasing the holster to her sidearm, she returns to her knees. Four more rounds open a blossoming inferno of molten blood in the next demon's chest.

The howl is wet and hissing as the dying monster sits down hard on its ass, the dust of the cracked earth kicking into the air. The orange fires of its eyes cool into solid pebbles and roll from their sockets.

A roar shakes the world around her. The wall of mist rattles and threatens to break.

Rifle back in her hand, she moves forward. The world of gunfire and death returning in a mad rush. Shapes begin to coalesce. Men in uniforms, rifles raised and cradled as they fire into the enemy's midst, pushing forward through the orchestrated march of the dying and the desperate.

She follows suit. Weapon ready, she keeps a clear sight of the position forward. Arm steady, she takes a deep breath, the taste of poison burning her tongue and speeding the beat of her heart.

"Grenade out!" a man's voice calls, the words almost lost beneath the chatter of exploding gunpowder.

Coleena drops to one knee and the world no more than a dozen yards in front of her erupts into a shower of dark earth and smoke.

An angry growl defies the combat and they continue forward. A cut through the battlefield opens on the horizon. Reinforced dirt, hand cut and packed to mark the ground they have fought so hard to keep yet have slowly given away piece by piece.

Five feet deep, barely three feet wide. Coleena jumps in. Men and women follow all around her. Dozens of faces. Blood stained and dirty. Tired eyes and hollowed looks. All grit and determination. Fighting to the bitter end, a need for survival and a defiance born of human resilience.

"Wall up, rifles at the ready," Arkens orders.

There he is again. Stoic in his stance, his presence a solidifying rock that helps keep them all steady.

Coleena turns with the gears of the war engine, thousands of pounds of human flesh molded into a fighting edge, ready to cut both the attacker and the user.

Movement shakes the horizon. A wall of smoke and unforgiving terrain. Scrub brush and open fields ending with a mausoleum of scorched trees, the last remnants of the forest bordering the former country of Orlasara. Soil dried to salt beneath a relentless sun brightens the chocking smoke. Where there is resilient turf refusing to die away, the surrounding ground has been blown to bits beneath the concussion of bombs and clawed feet.

"Here they come!" Arkens barks.

The warning is given though none is needed with a train of monsters shaking the ground. Dirt finds a way to rattle and pebbles shake. Howling and hissing, crying and roaring, the demons rush from behind the clouded wall of dirt and smoke.

Claws rip into ground, pulling them forward with all disregard for death and loss of life as bullets cut through them like angry bees. Their blood spills, cools, and turns the ground to molten glass. Coleena screams right along with the monsters and her fellow soldiers. Her frustration, her relentless anger releasing with each ejected piece of brass as another projectile is sent into the enemies she was born to hate.

The monsters draw closer regardless of their efforts. Bodies heap upon one another, a small wall of living stone turning into a growing barricade of hardened rock. A Banshee leaps over in a single stride, its wide glowing belling a perfect target as it wobbles and screams in its high-pitched wail. Bullets send glowing yellow rock spewing in a dozen directions, the thin stone of its abdomen bursting like a water balloon, its contents spraying over the edge and into the trench line.

"Ah!" the man next to her screams.

Flesh burns and hardens as the magma cools. Coleena covers his line of fire as he drops to his knees. The fallen enemy topples to pieces less than two feet away. Three more jump the growing pile of hardening corpses. More rock explodes, the heated blood melting everything it touches. Burns peel away with ripped uniforms. The screams of the dying and injured fade as the monsters are almost on top of them.

"Keep fighting!" Coleena orders as much to herself as to the others.

The end of her rifle glows red and the smoke blocks her vision.

Nothing seems to matter. The enemy is on top of them. Aiming is of little use. Holding back the trigger and keeping the new magazines flowing is mechanical in operation. Demon bodies begin to fall into the trench beside them. Banshees give way to a mix of Gorgoths who rip into friend and foe alike. Over seven feet tall, the first bastard topples as bullets shatter its kneecap, the lower half of its legs splitting away in a spewing mess of orange rock splattering across the ground. The monster howls, bullets chipping away at its exterior as it claws its way forward, six-inch talons digging into the hard dirt and pulling it closer to its next victim.

Coleena's rifle goes empty. Reaching into her belt, the satchel flattens against her hand, and she has nothing left.

The man at her feet continues to scream. Half his face is scorched black, the blood beneath his hands running in thick rivers between his fingers. Reaching down, she tears at his belt. Two more magazines and he is dry. Securing them within her grasp, she goes to reload her weapon.

"Ah!" the scream tearing its way from her throat is unstoppable as a searing heat slices through the flesh of her back.

Rolling away from the pain, her rifle drops, and she hits the bottom of the trench beside the screaming soldier. Standing above her, a Gorgoth growls its dismay. Teeth as long as her fingers and pointed into needle like tips open and close with anticipation of the death it will soon taste. Pulling her sidearm from her belt, the recoil rips at the openings bleeding through her uniform as the bullets punch holes through the beast's head. Blood and brains splatter in sizzling piles. Bright orange blood goes dark. The demon slides forward, several hundred pounds of dead weight pulling it along.

Coleena scrambles to get out of the way, the slow decent of the enemy quickening with gravity. The crunch of solid rock crushing the fallen soldier next to her is a horrible popping noise as organs burst and bone shatters into splinters. Reaching her knees, she scrambles for her rifle. The arm of the monster lays across the barrel, the metal bent into an odd angle and the grip resting in a pool of red blood.

Holding her pistol, her last weapon, she looks up and down the trench.

Men and women stand against the edge, weapons

barking death and destruction at the approaching enemy. Banshees and Gorgoths have broken over the edges and fight those closest in hand-to-hand combat between the narrow earth walls, filling the tunnel with screams and death. Coleena goes to stand, the searing pain of her wounds burning through her back and down into the hamstrings of her legs. Another Banshee makes its way over the edge, squat legs bracing as it falls into the trench beside her.

Three bullets splatter its liquid brain against the wall, the smell of sulfur and cooling rock thick in her nose.

Another Gorgoth breaches the barrier and falls down into their newly claimed territory a few dozen feet further down the trench. Men jump on top of it from both sides. Talons rip through human flesh and bullets splatter heated gore everywhere as enemy and ally begin their quick decent into madness. No one lets out a shout as the grenade is dropped at their feet. The eruption shakes the ground. Rock and smoke races its way toward her like a freight train. Coleena drops to her knees, her arm covering her face and neck.

"Retreat!" a voice screams the order.

This time it is not Lt. Arkens. She looks and she cannot find him. The fighting is chaotic. All lines are broken and the masses of bodies piling up is uncountable. Those still capable begin to throw themselves over the dirt wall in the direction that they had just fought to claim.

Just like that, their first moment of victory is lost and already forgotten. Unable to allow herself to hesitate, Coleena climbs out of the trench, her back to the wall of enemies being held down by suppressive fire. Unwilling to let them leave, a Gorgoth leaps the trench and slams into two men less than ten feet to her left. All three go down in a heap, the screams of the men drowning beneath the roar of the monster. Veering toward them, she keeps her pistol at the ready, letting the monster climb itself up from the pile.

A bullet tears through the back of its shoulder, the slight victory forcing the beast to pull itself away from its victims. Ignoring the threat, she is unable to stop the creature as it slams its gigantic fist into the side of the man's head lying beside him. Bone cracks open and blood splatters as Coleena fires more into the monster. Dirt kicks up around her feet as bullets from those covering their retreat try to take the Gorgoth out. Roaring, the demon lifts itself to its clawed feet, each toe digging into the ground and the body of the second man dangles from its outstretched arm.

Coleena stops running and her weapon goes empty. Red fires glow brighter than the sun beneath its darkened brows of stone and a small grin pulls at its stone lips as it looks down at her. The moment passes and bullets from the mounted machine guns tear through the rock skin of the monster and the flesh of soldier alike as she falls to the side, blood and molten rock spraying its way all over her. Ignoring the pain and the burning, she crawls away as the corpse of the monster and its victim fall into a disgusting mangled mass beside her. Dust and burning smoke obscure her vision, but she forces herself to crawl, head down and her own fingers digging into the dirt. With each agonizing movement, she forces herself forward, not in the direction of victory, but back to where they had started.

Another battle. Another loss. Bullets fired and lives spent. A war without ending and the possibility of defeat without a single victory.

2

———

"Now you understand what I'm telling you, don't you, Captain?" the doctor asks.

His voice is steady, a monologue of emotionless turmoil as he lays down the sentence. Coleena does not want to answer. Put a few CCs of morphine in her veins and let the darkness take her. The fire in her belly tells her to rip his guts out and spill them across the tile floor. Maybe he'd like to see how he would react if he was stuck trying to put his own life back together instead of ruining everyone else's.

"Of course. Torn muscles and sliced tendons. Limited movement across my chest and shoulders, and immediate dismissal from active duty. A death sentence if I haven't heard one before. Do I have it all, Doctor?" she replies.

A thin pencil mark of an eyebrow below a bald head lifts and the medicine man makes another check mark on his chart. If she didn't know better, she would guess he was angry because she got everything correct.

"It could be a lot worse, Captain. These injuries won't hamper much of your life since you are a middle-aged woman. Not everything in life is killing monsters, you know. Maybe now you could find a hobby once you're back in the real world. There is plenty that can be done around the kitchen or house once you've got all this adrenaline junkie stuff out of your system," he says while sliding the clipboard against the frame at the end of the bed.

"Go fuck yourself, Doc. Don't you have someone else's dreams to destroy?"

He shakes his head with a tsk-tsk sound and pulls his white doctor's coat tighter around his midsection. With a click of his heels he heads out the door. In burning frustration, Coleena buries her face into her pillow, the exertion already almost too much for the healing wounds across half her body.

The echoes of moans and the cries of the dying surround her no matter how much she tries to block them out. Shadows draw long patterns across the wall of her room, dark curtains pulled tight to block the windows and keep the sun away from those unaware that the end has reached them and there will be no tomorrow.

What few unrelenting bright rays of light are able to cut through enter the room like bullets seeking targets. In the end they are more like moving spotlights against the sterile white walls and shiny floor scrubbed free of blood and shit. The smell of alcohol, anti-septic, and lingering disease mingle like lovers and the hum of death-denying electronics play chorus to the injured and those who sit by their side. Coleena bites on her lower lip, the slightest taste of blood warming her tongue as she drives her chin into the pillow even more. Even this cheap comfort smells like plastic, a reminder of what will one day be zipped closed over her cold body. White polyester and impossible to get anymore uncomfortable, she cannot think of any place she would rather not be than here. Any movement of her body sends fire racing down her spine, the flesh within her freshly stitched wounds pinching and threatening to pull apart and bleed her out on the floor.

Warm, salty tears burn the edges of her eyes, and she fights back their onslaught and relentless need to roll down her cheeks. Loose strands of dirty blond hair tickle the edge of her nose and no amount of blowing moves them enough to relieve the annoyance. Even lifting her feet into the air, bending at the knees as she lies on her stomach, face down and useless, is a monumental effort. Something that she feels should be celebrated, but instead it is nothing more than the obvious sign everything is destroyed, and her life will never be the same. The first tears of this hour, relatives of those already drawn since she woke up from surgery, begin to fall. She can no longer fight them, the war of her own emotions lost like the battle that rages miles to the west, the familiar sound of bombs mixing with the pops of gunfire echoing into the afternoon light of her already fading memories.

Why me?

Why now?

The questions do not stop. They will never let her forget. Long after the wounds heal and the scars begin to fade, she'll remember where her last battle was fought. No amount of consideration will let her think differently. She is meant for this war. Her sole purpose is to fight the dragon and its minions, but here she lays. Crippled from the fighting, the vision of the last demons she will ever kill dies as she struggles to remember the monsters laying on the corpse littered ground of a field she'll probably never see again. Taking a deep breath, she buries her face into the scratchy surface of the pillowcase. Maybe if she keeps her face here long enough, she can end it all.

Is it possible to smother yourself?

She can still feel the rock grinding beneath her boots and hear the howls of the monsters that died before the onslaught of her weapons. Taking her own life shouldn't be that hard.

Press her face a little harder.

Hold her breath a little longer.

Slowly, she lets the warm, stale air escape her lungs. The burning of the wounds across her back spreads its way over her bruised sides and the organs of her gut pinch with pain. Yes, this is it. If she holds on long enough, they'll never catch her in time. She won't have to live with this suffering or embarrassment any longer. Her fingers dig into the edges of the bed, broken nails cut into the edge of the shitty mattress and it's two inches of eggshell torture.

"Captain Armigera?" a man's voice asks, low and gravely. "Coleena, are you OK?"

"Gah!!" Coleena gasps and pulls her face from the pillow, a momentous effort. "Who's there?"

Fierce, nausea creating pain rips through her body and the world spins. A dark figure stands over her, all shadow and bulk as it dominates the dim light filling the spaces around the confines of her new hell.

"Someone looking to see if his best soldier is going to find a way to get her lazy ass off this gurney and back on the killing field where she belongs," the man answers.

Major Greissler. A bear of a man if she was ever to imagine one. Skin so dark he makes the shadows look pale and the darker hair protruding from the opening of his collar speaks loudly of the fur coat waiting to burst its way out if it's ever given a chance. He smiles down at her, white teeth gleaming and the crisscrossing pale scares that x over his left cheek flexing as the look of recognition crosses her face.

"Forgive me, sir," Coleena answers before trying to shift onto her side. The pain and pinching of her gut forces her to regret even the silent thought that let her think she could even try. "I think my luck has finally run out. You're going to have to do without me out there. My ticket has been punched. I've killed my last demon."

She tries to fight back the tears setting fire to the edges of her eyes, but the look on his face drags them out faster than if he wrapped a rope around her waist and pulled her through the hospital with a transport truck. Lips pulled tight, his eyes shine with a glare that seers through her mind, telling of the failure her life has become.

"Not exactly the words I would have ever thought I'd hear coming from your stubborn lips," the Major says as he pulls up a chair from near the wall, the metal legs cutting a piercing noise through the room. Men and woman groan in protest from outside of her little dungeon, the sound slicing through them as easily as it makes her want to rip her own ears off. None of them can do any more than she can, and the protests die off quickly. "For the longest time I thought there wasn't a thing in this world that could kill the fight in you. But maybe even I'm a little stubborn in all of this. You're human just like the rest of us."

"Are you sure you didn't take a shot of some of my missing meds, Major?" she asks, fighting the rage of her torn muscles to wipe away the tears spreading their way across her face. "Sometimes I did feel like a machine. Out among the others and watching those monsters bleed all over the ground, of course. I could have done it for days without stopping. You know that?"

His grim visage turns up a few degrees as he settles into the chair, his bulk creaking the four-legged base not meant for a man his size.

"You've survived more than anyone I can imagine. Years on the front line, Captain. Even I was carried away before a single one of these monsters could lay a claw on you."

He runs a finger across the puckered flesh of his face.

"Like I said, Major. My luck finally ran out. The ticket that sends me home is finally punched. Size me up for my pine box now and let's get this over with."

This time the man chuckles something from deep within. One of those big belly roll laughs that has him rocking his seat backward and the protests from the peanut gallery in the connecting hall are loud and persistent. He ignores all of them.

"There it is. That stubborn streak of yours. What do you think, the only reason you breathe is to fight the dragon? No consideration that there is possibly anything else you can do in a world that hasn't fallen off the cliff yet?"

Coleena groans and buries her face in her pillow, a small growl escaping as she rubs her head back and forth before looking back up, his bright eyes of hazel brown burrowing deep into her.

"Now you sound like that asshole doctor who reminded me there is more to life for a middle-aged woman like myself. Let me be honest with you, Major. Nothing in this world is worth more to me than fighting the dragon. It is the single most devastating thing this world has ever seen, and no one will be safe until it is dead. A life not spent fighting for that single cause is a life not worth living. If you are here to convince me otherwise, Major, then I'd ask you to do me the professional favor of going back to the doctors and tell them you've done your best. There is nothing here for them to save, my soldiering days are over, and with it, my life."

Silently, Greissler waits, his arms, all cords of rippling muscle, crossed over his chest. Refusing to look at him, Coleena buries her chin back into her pillow and stares at the wall. She can finish this final kill when he finally leaves. One final act of desperation from a washed-up soldier. Taking a deep breath, the sob she has been holding sends wracking pain through her body and her reality crashes down around her.

"I really would have expected different from you," he says, his voice low and with an uncustomary tone of caring.

"Is there anything else, Major?" Coleena asks impatiently when she can't stand the waiting anymore. "I have more than enough time ahead of me to think of everything that I could still be doing if this hadn't happened."

She looks over at him, his eyes narrowed, and the wide chin of his face pinched between thumb and index finger.

"Yes, Captain. There is something else," he says slapping his bear paws for hands against his knees. "When I first received this request by General Whitaker, I passed it off as nonsense for a unit such as ours. No way was I going to lose any of my best soldiers for such an order. Easier to let the request fall off as missing in the heat of combat than to restructure a battle plan that already wavered on the edge of a knife, but now I'm not so sure."

"What request? Don't tell me she is asking for something that I possibly could do. If she's getting into the whole 'PR' thing and hiring washed-out has-beens like myself to drum up community support, you can count me out," Coleena says, the sarcasm deep and sharp in her voice.

"PR? General Whitaker doesn't do 'PR'. You know that as well as I do. But this is different. Of course, it would be nothing a woman of your skills would be interested in. It doesn't involve killing dragon spawn, or probably even risking your life, so I'm not even really sure why I bring it up. Let alone why I'm even here."

"Honestly, Major, I think you are full of shit. Just get on with it. We both can agree you are wasting your time, but if I have to listen to this charity to get you out of here, I will. In case you already forgot, I want nothing to do with anything that doesn't involve our war here where the fighting really matters. There isn't a single thing in this world I'd rather do than be here until we either win or you finally carry me away in a body bag."

With a sigh, Coleena goes to turn away again but the slightest catch of a grin on his face keeps her from turning.

"How about something that possibly could save thousands? A chance to make something of yourself other than another name on the list of those smothered with hospital pillows?"

Turning away from him, the wet spots marking the evidence are thick and have her eye-prints all over them.

Bastard.

Coleena can feel the heat burning at her cheeks. There should be no shame in this. One final act that she can control. Her life determined by her choices, not the damn dragon and his demons. Sticky salt dries on her skin. She balls her hands into fists and grits her teeth in defiance.

"You're talking to the wrong person, Major. I'll be lucky if it doesn't take years for me to gain partial movement back, let alone be able to take on anything that could save thousands of people. I appreciate your generosity. No one knows what we've been through in this war more than you and me, but I could do without the condescension. I'm out of the fight now, sir. Find someone who can actually complete whatever it is you are asking for. I'm not a charity case."

With a deep sigh she goes back to staring at the wall. Too much pain looking at the man she has fought beside for so long in the face.

"That's the thing, Captain. I've already thought about this, long and hard. I can't give you the order, in your state the General herself would be lucky to force you into this, but against my better judgment, I'm offering you this chance. One last mission. Thousands of lives on the line. Give us one last fight. Show the dragon that no matter how many times you fall, it will never defeat you. Let me know in the morning what your decision is. If you still have fight buried in you somewhere, I'll give you all the details you need. If what you say is true and laying here in this hospital bed is really all there is left, then I salute you, Captain. It's been a good fight and I hate to see it end like this."

Greissler slides the chair out of the way as he raises himself back to his full height. Shadows fill in across his chiseled face and the bright glow of his eyes take in the full breadth of her before he turns to leave.

"I thought you said this wouldn't be fighting the dragon," Coleena says.

The Major doesn't turn but there is a small laughter hidden in his words. "You never know, Captain. There are still many things that can surprise us all, even a battle-hardened woman like yourself."

He clears the room in fewer steps than should be allowed, his stride long and confident.

"I doubt that, sir. Not anymore," she calls after him.

He waves with the back of his hand.

"Talk to you in the morning, Captain. Get some rest."

Coleena drops her face back into the pillow. A mission?

Flexing the muscles between her shoulders, the pain from the injury drives into her mind like a red-hot needle skewering her brain. Does she really have an option? The smell of the salt stained cloth is warm and too familiar as it fills the empty spaces within her. Yes, she has an option. Even if this isn't fighting the dragon, doing something that could save thousands would be better than this. She grits her teeth and pushes against the pain.

This fight isn't over yet.

3

———

The sun rises to the east. Angry and red. Hot, sticky, and pissed off as the morning cuts the night short and stiffens the work of those already too weary from a lack of sleep and even fewer supplies.

The air in Meclav has a stench to it. A lingering smell of refuse and burned oil. Dark. Festering. As if the gears of war are stuck here, grinding and shaking as the engine's pistons pump red-hot and are on the verge of seizing. The cranks of everyday life bend and everything is unwilling to give to the reality of joints welded shut into unchangeable formations.

Coleena lets her head rest against the truck's door frame. No plastic or cloth. All cold and unforgiving metal. Her back aches. Three months and the pain has lessened to a dull ache. At least the stitches are long gone, just like the physical therapy she left a hundred miles in the dust. Rolling her shoulders into a better position does little more than pull the tight strings of muscle into a stretch that creates unwanted groans as everything stiffens. She has more movement than she ever thought would return. In her mind she is one hundred percent. To those damn doctors she will never get past sixty.

What the fuck do they know?

Even at that she is better than the green horns choking the front lines. Stupid bureaucratic bullshit.

She sighs. They could have at least shipped her in something more comfortable than this. A troop transport truck. Stomach churning shit green and empty of any soldiers other than her. If she could still call herself a soldier. Her paycheck still says so, but the fact that they are driving in the wrong direction reveals the true story. The bumps of the beaten road jar her body to the point where it feels like a broken mess ready to spill to the floor of the wide cabin. Minimally outfitted with only cold leather seats and a silent driver, she can feel the sense of urgency in their request for her assistance like she can the gratitude for her years of service.

Her eyes slip shut and her mind drifts, exhaustion taking over without her consent. The last time she laid her eyes on the dragon flashes across her vision. Wings as wide as several city blocks. Fire erupting, consuming everything it touches and the screams of those dying etching their echoes into her mind. A flare of anger sends a pulse through her veins that burns like hot coals. Her fists squeeze tight and for a moment all thought of rest turns to ash and blows out with the wind running through her hair. Scarred fists of fury grip the air above her knees. The moisture in her throat whisks away leaving pure unrelenting hatred for the beast who burned everything she ever knew.

Her whole world, gone like it was nothing but a mound of ants fighting a forest fire. No one ever had a chance. Not a single thing worked against the magic and the monsters.

The more they killed; the more would spawn. An endless stream of hydras multiplying with every death.

Then they ran. Humans found they could do one thing correct and that was to hide. Shelter behind their walls, so far away from the dragon that they were of little consequence.

A bitter taste fills her mouth, and she spits it out the open window. Cold and wet, it doesn't make it far before leaving a sticky streak across the side of her face. She wipes it away before setting her head back against the emotionless headrest that thinks little of her comfort. Taking a deep breath, she lets it settle as she holds it tight.

The anger eventually cools, and she feels hollow on the inside. Not much different from the dark shells of people's lives passing by as the truck continues into the heart of Meclav. Abandoned buildings and broken houses line the streets. Windows boarded with peeling wood, trash blowing in streets in dire need of repair, and everything bleached a sandy color beneath the scorching summer sun.

Squinting, she wipes away at the sweat collecting at the line of her blond hair. It's still first light and the heat is already here. The air stuffy and thick enough to choke out a grown man.

The driver sitting beside her is little company. Hasn't said more than a dozen words since he picked her up in Starlensburg. Older. Wiser. The gray hair lining the edges of his dark ball cap tell as much as the deep lines cutting canyons around his bloodshot eyes. Sparkling an unnatural green against his sun leather skin, the emeralds do not alter from their forward directive. The roll of his belly bounces slightly as the front tires dig deep into a pothole the size of a full-grown dog.

"So, how long have you been in the army?" she asks.

Probably her fifth attempt to make this whole procession seem less like a funeral and more like a courtesy call.

The man takes a deep breath and looks at the mirrors on each side. Watching the dust kick up behind them, a few squads of jogging soldiers pass, and he tightens his grip on the wheel. As before, their conversation dies before it ever begins.

Coleena settles deeper into her seat, fingers tapping on the open windowsill. The skyline of the city fading from a bright red to harsher yellow as the morning continues its march across the day and the sizzling of her skin begins its new assault.

"Not much of a speaker, I guess. Wouldn't blame you. Really not much to talk about. I heard the General can be a real bitch. More like a cunt if the word from the men on the line are correct," she says.

Pulling down the flap above the front window, Coleena uses the provided mirror to pick at a piece of her last ration stuck between her teeth. Yellowing and honestly a bit sensitive to anything cold or warm, the hardened cheese between them still tastes sour as it breaks loose. She reminds herself to do a good flossing the next few days of leave she is given. Sniffing at her shirt, a good bath is also needed. Even if it costs her a month worth of water rations.

Dry soap and desert filtered water can only go so far. She gives the driver a quick glance one more time and if he has noticed how she smells, he is keeping it locked away like he is everything else.

Approaching the center of the city produces a lot less fanfare than even she remembers. Here, near the center of the city, life returns to normal. Buildings show signs of life. Open windows, where clothes are hung over metal railing to dry, sport boxes where potted plants struggle to survive and give this monochrome world some much-needed color. Families of the soldiers stationed here she guesses. A level of comfort for the men and women before they find themselves sent to the front lines to die. The inevitability is written on the faces of everyone she passes. Somewhere deep inside of her she can already feel the jealousy sinking its teeth in. The stiffness in her neck a quick reminder that no matter what she does, there is no going back.

A guard post of a single windowed shack and layers of sandbags manned by two Spec-Ops with their standard double slashes of red on black waits as the truck slows to a halt. All bravado and no bite if anyone ever bothered to ask her. Their ranks must be stretched as thin as everyone else if these men's lazy eyes and even more tired looking dogs are any indication.

"Papers?" one of the guards asks.

Tall, with bolder like shoulders. His uniform barely fits, and the rolled-up sleeves means he hasn't been checked on by upper command in far too long. His eyes trace the interior of the truck as the driver pulls the documents from beneath his visor. The other, a much slimmer recruit with barely a whisker on his chin, leads his shepherd around the back, its wet nose barely spending a few moments at any point before finding itself back around to the front.

Coleena lets an arm drop out the window, a finger length of dried beef held between finger and thumb. The closest dog spares a quick glance and then lays back down at the guard's feet.

Yeah, she doesn't enjoy them anymore either.

The guards wave them through with no solute and little more than the back of their hands. Coleena watches as they fade into the distance of the side view mirror. Neither man nor dog look back. They lean against the booth of the checkpoint, dust kicking up around them, and as quickly as they appeared, they are gone into memory.

A bit more subdued than when their battalion pushed out years ago. To a parade of hundreds, if not thousands, they were going to bring the fight to the dragon. A new era for mankind when they finally stopped hiding behind their walls, living from day to day keeping the monsters at bay.

No, they were going to show them all that it was time to take back what belonged to them. Reclaim what was taken. That was then.

Her ride squeals to a stop, the brakes grinding with rust and grainy sand. The front of a wide slowly rising set of concrete steps remains empty and cracking beneath the inch of dust layering them. Four sets of twelve. The memory of her counting every single one the last time she was here vivid in her mind. Forty-eight and then the pillars. A monolith of historic ingenuity built into a dome five stories tall. Made of stone, the story says this building has been in use for more than six hundred years. Looking at the small breaks in the rock running from entry to curved roof, like spiderwebs stretching their way across the stone, a quick feeling of stepping into the past grips her gut. A past that should have never let them go.

Coleena can't imagine anything remaining from a world lost to them all. Entire cities were destroyed in the days following the attacks twenty-five years ago. But somehow this relic remains.

Three flags flap in the wind above the entrance roof. A slow curling of fabric to announce their arrival. One a dark starless night with a red slash of lightening to signify the tip of the spear the Army will be in its fight against the dragon and its hoard. One is a silver sword on a blue recess background with three stars, one on the hilt and two on each edge of the guard. A symbol of the church and its unified fight against the demons who have taken so much from them all.

Then there is the last. A red fabric with a single white star in the center. The Unified Government of Azhana.

It's amazing how a single act of fear can bring people together. The world was at war. Then it dies and the people who remain forget everything.

At least temporarily.

"Thanks for the lift," Coleena says.

She slams the door behind her. The building, the central heart of their entire operation, looms over her.

"Ten years," the driver says. His voice cracks like the gravel beneath the tires of the vehicle he drives.

She turns to him, but he does not look at her. Checking his mirrors, the engine revs and the tires crunch the dirt and stones as they groan and begin their slow turn.

Ten years? One of the older ones. Is that what she is going to be doing when she completes whatever it is that has brought her here today? Driving one of the few remaining vehicles and running errands for the brass?

She shrugs her stiff shoulders and straightens up the front of her dress-shirt. Six rows of pinned metals scratch against the skin of her breast. The weight of the cheap metal heavy against the fabric and useless behind the memory of everything it took to get them and what little they mean against an enemy that is relentless.

Taking the steps slowly and gritting her teeth each time, she reaches the top and the shade provided by the stone roof does little to dissipate the heat. Shadows move and the sound of shuffling feet follows her, but there are no guards on the outside. Nothing but silent pillars and vacant doorways.

A relic to the past. Left to rot and crumble like the dust around them, though it will probably outlast them all.

Pushing open the wooden doors, a gust of wind hits back, the smell of sweat and burning candles heavy in the air. Soldiers and clerks mill about the first level. Dressed in similar uniforms to her, the dark with the red sash, they move about their business with shoulders stiff and looks of sternness tattooed to their faces. The civilians, watched closely by the later, go about their work with faces down and hands moving quickly. Most wear loose fitting clothes of dull colors. Long dresses and head wraps for those she assumes can afford them. Anything to help stop the sun from scorching their skin.

Coleena makes her way over to the table at the very center of it all. A semi-circle with piles of paper stacked all across, barely an inch of surface visible. A clerk sits there, her dark skin and round cheeks a contrast to the bright red hair that easily takes its ideas from the burning light of the morning sun.

"Captain Armigera here to see General Whitaker," Coleena announces.

The woman's head doesn't move, her eyes shifting up momentarily before returning to their own business. Long nails flick at paperwork sitting in front of her, handwritten messages scribbled from edge to edge, the yellowing parchment thin and brittle beneath her touch.

"Uh hum," Coleena clears her throat.

"I heard you," the woman answers.

The thick curls around her head wave over her shoulders as she finally looks up, the smile beneath her ruby lips and bright brown eyes a glow within the dark confines of the building. A small tag has the name Emmra written in dark ink.

"I was called back from the front lines to see the General," Coleena says, this time hoping the fact that she came from where they actually do the fighting would get the woman to move a bit faster.

Eyes narrow and Emmra examines the lines of plastic and metal hanging from Coleena's shirt. She fights the urge to ask if the woman even knows what they mean.

This glorified secretary ruffles the papers before her, piles them neatly, and then pushes them to the side where they should have knocked over everything else, but somehow, they fit without touching another pile.

"Of course, you are. You were supposed to be here at 0500 hours." She glances at the ticking clock at the far edge of desk opposite of her. "You are almost thirty minutes late."

Coleena's hands can't ball into fists any faster. The fire in her blood that has kept her alive for so long ignites like gasoline hit with a match.

"I was never given a time to arrive. My orders were--" she begins.

Emmra cuts her off with a hand up, palm out.

"The General is up on the third floor waiting. Take the stairs to the left and I'll let them know you are coming."

The woman sets her attention back to a separate set of papers piled in front of her and doesn't say another word.

Coleena bites down hard on her teeth, the urge to jump across the counter almost unbearable. With a deep breath she nods and heads towards the stairs. Soldiers and civilians watch, some openly and others with sideways glances as she passes. A quick thought wondering if they know why she is here passes through her mind, but like a shadow at night, the idea is gone. No need to worry if they already know, because she'll find out soon enough.

4

―――――

Sixty-two steps. All cut into stone. Walls of mortared brick, and the entirety of it cool to the touch. Sharp edges like broken teeth catch the soles of her boots making the long walk more painful with every step.

Coleena's movement echoes through the empty, narrow stairwell. Her rubber heels slap with a rhythmic tune, answered only by the thoughts within her own mind. At the top, out of breath and cramping all the way down her spine, she pushes through a wooden door, unmarked and unassuming.

Through the entry, a long hall awaits. Something she would imagine a catacomb buried hundreds of feet below ground would look like with dull gray walls full of shadows and secrets. Lit with candles between closed mahogany doors, the regularly spaced flames dance in the stagnant air and darkened ghosts spread across the walls. Two men stand at the far end, their silhouettes barely visible from where she stands. Their uniforms identical in every way to the one she wears, but this time they are armed. Rifles held across their chest they make no move as she begins her slow meandering walk toward them.

Statues watching her approach, they are twins from their faces shaved cleaned of all stubble around their cleft chins all the way down to their polished boots reflecting similar images of the candles flickering on the walls. This part of the building feels empty. Devoid of life and time. A hollowness to its sound and stagnate air. Only her and these two guards. She isn't stupid though. The General, this single woman, means too much to humanity's existence. There has to be a full platoon with each soldier armed to the teeth between her and any potential enemy.

How many could be hidden up here? A dozen? More? The quick thought of what it would take to reach the end of the hall and get through with a hostile force calculates in her mind.

Too much. But if you were crazy enough...

Coleena mentally shakes her head and approaches the two men after what feels like a mile of walking. Those days are in her past. She'd be lucky to get past a squirrel holding six nuts, let alone any number of guards protecting the General.

"Captain Armigera reporting as requested," she states.

Neither man moves. She watches their throats, waiting to see if they prove to be human at all. Maybe they are statues.

"Password?" a man's voice asks from the empty hall behind her.

The sound is like pushing air through a helium balloon and scratching knives at the same time.

Startled, Coleena hops on her heels and spins. A sharp pain followed by a dull ache tightens her thighs and lower back into one solid mass punishing her for her forgetfulness. The approach of the diminutive man is as silent as it is deadly. Barely reaching her shoulders, his mop of brown hair falls loosely over thick brows that stop just before the eyes.

There is almost no way of describing them. Emerald green. A sea of color ready to swallow her. Words do not come easily, the air in her lungs locked prisoner behind invisible chains and any answer to his question is frozen in her mind.

"You should have been given a code by the secretary downstairs," he adds, the jolly round cheeks bouncing as he goes from smile to a firm businesslike smirk.

With a flick of his wrist he marks off a check on the steno pad resting in his hand, the tip of his pen scratching the paper with practiced ease. Hardly a movement puts the written notes into a deep pocket tucked within the red fabric of his full body robes cut long enough to rub across the floor. Eyeing her up like a man examining merchandise, he looks to mark a second check, this one in his head. He then steps around, placing himself between the two guards and his nose somehow pointed down to her though he barely reaches past her chin.

"I wasn't given any password. Maybe a bit of attitude and directions to follow the stairs until I found myself on this floor. If this is the wrong area--," Coleena responds.

Lifting his hand, he stops her. The pen reappears as does the pad. Another check mark and a few notes scribble across the page before once again performing their disappearing act.

"Never said that you were in the incorrect place. You are here to report to General Whitaker, correct?"

Coleena snaps her heels together, stiffens her legs

making the same mistake, and does her best to roll her shoulders back.

"Captain Coleena Armigera reporting as requested."

The man clicks his tongue and gives another once over with those deep green eyes.

"Yep, as they always say, Captain Armigera. Let me see if the General is ready to receive you. Let me warn you though, she is a busy woman. She will suffer nothing but short answers. Stay on point and be quick about it. There are more important things for her to handle than anything you have to present to her."

"I was ordered--"

He doesn't wait for her response and turns to the door. A double knock precedes a slow turn and the little man slips in through the opening and disappears leaving her with the silent sentries.

"Little prick, isn't he?"

Neither man look at her. Not even the slightest movement of their large frames and cold eyes.

"And you two could use some work on your manners," she adds as she steps back.

The wall is a sturdy support as the wait begins to drag. There is no signal from the other side that the General has agreed to see her, and the strange man has yet to return. Time moves slowly, a turtle crawl she has no way to count.

Is she going to spend the entire day up here? Peering at the now counted dozen doors that line the hall, she looks for any sign of light from the windows beyond the barriers. Maybe seeing light will give enough to let her know if there is still anything left to this day, but the candles are her only hope. Half burned down, the little pools of wax drip down slow waterfalls and cool into mounds as the sizzle of the flame sings into the empty air, stuffy and warming beyond comfort.

"The General will see you now," the man's voice returns.

There he is, standing in front of the door. She never even had the chance to catch the movement of his arrival. One moment she is by herself except for the inhuman statues and the next he is right there beside her.

"Has anyone ever told you--" Coleena starts to ask.

The man checks another box off of his notepad, a small tsk escaping his closed lips.

"Told me what?"

Coleena shakes her head.

"Never mind."

Turning away from her, she is led to the door and on dead silent hinges, it is opened to what lays beyond. Coleena eyes the two statues as she draws closer. On her approach, they do not move, but somehow, she can feel their eyes following her as she passes between them. Their glare burns into the skin of her back, and she can already feel the bullets ripping through her body as if she were the enemy they were waiting for.

"Come in, Captain Armigera," a woman's voice beckons from the inside.

As smooth as silk, the words do not order, but instead call to her as a friend, a companion coming for their weekly dinner.

Passing beneath the entryway, the room on the other side is an entirely different place. Wide windows let in enough light to burn her eyes and Coleena squints as the door shuts quickly behind her.

Thick cut slabs of rock are chiseled between mortared stones. Single candles burn on each windowsill. She counts twelve. Twelve sets of dark uniform colored curtains sit pulled back, silk blinds flapping in the wind that feels both refreshing and cool as it circulates the room.

A chill runs down her spine at the light touch of the cooler air. This is an entirely different world.

"Thank you for responding to my request so quickly," General Whitaker says from behind her desk.

Stained Mahogany, sharp edges, and cleared of all possible unnecessary items. A single steno-pad with a pen rests at the very center. This woman has every detail checked and straightened. Her reputation of being on point one hundred percent of the time is not an exaggeration.

Coleena snaps to attention, her mind refusing to remember what her body will not forget, and she clasps her hands to her side. A quick salute, and she goes back to trying to be a statue.

"At ease, soldier. I didn't ask you here for a private audience just to see you play the role of mindless drone."

Coleena lets her arms fall loose, unable to get them to her back comfortably, and relaxes her legs enough to stand ready on the soles of her feet. She watches the woman opposite of her rise and leave the safe confines of her desk.

Tall and formidable, the General is nothing of the forty-five years she is rumored to be. Broad at the shoulder, she is easily a head taller than Coleena with a full dress of brunette hair that falls in waves down to her shoulders. Sun kissed skin sparkles in the light around round cheeks burned permanently red. If it wasn't for the scar on her face, a deep white line that runs from the right side of her nose through the dark leather patch covering her eye, she'd be more model than war General. There is no doubt in her mind that this woman could handle any man of the line. Unarmed or not.

"Why am I here, ma'am? If I may ask?"

General Whitaker beckons her closer and leads her over to a window. The sweet smells of the deep summer work their way through the opening, full of warmth and the ripening fruits of a land once adorned by the trade of exotic delicacies grown locally and sold for massive profit. Somehow the stench of the entire city avoids this room like the plague itself.

"Do you see what is laid out before us, Captain?"

"Meclav City, ma'am?"

"Yes, if you want to be exact. But tell me what you see, not with just your eyes."

Coleena takes a moment to really look, the sights processing a lot slower than she wants them to. At this vantage point she can see the circular formation of the city. Streets built into giant ovals, creating a bullseye ending here at this very structure. Below, the soldiers of the army are little more than toys going about in formation. Workers and soldiers, the few authorized vehicles transporting them and equipment. The smoke of the war machine rises high into the afternoon light and a storm rolls toward them from the horizon to the west.

"I see a city ready to defend itself, ma'am. Thousands of ready soldiers, all willing to throw themselves at the enemy. A blockade of obstacles built to prevent the monsters from having a straight line to the heart of what it means to fight for us."

"Good answer. Perfect for a soldier of your caliber," Whitaker says without turning away from the window. "And who would the enemy be, Captain?"

"Ma'am?" Coleena asks.

Placing her own arms behind her back, Whitaker leans up against the stone sill. Shadows created by the wall draw deep caverns across her face of strong edges and hidden thoughts. A career of stories etched into her skin show the years secreted away by unknown magic.

"Who do we fight against, Captain Armigera? Who stands in our way and for whom do we spill sweat, blood, and tears? Tell me the purpose for all of this? Why do you fight, Captain?"

Coleena steps forward and watches the approaching dark clouds. A roll of thunder crawls across the world, a gust of dry brittle wind following in its wake.

"We fight the dragon, ma'am. Its minions are born and bred for one purpose and that is to destroy us and wipe us from the surface of this world. We are the only thing that can stop them. It is kill or be killed. The people of the United Citizens of Azhana depend on us. Ever since--."

"Ever since that demonic lizard and its devastating army wiped out more than half this planet, we have been telling ourselves that. If it was that easy, then at least we could be on common ground. Kill the monsters, bleed them solid and crush their lifeless husks until they are the pebbles beneath our feet," Whitaker says and turns back toward her desk. "Has anyone told you the story of what was really happening during the war when the dragon came? Before this whole world turned to shit, and we handed it to them in a fucking wicker basket?"

"A war raged across the entire known world. Then during one final battle the dragon was released. Neither side was ready. The monster and the demons it brought with it wiped through men and machines. Bullets slowed them down and bombs held them back, but in the end, we lost. We all lost. I remember it as clear as I do this morning, ma'am. I was there that day."

"Yes, I've read the report on your past, Captain Armigera.

The losses in Obrathe were staggering. Did you know my father was there that fateful day?"

Coleena, remembering the look of her own parents rushing her into the safety of the nearby forest as the men who saved them stayed to fight, feels the old familiar pain in her stomach return. Her metal dog tags burn against the skin of her chest, the need to run its smooth texture between her fingers almost irresistible. She takes a deep breath and pushes it away. This is something she cannot dwell on, or it will be the death of her one day.

"I've heard as such, ma'am."

Whitaker nods and reaching behind her desk pulls a leather journal from one of the drawers. Corners wearing, the red leather looks to be a lighter shade of white and brown in thumb sized indents across the surface. The paper between the binding curls from years of use and time.

"Like so many, he never made it back. Many survivors told stories of how he stood at the head of command, ordering lines of fire on the enemy and then worse as the dragon swooped down on them all. But that is not why we are here, Captain. Though we both share a common bond of being connected to that city of nightmares, I am more interested in knowing what you know about the truth of what happened."

Whitaker sits on the corner of her desk, the edges of her black uniform sharp and to the point as she flips through the pages of the tome.

"The truth, ma'am? I know nothing more than what everyone who survived knows. What else could there possibly be than that dragon?"

The General stops as she reaches the last few sheets held between the worn covers.

"We were betrayed, Captain. From within our own ranks

there were those working their own schemes. Secret plans and actions that put us into this very mess. I'm not sure what magic they worked, but they are the reason we fight today. Their cursed mechanics brought these demons to our world and in my father's own words he documented what they knew before it was too late."

"We brought this dragon to the world? Mankind summoned it? Who would do that?"

General Whitaker puts the book down and runs a hand through her hair, her eyes closed and lips cutting a thin line.

"Power, revenge, worship of the apocalypse. Take your pick. What we knew, we found out too late. What we discovered wasn't enough to explain it all. That is where you are coming in."

Coleena turns and looks back out the window. Suddenly, the storm in the distance is a lot closer than she remembers. A flash of lightening streaks across the sky cutting a jagged line that leads the way for a boom of thunder that rattles even the walls of this ancient building.

"What do I have to do with this? I'm just a front-line soldier. A grunt out there fighting these monsters."

A firm hand finds its way to Coleena's shoulder, the pressure heavy, yet strengthening.

"The average man or woman survives how long out there cutting their teeth against these monsters? A week if the fighting is heavy? Maybe a month if they are strong and lucky. How long have you been out there?"

Coleena takes a deep breath and tries to count the passage of the years. It feels like a lifetime, but she knows that isn't correct. All of it blurs into one large battle. This has been her entire life. The only thing that she knows or wants.

"You've been in the army for eight years and nine months. Ten tours to the front lines and up in the thick of it for sixth months now. More than a thousand times the average soldier. You have a knack for being a thorn in the side of the dragon and I could use someone with those skills."

Turning, the hand on her shoulder drops and Coleena takes a long hard look into the eyes of the woman in front of her.

Cold.

Hard.

Determined.

"I'm sorry to report to you, ma'am, those days are behind me. I figured the news would get to you before my arrival, but my luck finally gave out. I may have lasted longer than any of the others, but the damn monsters finally got me," Coleena says, her head dropping away from that face and its judgmental eyes.

Whitaker slides around her so she can sit on the windowsill, a long look casting its hopes and dreams over the cityscape.

"I'm well aware of your injuries and their current state of repair, Captain. If I for a moment thought they would hamper your duties in this matter you wouldn't be standing here in front of me. My aid, though peculiar as he is, is not one to be bothered with wasting time. He is a stickler for schedules."

Coleena nods and raises her chin, the muscles in her back screaming as she tries to stiffen into a ready stance once again.

"What are my orders then, ma'am? Ask and I'll do what I can to see it done, though if I'm going to be honest, I don't see how I can be of any help. No matter what it is you need."

A small smile twitches on the General's face, the smallest break in the stone exterior.

"Unlike what we had hoped, we have come to believe those who brought this monster upon us did not perish with the others when all hell broke loose. There are still sects of the dragon's followers causing havoc across our cities. We need someone who knows the dragon, inside and out, to hunt them and flush them into the open."

"These people still exist? There are those who would still think the dragon is a good thing?" Coleena asks.

The revelation stops her mind cold. How could this be? Is it possible people could be so ignorant? All strength drains from her body, a cold shiver running through her injured flesh. She slowly lets her body slide and settle onto the windowsill beside the General.

"Some people have lived their entire lives away from these demons, Captain. They don't remember a world without its presence and to them, it is nothing more than a rumor to be forgotten. Their lives revolve around the day to day, not the certain death waiting for them outside their protective walls. This is what we fight against, Captain. Ignorance and complacency. Whenever those two get together, there is always someone ready to step in and take advantage."

"What is their end goal? Lead everyone to their death? What is it you think we can do to stop it?" Coleena asks, her eyes locked on the storm already casting shadows across the furthest reaches of the city.

A smile creases the corners of Whitaker's face. A small hook pulling at the thin pink flesh.

"Do what you do best, Captain. They work for the dragon. Human or not, they are not one of us, and we give no ground to those who would serve such dark purposes. Flush them out, end the threat against our people. Some will not trust you; others will outright hate you, but we are the only ones equipped to end this threat. They might not realize that now, but one day they will, and we need to be there when it happens."

"How far does this extend, General? I can't be in more than one place at a time."

Whitaker nods and walks over to her desk, putting her father's journal to the side she slides a map to the front edge of her desk.

"Best place to start anything, Captain. Right at the heart. Parliament City. There have already been incidents there and if we are going to find the head of this monster, it's going to be there."

Coleena looks at the little black dot beneath the woman's finger. Parliament City. She hasn't been there in years. Not since she enlisted on her first day of freedom.

"I'll do my best, ma'am. Whatever that may be," Coleena says, her eyes leaving the map and her mind spinning like a top.

"That you will, Captain. I'm counting on it, and so are the people who don't know how much they need you. How much we all need you."

5

Parliament City.

She was here only once prior to enlisting and that was a lifetime ago. Years have reduced the memory of the city and its busy streets from the vivid picture to what can no longer be real. An imaginary life that is no longer hers.

Her entire world living with protective walls, imagination and delusion refusing to acknowledge reality. All of it broken down by battle and death into a single solitary struggle to survive and continue the fight. One single point of worth and determination. Rolling her shoulders sends pain and bad memories shooting through her mind. All of that fighting against a relentless enemy lost and now nothing remains but the minor hope that something new will come along to fill the void.

Of course, nothing could possibly help in such a cluster fuck of a traffic jam. The horn of her government escort truck honks but the pileup of men, women, and non-moving vehicles do not care. They remain seated in the heat that is beginning to choke her. Sweat beads on her head, her throat is dry, and her skin burns sitting there and waiting. Hundreds of people and dozens of vehicles sit stationary and block their path. Families meander on the two-lane highway leading toward the city walls. Fathers carrying children on their shoulders as they step on and off the broken pavement, their clothes filthy and dark circles blacking out their eyes.

The clouds above threaten further torture. A storm brewing, a threat to wash away what little these people carry on their shoulders or keep tucked within their folded arms. Laying her head back to rest against her chair, the scratchy cloth fraying at the edges is little relief to her pain, but nothing compared to the people outside. The pinching grabs at her neck like a vice slowly losing its bite. The words of her therapist reciting the required therapy she needs continues its unending torture in her mind, and she grits her teeth. Never one to take orders from anyone without an additional row of medals pinned to their chest, she rolls her head in a slow circle and feels the bones beneath pop.

Large circles, clockwise and then counterclockwise. Every hour followed by thirty-minute stretches to keep the muscles loose and supple. Coleena spits out the window, the dry air assaulting the moisture in her mouth with renewed vigor.

Fuck those ideas. She can beat this. There isn't anything in this world she hasn't beaten before.

"Fucking asshole, city whores and their incessant needing to be coddled," the man driving the truck says.

He's not the same that brought her to Meclav. His eyes burn with enough hatred for the crowd in front of their vehicle that part of her wonders how close he is to running them all down. Gaunt cheeks chew as his jaw works overtime and his knuckles bleed white as he throttles the steering wheel for every last ounce of life the poor thing ever had. Veins pulse up his neck and the wrinkles spreading across his forehead are blade thick, angry red, and dripping sweat like rain on a spring day.

"Calm down, killer. It's not like anything we say here is going to make them move any faster. Look ahead, where are they going to go?" Coleena says pointing past the multiple rows of blockage stopping their forward movement.

Gigantic doors remain locked, iron braces holding firm as the outer wall of the city holds them back. Wide enough to swing and let in three times the number awaiting outside, the barrier is closed, and no one is going anywhere. She can hear the voices of hundreds mingling into a chorus of anger and the heat lends a helping hand making everyone uncomfortable. An urgency keeps them pushing. A rumble of thunder in the distance giving them a drive that any other time would be defeated.

Taking a deep breath full of dust and the taste of salt, she leans out the window to get a better look of what lays before her. Like being transported to the past, she can see for miles in each direction and nothing passes the endless stone wall. At one time as black as night, but now dusty and gray for as far as she can see. A flat face of impenetrable protection. Parliament did itself a good job protecting the last bastion of humanity. Forty feet high and more than double that deep, the walls circle the entire city. Stone cut with the last remnants of technology before most of it began to fade into history, the surface is as smooth as ice and the shadow it casts is dark and ominous. Battlements set their watch along the walls on both sides of the closed entrance. Helmets worn by men and women of the city guard pace along the top, their eyes watching the growing unrest below.

A world wonder cut from the pages of myth itself, Parliament City is made for the ages, a testament and silent message to humanity's enemies that no one will go quietly into the night. Mankind will fight, it will claw itself free no matter the cost, and in the end, it will be free.

The driver, Yariel lets down on the horn again, a blaring siren cutting the tension and thick humidity like an ax trying to cleave its way through a fly infested swamp. Wrong weapon against an impatient, yet relentless enemy. Coleena has had enough. Unbuckling herself, bones pop and muscles pinch as she pushes the door open and swings her legs out into the sweltering heat of the day. Even with the incoming dark clouds, her skin sizzles under the assault of the sun. The buzz of insects echoes in the distance. The world's chorus hidden beneath the moaning and desperate cries of the unfortunate stuck out here with her.

"Find me inside the city walls if you need to. I'll check myself into the barracks once I get through all this shit," she says without bothering to look back.

The man grunts his disapproval and lays down on the horn again. Some faces turn, most do not. It really isn't like they can do anything about their situation.

Coleena stretches her back, hands on hips and lets the stiffness of the three-day ride work its way through her muscles. The humidity here tastes like the sand itself is suspended in the air, and she can feel it grit between her teeth. A brief cough plagues her lungs and there is a taste she recognizes immediately but did not expect.

Ash.

Tangy and filmier than grit. Hacking back, she spits on the ground, grayish bubbles popping on the surface of the dirt beside the road.

Why is there ash mixed in with the air? In such a populated city it shouldn't be such a surprise that there would be fires burning. Even through the sweltering heat of the summer and early fall, people need to eat. This is thicker. More recent and there isn't an open fire for as far as she can see. Nothing but a mile of bobbing heads and the glare of the sun reflecting off the roofs of the few vehicles permitted to pass between the cities of Azhana.

Coleena looks back at her ride, the evil glare of the driver clearly visible through the windshield. She turns to walk herself to the gate. None of them are going anywhere, and she doesn't have time to waste standing around.

Passing and sometimes pushing her way through the human equivalent of constipation, the closer to the closed gate she gets, the tighter the quarters draw. People are shoulder to shoulder, voices raised and angry as hell. She begins to wonder even if she makes it to the doors, what are the chances she is actually going to get through? The transfer papers folded neatly into the back pocket of her pants weigh as much as the real chances they'll matter more than the pleas and threats of everyone in front of her.

She can let none of this stop her. She has a job to do and the feelings and thoughts of hundreds of everyday citizens matter little to getting the assignment completed. That is something she understands. This is something she can hold on to.

"What the fuck do you mean the gate is closed until further notice?" an angry man barks.

Red cheeks puff out with sweat and tension. The fellow presses his fists into his side, suede jacket held open and large belly exposed. Thick beads of sweat run down his face to make their way to the large stains building beneath neck and pits.

"As commanded by Parliament, these walls remain shut until further notice. No traffic in or out. Grievances can be filed with the city clerk when the doors reopen," a man dressed in the uniform of the wall guard responds.

Not much different from the uniform that she most recently wore herself, all black even below the fiery sun. Replacing the red sash from shoulder to hip sits a shield across the chest and torso emblazoned with the fires at the heart of Azhana itself. She remembers what they used to call them.

Gate Jockeys.

Real hard asses with the ability to swing a door open-and-shut. The men and women who couldn't cut the training for real combat. Reduced to standing watch over a wall hundreds of miles away from any real fight.

Her heart drops as the memory skips away with the children playing in the dirt beside the road and the reality of what the uniform really means slams home. The feeling of her second skin, black as night with its red flaming sash and how much she misses it is still as raw as the scars and puffy tissue covering the space between her shoulders.

"And when will that be? Next week? Maybe a fucking month from now? How are we to survive out here? Do you see a fucking grocery store waiting to open its doors so we can eat? How are we going to house ourselves?" the angry citizen argues throwing out a million questions.

Cold and professional, the soldier waits and does not respond, his eyes locked on the clipboard held steady between his hands. Finding no recourse coming, the fat man spits on the ground, gathers his unneeded jacket tight against his frame and stomps his way back to a much more frightened looking family of wife and three young children. Coleena gives them less than a moment's glance and turns to the soldier.

"Captain Coleena Armigera on assignment from General

Whitaker in Meclav. What is reason for the shutdown, officer?" Coleena asks.

Without a word the man looks down at the papers in front of him. He doesn't move a single sheet.

"By Parliament Order 247-A6, these walls are shut to all traffic until further notice," the man recites.

"Look, officer," Coleena starts as she searches his chest plate for any sign of his name. "Officer Kaelobs. I'm not sure you heard what I said. My name is Captain Coleena Armigera of Azhana's First Battalion, Second infantry, and I am on direct orders from General Whitaker."

Closing the short distance between them, Coleena is far less surprised than he is that they are eye to eye when he looks up.

"I heard you the first time. Parliament Order..."

"Do not read that to me one more time, officer. I have my orders right here, signed by the woman herself, and I do not think some fucking political declaration is going to prevent me from seeing the inside of these walls."

Reaching into her back pocket is a test of wills as the muscles, on fire with the adrenaline running through her veins at the need to strangle this asshole, cramp and protest her attempts to retrieve the orders typed out by Mrs. Emmra herself.

There is a silence in the air as the man reads the documents, his hands less than gentle as he flips them over as if to judge the authenticity himself. People within earshot are already beginning to protest her ability to ignore what is so easily keeping them out in the torturous world deemed too uninhabitable by those within.

"I'm sorry, ma'am...," he starts.

"Captain," she barks back, finding less pain cramping

her shoulders as the words she does not want to say threaten to cut the tip of the man's tongue.

"Orders are orders, and I still have to follow them," he says and hands her back the papers.

Coleena folds them with an exaggerated pinch of her fingers and slides them into her front pocket this time, her jaw set, and the next set of words picked very carefully.

"Officer Kaelobs, let me be very clear here. I am not sure what has happened to force you to refuse all of these wonderful people, nor do I give two shits. I am on direct orders from the Army of the United Countries of Azhana and I intend to complete those orders. Included within these commands is to take all reasonable and needed actions to complete my mission and right now the only thing stopping me is you, your career, and these walls. As the gods above are my witness, I may not be able to move the gates myself, but once I do find my way inside, and you can be assured I will find my way in, I'll make it my sworn duty and first official action within to make sure that the only part of this wall you ever see again is the one guarding the city waste as it dumps itself into the Niarane River. Maybe you'll find fulfillment in the idea of protecting the great people of Parliament City from its next battle with the shits. Do I make myself clear?"

The small knob at the front of the man's throat bobs as his eyes scan the clipboard and subsequent papers clipped to it.

"P... Parliament Order...," he stammers.

"For fuck's sake, man," Coleena cuts in. "I'm not asking you to throw the doors open and let all these people in. Shit, you don't even have to open them at all. Just point me in the direction of the nearest entrance that WILL open, and I'll quietly report to the barracks and the officers within. There will be no reason for me to even remember your name, but it will give me a reason to remember the courtesy you have shown me by not impeding my progress. Nor will the woman keeping the fucking dragon and its minions at bay so you can stand out here making all of these people's lives miserable need to find out. Are we clear on the priority of your shitty orders and empty pieces of paper?"

The man doesn't answer but instead looks at the other guards standing silent like statues on each side of the massive entry. None of them are going to help. He either makes the right decision now or she'll do far worse than she has already promised. That she is sure of.

"All right. Petty Officer Tucker over there will lead you to the EVAC door to the west. It's a little bit of a walk, but from there he can lead you back to Congress Street and from there the reporting station is impossible to miss," Kaelobs says with a nod toward the man to her left.

Young, broad shouldered, and blond with too much sun, the soldier doesn't even move a muscle other than those to move his eyes from her to the crowd champing at the bit behind her.

"Good choice, Kaelobs. Good choice," Coleena says. With a nod of her own she moves off toward the man who will get her through. "Your lead now, Tucker. Let's hope we aren't going to have any trouble with you like we did your friend Kaelobs here."

The soldier says nothing. Spinning on his heels he is quick to lead her off along the wall and to the door that will get her passed all of this mess.

6

If she didn't see it for herself, she would never believe it.

Soldiers marching through empty streets. Black uniforms with red slashes pressed into wrinkle free mirrors and marching orders bringing squads up and down narrow paths in perfect order. Red flags billowing in the air, quickly erected fences gleaming in the mid-day sun. Razor wire topping it all; sharp and threatening. All of this from her first steps into the city.

Men and women at arms lined up, weapons on shoulders and ready for orders. Officers barking and the sounds of the war engine coming to life, all within the confines of the protective wall. There are no onlookers. No citizens lined up against the fence to watch the war demonstrations or their family members performing their honorable duty. Only the membership to the cause that ties them tighter than blood is allowed here, a sanctuary where the fears and the memories of what you leave behind is kept in the darkness where it won't become a hindrance. A weapon to use against you.

Where there are no people, the city itself is the only allowable onlooker. Buildings made of twisted metal, welded and bent together in unimaginably uncomfortable shapes. Broken windows with rusty corners and empty flowerpots glare down at them all, dark set eyes watching and passing judgment where their own courage refuses to let them become one of the chosen. The shadows stretch for as far as she can see. A hodgepodge of sizes, a child's mess pressed together to become one of the world's largest remaining cities. A disaster squeezed into a sandbox protected by stone. Parliament City at its finest.

Then there is the smoke. Giant clouds of it lifting into the air. Dark, bulbous, and carrying that taste of ash that has been with her since she left Yariel and his truck back on the road outside. Somewhere deeper in the city something burns. Actually, several things must be burning. At least three different areas turn the sky a deep red color and the surrounding air is gray and choked full of the ash not yet carried outside the city walls.

A deep roll of thunder growls in the distance. Echoes of the pounding rattles through the city and the thick smoky air gets a touch of chill before she is smothered with the oppressing heat once again.

"What is going on here?" Coleena asks.

The young soldier does not answer. Watching his own steps as he leads the way down from the guard entrance to the city wall, his face remains away from her leaving only the back of his head, neatly trimmed without a hair out of place, as her answer. He stops at the bottom of the metal stairs, the clanging of his boots silencing and quickly being overtaken as a squad of men, marching two abreast, pass by, their faces as stoic and stone-like as his.

She stops as she reaches him, the muscles of her legs

finally loosening but those crisscrossing their way over her spine tightening and sending needles up to her neck. The silent soldier nods and begins again without a word.

Not far from the wall itself they pass beneath a checkpoint, a guard-post made of sandbags four stacks high and ten wide blocking all but a man's width walkway cut into the razor wire. Without stopping, they find their way into the military encampment within Parliament City. Tents, rectangular and carrying the same dark cloth of their uniforms, sit side by side at the regulation three by three pattern. All have their front flaps open where she can see mirror images of bunks sitting tucked and empty deep within their shadows. The men and women who sleep within them are not here, all of them somewhere drilling or tending to other duties that they are assigned.

Turning her eyes away from what she knows she will never experience again, she follows her guide deeper into the sanctuary she once called home. One building, the only one made for permanency, stands at the center. Metal sheeting rusts along the walls and a door of cheap pressed board sits shut across the front. A single lantern hangs above the entryway, out of place and out of time. More like a large shed than command post, she can imagine the pile of tools and empty buckets piled within. The smell the cleaner and stale water hiding and waiting for the chance to escape at the first crack of its worn exterior. The windows along the side are blacked out with curtains on the inside, dark eyes watching her every movement.

"Am I going in there?" Coleena asks.

His response is a nod and blank stare as the man turns to look back at the city's protective wall, his back to the three steps that lead up to the front door. A small wind carries the chocking ash and puts the lantern into a scratching swing of rusted hinges and painful glass. She gives him a hard look, her eyes narrowing and taking in the soldier for what he is. Young. Hardly a scratch on his face and his eyes bright beneath his dark cap and hardened stair.

There is nothing else to say, so she turns to the door ahead. Sign painted in a flat white that darkens at the edges says office and the thin wire used to hang it from its nail is rusty and has seen better days. He does not solute her as she walks away, nor does he make any announcement of his departure. Instead, the moment she reaches the building's entrance he is gone and the world around her already seems to have forgotten her arrival. Pointless and alone. No one looks her way. The world passes by and she stands there unchanging.

A quick rap upon the wooden panels of the door brings a quick response of boots on floor before the handle turns and the building opens up.

"Name and rank, soldier," a gruff older man demands.

He's her height, though in his younger years she can imagine him being a monster among men. Age has stooped his posture and turned his non-regulation hair white and thin. The widening of his shoulders tells the story of the strength lost to the passage of time. Deep wrinkles darken beneath deep set eyes of hazel brown and a thick stench of tobacco clings to him. He chews on something between a wide jaw and for a moment his gaze sweeps around her, somehow seeking to find what is hidden behind her. Much to his disappointment, she is the only one standing and waiting.

"Captain Coleena Armigera. I'm to report to the city barracks upon my arrival. After that, my orders get well...," she says.

"Spit it out, soldier," the man says, his voice somehow growling more like a junkyard dog than a man.

"I'm not really sure, sir. My exact instructions were to see myself to the city, check in with the commanding officer stationed within the barracks, and then find a way to make myself useful."

Part of her argues that withholding information to a superior officer is a lie unto itself, but up until now, she is still telling the truth. Outside of her real mission, this is exactly as far as she has been told what to do. After this point, General Whitaker was very clear the rest would be up to her judgment. Whatever that happened to be.

"You do look like you could use a weapon. Ever shot at anything, Captain?" the soldier asks, his eyes now tracing her outline as if he finally realizes it is only her.

"Well, yes, but," she starts.

"Let the Captain in, will you, Tul?" another man calls from the inside of the small building. This voice is much younger, though there is no lack of sternness in his command. "There is no reason to force her to stand out there on display when we both are well aware that she is here by orders of the General herself. Stop being a bloody busybody and step out of the way."

"Can never be too sure," Tul growls, but does as he is ordered. The smell of tobacco is nauseating as she slides by him, his step to the side opening enough room that she is almost forced to press herself against him to squeeze around and through the door.

"Captain Armigera reporting for duty, sir," Coleena says as she gets around Tul and brings herself to attention.

The gloom in the small confine of the building is choked with candle smoke and the solid black curtains create a sauna as thick and oppressive as the heat across the front lines.

Vanilla. The entire room reeks of the stuff, and she doesn't know which is worse. The stench of Tul's cigarettes or the fake bakery vanilla pressing itself into her skin. An invisible enemy using grievous methods to find its way inside her body. Clenching her gut, she holds back the need to vomit.

Coleena can feel the sweat sprouting like new spring leaves across her skin within seconds and the dim light cast by the tiny flames give everything a soft appearance. Almost as if there are no clear edges to anything, even the square card table where the man from inside sits.

Stacks of paper rest in uneven piles and a deep tin of coffee sits stained between them. An old beaten down couch gives itself up beside it, the center buckling beneath the weight of the man waiting with a folder held closed within his fingers.

"Please, Captain, have yourself a seat," the man says. With a wave of the manila folder he indicates the aluminum foldout chair waiting beneath a book sized piece of board holding three candles burned into blobs of dried wax in the corner.

He's round in all ways possible. Puffy cheeks as red as cherries even in the dimmed light. His hair is non-regulation length and shaped more like a bowl to further accentuate the shape of his head. Buttons struggle to hold his girth within their restraints as he leans back into the cushions of the couch. Dark circles of sweat soak beneath his arms and double chins. Silver dog tags hang from his neck, gray sparkles of polished metal hooked to a finger thick chain resting upon his exposed chest. None of it compares to the bright twinkle of his eyes. Beady little things watching her every movement. Parts of her wonders if they blew out all the candles at once if she'd still be able to see them reflecting back at her, cat like and full of distrust.

"Thank you," she says before pulling the chair out and sliding it next to the table.

"Before we begin, Captain, I want to introduce myself and my associate. I am Lieutenant Major Lawrence Mason and that is Petty Officer Tul Bornoik. I have been made well aware of your coming arrival, though the specifics of your purpose here within Parliament City has been left, how should we say, vague?"

"I was telling Officer Tul that...," Coleena starts.

"Let me be honest here, Captain Armigera," Mason says with another wave of the folder before he places it down to rest atop his coffee tin. "We both know General Whitaker sent you here for something of her own making and that whatever it is you are not going to tell me. I normally am a man who loves to play these games of intrigue. We could spend hours here seeing how good you are at lying and just how devious I can be in getting the answers I want to know, but as you can see, we don't exactly find ourselves allotted with all the conveniences usually afforded people of our station here in the city. The politicians and their panicky ambitions have this place locked up like a virgin asshole and everyone from myself to the janitor fixing the fucking toilets of the capital building are on high alert."

Coleena crosses her arms across her chest, an act she again regrets immediately.

"Yes, I noticed. I was barely able to even get within the walls themselves," she adds.

"I was wondering about that. I see our esteemed leader may have picked someone with more skills than I've been led to believe seeing as not a single soul is supposed to be allowed to enter or leave our great city until further notice," Mason says and picks up the folder. He opens it and flips a couple of the papers within over. "How exactly did you do that?"

A smile sneaks across her face.

"I may have let a certain man outside believe that he'd find himself guarding that same toilet that needs repair if I found myself delayed. I'm taking that this sewage problem is something to be feared here within the city."

Now it is his turn to smile and a small chuckle breaks the silence between them. Tul, who stands like a shadow in the corner near the door, offers his own grunt that quickly fades into a dark glare she can feel burning a hole into the side of her head.

"Clever and witty. Doesn't exactly say that on your report here, but the army isn't exactly known for being as thorough as it should be. I'll ask this once, Captain. Are you going to tell me why you are here? Maybe we can skip this whole cat and mouse routine and get right to the good parts."

Coleena takes in a deep breath, the acrid smell of the candles burning her chest.

"General Whitaker has her reasons, Lieutenant. I am here to pay a courtesy call and then be on my way. But I can see you already understand the reasons I am here. I do have questions of my own, though."

The man's smile grows larger, and he places the folder back on top of his coffee cup. A long finger, tiny scars of white crisscrossing their way across knuckles and skin, taps at the tip of his chin.

"Ask away, Captain. For the moment I am at your disposal."

She leans back, a quick turn of her head catching a

small glimpse of Tul who has not moved from his post in the corner.

"What has happened here? I can see the different fires raging across the city and it smells like a war zone out there. Last time I checked the dragon wasn't within a hundred miles of here."

"Not all wars are fought with dragons and demons, Captain. But you are correct. The dragon is nowhere near here, yet we have our own problems to solve. Two days ago, there was an attack. Actually, several attacks and some very strategic points were bombed within the city limits. Nothing indicating a direct danger to Parliament or the sniveling politicians within, but more than enough to get their panties in a bunch and to force them to shut this place down like a fort under siege."

An attack in Parliament City? Did the General know about this before she sent her? Could this be related to the same cult of worshipers from before the destruction?

Too many questions, not enough answers.

"Do we know who did this? Has anyone claimed responsibility?" Coleena asks, her legs cramping and the muscles in her back screaming bloody murder in this tiny tin can of an office.

"Tul and I were under the impression that might be why you are here, Captain. Not much of a coincidence that the city is attacked and suddenly a messenger from the General herself shows up on our doorsteps."

The attack was two days ago. It took her three just to get here. Could this be a simple coincidence?

"Why would that be so strange? Men and women are sent back from the front lines all the time. Almost an endless train of injured and dead sometimes," Coleena returns, the knowledge that it should be her on that very train not forgotten so easily.

"It's not exactly rose petals and wine between Parliament and the General, Captain. She may be the one responsible for keeping the dragon and its minions at bay, but here, this far from the fight, she is sometimes considered more of a thorn in the side of progress. Without our presence and these attacks, it's not that much of a stretch thinking people might forget there is even a war going on. Out of sight, out of mind if you want to think of it that way."

Coleena sighs and pushes herself out of her chair. The muscles in her legs cramp, and she uses it to keep her balance.

"Unbelievable. Without this war, we'd all be dead, or worse. Probably hiding out in some cave somewhere waiting to die. Don't people realize that?"

Her blood is boiling, forcing the muscles to relax though the screaming aches are tearing her spine in half.

"People don't want to know how close they are to death, Captain. How would we sleep if we didn't have the ability to forget what is out there and only worry about what we see? It's the way of the world and you really can't fault them for it. Life has to move on. It always does and always has."

"Typical," Coleena responds. "And then we try to blow each other up? We start looking at each other as the enemy?"

Mason pulls her file away, picks up his coffee tin and takes a big swig of the contents inside.

"Now that is where we think you come in, Captain. Up until now we would see nothing but the occasional petty city crime. Murder, robbery, even a few kidnappings. People always want what others have and there are those who refuse to get that which isn't theirs the legal away. This is different. This was planned and by someone with more connections than your normal thug or angry anarchist. Weapons are outlawed here in the city. We still have them because you can't get rid of them completely when there were available like candy before the world died, but primarily, they are not capable of doing harm on a large scale. These explosions. This attack. This was coordinated and used something that should never have been able to find its way beyond these walls. Explosives, Captain. Whoever did this has connections, and we need to find them before they can do it again."

"Any leads on where to start?" Coleena asks, her throat suddenly dry with the realization of how big this may actually be. She's a foot soldier. Not an investigator. The thought of stopping whatever comes next rests entirely on her shoulders as a burden unlike anything she has ever felt.

"No, but I know a guy. He's a loner not much different from yourself. Works as a detective in the city police and if anyone has anything to go on, it would be him," Mason answers.

"Good, let's bring him here and get started," Coleena says.

"I warn you, Captain. This isn't fighting demons and there are rules you will have to live by while you are behind these walls. Our friend won't be coming here as all civilians are forbidden from finding their way onto military grounds, but it won't be hard for you to find him. Tul will set up the meeting for tomorrow morning. Why don't you take a break, Captain? Get something to eat and I imagine some badly needed rest. We can find you a bunk here and set everything up for tomorrow."

Straightening her uniform, Coleena glances at Tul in the corner and then back to Mason.

"Very generous of you, Lieutenant. I could definitely use something to eat and rest would not hurt. I'll meet your man in the morning and then I'll be on my way."

Mason does not move from the couch. He nods and Tul is quick to peel himself from the corner and find his way beside her.

"Fantastic. Well, Captain, I wish you a good rest of your day and I hope to hear good things from you."

Coleena gives the man a quick nod and turns toward the door, Tul sliding in behind her as she passes.

"Oh, Captain," Mason calls. "I do hope that the General hears how receptive we've been since your arrival. The man outside isn't one of ours, but we take care of own in the Army, don't we, Captain?"

"Yes, Lieutenant. Once Army, always Army."

The smile on the man's face is tilted to the shadowed side of his face, the candles behind him darkening.

"It is good to meet you, Captain. I look forward to working with you."

Without another word Coleena lets herself out the door.

7

———

A red morning. Thick with heat, choking with ash, and the horrific taste of death that refuses to move on and will not let them forget. Coleena forces herself to take a deep breath, the result burning at the back of her throat and the sweat on her skin a sticky film refusing to cool her body. The promised storm of the night passed them by as nothing more than a threat, the humid remains left to linger and torture them all.

Muscles burn, cramp, and are all around angry as she lifts her arms over her head and does her best to open her lungs. Her wet hair is the only cool part of this city as the thick strands run between her fingers. Dark smudges of ash smear into an oily residue, black and full of grit. Looking at the people she has passed this morning, she can only imagine she looks no different than they do with a fine layer of dust and gray soot coating her skin and uniform.

These morning runs, or closer to jogs compared to what she used to do, are part of the routine to keep the muscle damage at a minimum. Keep the tissue fresh and supple. Do not let up. Sitting idle will do more damage than pushing

64

the injuries to their limits. She grits her teeth at the thought of the routine that she is forced to maintain. Self-indulgent assholes and their recommendations. Maybe they should feel what it is to run with a body wanting to peel itself apart piece by piece.

Hacking forward the phlegm from the back of her throat, she spits and lets it splatter on the worn asphalt beneath her boots. The cracks and holes run deep. She is several blocks into the city and the damage from the attack is clear.

Parliament City, once heavily layered by station and class, is a skeleton of its former self. First within the wall, the poor districts clung to life, the homes and businesses in bad need of repair. Crime, homelessness, and the decrepit existence of people who can barely eat on full display no matter where a person would look.

Now, that same feeling of loss and emptiness begins to find its way further into the heart of the city. Buildings lean heavily against one another. Where the city streets first start, the lean between structures is more of a fading and shifting until the mass and bulk of the homes and businesses hold themselves upright by pure determination. Here, closer to the center of the city, the rusted metal gives way to sun blasted rock held together with mortar and chipped away by time. Spider veins of black run from the foundations buried deep within the ground to the roofs that buckle beneath the damage.

Entire floors and buildings have shifted or been erased entirely. The evident lean seen in the poorer populace has turned with the tides into an all-out embrace as the more capable structures fall victim to the violence wrought by the explosions. Commercial buildings with merchandise still visible beneath bowing ceilings, windows cracked and the insides gutted by looters and fire. The disease that festers in the lower quarters now encompasses half if not more of the city. Merchants and people alike struggle, while those in government sit in the center watching everything die around them.

She has seen this before. Cities turned to rubble, lives reduced to pebbles, and rock ground into dust.

No matter how far she gets away from the war, the war will always follow her. This is a different battle. New enemies, unseen rules, yet in the end it is them or her. People die out in the sands or find themselves snuffed out laying in the streets of their own home. They are no better here than they are out there. Their walls can't protect them, nor can the distance. The darkness will always find them. It is what it does. It is the only thing it can do.

She takes another breath, the polluted air burning her lungs, and she makes her way further up the street. Path narrowing with debris that has not been removed, Coleena finds her way around large stones and toppled carts with their wares of homemade items crushed and forgotten. Rounds of string and tape cordon off areas where the ground beneath is broken into deep grooves large enough to swallow a person whole if they are careless enough to fall victim to the gaping maws.

The sounds of the city become a loud storm of commands and angry voices the closer she draws to the inner realms where the terror becomes real. Scorch marks, black and wide, set their tattoos on everything that still remains solid and in place. Men and women marked as police with their dark blue uniforms and flattop hats stand at corners, arms behind their backs and their eyes watching everyone who draws near. Most are armed. Revolvers and other pistols at their sides, batons looped and ready in case the need arises. Not an unexpected revelation, but still uncommon. Most firearms are commissioned for military use, but now that the war has reached their own borders, she can't find the fault in their logic. Though she hopes that they are adequately trained for there is nothing worse than an untrained person with a gun given the right to use it.

A perimeter has been set. Two blocks deep by her best judgment as she slows to a sensible walk. The muscles in her legs scream their thanks with the tips of angry knives cutting rivets into her insides and her heart pounds like a drum beneath her chest. Every building this close is nothing more than a burned husk. Empty and dried out, she can see the blasted windows and the scars stretching up the rock that did not fall to the ground.

Giant cracks run the length of the paved road, fissures cutting through the asphalt and copper pipes wrenched free from their burial places to reach high into the air. Citizens mill about where they cannot get past the police officers. Small clusters of them. A pair or two here, a half dozen there. Parents holding the hands of little ones, eyes gone dark with worry. They wait for word on survivors that will never come. Coleena tries not to shake her head at the heartbroken looks of their faces. Refugees all of them. Even here in their own homes. Dark ash and dirt smears across them all. No sleep. Probably no running water either. All of what they would call normality blown away with the smoke and ash that carried their hopes away.

Let them grieve. It might not be worth a damn, but it's their right. She wonders if anyone would do the same for her.

"You will have to turn around, ma'am," a woman says, her words sharp and to the point.

Coleena regains her composure and realizes she has

found her way to the officer waiting at the corner. Taking a deep breath, she stretches her aching shoulders with her arms over her head and lets the tiny amount of emotion that had somehow escaped its prison find its way back behind locked doors.

"No problem, officer," she says. "Just trying to get a little exercise in before the heat swelters us all."

The woman is a stone, albeit a small one. Long beaked nose, shut cut brown hair tucked in beneath her cap, and matching eyes watch as Coleena doesn't move. Her attention does not waver as it takes in everything in all directions. A steady glare that reflects within the deep hazel eyes, as hard as the mahogany they resemble. Well trained. Dependable. Could use a few more like her out on the front line.

"Citizens are to remain outside the marked perimeter and off the streets outside of curfew. Direct order from Parliament," the officer continues.

She doesn't move a single muscle. Coleena wipes away at the sweat building on her brow. Maybe too well-trained.

"Understood," Coleena responds. "I am wondering, would you happen to know where I could find a Detective Roland Summers? I have an appointment with him later this morning, yet it is a long way to run back down to the Army barracks if I could find him here or at least closer."

Doesn't seem like a bad idea to drop a name or two now. Maybe she could actually get something done instead of waiting.

"You will have to take that request up with central command, ma'am," Officer Payseur responds, the little name tag barely visible against the dark blue of her uniform.

"Humor me. Where would I find central command?" Coleena asks as she rolls her shoulders back and forth. The muscles in her back tighten with the movement but do not argue as the feeling of being approached from behind begins to build. Watching Payseur's eyes momentarily flicker to the area beyond where she stands confirms the feeling.

"Central command has been--," the officer starts.

"When are you going to let us in there to find our families? What are we doing just standing here? They are dying in there!" A man behind Coleena barks.

Slowly, she turns.

"Please, stay calm," Officer Payseur cuts in. "By direct order of Parliament--."

"Fuck Parliament!" the man shouts and pushes forward, a crowd of six more behind him. He's a big fella. An inch or two taller than Coleena, broad shouldered and going gray around the ears. A thick neck strains below his wide jaw, and she can see him chewing the words before he lets them out. "They are covering up what they know. They don't give a shit about us. All those fucking bureaucrats taking our money and now our rights. We should be in there, finding our fucking families!"

Stepping up to force the issue, the man presses into Coleena, and she braces a leg back to stall his movement. Good sized or not, he's no more special than the ones behind him.

Worried.

Heartbroken.

Scared.

His ash covered and sweat stained shirt wrinkles against her skin and smells horribly of salt and body odor. With a little shift of her weight she gets him to step back.

"Listen to the officer, sir. She is only doing her job. Once the police and the detectives--," Coleena says.

"The fucking police? You think they are doing anything

in there?" the man barks back. "They stand out here, guns in hand and hold us back like we are the fucking enemy. They aren't in there looking for answers or for those we can still save. It's all a damn smokescreen. The real criminals are in there right now covering up what they did, and these fucking pukes know that I'm right."

He goes to shove a thick finger into the chest of Officer Payseur and damn near pokes Coleena in the face.

"Sir, if you do not calm down and disperse, I will be forced to bring you in for--," Officer Payseur says and pushes up beside Coleena.

The man is not here to discuss or negotiate anything. His first strike hits the shorter woman across the jaw and the distinct crack of bone breaking is loud and clear as she drops to the ground quickly. Like a tidal wave the men in the back who seem to have doubled begin pushing forward.

Coleena grabs the man by the shoulder as he pulls it back to strike the fallen officer again. Muscles bunched in his arms, those in her back engulf in pain as she holds him there.

"What the f--," he starts.

Now it's her time to cut him off as she drives her forehead into his nose. A similar crack snaps the air and stars sparkle before her eyes as the world momentarily spins. All chaos ensues as those behind begin tripping over the man's fallen form, several of them spilling over him to sprawl over the fallen officer. Ignoring the pain in her head and body, Coleena tries to push and pull her way to Payseur but the flood is growing out of hand.

Hands claw and scratch at her skin. Her blood boils as one man tries to sneak a quick kick into the fallen officer's prone form. Her fist slams into his groin turning his howls of anger and victory into a yelp of pain as he trips back and becomes a victim of the mob himself.

A fist connects with the back of her head, a flash of light brightening her eyes as she drops to her knees. Growling, she grabs the nearest knee she can, lifts with every ounce she can muster from her strained muscles and flips the man onto his back. Falling forward puts her on top, knees pressed painfully beneath his shoulders and her fist feels nothing as it cracks the side of his face.

Screams and shouts fill the air. There is no way to tell how many of them are her own as she pounds her fist into the man's face over and over. A body slams into her, rolling her into the asphalt. Biting, she finds a piece of flesh and the yelp and taste of blood returns her to where she should be.

This is war.

This is home!

A chunk falls from her lips as she rolls away, chin warm and sticky she tries to get back to her feet. Knees wobbly, she sets one boot to the ground before a pain cracks her ribs from behind and drops her to the pavement. Gunshots ring into the air and people being to scatter.

Coleena tries to get up. Something heavy slams down into the space between her shoulders and presses the air out of her lungs. Gritting her teeth, she tries to crawl forward. She can see Officer Payseur sprawled across the pavement. Blood pools beneath her head.

"I need to help," Coleena grits through her teeth.

"You aren't going anywhere," a deep growl says. To settle the point, Coleena feels the pressure between her shoulders grind into the bones of her back. "Make another move and I'll make sure the street beneath your face is the last thing you ever see."

The click of a revolver setting its hammer back is all she

needs to hear. Tongue bit between her teeth, she watches as dozens of black uniformed officers swarm the rioting men and women. Many try to scatter but the roundup is almost methodical. If she wasn't in so much pain and staring at the young officer's body which still isn't moving, she'd almost think this was planned.

8

Crowded room full of bodies that smell of sweat and desperation. The air is so thick with it, Coleena wipes away the feeling of its sticky touches as the dried blood flakes away from the skin of her hands, arms, and face. Pressed uncomfortably shoulder to shoulder with two women who smell and look like they haven't showered in days, she waits in the cage like an animal. Twelve of them in total shoved in without a second thought. They couldn't pack them in any tighter if they tried.

Injuries hang over them all like badges of honor. Dirty rags tie back bleeding wounds, scratches scab over, and at least one of them coughs through broken ribs. A single fan, the stupid little box type, sits on a chair outside the bars blowing enough warm musky air to circulate the stink and nothing more. Sighing, Coleena rests her head back against the cage. The cold steel is a comfort against the throbbing of her brain. She closes her eyes. The fire running through her muscles has turned everything into one giant angry cramp.

Her hands shake where they rest against the bloodstained fabric of her pants. Balling them into fists, she can stop them momentarily.

"Why me?" she whispers.

Others mumble words as well. Maybe they are answering, their minds linked with the will of the gods and able to give her insight into what she did wrong. Or more than likely they are as desperate and lost as she is with little hope or idea of what to do next.

"You one of them?" a voice asks.

Female. Husky from too many cigarettes. Coleena opens her eyes. No one is looking at her. She ignores the question and shakes her head to loosen the ringing in her ears. Probably just a figment of her tired mind.

"Not answering the question makes you look as guilty as fighting to protect that Blue Jacket," the voice returns.

This time Coleena sits forward, her back stretching with temporary agony before relaxing into the movement. The woman across from her is staring her in the face. Thick set, wide shoulders roll forward. Bandages cover all her knuckles and a good shiner reflects a bright purple from the single light hanging a dozen feet over their heads. Thinning dark curly hair with a serious amount of pepper covers her head as she drops her gaze down to the floor, shaking it back and forth like there are cobwebs she desperately needs to fall out. Within a moment, she returns with her granite stare.

"One of whom?" Coleena asks.

She has been in the city less than a full day. She doesn't even know who "them" is.

"Don't give me that shit," the woman answers. Shifting and seating herself back against the opposite set of bars, the woman is a burly one. Years of hard work have built her a stout body that the test of time has yet to find a way to chisel it away. "I saw you fighting to protect that Blue Jacket. You were talking to her before all chaos broke out. I immediately spotted you as one of them until you ended up here. Get a little too overzealous and forget which side you are on?"

Coleena crosses her arms across her chest. Not often she finds another woman willing to meet her eye to eye.

"That woman was a police officer. She was only doing her duty. What was I supposed to do, just let them kill her?"

With a sigh, the other one rolls her head back, the muscles in her neck flexing.

"Would have served her right. They've killed a lot more of us than just her silly little ass. Maybe if more of them begin to drop they'll realize that we are on to them. You know, I still think you are one of them. Maybe it wasn't a mistake you are here. Maybe it was all planned just like that little sudden raid of theirs. Sound about right? I bet they are listening in right now, hoping with their greedy little smiles I'll spill some information you can take back. Fucking fools if they think I'm going to fall for something this simple."

Words suddenly become hard to come by. All reason has obviously left this place in a trail of dust and there is no logical explanation for anything.

"I have absolutely no idea what you are talking about. I'm a captain in the Army, and we are sworn to protect the people of Azhana. That includes police officers and scum like yourself," Coleena answers, the blood inside of her quickly flaring back up, warming the muscles ready to snap in tired anger.

"Army all right. Now that I think about it, it kinda makes sense. Got a few good punches in there before you went down. Should really teach you bastards how to fight without all those guns and bombs of yours. The real war is right here little miss 'I protect the people of Azhana'. Maybe one day you'll see real combat for yourself."

The hilarity of the comment is almost too much for Coleena. Others in the cell with them groan and mumble and it's all too much. Her eyes are so tired, and it hurts to press them shut. She does everything she can to stifle the laugh, her eyes watering between the pain and ignorance when the bars to the cage rattle with an ear-piercing crack. Baton making its way one rung to the next, the other women begin to moan and move as a guard makes his way over to the door.

"Captain Coleena Armigera?" the man asks.

Dressed like all the blue uniformed officers from the street, the man's eyes barely sweep the cage as he lets his stick whack against the cell a few more times. Coleena leverages herself off the bench to stand. The man's jaw is set. He shows no emotion. Like a robot, or worse, a statue, he waits.

"Right here, officer," she answers.

"You really are one of them," the woman grumbles. "Remember, I didn't tell you anything. Those pencil dicks can go suck themselves off if they think they are going to turn me."

"Go fuck yourself," Coleena says in a whispered tone.

A couple of the others get shifted violently out of the way as the woman goes to push herself off the bench, but a good resounding slam of the guard's baton settles her down.

"Come with me," the officer demands, his eyes settling on Coleena. "You have visitors waiting for you."

"Visitors, yeah right. More like accomplices," the woman cuts in before turning her head back to the floor.

Coleena nods to the guard and waits as he gets the door open with a key from an overflowing ring hooked to his belt. No one tries to rush as she makes her way out, the whispers and weak protests of the inmates all that follows in her wake. The officer leads her down along the front of six more identical cages. Boots tap on concrete floors and the baton cracks against every steal bar as they make their way past all the others held down here in this makeshift dungeon. Every available space is crammed full. Heads down, the locked-up citizens don't bother to look her way. Many carry the same injuries as those who came in with her, their clothes doing very little to cover the marks beneath the ash and dirt from the attacks. Some are different though. She doesn't get much more than a glance, but there are those who look like tired and beaten but clean beyond the filth of remaining in a prison.

"Are all of these people here from the riots?" Coleena asks.

The guard does not turn, slow his walk, or answer. Continuing forward, he keeps them moving. Cages end with a stairwell that brings them to the floor above. The stink of the human cesspool quickly fades into a warmth made of lavender candles and fresh coffee. Dim single bulb lighting is replaced with a soft touch. Stone fades away and is replaced with wood painted a neutral white color and the cold floor is carpeted and clean. Coleena's mouth waters as they turn way from the sound of people talking in pleasant tones from open offices with potted plants by their respective doors and make their way in the opposite direction.

Cold emotionless barriers made of steel with single windows line the hall that was within such a short distance of what seemed so peaceful and business like. Here the harsh realities of being locked up return with a slap across the face, and they stop at the first new hellhole. Taking his key ring from his belt, the guard opens the door and waits for her to step in.

"I thought you said I had visitors?" Coleena asks as she makes her way into the room. Bright white light assaults her eyes like a hot poker and small tears burn at the edges of her eyes as they adjust. "What am I supposed to do--?"

The guard slams the door behind her with a final crack.

Alone.

Silent.

An empty steel table and two uninviting chairs.

Her muscles ache and welcome the offered relief regardless if her captors think of it as such. With a sigh she takes the chance and sits down on the one opposite her entry. At least she is going to see them coming, no matter who they are. The sound of air filtering in through the vents near the ceiling creates a whine that buzzes in her ears. She closes her eyes and lets her head roll back.

"Great, one more problem to deal with."

Time passes slowly. The hum of the air begins to grow, and a dull ache builds in the back of her head to replace the splitting pain that once was her every waking moment. White walls stare at her with no emotion, and yet she begins to hate them. At least the women down in the cells were easy to understand.

People fighting for their homes. Their anger misplaced, but the fight she can understand. But why Parliament? Why are they so certain that the government has anything to do with this?

Questions remain unanswered, the empty flat boards of the walls painted clean and bright watch her, refusing to give the secrets that they know. There is no way to tell how long it has been as the sound of keys working their magic opens the door. Coleena does not move as the men walk in.

Lieutenant Mason and Petty Officer Tul are not expected. Somehow the fragrance of the man's vanilla candles carries with him even here. He looks like even the excursion to the police barracks isn't enough to get cleaned up. The sweat stains under his arms are larger than before and the collar of his shirt still hangs open, his dog tags brighter than ever in the harsh light. Tul, silent and carrying his permanent glare of suspicion, settles himself into the corner where there are no shadows to hide him.

A small amount of tension lifts itself from her shoulders as they enter.

"Finally, a bit of sanity in this damn place," she says, pushing herself from her chair. Cramps ball in furious protest as joints crack, and she struggles to lift herself up.

"Don't bother getting up," Mason says, his hand kindly waving her back down.

Another man steps in behind the two soldiers and the door is unforgiving as it slams back into place. Her third visitor gives the barrier a quick glance before turning to her.

Middle aged. Serious eyes deep-set beneath sun darkened skin and a chin wide and strong. He tilts to the side as he looks at her, his appraisal locked behind the stone visage of his appearance. Then Mason steps out of the way. The man's lean isn't limited to his need for a clear line of view. Relying heavily on a cane, the stranger and his trench coat sway to the side as he waits. Thick gloved hands strangle the top of the polished oak rod.

"Captain Armigera, I would like you to meet Detective Roland Summers," Mason says.

Coleena goes to stand again, but the detective waves her back down like they did upon their arrival.

"So, you are the one I went to look for?" Coleena asks.

The detective tilts his head before taking off his Trilby cap and letting his dark hair settle down. Now there is a style she hasn't seen in ages.

"Is that before or after you decided to start a riot and assault a police officer?" Detective Summers asks.

"I--," Coleena starts in protest.

The Lieutenant chuckles. "Don't worry about that, Captain. We are fully aware that you would never have had anything to do with such a violent protest. From a few reports I've gotten my hands on, you got a few good licks in there before the whole mess got itself taken care of."

"Yeah, if you want to call it that," Coleena adds as she rubs at her ribs and winces at the sharp needle like pain running through her back and over her kidneys.

"But we aren't here to discuss your fighting prowess, Captain. Since the men outside also don't seem to be on the side of prudent investigation, I think it would be best that we make this quick," Mason adds and waves Summers over to the table where she sits. The detective takes his own seat and Mason wraps his big hands around the back of the chair. Like a silent stalker, Tul remains in the corner, his eyes watching and his lips no more than a flat line. "This is the man who is going to help you get the answers that you need. He's a good fellow and the best you are going to find on the force. More than twenty years on the job if you count before all that bad business with the dragon and such."

"Nice to meet you, detective," Coleena says, leaning forward with her elbows on the table. "First off, when am I getting out of here. Until I find that out, the rest of why we are here means little to me."

Placing his dark colored cap down on the table,

Summers runs his hands through his hair and takes a breath. Long, deep, and steady.

"My C.O. is already working on that. They aren't too pleased with letting ANYONE who was involved with that riot out, but the Lieutenant here helped me put in a good word for you. We swore to the church itself that you had nothing to do with this event."

"An innocent bystander who tried desperately to help that stricken officer I think is more like it," Mason adds.

The detective nods in affirmation.

"As I was saying, we hope that all of this will be cleared up shortly. Until then, I want to know what you have already discovered for yourself."

Coleena sighs and leans back into her chair, her head rolling over her shoulders and stopping to gaze at the bright light burning above them.

"Not much. This was my first time back since I enlisted and a little wrong place in the wrong time put me here. A few assholes mentioning that they blame this attack on Parliament itself. You know, the usual crazy government conspiracy accusations," Coleena answers.

"Anything specific? Any names?"

Coleena shakes her head.

"Nothing that I would consider worth a damn. Lots of mumbo jumbo that this isn't the first time this has happened, and a few dead cops is nothing compared to the number killed constantly by Parliament itself. Does this make any sense to you?"

"I wish it did. To be honest this attack took all of us by surprise. This is the biggest city in the remaining world, so we have our problems, but nothing like this. Lieutenant Mason filled me in on why you are here, Captain Armigera, so I was hoping you might have a few insights that would break this right open."

"Sorry to disappoint you, Detective. I am here to offer what assistance I can, but I bring little with me other than what you see in front of you," Coleena says.

"Then back to square one I would guess," Detective Summers replies. "Back to square one."

9

———

The sun is a distant memory when the doors to the jail finally open and Coleena finds her way back out. None of the stench from the fires and the bombs remains, the remnants of the attack no longer evident in the air. The scars will remain, but the lingering torture reduced to aftereffects that will linger for years.

A sour smell, of sweat and unwashed bodies has moved in. Rotting trash and too many living things crammed together within a tight space. A living city. On its last legs, but at least still alive. This is the Parliament City she remembers.

Lights flicker across the landscape, a thousand ground level stars dancing in the darkness among the blotted-out skeletons of buildings spread between her and the walls to all sides. A cage holding them in. The ever-present watchful eye of those stone barriers keeping them in. She rolls her shoulders in big loops to break the tension squeezing her tight.

No cars move in the streets, of the few she figures they

are even allowed. The curfew is in full effect as patrols of officers walk in threes, visible with the lamps they carry in their hands. Coleena waits at the end of the stairs, her muscles and lungs enjoying the freedom of being outside regardless of her need to lean against the handrail she used to keep from falling. The silence of the city. An abnormal feeling subdued and frightening. Like everyone is on a knife's edge. At least now she is in the open and free of the cages and closed in hallways.

"Hopefully you'll catch a break soon, Captain," Lieutenant Mason says as he steps up beside her, the sweet smell of his vanilla candles still clinging to his skin and clothes. Regardless of how helpful he has been, that flavor turns her stomach.

He puts one big paw of a hand on her shoulder and gives it a squeeze. Revulsion sinks deep down within her, and the pain isn't enough to stop her from rolling her shoulders again when he finally pulls away.

"It would be good for us all if we can end this quickly," Coleena says while making sure her face is pointed away.

"That would be for the best," Mason somehow finds a way to mock before tapping her on the shoulder with the palm of his hand again. He may have helped her out, but that damn smell. "You know where to find us if you need any further assistance, Captain."

Without another word, Mason and Tul turn down the street and begin the long walk back to the barracks, their military uniforms keeping the warning looks of the patrolling officers at bay.

"A hardworking bunch, those two," Detective Summers says as he steps up beside her. A ghost hidden in the darkness she didn't even know he was there.

He's half a head taller than she is even with the lean of his cane. Filling out his long coat, he'd be a formidable man without the crippling injury. She rolls her shoulders again without even thinking about it, the pinching of the muscles and ache of her bones a quick reminder she isn't much different herself.

"Really can't expect much else. They are army. Investigating matters like these aren't exactly in our job description," she says. "Have you known them long?"

Summers spares the departing men a quick glance.

"Met them not long after the initial refugees started piling into the city. A real bad time back then. Violence, fear, and always those willing to take advantage of others regardless of how bad the world has just broken. The army that wasn't fighting back the dragon, before we even knew it was a dragon, was all that kept us from falling into chaos and anarchy. Rounded everything up, kept order, that kind of thing. Good men from my experience with them."

"Could use every single one we can get," Coleena adds. "Sometimes I wonder how we keep it going. Men and women die every day on the front lines, sometimes in the hundreds before the bloodshed has finished. But they just keep coming. An endless onslaught."

"Someone will figure it out. This won't be the end of us all. If we've lived this long, we'll find a way. Part of me at least believes that."

"I hope so, Detective. I really do," Coleena says, her voice fading with the final words.

"What is in YOUR job description then, Captain?" Summers asks, changing the subject. "You aren't exactly on the front lines anymore. Unless you count punching it out with a few rowdy men and women."

Coleena spares him a quick glance. His eyes are locked on the darkness of the city, small flickers of light reflecting in the dark irises that watch everything.

"Definitely not this. I was raised for the battlefield. Police work, interviews, and collecting evidence? Honestly, not sure where I can be of any help," she says.

"At least we both can agree we are starting on a good foot then," Summers says tapping the inside of the shoe on his good leg. He steps away and heads in the direction opposite of the two army officers.

"What do you mean by that?" Coleena asks, a quick pickup of her own pace gets her up beside him.

"Tell me why you are really here, Captain. There are no ears to listen in and if we are going to work together, it would be best for both of us if we don't start on a lie," Summers says.

"I already told you. I'm here to offer what assistance I can. I'm a soldier, not an investigator."

"Yet, General Whitaker pulled you from all the men and women of her ranks and put you here with me. A highly decorated captain with no skills of note to aid in the apprehension of those responsible for the largest civilian attack since the coming of the dragon. Am I missing something, or are you hiding more about your abilities?"

Coleena pauses, and he doesn't bother to slow, his limped gait moving him away at a snail's pace. How much can she tell this man? He's correct. There is no one around. The streets are deserted other than the patrols and judging by the nearest waving lamp, she'd have to yell for them to hear her.

"Like I said, I'm built for the battlefield. Nothing more, nothing less. This is new territory for me, Detective

Summers. I'm not really sure why General Whitaker would assign me this type of work," she tries to lie anyway.

The clicking of his cane stops, and she almost walks right past him as she catches up.

"No one is 'built' for the battlefield, Ms. Armigera. People are flesh and blood, plain and simple. Some of us find a calling for death and mayhem while others see it as their duty to stop such individuals, but I do not believe in such predestined outcomes. A lot of people have worked very hard to survive in a world lost to such madness; I'd hate to believe it had nothing to do with everything we have lost along the way."

With a sigh, Coleena looks up at the stars. The memory of that fateful day still so vivid after twenty-five years.

"There are things I've seen out there, Detective. A lot that I cannot explain. Maybe you are correct, and this world is nothing more than a long list of circumstance that has led us here, but deep down I'm not so sure."

He begins walking again, and she falls in stride beside him.

"So, you are a religious person I take it?"

With that question, she chuckles.

"Religious? You can keep that shit to yourself. There are a lot of things going on out there between us and the dragon. So much that I can't even explain half of what I've seen. Whatever gods there are they are playing some sick game and if I had my way, I'd put a bullet in their head without hesitation. So, no detective, I am not a religious zealot. I'm a simple woman with a vendetta against a giant flying lizard. One who wants nothing more than to help the people of this world survive. I may desperately want there to be a reason for all this shit, but I don't think we are going to find it in some damn book. Let alone listening to some preacher go on about a reckoning or penance. They can keep that horse shit piled in their own houses."

Summers chuckles as the darkness of the street thickens bringing the spaces between buildings into a narrow focus. She can feel it all closing in around them. A slow suffocation as the sound of their shoes and boots echo into the night. A solo chorus both dreadful and dreary. They turn away from the main street and into a side alley with a quickness that she is barely able to follow. Here she can barely make out the walls but now there is no doubt how tight everything is growing. If she were to stretch her arms out she'd be able to touch both sides with little effort.

The lights from distant buildings, not vacated and abandoned, fade into the distance. Coleena can feel the muscles in her arms and legs begin to tighten as the little hairs in the back of her neck begin to straighten. A swirling in her head does not help with the dull ache that has yet to go away.

"Amiable aspirations, Captain. Still, none of this points us to why you are here. I understand you were hurt on your last tour, and though I can relate to your plight, I doubt the General is the kind of person who feels putting two cripples together is a gesture of good faith," Summers adds, seemly oblivious to the darkening path.

"Do you have any idea where we are going?" Coleena says, ignoring his continued questioning.

"Yes, I do, Ms. Armigera," he answers, his voice suddenly hushed. "There are secrets between us and if we are to work together, I believe it would be best we get them out into the open."

Without a sound, the man steps to the side and into the ink black of a small alcove created by slight ajar brick walls. What little outline he has disappears into the void. A firm hand grabs her arm and pulls her in to join him. She can feel him press beside her as she slides up against the stone wall. The space they occupy feels like an open coffin. If they were any closer, he'd be right on top of her. Which with his smell of sweet pine and the saltiness of sweat, he is a load better than Mason and that gods-damn vanilla.

"I told you there is nothing more to me than what you see here," she whispers back.

His shoulder presses tighter against hers as he leans closer.

"We are about to test that theory," he whispers, and she can feel his finger go to his lips more than see it.

Silence envelopes them as the city slumbers in its midnight dreams. The darkness is so complete all she can see is little imaginary white lights flicker within her vision. Summer's breathing is calm but short as he stays pressed against her, his form comforting where it isn't disturbing. A few distant shouts echo into the night, voices lost among the tightening streets. The creaks and groans of a world falling apart sing their dreadful song and it is a tune she has heard for far too long. Coleena is about to demand to know what is going on when the surface of the still air cracks with the sound of boots on asphalt. The approaching steps close in on where they hide.

A patrol?

No lamplight precedes the arrival of the trailing group and by the sound there is close to six of them. Coleena's mouth goes dry and the fire in her belly ignites. Maybe they let a few of the other rioters out. Trying to get home themselves, they have followed the same path and without noticing they will continue on their way.

Detective Summers puts a warm hand onto her arm and gently pushes her deeper into the ink thick darkness. She can practically feel the man's heartbeat through the cloth of his jacket, his presence smothering her. For some reason he seems to be trying to shield her with his body. Coleena can feel the tailing group reach them more than she can see them. They are right upon them. If she reached an arm past Summer's protective cover, she'd catch one in the shoulder if not the face.

The boots stop.

"Wouldn't be looking for us, would you?" Summer's asks.

Blinding red light flares and Coleena jerks back in surprise and pain. Men scream, the closest two falling back as they do the same. Crippled or not, Detective Summers jams his cane into the belly of the closest man who falls as the breath ejects from his lungs. Screams turn to hollers and threats as the next catches a handle to the jaw and drops. Coleena no longer feels Summer's protective presence as the brawl spills into the alleyway. More men's voices cut into the night followed by the short abrupt yelps of pain as the officer moves in and out of grasping hands, his cane a weapon that keeps them at a distance.

There are six of them. Two try desperately to pull themselves off the ground. One remains sprawled, knocked out cold with a deep divot curving in the side of his jaw about the size of Summer's cane handle. Another of the attackers, a big burly man with chest and shoulders as wide as a car door circles around where the detective crashes into the far wall, his shoulder driving the air out of another man.

Coleena moves in quietly.

Bone cracks beneath her fist as she drives it into the base of his neck. The behemoth stumbles forward, the pain in her hand numbing as he catches his balance and rolls his head to the side to crack the bones again.

"There you are, you stupid bitch," the man growls,

crooked teeth beneath a broken smile reflecting the harsh red glow of the flare.

"Come and get me," Coleena challenges as she backs away from those trying to find their way to Summers.

The man pops his knuckles as he approaches, his girth filling in the narrow space between walls and entrapping her with no more effort than his presence. She can smell him. A cologne of beer and grease. Beads of sweat run down his face and over his pudgy cheeks. Coleena puts up her fists. She was never great at boxing, much preferring firearms than a test of weight against strength.

"We have a message for you," the thug says through his grinning teeth.

Opening both arms wide, the man goes to lunge forward and grab her but his whole-body rears back as his right knee buckles. Not missing an opportunity, Coleena drives forward, her hands wrapping the man's clammy hairless scalp and driving her knee into his face. Cartilage breaks and blood spurts as he groans and begins to topple backward. With a flop he hits the ground, his leg bending awkwardly. Two men have Summers pushed up against the wall right behind the fat man, his cane dropped to the ground where it fell after smashing the thug's leg from the rear. Coleena stomps on the man's wrist and lets the little bones grind beneath her boots.

He lets out a howl, but not before she hears a sound she would not mistake in a thousand years. A blade finds its way out from a sheath. Both men who hold Summers struggle to keep him standing against the wall. A dark river of red runs from the officer's lower lip and it takes both men everything they can to keep his arms up and out of their way. A third is hunched at his abdomen, a hand holding the pain back and another held tucked in along his side.

"Summers!" Coleena shouts.

Charging forward, she crashes into the approaching man, the top of her head connecting with the side of his face. Light flashes before her eyes, and they both hit the far wall. The attacker crumples to the ground and her world spins as she finds the ground catching her as well. Vomit rushes into the back of her throat and the ache in her head is now a splitting mess as it feels like her head is cracked in two. Groaning, she rolls onto her elbow and shoulder, the muscles in her body screaming as the man who toppled with her does the same.

Their eyes meet.

His are dark, almost entirely black in the dying red light of the flare, and they widen at the sight of her. He lunges forward, knife aimed right for her chest. Searing pain racks across the outer part of her forearm as she keeps the weapon away. He's all arms and teeth as he does everything he can to get on top of her. World spinning, she wraps her hand around his wrist and tries to lock her arm to prevent him from getting it any closer. His eyes narrow as he begins to drive his weight into her. Pressing his other hand onto the back of the knife, it inches closer as her arms begin to lose the fight.

Those dark eyes watch as her end approaches. A little flicker catches them and the warm glow of the fire illuminates a featureless patch that makes its way across his cheek. She cannot keep him off of her. The tip of the knife stares down at her heart. Blood fills her mouth. Her muscles are giving in.

The blade moves closer.

This is it; this is the end.

"Ah!" a man screams as he topples backward and into the one atop of her.

His weight shifts but he does not let go. Adrenaline surges through her as the pressure lessens and instead of trying to push him away, she pulls his arms upward. The knife drives forward and the edge catches the flesh between her neck and shoulder. Fire rips through her skin, but she shoves it into the back of her mind. Wrapping her arms around the man, she squeezes as tight as she can and pulls him against her. Her teeth find the soft skin of his ear, and she bites down until they meet. Ripping violently, the man's ear tears in her mouth and a bright orange light flares into the darkness of the alley.

Her eyes go blind with the sudden flash. She squeezes them shut and goes to roll away. Hot searing pain burns the side of her face as everything is lit up in a glaring yellow light. Her attacker rolls away, the knife dropping beside her. Scrambling, she wipes at the burning liquid searing the flesh of her face and part of her shirt catches on fire in the process. The man is howling as he crawls and pulls at the wall to reach his feet. Everyone stops as the man catches his footing and stumbles trying to flee into the night. Legs buckling, the man struggles, finds his balance, and disappears into the shadows.

Patting her scorched clothes, Coleena scoots across the asphalt until she hits the wall, her face such a mess of pain she can barely feel it and the smell of burning meat fills the air. A streak of yellow light follows the sprayed blood. She tries to process what she sees. Three men sprawled across the alley. Summers pressed up against the adjacent wall, his face in his hands drenched with blood she cannot tell is his or not. The two remaining men run in the opposite direction from the one she bit. At her feet, Coleena does not understand. This isn't possible. She is in Parliament City. That was a man trying to drive a knife into her heart and kill the detective who just happened to be in the wrong place at the wrong time.

Down by her boots, smelling of burning oil and seared flesh, a spray of yellow magma cools. Even with all the pain, Coleena knows that Parliament City's problems just got whole a lot bigger.

10

Pain killers are never enough.

Not for the stitches. Never for the burns. Even muscle aches and swollen joints barely react to the simple drugs. Coleena grits her teeth as the needle pushes through flesh and the doctor hums a small tune as he does his work. A perky song. One of those you would hear a child sing while skipping along a street in the spring.

She wants to rip his tongue out.

Heart monitors beep. People cough in the distance. A wet hacking that sounds heavy and full of stuff it should not be full of. The whole fucking place smells of antiseptic and the sound of plastic wheels over tile scratches at the insides of her ears as she sits forward, shoulders hunched so the man who calls himself a doctor can tear apart her shoulder. She watches as shadows move back and forth behind the curtain that separates her from other patients. A single piece of cloth decorated in tiny dinosaurs. Did they steal this from the children's ward?

Slippers worn by medical personnel slip and glide across the floor as they go from patient to patient. A few yelps of pain and sobs full of wet tears fill in the gaps between the constant beep of monitors. A rolling cart jingles like a loose chain as it goes by, but the two sets of boots standing watch outside her curtain do not move.

Black.

Thick soled.

Military.

The guards have not left their post since they arrived.

"Ah!" she yelps as the needle hits a nerve and the butcher pulls the cord tighter.

"Just a little more, Captain Armigera," the monster assures her, his voice quickly returning to the happier tune he just started.

Small tears burn the edges of her eyes though she has been through this a thousand times. She doesn't care what other people have told her. There is no getting over the little prick of metal as it pushes and pulls its way through your body no matter how many times it happens. Tracing the white tracks of scars all across her body tells her it has been one time too many.

A jagged line over the liver and kidney of her abdomen, an inch wide and six long. Crisscrossing twisted branches over the muscle of both upper arms. Beneath her pants it's a scatter shot of street drawings across her thighs that would make tree roots look uniform. Then there are those fresh ones holding her entire back together. She can feel the bastard's gloved hands working across them as he seals her shut once again. Another sharp pierce lights a fire that reaches up her neck, and she groans instead of turning and shoving the stitching needle into the bastard's eye. The pulling of the crinkled curtain takes her away from her murderous thoughts.

"Do you mind if I come in?" Detective Summers asks.

Without waiting for a response, the man walks in, his gimped leg leaving him to lean heavily on the cane as he passes the pathetic barrier and lets it fall into place behind him. A few stitches close a cut over the man's left eye and bruising darkens the skin below the right. Dark shadows draw a gaunt look to his features and the harsh hospital light puts ten years onto his stubble and chin.

"Not like I could stop you," Coleena answers with a nod to the two sets of boots outside that still haven't moved.

She doesn't bother covering up. Her shirt, bloodied and torn, sits crumpled on the chair next to her bed. All semblance of modesty left when the Army introduced her to communal bathrooms and a life with a family where the men outnumber the women more than one hundred-fold.

"I think that will be it, Captain Armigera," the doctor says.

The quick snap of his gloves gives her little warning before he pats her on the back sending a vice down her spine. He doesn't know how close she is to jumping off the table and strangling him as he gives her that placid look a man gets when forced to talk with a child that isn't his. His brown eyes, the left as lazy as he is, barely moves from her chest as he puts a few markings down on the clipboard at the end of her bed.

"If that will be all, doctor, I'd like a few words with the Captain," Summers cuts in.

Noticing the Detective for the first time he lets his gaze bounce a few times between them before settling on the report in his hand.

"Right, well, yes. That should heal in a few days. Keep a few aspirin on you for the pain and within five stop by the field station to have them removed. They should be able to do that for you, correct?"

Coleena can do nothing but growl.

"I'll make sure she is taken care of, doctor," Summers reassures the man.

Without another word, the jerk is out the curtain and turning to his next victim.

"Fucking asshole," Coleena mutters.

"Doctors are in short supply," Summers says. "Those we don't lose to enlistment in the Army are busy working on the victims of the attacks. A few stitches here and there are hardly worth their time."

Coleena lets her head roll back, the tightness of the skin at her neck numbing as the pain medication cuts in and out of her system.

"Didn't escape without a few of your own," she says.

Summers lifts a hand to the jagged mark etched into his face.

"I've barely just met you and I see you're not one for disappointing."

"You're not blaming me for this shit," Coleena cuts back. "I have no idea who those men were and why they were following us. If I remember correctly, you are the one who caught wind of our tail and decided to do something about it."

Using the tip of his cane, Summers pokes at her ruined shirt and pulls at it until it falls on the floor. With a grunt he lets himself settle down and runs a hand through his dark hair.

He looks tired. More than the swelling of his beaten face and the torn skin over his knuckles. If she didn't know better, she would guess that he hasn't slept in almost a week.

"It's the city. Stay here long enough you'll begin to pick up things that don't belong. There should have been no one near us at that time and along that specific path. No merchants. Very few services. More like a shortcut between the jail and the Western District Special Crimes Unit. During the day the twists and turns are enough to get a veteran lost, at night it should have been a nightmare. Wasn't hard to know they weren't there by accident as neither were we. Plus, they weren't doing the best at covering their tracks which either tells me they are new here and didn't realize their mistake, or they didn't care."

Taking a deep breath, Coleena lets her fingers run over the cool silver chain of the dog tags hanging from her neck. Her fingertips can trace every letter on both plates.

"Six of them probably wouldn't care. There were only two of us and neither you nor I are exactly in the greatest of shape. Probably figured it would be easy. Almost was."

"You are wearing two different sets," Summers says, a quick and abrupt change of subject.

Coleena goes to answer but finds no words. She closes her mouth and waits for him to speak again, but he doesn't. Watching his eyes, they do not move from her chest, though the look tells her it isn't for her tits.

"These?" she asks. "Yeah, one is mine. The other I was given back when I was a little girl."

She lets the tags drop back down onto her chest and slide beneath the cloth of her sports bra.

"Was your father in the Army?" Summers asks.

Coleena laughs. A good belly roll that she lets her push back until she is reclined and resting on her bed, her hands resting on her belly and tracing the rippling scars there. The pain from her shoulder and face pinches and then lessens.

"In the Army? Oh, if you only knew my father, you'd understand how funny that really was. Didn't think I had that left in me," Coleena says as the good chuckle finishes. She lets the sound of the heart monitor tick away in her mind before continuing. "My father was a good man. Caring and gentle. He was no soldier. When the dragon came, he did what any smart person would do. He hid. My mother was always the strong one. A real fighter at times. Both of them working together helped us survive those first few years. A lot of people died of more than just the dragon."

Summers doesn't move, his eyes watching and waiting.

"Yet you joined the service the first moment you got the chance," he says.

"Not exactly right away. My mother was adamant that it was another name for suicide and kept me from joining. Once she died, I signed up."

"Didn't spend time grieving?" he asks.

"Grief is for those who lose their loved ones every day to those demons. My tears dried up with the thousands burned in their homes when that monster spread its wings over Obrathe," she replies, the soft caress of the bed no longer very inviting.

Sitting up, she reaches into the top drawer of the single dresser by the bed. Neatly folded white cotton shirts line the inside. The chances any of these fits are slim to none.

"Those are two different sets of tags. An uncle? A close friend?"

Coleena throws the shirt over her head quickly, the neck hole pulling at the bandages covering her cheek as she forces herself through. With a quick tug of the chain she makes certain the silver tags tuck under the collar of the fabric.

"Aren't you being a little inquisitive of my past that has really nothing to do with this investigation?"

The corner of his lip pulls up tight, and he leans back into his chair, his leg stretching out before him.

"I like to know what I can about those I work with. We

still haven't finished that conversation of why you are really here, but if I have to, I'll start with getting to know you."

She rolls her eyes, sits on the bed, and pulls the shirt away from her belly where it clings like a second skin.

"Not an uncle, and I've had too many friends killed out there. If I was wearing the tags of every one of them who we lost I'd have a hard time just getting out of bed," Coleena says.

In a show of finality, she swings her legs off to the side of the bed again and her boots hit the floor with a clap. Lifting herself up sends pain rippling through her legs and the world spins as she loses balance and slides back onto the thin mattress.

"Not exactly doing the greatest at that right now anyway," Summers says. Leveraging his weight with his cane he rocks himself back onto his feet and extends a hand to help her up.

"Thanks Captain Obvious. Not exactly a spring chicken yourself."

She accepts the help and with a tug she is back on her feet.

"You are more than welcome, Captain. It would be best that you keep your strength for what comes next," Summers says.

"What do you mean? Aren't these guards yours?" Coleena asks.

He shakes his head slowly no before moving his face close to hers. She can feel his warm breath against the tip of her ear.

"Parliament has an envoy waiting for a debriefing once you got out of recovery. It seems our little incident has drawn the attention of those higher up, and they want nothing to come between them and what we may or may not have found out," Summers whispers.

"That seems quick. How much do they already know?" Coleena asks, the boots waiting outside the curtain no longer so welcoming.

"Unless you confessed all of your sins to the good old doctor before he left, I haven't even filed my report yet," Summers adds.

Coleena has no words. She hasn't told anyone other than the first officers on the scene and that was hardly worth Parliament's attention. A couple of downed thugs. An officer and a military contractor mugged on a city street. That couldn't warrant anything like this.

"Can we trust them?" Coleena asks.

Summers shrugs his shoulders before pulling his jacket tighter and putting the cap he seems to never be without back on his head.

"After last night, I'm not sure who I can trust. Something is going on here, Captain, and I've got a sick feeling this attack was just the start."

Coleena nods in agreement. This can only be the beginning, yet she isn't sure she wants to know where this is going to end.

11

When she first came to Parliament City there was no other place that she wanted to be than within these walls. Stoic and ancient. A monolith to the human condition and the resilience needed to survive.

Now, she isn't so sure.

Congress Hall. Parliament's home and seat of power.

Long tapestries of exotic colors feel muted as they hang from a domed roof dozens of feet above their heads. Thin streams of light cut their way to the floor, frail and weak as they filter through the glass. Dust marking age and stubbornness floats itself through the stale air. The images sewn into the hand-woven threads of the rugs against the walls and below their very feet depict memorable images from the history of Azhana. Yet, instead of giving her the pride she once sought, they bare down on her. The vigilant eyes of the gods do not watch the heroics of the men and women who fight across the field, they cast judgment of all who come before them. Even those who now walk these marble floors, decorated with aged crafts from the edges of the known world, fall victim to their weathered looks of disdain and scorn. All who are unlucky to step within these walls are here to confess their sins before the tribunal of their lives.

Boots echo through the cavernous entry as Coleena and Summers follow their issued guards. Empty and hollow, the building is a crypt with eyes everywhere. Dark shadows of human statues watching without moving, judging and waiting.

Moving slowly, she stays close to the detective's broad shoulders. This is not correct. Nothing feels right about this. She should have no worry being here. This is what she fights for. The people of Azhana. Parliament is nothing more than an extension of those people. So, why does this feel so strange?

They stop at the back of the hollow bowl of a room. Two soldiers wait on each side of the closed oak doors. Black uniforms. Red slashes. Stone faces. Without the flesh on their bones she would almost guess they are the same monsters she has fought against the last several years.

"In we go," Summers whispers.

He pivots slightly on his cane to allow her in through the door first. The men standing watch do not move and the two leading the way enter swiftly to take position on opposite sides once through the opening. Coleena follows and regrets the decision the moment she makes her way through.

A long semi-circle table. Sharp as a blade, the surface shines in the light of the chandelier above. The walls are empty but for stone filled with shadows rising high enough to disappear in the gloom above. This is a trap, a cage she'll never get out of. Two chairs wait empty in the center of the silent auditorium. Side by side she can almost make out the invisible bonds that will hold them down should they be foolish enough to actually take a seat.

Hard cut faces watch them come to a stop as they force themselves to continue until they reach the center. Neither of them gives any attention to the two chairs. Chiseled jaws and narrowed eyes watch silently, statues waiting for them. Coleena knows they are considered guilty already and they haven't even done anything wrong. Politicians in their fine suits. Men and women, all of them solidified in their choices in a room full of the certainty of their power.

What has happened here?

"Welcome, Captain Armigera and Detective Summers," the woman at the center of the table starts.

Silver hair flows around the sides of her hardened face. Deep brown eyes watch as muscles pull tight beneath her stretched skin of pale wrinkles and sharp features. A woman who is not to be messed with. Hands age marked and rippling with veins still emanate power as they shift paper documents into a neat pile. Coleena sets herself at attention instead of sitting, the muscles in her back screaming as the bones of her shoulders pop.

"It is our honor, Senator Reza," Summers says.

He is less stiff, the lean on his cane suddenly more extenuated now that they stand front and center. Coleena stays silent. He does not sit either.

"We have seen the reports filed from your investigation into the attacks, Detective," Senator Reza continues.

"I hope they have been sufficient, Senator," Summers replies.

"So far, the information has been sparse, Detective. It has been almost a week, yet you offer no further explanation on why or how this has happened."

Summers' shoulders roll back slightly, almost invisible to the eye, but Coleena catches the small movement.

"This was a very coordinated attack, Senator. Professionals with the means and the time to get everything correct. We are not dealing with amateurs who will so easily be caught."

Two of the other six senators ruffle papers set before them. All of them watch, thoughts burning behind their eyes.

"Do you know of the small rebellion we have on our streets, Detective? Have you heard of a group called Azhana United?" Senator Karagoz asks.

A heavy-set man with cheeks red and puffy. He reminds Coleena of the cooks from the mess halls of every military base she has ever visited. All sweat and high blood pressure. Too much of everything except hair. Ready to pop with bulging veins rippling across their multi-colored clammy skin. His bloodshot eyes are dull and angry. The chubby lower lip quivers where he isn't biting it.

"Nothing but rumors," Roland answers.

"Despite the snail pace of your investigation, Detective, evidence has been presented to the council here regarding the growth of an anarchist movement which goes by this name. Little more than a disgruntled gathering of unruly degenerates, they have become more vocal lately about their hatred for Parliament and everything this country stands for. They believe that the world would be better off with smaller, more tribal forms of government. Of course, these tribes would be led by men handpicked from their own numbers. Their central tenant is one centered on the removal of both the church and government. Has your investigation found anything along these lines?" Karagoz continues.

Summers shakes his head.

Azhana United?

Coleena has never heard anything about this. The senator's eyes narrow as the detective takes a moment before answering.

"Nothing but a few rumors and ramblings of crazy or drunk men, Senator. I have followed any leads that seem worthy but those have shown little merit and even less connected to the matter at hand," Summers answers.

"Yes, the matter at hand," Senator Reza cuts in. "As I see it, Detective, Parliament City has suffered its most gregarious attack since it rose to prominence and yet the detectives of this city's esteemed police force have shown nothing but detail empty reports. Almost an entire week and what do you bring to us?"

"My reports contain all that we have collected so far, Senator. It is our opinion that this attack, three coordinated bombings of highly populated commerce buildings, was completed by those with means and skills above your average 'degenerate'. The blasts at the bank and the Center of Small Business Planning were used to maximum effect. Their busiest hours with the greatest possibility of collateral damage."

"Yet, here we sit with little more than the facts of what was done and not who did it. Do you have any leads, Detective? Any suspects within your custody?" Senator Karagoz cuts in.

His bulging little eyes shift to Coleena and regardless of the pain she stiffens her shoulders and back, her mouth shut until spoken to.

"Besides those arrested during the riots of the other day, no, Senator. Our investigation continues and every day we hope to draw closer to the answers we all seek," Roland says, the tone of his voice raising ever so slightly.

The senator holds his gaze on Coleena a moment longer before turning back.

"What would you say if we told you there has been other evidence presented to us, Detective? Concrete proof that the city police is chasing ghosts and wasting the precious time of the citizens who await answers for the pain brought to their lives. These rebellious degenerates must be brought to justice before they can bring harm to more people, Detective. Do you understand that?" Reza asks.

Summers shifts his cane in front of his feet and leans forward.

"Any leads that can be provided, Senator, would be greatly appreciated. The detectives of the city police will gladly turn over every last stone until we find who did this and bring them before the courts. I give you my word that we are doing everything within our power--."

"Power. Yes, Detective, we are well aware of the police 'power' within these city walls. If it wasn't for the fact that you have proven less than capable of utilizing such information, we would gladly hand over all that has been presented to usher an appropriate end to this travesty. But, alas, we are not of such confidence, Detective. Parliament's resources are of vital importance, and we cannot risk losing all the work we have succeeded with so far. Unless you can prove that you or any of the men and women of the police force can make use of these resources, then we will have to continue this investigation outside of your meager abilities," Senator Reza continues.

"Understood, Senator," Roland replies.

"See that you do, Detective. We grow impatient with what you have done thus far, and the people of Parliament city deserve better. In fact, Azhana itself, cannot wait for the wheels of justice to finally get moving. We must strike while the iron is hot, Detective. There is no other way," Senator Reza says.

"I agree," Summers responds.

"See that you do, Detective. Now, let us discuss another matter that disturbs the committee as much as it does intrigue us, Detective," Senator Reza says as she lets her gaze fall onto Coleena.

Muscles tighten, heels click, and her throat is cotton. Staring straight ahead, Coleena does her best not to match the older woman's eyes.

"If it would please you, Senators, let me introduce Captain Coleena Armigera of the Azhana armed forces," Detective Summers says.

A few muffled words find their way out of closed lips as half the senators shuffle papers before solidifying their eyes on the hole burning through her chest.

"Captain Armigera. Yes, I see that you first returned to this city just a few days ago," Senator Reza starts.

"Yes, ma'am, that is correct," Coleena answers.

"Tell us why you are here," the senator continues.

"I was assigned here by General Whitaker to aid in the investigation involving the attacks that have plagued this city, ma'am," Coleena responds.

"So, the General herself felt these attacks, committed by citizens on civilian ground, warranted interference by the men and women of the armed forces? Does she have as little faith in the police force here in the city as some have already reported?"

Coleena can't help but spare Roland a quick glance before answering.

"No, ma'am. I believe General Whitaker thinks as highly

as I do of the men and women who have taken their vows to protect the people of Parliament City. She believes that such a travesty should bring all resources to bare when apprehending those who would do such a thing. Having been injured in the line of duty, General Whitaker felt that my skill set would be of better use here as a consultant than a retired ex-soldier."

"Very generous of the general, Captain Armigera," Senator Karagoz says. "Of this skill set of yours, what do you see will be most beneficial in helping Detective Summers here? Maybe something that can be used by the other detectives on the force who currently spend little time moving forward with their investigation as well."

Coleena tries to choose her words carefully.

"I have seen many things within my time on the battlefield, Senator," she starts, the trickling sweat on the back of her neck sending painful shivers down her spine. "I have witnessed devastating attacks from all angles. I believe that the General thinks with my trained experience in the heat of battle, I might be of use to the detective and the other officers of the police force."

"Battle tactics and war, Captain," Senator Reza says. "Are you telling us that there is a war raging within our city walls? Is this an invading army trying to overthrow the government?"

"No, ma'am. The General feels--," Coleena tries to answer.

"Or would it be more logical that maybe the General has a personal stake in all of this? Did you know she has been very outspoken in her distrust for the decisions made by some of the very men and woman who sit before you?"

"No, ma'am," Coleena says.

"Your General Whitaker has not been very kind to those

of us honored to serve the people of Azhana. To be honest, there are many among us who feel that if she was not so protected in her position by the subservient men and women of the armed forces, there would be reason to have a change of leadership within your own ranks. Maybe then we could see a real change in this little war of yours with the supposed dragon," Senator Reza says.

"Supposed dragon?" Coleena asks. All words are lost, her mind blank as she stares into the cold faces of the politicians in front of her. "I'm sorry, ma'am, but there is no supposed about these monsters. People are dying day in and day out fighting the demons that storm our front. If it was not for their bravery and the blood we spill every day, there wouldn't be a Parliament City still standing."

"Yet, Captain, we don't see any of that here. Actually, other than these reports written by the General 'herself', not a single person within these walls has had a problem with these demons in twenty years," Reza continues.

"That does not mean it doesn't exist. Are you telling me, Senator, that you doubt the dragon is real? Millions of people were killed when that monster sprang from the earth. I was there that day. I watched an entire city burn!"

Coleena can barely hold in the fire burning through her blood. This is ridiculous. What is going on here?

"We know the supposed history, Captain. But one would think with an army so capable as Azhana's, we'd have more to show than rumors, reports, and lists of dead soldiers. Where is the dragon? Why can we not fight it? Isn't there a way to shoot the damn thing right out of the sky?"

The urge to rip the hair right out of her head is unbearable. Coleena looks over at Summers who shakes his head with barely discernible movement. She cannot hold back.

"This THING is not of our world, Senator. Its minions

and demons are made of solid stone and bullets hardly do more than keep them at bay. We can't even get close enough to the damn monster to try to 'shoot it down'. We die every day just to keep the bastard as far away from here as possible. Even that seems to have failed."

The words are out of her mouth before she can stop them. A dead silence blankets them all and the walls close in around her.

"And we reach the point why we even decided to entertain this farce you bring to our doors, Captain. We have read a report that you believe you found one of this 'dragon's' minions within the walls of our city. Some kind of hybrid between man and monster," Senator Karagoz says.

"I made no such report," Detective Summers cuts in.

"We weren't speaking to you, Detective," Senator Reza interjects.

"Neither have I," Coleena adds. "We were attacked on the streets last night and in that altercation, I was injured. The detective here saw to it that I was taken care of and after my release I was brought here. I have issued no report stating that we have found anything related to the dragon within these walls."

"So, you deny having fought a man who bled molten blood onto that wound covering the side of your face, captain?" Reza asks.

Coleena puts a hand up to the patch of gauze taped to her cheek. She can feel the heat beneath her palm and the numbing of the medication beginning to fade quickly.

"I did not say I deny that is what happened. I simply stated--," Coleena starts.

"Regardless of who filed the report, are you here to tell us that these statements are true? Are we to believe that man and monster are now breeding, and they are here bombing our city?" Reza cuts in again.

"No, Senator, I didn't say that."

"So, there are no human-monster hybrids attacking you at night? That wound on your face is self-inflicted. Maybe your time on the front-lines took away your ability to cook and you suffered an unfortunate kitchen accident."

"That is not what the captain is trying to say, Senator," Roland interjects.

"Quiet, Detective. We are speaking to the Captain and if we decide that your opinion is worth noting, we will tell you," Reza says, her voice bitter and sharp as a knife.

"Senator, yes, we were attacked last night. During the fight I was hurt, but I also got a chance to rip away part of an ear from the man who attacked me. When he started to bleed, I was burned by molten rock," Coleena finishes by taking her hand away from the large gauze covering part of her cheek.

"And you are absolutely, without a doubt in your mind, certain that this attack was from a man?" Senator Reza asks.

"Yes, ma'am. It was dark in that alley, but the flare dropped by the detective was enough for me to be certain of that. He tried to drive a knife through my chest, and I was close enough to smell the heat of his breath. There is no doubt that this was a man."

"A man who bleeds rock," Senator Karagoz adds.

"It would appear so," Detective Summers finishes.

The senators all look at him, the hard glares a reproach that would make a young child run to the corner. A small part of her wants to as well, the larger wanting to jump over that polished table of theirs and strangle every one of them to death.

"Dragons and their demons. Men who bleed rock and a

hybrid monster using bombs to attack our city hundreds of miles away from the so-called beast. What is this world coming to?" Senator Reza asks, more to herself than anyone.

"Is there anything else you want to add before this committee, Captain Armigera? Any final statements before we convene with our final judgment?" Senator Karagoz asks.

"Wait, judgment?" Coleena asks, unable to hold back the shock in her voice.

She looks over to Summers. His eyes are as wide as hers, but the glares of the politicians in front of them keep him at bay.

"Then if you have nothing else to say for yourself," Senator Reza starts. "I am one who has not changed their opinion since the meeting started. Is there anyone here who has had a change of heart or are we all still in favor?"

All of them give slow nods of their heads. Seven confirmations without a single dissent among them.

"Wait? You all had your minds made up before we even started? What is this? Are we in the middle of some fake trial?" Coleena lets the words flow unrestricted from her lips.

"You have had your chance, Captain," Karagoz says.

"Chance for what?"

Roland's face is concentrated on the tiles of marble at his feet and his shoulders are slumped, his full weight on his cane. He does not look at her. He must already know.

"The senators and I have come to the conclusion, Captain Armigera, that for the security of our fine city, your pass to remain within these walls has been revoked. Though most, if not all of us, would question openly what the General is doing by sending a woman such as yourself here, we have given enough to her flights of fancy in allowing your escapades here within Parliament City. This is a time of great danger, and we cannot afford for distractions to take us away from what must be done. Those responsible for these attacks will be found and punished. With or without the help of our police detectives, we will get the job done ourselves."

"You have got to be kidding," Coleena says.

"No, Captain, we are not. By Parliament proclamation, you are ordered to leave the city limits within the next three hours. A message has already been sent to General Whitaker that she may come and retrieve you at her pleasure and that her rendezvous with you will be outside our city walls. Be warned, Captain Armigera. The city wall guards, the police force, and even the detectives will all be made aware that if you find yourself within Parliament City again, you are to be detained immediately. Next time it will not be so easy to get yourself out of the prison cages, Captain. I would take this one chance and do not show your face here again."

"You can't do this," Coleena says. " I am a citizen of Azhana. You can't just ban me from the city."

"This is Congress Hall. We make the rules by which all Azhana citizens must live and if we say you are banished, do not for a moment think otherwise. The survival of our way of life is at stake here. We cannot afford to have anyone, especially such a decorated officer like yourself, spreading such false rumors. Dragons, demons, and now hybrids. What has come of this world?"

"Roland, say something," Coleena pleads.

The detective says nothing. His attention is still locked on the floor.

"He will not help you, Captain," Reza starts again. "You have three hours. If you are not outside of these walls by then, you will be considered a criminal and the law here is harsh for those who do not abide by it. Take this time, Captain. Make the correct choice."

There are no words. Coleena cannot say anything. In shock, they lead her and Summers out of the room. Everything is a blur. The attacks. Those men in the alley. What is going on?

Stepping out into the heat, everything returns to focus. With a crack the doors slam shut behind her. The fire in her belly burns with a white-hot flame. This is not over. One way or the other, she is going to find out what is happening here.

12

———

Three hours.

She has barely been in the city for more than two days and now she has three hours to leave. Rendezvous with the General outside of the city walls. Who do these politicians think they are?

For one the weather outside has become as miserable as she is. Hot, humid, and sticky. The heat itself has a taste and it's too close to the flavor of rotten food and piling shit. It may take longer than she wants to get the disgusting film of this city out of her mouth.

Sun glare reflects off every surface.

The stone.

The dirt.

Even the faces of people as they walk by reflect the light with a blinding brilliance that hides the filth beneath. She squints her eyes in frustration and pain. Life as she expected it to be returns to the streets of Parliament City. Pedestrians filling the sidewalks, roadways, and everywhere in between. The sounds of a thousand voices. Talking, whispering, and shouting. The city is a living and breathing thing. Hundreds of people pushing to go on with lives that must in some way return to normal if that is what they want to call it.

What is normal anymore?

This is not it, not to her. People are strangers here. No more than faceless shadows passing by in the street. Clothes of every imaginable color pulled tight to keep from breathing the choking dust and head-wraps preventing the relentless sun from scorching their scalps. Coleena puts a hand to her own head, the blond strands greasy and thin beneath her fingers. She can feel the heat warming the skin of her palm. The side of her face begins to itch, and the pain medications fade to a distant memory as her neck and face stiffen from the trauma.

No dragon?

General Whittaker plotting to take down Parliament?

This is not the city she remembers as she shoulders her way through the crowd, men and women moving quickly out of her path as if they can feel the hatred radiating from her like the heat. A different country entirely, she is a stranger between the walls that should make her feel at home. Maybe twenty more minutes of this pushing and shoving, and she'll be back to the barracks. The red flags marking off the military zone lay limp in the distance. She can almost feel the same relief she did so many years ago return at the sight of them.

"You all right?" Summers calls to her.

The ground no longer has so much of his attention, and he moves up beside her, weight heavily tilted to his cane and life returning to the eyes that will not look her in the face.

"Let me see. I've been here, what, maybe forty-eight hours? I've been arrested for instigating a riot and attacked by something I can't even describe. I've been left with brand-new scars across half of my face, and now I'm ordered to leave the city for creating panic," Coleena answers. "I'm going to have give you a no on that one, Detective. Or is it written somewhere down there on your shoes?"

She cannot let this pass. Planting her feet, she lets the crowd bend and mold its way around her. This single spot is hers at the moment. No politician, no police officer, and sure as hell no cowardly detective is going to take it away from her. In that pseudo trial he was as useless as they made him out to be. No fight. Absolutely no defense. He took all of it with his tail between his legs and did nothing to protect her. What a great part...

The words refuse to cross the tip of her tongue. Poisonous just to consider it for a moment.

"I probably should explain myself," the detective answers.

He sighs taking in a deep breath, and she begins to walk away, leaving him behind her. Fuck, he isn't even worth the time.

"Best do it while we get ourselves moving. Remember, I now have less than three hours to get out of this hellhole and time is a wasting. That cane of yours better be able to keep up," she yells back at him without another glance.

Deep down she wants to regret that statement, but she can't. The war inside of her will not let it happen. Half wants to leave this place in the dust and forget she was ever here, while the other needs to figure out what is going on.

Can the war actually be this far out of their minds?

She shakes her head.

No, there must be something else.

"We both know what they did in there is wrong, Captain. They are getting information from a source that has nothing to do with you or me. I'm beginning to suspect that this problem goes a lot deeper than we want to believe."

Coleena wheels around on him fast enough to elbow an old woman, bent with age and a heavy three rolled pack on her back, forcing her into a stumbling walk. Dust kicks into the air as pedestrians continue to filter around her and Summers with a strong arm helps right the woman and keep her on her feet. None of the other people spare any of them even the slightest glance. The streets are packed regardless of the heat and busy lives leave little room for others. Center city is still blocked off, the dangers still evident where the bombs did the most damage. People are forced to find new routes, keep their lives going regardless of what was taken away.

Summers shuffles up, shoulders jostling him back and forth in a human example of bumper cars.

"You are giving me reason to believe those assholes in that building aren't too far off in their assessment of you, Detective. I might be a soldier, not accustomed to the work you do here on the streets, but even I can see this problem is deeper than a few angry citizens wanting to be leaders. Or all the pits in hell protect us, they may want to be politicians. This place has a big fucking problem on its hands and yet no one wants to do anything about it. Do I seem to have it correct, Detective?"

Summers stops in front of her. Beads of sweat run down his forehead and his cheeks are rosy red beneath his dark eyes, the swelling around the right one about to close it entirely. Not a good look for the man. Makes him look pasty and old.

"Correct on all accounts, Captain. The real question is what are you going to do about it?"

Coleena throws her hands up in disgust. Turning back into the crowd, she pushes her way through and works her way against the flow. The great walls loom dark in the distance. Closing them in. The rock thick and solid. What good will it do if the danger is already here?

"Let me think on that, Summers. I have to be outside these city walls regardless of what I think is happening here. Maybe I can try and help from there? We both know that is probably of little use, but if we are going to sit here and play imaginary friends for a moment, let's think on this a moment. If I don't follow their new 'proclamation' I might just become the most wanted woman in Parliament City. And if, that is a big fucking if, I follow their instructions but still find a way to interfere inside the walls I doubt they are going to consider it any different. Are you going to arrest me on sight? Cuff me and shove me in a cage with all those other people?" Coleena yells, the distance between them already beginning to grow. "Do you think for a moment they won't step in if they find I'm working on this case from outside their protective walls? Does their influence really end with that stone? Does it, Detective?"

"What Parliament doesn't know won't hurt them. There are good men and women on the force, Ms. Armigera. Many of them I would trust with my life. If I tell them I trust you, they will do the same. The city is a big place. Shouldn't be hard to lose a single army captain among so many individuals."

"Now you decide to grow yourself a set of balls? Disobeying orders. Where were they when we were in there getting our asses handed to us? You were a sick fucking puppy with its tail between its legs. What in the seven hells is wrong with you, Detective?" Coleena demands.

Halting beside her, Roland removes his cap and wipes away the sweat soaking his brow and replaces it over his greasy hair.

"I'm no coward, Captain. We have to get a few things

settled between us and a lot of it has to do with what happened in there. If you would give me a few moments to explain, preferably in a less open area, I think we both have things to get off of our chest," Summers says while casting a long hard look on all the people passing them by. "You still have enough time to sit down with me. Why don't we do that? After we are done you can decide if you are really going to leave the city or if finding out what in the world is going on here is enough to keep you around."

Coleena sighs, plants her fists into her hips, and lets her head roll in a big circle to stretch the cramped muscles of her neck. The bones pop, and she can feel a little pressure release though the pinching and burning of her face forces the lid of her right eye to twitch.

"You've got one hour, Detective. If what you have to say doesn't change my mind, then I still have plenty of time to get out of here. Once I'm through those doors though, this whole investigation is over for me. I did my best with the time given. I was never meant for this type of work. We both know it, but I'm willing to listen to whatever it is you think will change my mind."

A small smile lifts the corner of Roland's busted lips, and he gives her a nod. Taking the lead, he helps push their way through the crowd. People are reluctant to give up their spaces even to a man of the police or woman of the army. Words are growled and a few distant threats are barked, but they make their way past all the stink and filth. Ducking through a side alley filled with bits of trash, piles of dirt, and a dead stray cat, she finds them heading in a direction opposite the barracks. A few blocks further down, Roland turns right onto a street less traveled and practically empty.

Some thin looking kids, all bones and knobby knees play stick ball with a broom handle, and they haven't even bothered to remove the actual broom end. Clothes barely hang onto their bodies with enough holes she is surprised they know which to put their arms and legs through. A few more cats. Several loose chickens and more boarded up doors. Deep cracks in the road and walkways make it treacherous to even step without keeping your eyes on your feet as you move forward.

"Not going to bring me to one of those places where I get to fight for my life again are you? A girl can only take one of those a week and you've used up your entire allowance," Coleena says.

He shakes his head no.

"It's a little place we can speak privately. Rare in a city this large," he answers and continues leading the way.

Two blocks later they take a left and step into what has to be one of the poorest neighborhoods in Parliament city. Compared to where she just was, those kids and their makeshift game look well-fed and at least the roofs above their heads were probably less likely to fall. Houses here have never heard of the word straight. Boards making up the outer walls peel paint like a rifle drops bullets and the lean to their foundations gives Summers a run for his money. Most look collapsed. The cracks and openings traversing the road have made their way up the walls. In some places entire windows have collapsed onto themselves. If it wasn't for how far away from the actual bombing this place is, she would guess this is where it happened.

Clothes and towels of mismatched fabric look stained beyond recognition and some are barely more than thread as they dangle from loose lines. Trash piles up on the corners and front porches. There are more boarded doors than those with actual use still left to them.

"You sure we are in the correct place?" Coleena asks.

Of the few people out on the street, most don't bother to turn when she notices them staring. Old women sweeping up dust that will return in a matter of minutes. Rail thin men wearing little more than pants with skin burned a deep brown by the sun and hair as unruly as a stray dog. Their eyes are what stops her.

Questioning.

Hungry.

Feral.

The small flame in the pit of her stomach churns and readies to ignite if any of this goes sour. These may be old women and men lost to whatever ails them, but something about this place does not feel right. Forgotten and left to die, this is the home of Parliament City's desperation. People long forgotten. When all hope dies, anything is possible.

"Like I said," Summers says as he turns the handle of the third house since they turned onto this street. "A place where we can talk privately."

All smoke and mirrors. Coleena is in a new world when she steps in where Summers presses the door open. Shadows hold sway in the dark and gloom, but the air is warm and thick with the smells of fresh roasted coffee. There is a slight hint of alcohol, but it's an aftertaste where the tongue lavishes on the sweet notes of berries and roasted beans. Unlike the sun blasted exterior of faded purples and browns down the street for as far as she can see, inside this room everything is spotless. Not a mark or grain of sand on the floor where small round tables made for couples wait beneath the window and in secluded corners. Even the bar across from them is gleaming beneath the candlelight and the rays of golden sun making it in through the paneled window in the front. A checkered board shadow where two of the panel boards have been knocked out pattern the polished top where empty glasses sit on folded cloth napkins.

"What is this place?" Coleena asks, her tongue thick and wet.

A cool breeze sends shivers up her spine as the door behind the bar swings on smooth hinges and a woman a good head shorter than her shuffles in with a tray between her thick arms and a towel thrown over her shoulder. Her flannel dress creates a wide sway of her hips, and she would draw the attention of anyone in the room if it wasn't for the fact that Summers and herself are the only ones currently in the establishment. A warm smile brightens her homely face and eyes of a perfect sea blue sparkle as they find Roland standing beside her.

"This is Mama Filiz's little diamond in the rough," Roland says before bowing down to kiss the old woman on the cheek. They redden as her smile grows wider, and she gives a small chuckle. He takes his cap off to run a hand through his hair. "Best coffee and soup from here to the remains of Obrathe, and Beggar's Town likes to keep it that way. Plus, it's a secluded getaway for the patrolmen and C.O.s of the department so people know to keep it a secret as well as leave it alone."

"My mama taught me everything I know, and she was born and raised in Obrathe," Mama Filiz says. "Second best soup after hers, may the gods protect her soul."

The round women waves her hands to the table in the corner furthest from the door.

"I'm from Obrathe myself," Coleena adds as she slides her way into the offered chair facing the bright window.

Roland takes his time sitting with a grunt as Mama Filiz disappears and quickly returns with two steaming bowls of soup.

"You will find a lot of refugees from Obrathe within these city walls," Summers says. "Spread from here all the way to Parliament itself."

Coleena nods with a smile as Filiz slides a plate with a small bowl of the creamiest looking tomato soup she has ever seen in front of her. She wants to say something but the inside of her mouth waters to the point of uselessness at the warm smell of tomatoes and basil.

"Go ahead and eat," the woman says. "I'll leave you two in private, but I expect both bowls to be empty. Especially yours, Mr. Summers. You don't look like you've been eating enough."

She pokes him in the gut before turning away.

"I'll be OK, Mama Filiz," Summers says.

Between delicious bites Coleena adds, "You didn't bring me all this way to fill me full of soup and tell me what I already know. Obrathe was the capital before it burned to the ground. Of course, if Parliament City was going to flood with refugees it would consist of a lot of them. Not exactly hard evidence, Detective."

He shakes his head, his right hand flattening his hat on the table and a thumb rubbing a pattern over the soft material.

"That brings me back to the real reason you are here, Captain," he answers.

Coleena pushes her bowl away. Already empty and her stomach wanting more.

"Look, we already tried this. I am not hiding anything. I'm here to use whatever skills I can to help you find out what is going on in this city and that is it. Are you telling me you secretly think General Whittaker is trying to take over the city? Is that what this is all about, Summers?"

He doesn't answer right away. A few bites of soup pass

his lips as his eyes move from her to the empty shadows of the vacant restaurant.

"Then this might come as new information for you, but I have not put everything in the reports that I send to Parliament. I have found information that could help lead us to where we need to go, but I've withheld it from them and pretty much everyone. Even others on the force."

"And what would that be, Detective?" Coleena asks. "I don't exactly have all the time in the world, and I am not known for my patience."

He pushes his bowl away, empty just as he was ordered to do.

"I think I can believe that one," he says with a small grin. "Have you ever seen a dragon symbol before?"

Coleena leans back into her chair, her eyes on the window where several people walk by, nothing but shadows passing across the glass.

"What kind of symbols? I've seen dozens used to mark information in regard to plans for our fight with the dragon."

"Not those kinds of symbols, Captain. More like a brand. A dragon silhouette with flames and a crescent moon. Probably easy to mistake for a phoenix but distinctively different unless the legendary birds also breathed fire."

The heart in Coleena's heart skips a beat, a choke forming in her throat. She has seen this before. The first time only a week ago.

General Whittaker.

Her father's book.

"Wait a minute? You've seen a symbol like this? Where? Here in this city?" she asks.

"Tell me what you know, Captain," Roland says, his hand bunching his little hat into a tight ball. "What do you know that I don't?"

Coleena doesn't know where to start. If what the General told her was correct, then...

More figures pass by the restaurant's window. She watches them go by as the thoughts circle like angry bees in her mind. Pain ripples down her cheek, across her neck, and down her spine. What can she tell him?

"General Whittaker, she...," Coleena starts when the activity in the window catches her eye again.

"What, Captain? What did Whittaker send you here to do?" Roland insists, his attention fully drawn to her.

Pushing her chair back, Coleena gets up, her pain and misery momentarily forgotten. She shakes her head to clear her thoughts as she moves toward the window.

"She...she has information that has been kept in archives since the World War and the emergence of the dragon. Handwritten letters and notes from her father. There was this organization..."

There is movement out in the street. Men, several of them standing together in a small circle, huddled over a rusted and beat up trashcan.

"What type of organization? Captain, are you listening to me?"

Coleena makes her way to the window, her eyes squinting in the bright light.

"More like a cult than an organization. Her father believed they were responsible for all of this. For everything."

"So, what you're telling me is if this symbol has anything to do with this cult, these people survived the devastation that wiped out more than half the known world, and they are here, in my city?" Summers asks.

Pivoting with his cane he finds his way to his feet.

"I'm...I'm not sure," Coleena responds.

Those men across the street, they don't look like they belong here.

Their coats.

Long flowing cloth of neutral browns and whites. Heads hidden by large cowls and one of them turns her way. Her heart stops.

He looks right at her. Red eyes stare at her, the fires within burning bright even at this distance and in this oppressive heat. Then there are the scales. Black, charred. They look like stone growing its way across his cheeks. He smiles.

"Summers, get down!" Coleena screams as she dives for him.

Deafening thunder shatters glass and buckles the walls as their world erupts in a cataclysmic earthquake that blots out the sun and puts them all into darkness.

13

This isn't what death feels like. It's definitely not what it tastes like.

Gritty.

Dry.

Too much like sand, dirt, and that horrible coating ash this city is so fond of.

The world rings in an endless siren and everything is gray. Her skin, her clothes, the walls where they haven't collapsed, and even the air. It's everywhere. Her lungs burn as each breath is a choking hazard. People scream and cry. Shadows move in and out of the foggy haze as she stumbles getting back to her feet.

Everything spins. The ground moves beneath her feet. Her knees wobble, but she stands with the help of a table that shakes with the effort. Her only lifeline, this sturdy piece of the world, is covered with bits of rock and dust just like everything else. Mama Filiz's restaurant. So immaculate. A diamond buried beneath so much rough. The gaping hole in the wall tells the story of the business' demise.

More violent coughs rack her body and her vision

clouds at the pain as it shoots through her spine and threatens to rip her face in half. A warm liquid, dark and salty, drips from her eyebrow. She wipes it away. Looking at her shaking hand it takes a moment to put it together. Black and sticky. She rubs it between her fingers. Warm and staining the skin beneath. Putting her hand to her forehead sends a piercing agony through her scalp.

Blood.

Great, another scar.

She can hear sirens in the distance. The sun is blotted out as a choking, poisonous cloud hangs over everything. Bits of wall, rock, and road crunch beneath her boots as she walks forward on uneven steps.

"Summers, you OK?" she calls out.

Is she yelling? She doesn't know. All she can tell is that she doesn't hear any response from him.

Shadows move in and out of the cloud. The door where she entered shortly before all of this nightmare is gone. No frame, no wall, only support beams that are bent at horrible angles and charred almost to their core. How in the pits of hell did this not collapse and kill them all?

Looking around she cannot see Summers anywhere. Tile and wooden planks litter the floor. The place where their table was is a pile of rubble, and she sees no bodies.

"Mama Filiz! Are you OK?" she calls out.

Still no answer.

The sirens draw closer. A wailing rattles the inside of her ears alongside the ringing that won't go away. She has felt this way before. When bombs or missiles go off too early or too close. Closing her eyes, she lets the world stop spinning in her mind before opening them again.

Those men, where did they come from? Why were they here? The questions barely hit her mind, and she already has the answers. They were here for her. She knows who they are, and they cannot let her live with that information.

Outside the restaurant, the world is in chaos. Rubble is everywhere and the road is a new crater opening itself all the way to the front of Mama Filiz's front door. Men and women shout for help and wail in pain all up and down the street. The pounding of boots echo in the distance and Coleena feels the strength in her legs drain. Finding a piece of the building next door reduced to little more than broken cinder with sharp edges and scorch marks, she sits down. Nausea pains her stomach, and she bends forward to stop herself from puking all over the pavement.

The sound of the marching men is all around her. She can't see them, but they are here. Maybe those responsible for all of this didn't get far away. Taking a deep breath burns her lungs and the edges of her eyes water as her body screams in agony.

"Summers!" she screams through choking breaths.

No answer comes back. The world is a haze. Devoid of life other than the ringing threatening to destroy her ears. Shadows move all around her. The military, the police, she doesn't know which, but they are here to help clear everything up. A small chuckle wracks her body. She can't leave now. Not after this. The dragon is here and if that is the case, then she must be as well. But what is she going to do?

Straightening her back, she sits up and lets her head roll until she is looking at the sky. The sun is a yellow bulb burning itself out to get through the hanging cloud of dust and destruction.

Yes, yes, she will stay and see this through. Parliamentary proclamation or not, this is now her fight and there isn't anyone in this world more dedicated to the destruction of the dragon than her. Inside she can feel the fire in her stomach begin to burn, the muscles in her aching body start to loosen.

"Captain Armigera?" a man's voice asks behind her. The words are gritty and barked.

Probably too much dust in his throat already.

"Yes?" she answers, the twisting turn where she sits on the broken stone sends a flaring pinch through her spine.

Thick hands grab the back of her shoulder, wrench her arm behind her back and shove her to the ground. Pain erupts through her face as it cracks on the pavement and pressure begins to pop the bones between her shoulders. She can barely breath.

"You are under arrest," the voice cuts through the ringing and the pain. "Under Parliamentary order..."

"Wait, what?" she coughs out. "This is a mistake. I was given three hours to leave the city."

"Keep that damn mouth of yours shut or I'll gag you," the man's voice demands, his lips much closer to the back of her head now. "For instigating civil unrest, I am placing you into custody."

"You can't do this. I am a captain in the Azhanian Armed forces. Talk with Detective Summers, he'll tell you everything," Coleena says, her voice refusing to plead.

A twisting of her arm sends flashing lights across her vision and the back of her throat fills with bile as the grinding in her spine worsens.

"Tell that to someone who cares. Look what you've done here, Captain. This is all because of you."

Coleena lets her head rest against the gritty pavement as the pounding of boots continues around her. Hands twisted into an unnatural position; she is left there to lay on the ground. Nowhere to go. No one to help. Closing her eyes, she lets everything fade into the distance.

14

At least the dust is gone, but so is the life of her uniform shirt. The pain still remains and the bad taste it left in her mouth is a slime of mud coating everything from her teeth to the back of her throat. The cool bars of the cage feel good against her burning skin. It does nothing for the splitting headache that turns the lonely light bulb over her head into the single focal point of everything she has ever done wrong in her entire life.

Women cough and moan with their sicknesses and injuries. Coleena is back in the same cell she was before. The same hard bench. Shoulder to shoulder with the same stinking bodies. She can't move without the threat of pushing someone else to the ground. The shadows close in around her and this time the walls fall with them.

Like déjà vu she waits down beneath the city jail. This time she feels worse both inside and out. Holding her ruined shirt balled within her fist, metals and all, she presses it against her pounding skull. She tries to keep her eyes closed and runs her tongue over the inside of her mouth. Somehow the taste of dust and defeat helps keep the nausea down. She can't take a deep breath. The stench of all of them crammed in here like caged animals isn't moving since they turned the fan away when she arrived. That pathetic little box now aims uselessly down the hall and does nothing but buzz in the background while they all sit here.

"This couldn't get any worse," Coleena mutters to herself.

Her lips crack and the slightest taste of blood finds its way into her mouth.

"I see they sent you back," a voice she recognizes calls out.

Not wanting it to be the case, Coleena sighs. Opening her eyes, she watches as the stocky woman makes her way down the corridor between the wall and the cages. Her hands are behind her back, shoulders bulge where they are forced to accommodate the tight bindings around her wrists, and a new shiner puffs and darkens beneath her left eye. The guard she recognizes from before walks behind her, his robotic walk now carries a good limp.

"Having a pretty bad day if you wouldn't mind," Coleena says in return.

"I would say you aren't the only one," the woman chuckles and the man shoves her into the cage wall.

Metal rings and her head hits hard. A crack of bone and soft tissue loud enough that Coleena can feel it as well.

"You're lucky I didn't kill you back there you little bitch. It's whores like you that bring these things down on yourselves," the guard growls.

"I wouldn't use the word little around me, short stuff," the woman taunts.

For her effort she gets a punch to the kidney that drops her to her knees.

Coleena is on her feet without a thought. Reaching her

arm through the cage, her fingers graze the edge of the man's uniform, but are unable to get a grip.

"Back the fuck up!" he shouts.

Laughing, the woman on the ground begins to pull herself back to her feet as the others scatter to get as far away as possible. Coleena does not move.

"Don't bother fighting pencil dick here. He's quick on the draw but doesn't carry much of a shot."

A slap across the back of her head sends her reeling down to the floor and a flurry of keys gets the door to the cell open. Balling her fists, Coleena stalks toward the opening. Baton against the railing creates a thunder that spins lights in her eyes and her knees begin to buckle.

"To the far end, now!" the guard shouts.

The fallen woman continues to chuckle as she crawls her way in. Coleena moves only enough to allow her passage before bending over to help her back to her feet.

She's heavy. A lot of muscle bunches beneath layers of bulk as she regains her footing and slides back enough for her cuffs to be removed. The gate slams shut the moment the bonds are removed and with nothing more than an angry glare the guard leaves. All the other prisoners cower in his passage.

"You all right?" Coleena asks.

"Could be better," the other woman responds. "Name's Narin by the way."

She offers her big mitt of a hand and Coleena takes it. Thick fingers crunch down on bones and the grip is tight and without remorse.

"Coleena. Captain Coleena Armigera."

"Nice to finally meet you, Coleena," Narin says before shouldering her way to a spot against the far wall of the cage.

She sits and with a tender touch nurses the swelling beneath her eye.

"What was that all about?" Coleena asks.

Narin chuckles and then licks her lips with a wide pink tongue.

"Promised the asshole a little personal touch if he got me out of this shit hole for a few hours, maybe even some decent food for once. If you're following what I'm saying. After the deed was done, little prick recanted on his offer. And by little prick I'm not just calling him names."

Some of the other women can't help but chuckle. A few cheeks turn red but all of them still keep their eyes on the ground.

"Then he did that to you?"

"Little fucker is gonna be limping for weeks. I'd say I got the better end of the deal," Narin answers while dabbing the swollen flesh with her fingertips. "Doesn't look like you got the better end of an argument either sweet cheeks."

Coleena runs her hand through her ratty hair and all the pains of the last couple of days flood through her body. Muscles ache. Bones feel broken and her skin is on fire.

"Yeah, I think you could say that," she says back before finding her own seat closer to the door to the cage. "I'm just trying...trying to figure out what the fuck is going on around here."

Narin nods.

"Not exactly from here, are you?"

With a sigh Coleena stretches her arms over her head and lets the joints pop as she tries to relax her worn and bruised muscles.

"Wouldn't be a hard guess, now would it? No, I'm not from Parliament City. I'm originally from Obrathe, but I've just recently been assigned here. From the looks of my results so far, it's been one mistake after another."

Coughs and moans fill the gaps between them, and she can feel the dozen other women crammed in with her. There is nowhere to sleep, and the smell of refuse is becoming too pungent to keep ignoring.

"Wasn't always like this," Narin says.

"Not like what?" Coleena asks.

"Parliament City. Was a decent place to live once, and I'm not talking since the refugees started flooding in like the plague. That whole dragon and all."

She waves off the statement like it's nothing. Several of the other women mutter curses toward the vile beast, a few even cross wards over their foreheads and chests before returning to their far-off gazes of a world not located within these four walls.

"You believe in the dragon? You know it's real?" Coleena asks.

For the first time since the bombing, the world stops feeling like it's gone upside down and about to drop her off into an unknown abyss.

"Of course, I believe in the dragon. Not like I've seen the thing, but I don't have to see it to know it's real. Did you hit your head harder than it looks? This whole world got fucked by that flying rat and you think it's simple to just forget about it? What has gotten into you, army girl?"

Coleena can barely hold back the laughter. Of all the places.

"I didn't think it would be possible," Coleena starts. "But down here. In these cells I finally found one."

A few more chuckles feel good beyond the pain of her back cracking and the burn of her face stretching into tiny new tears.

"Found what? You think the dragon is funny?" Narin asks, the blood in her cheeks beginning to redden where her knuckles whiten as her hands ball into fists.

"Oh no," Coleena placates with her hands up. "I was there when the damn thing sprung from the ground. I know it's real and have spent almost my entire life fighting the fucking thing. It's what you said. You believe it's real. Shit, you know it's real. How is it you are down here, and all I find out there is people who've lost their fucking mind? God. Damn. Politicians."

Narin relaxes her posture and puts her head back against the bars.

"That's what I'm talking about. Things have changed and it started with them."

Sitting forward Coleena asks, "how so?"

"About seven years ago we had our summer election. Same old political mudslinging and all, but this ended differently. Rumors of interference from an outside source. Voter tampering, that kind of thing. Once these assholes got seated though, everything broke loose. New laws. People being assigned with no reason or skills to be doing what they were supposed to do. They even banned our news reporters. Man, I wish we still had a newspaper. I always loved that crossword on the back pages. Have you ever heard of such a thing like banning the news? How are people supposed find anything out or educate themselves if there is no news?"

"You think Parliament has something to do with all of it?"

Narin wraps a large arm around the woman sitting beside her. All dirt and grease filled hair; the poor thing looks like she's barely eaten in a week. Her clothes of a simple cotton shirt and wide-cut pants hang off her bones with enough space to fit an entire other person in with her.

"Why do you think some of us are here? Not everyone was in the middle of that riot you started," Narin says.

"Hey!" Coleena starts.

The older woman waves her off.

"Just making sure you are listening. I was there, I saw what you did and what you didn't do. But look at some of these poor souls. Do they look like the rioting kind to you?"

Coleena takes a good hard look at everyone. Many sport the remainders of bruises and cuts from the fighting, but then there are the others. She glances toward the cell closest to the stairs leading to their level. Hollow sunken eyes look back her way before turning back to the floor. No, they do not look like fighters. At least in the normal sense of the word.

"I guess the only question left is what can we do about it?" Coleena asks.

No answers or words of wisdom are given. She sighs and closes her eyes, the cold steel of the bars a slight comfort to the pounding within her head.

Time passes. No real way to tell how fast or slow. People fall asleep, heads sag, and the relentless buzzing of the light above their head never goes away.

"Get on your toes, Captain," Narin whispers.

Coleena's eyes spring open, the realization that she was even asleep washing over her. By the gods she is more tired than she remembers. Stiff joints ache as they move, her body feeling like the bomb went off directly below her chair.

"What is going on?" she whispers back.

The sound of boots on the hard floor quickly follows. Loud clops of rubber and the clicking of plastic that draws closer with every breath. Some of the women find the strength to reach their feet. Narin, cracking her knuckles, stands and gets herself up in front of everyone.

"Probably an inspection. Keep your hands to your sides. They can get a little grabby, but if you can ignore it for a few moments they'll be on their way," Narin adds as she makes her way up beside the door.

Coleena feels the blood in her body begin to warm as she stretches and makes it to her feet. Rolling her head sends loud pops through her ears, and she is ready for whatever this becomes.

"Prisoners to the back wall," the guard barks as he makes his way down the hall, baton swinging in wide circles as he walks with another man close on his heels.

Coleena cannot see who the other is, but he is not dressed in a standard guard or police uniform. He wears a scuffed-up dress shirt, puffy around the chest and abdomen but also rather gray and dust covered like the pants he wears. He keeps his head down and turned away. Maybe the shame of what he sees is too much.

Groans and curses echo through the dungeon, but everyone complies. Everyone except Narin and her. They wait, shoulder to shoulder by the door.

"You two. Are you deaf?" the guard asks as he stops at their cage.

The guard's new companion slides in behind, still out of sight.

"We heard you loud and clear," Narin answers. "If you're gonna come in here and get your rocks off by grabbing these poor girls, you can start with me."

A crooked smile crosses the man's face.

"I'll show you something about getting rocks off you stupid little bitch," the guard says as he fumbles with the keys on his belt.

His cheeks redden as he works with the large ring. Finding the correct one, he raps his baton against the cage, the shock a piercing crack that punctures the ear. Coleena does everything she can not to cup her ears and back away a step.

Metal hinges cry as the door swings open, their captor taking a tentative step between the open portal.

"I said get your asses back against the wall. We are here looking for a single individual. If you don't make this hard on yourselves, I'll be out..." the man says before his eyes roll into the back of his head. He topples to the ground unconscious.

Everyone stands there frozen in shock. A cane, broken in half, sways back and forth within the tight grasp of the stranger. Looking up, the cut over his left eye, the dark hair now messed and matted with dirt and dust, and those eyes are as recognizable as the sun of a new day.

Detective Roland Summers.

His smile is cut short as his leg begins to buckle, and he slides into the side of the cage door, a hand reaching out to prevent his rapidly increasing decent to the floor. Coleena jumps forward to catch him, his weight pulling hard on her as he stops halfway down.

"I thought I might find you down here," he says with a voice pained and weak.

"Get over here and help me," Coleena yells.

Hesitating for only a moment, Narin makes her way over after giving the stricken guard a swift kick into his ribs.

"Who is this guy?" she asks, her large shoulders and powerful legs a much better leverage for the fallen detective.

"This is Detective Roland Summers. He's a friend," Coleena answers.

Narin goes to pull away, the tilt of Summers' body quickly sliding back to the cage.

"It's all right," Summers whispers. "I'm here to help you out, Narin."

A look of shock crosses the woman's face. Her eyes go from the detective to Coleena.

"Wait, what is going on here?" she asks, the sudden look of bolting etching its way through her stone-like features.

"No time," Summers adds, his words labored with a wet, heavy breath. "Azhana United. The purge has started. They aren't waiting any longer."

"I thought you said that was all just bullshit, that's why you didn't put it in your reports," Coleena says.

Summer's head looks up at her, his eyes darkened and hollow.

"He is part of Azhana United, you bumbling moron," Narin cuts in, her eyes looking the stricken detective from head to toe. "That's how he knows who I am."

Coleena looks into the eyes of her partner leaning into the arms of the older woman.

"But? He just said Azhana United was rioting in the streets. Why is he?" Coleena asks then looks down at the fallen guard. "What is going on here?"

"We don't have time for this bullshit, and looking at the condition of our friend here, he has even less," Narin says. She shifts until he is standing straighter and a growing red patch spreads from below his rib cage down to his belt. "Azhana United is here to fight the rise of this new government and their reluctance to believe that dragon influence has breached the walls. We aren't some splinter cell, but a militia of men and women trying to save Parliament City. The purge is Parliament cleaning house. They are coming to kill us all!"

Coleena has no words. She watches as the small pool of blood beneath the guard's head begins to spread. Summers struggles to speak as he straightens and stiffens his wobbling legs.

"It is now or never, Coleena," he coughs out. "If you stay, you'll die with the rest. Come with us. The war starts tonight, and we need you."

What else is she supposed to do? Doubt runs rampant deep in her mind, but there is nothing else she can do.

"Lead the way," she says. Wrapping her arm around Summers' back and letting some of his weight shift to her, they turn to leave. "You better be right about this, Detective."

Without another word, they leave with hopes of disappearing into the night.

15

———

This is all too easy.

So easy there has to be something wrong.

No one stops them as they leave the lower cell block and reach the first floor. Voices, cut short with fear, whisper through shut doors as all three of them shuffle through the hall, bumping left and right as they drag Summers' feet across the floor. No one approaches. Potted plants have been removed leaving tiny stands empty and lifeless as they pass. Lights are dimmed, locked doors keep everyone barricaded safely away from the violence outside. Even here they can smell smoke in the air. No more lavender. Death and mayhem do not have time for sweet smells.

The sound of rumbling sets the small wooden pedestals shaking and the roof creaks with the movement. Both Coleena and Narin help Summers keep going, his legs hardly able to move enough to act like he is carrying any of his own weight and the red stain across his shirt actively drips onto the legs of his pants.

"We need to get him to a hospital," Coleena says, out of breath and sweating profusely.

Narin shoots her a hard look, eyes narrowed and lips cutting a razor straight line. The woman does not answer as they reach the front lobby. A single guard stands waiting by the glass doors, eyes out to the streets and hands interlaced behind his back. Neither of them hesitates as they continue forward.

"Officer, this man needs help," Coleena pleads.

With the slightest jump of shock, the man turns. His eyes are wide, and a bit of confusion strikes his face before it fades and training kicks in. He wasn't expecting the problem to come to him from behind. All the disturbances should be outside the precinct, not behind these locked doors.

"Please, we don't have much time," Coleena continues.

Now stone-cold, the young officer moves forward, his walk robotic as he tries to take charge. Probably barely out of training and judging by the clean edges to his face, the lack of scares, and how there is no dark circles under his eyes, this is definitely going to be his first rodeo. She can see the textbook steps running in the back of his mind, like a movie she has seen one too many times.

"What happened to him?" the officer asks.

His look of stern training fades slightly into indecision as the realization of Summers' injuries come into full view. Blood is pooling like a bag ready to pop where it pushes its way out of any opening in the man's shirt and his skin is ashen white where it isn't covered in mud. Coleena lets more of Roland's wait shift to her shoulder as the officer comes within arm's reach.

"The fighting, he was hurt," Coleena answers, but the words mean nothing.

There is no time to react. Narin's fist hits the man below the ribs and the air in his lungs evacuates in a large gush of warm breath that smells sweet and oddly of strawberries. His eyes bulge but all they see is her thick knee coming up in a horrible arc as it catches him square in the nose before flipping him onto his back. The man groans and tries to stem the blood gushing from his face.

"Let's get out of here," Coleena says and tries to shift the detective's weight back to the larger woman.

"Not until I'm done here," Narin says as she goes to climb on top of the stricken young guard.

"Don't!" Coleena screams. "We don't know if he has any part of this. There is no time. Roland needs help."

Arm cocked back to strike, Narin stops and turns. Coleena can barely keep her partner from falling and the man beneath her is as defenseless as a child. Eyes wide, face gone pale, blood seeps between his fingers, and he makes no move to defend himself.

"Piece of shit," Narin says before stepping back and taking Summers' weight completely onto her shoulders. "Lead the way, army girl."

Coleena nods and with the aid of the officer's keys, pushes the doors open. Smoke rolls through the air and large silhouettes of light flicker in small halos across the city. Buildings burn and people fight for their lives. There is surprisingly little gunfire, but where there are no pops you can hear voices screaming in the distance. Sirens echo into the night and without being stopped or approached they find their way down to the bottom of the steps and to the empty road.

The heat of the night lingers thick like a blanket. No stars break through the canvas of night and the fine layer of smoke coating the city from wall to wall.

They are out there hunting. Coleena can feel them. She

has done this before. The monsters are waiting, hoping and ready to pounce on the first mistake. Their enemy may be human this time, but it is all the same in the end. Until now, she didn't realize how much she missed having a weapon on her side. Standing out here in nothing but her cotton shirt and dress pants, she may as well be naked.

"We have to go this way," Narin says with a cock of her head toward the north.

Coleena turns to the south. Congress Road. Following it will lead her straight to the barracks. There she can find help. They'll find a way to clear this whole fucking mess up.

"The barracks are this way," Coleena says. "Surgeons stationed there can help him. We'll be protected."

Narin shifts the detective further up her shoulder and backs away.

"We have ways to take care of our own, army girl. If you're going that way, you are going on your own. I'll make sure the detective gets to someone who can patch him up. You can follow if you want. I don't exactly trust you, but if his word says you are good, we won't turn you away. Make your choice."

Coleena looks at the big woman. Her stone persona is back, and Summers is barely with them. She could make it to the barracks. Curfew or not, there are enough shadows and places to hide that she could make it. Once she is there, she can get word to the general. She needs to know what is going on. This is too big for just her. Political or not, the army can't sit and let the capital fall.

"I've got to try. Take care of him, Narin. I'll find a way to help from there and contact you once I do."

The big woman nods.

"If you change your mind or get the help you think you

are going to find, make your way to Hell's Toilet. Up by the north wall, you can't miss it."

Without another word she turns and heads up Congress Street before turning into the shadows. Sirens grow louder in the distance and there is no time left. Without another look, Coleena turns and heads back down the road where all of this started.

16

The streets are not all empty. Where shadows do not linger, patrols of police and Parliamentary guards search the shadows, looking and prodding into every crack and crevice of this city. They are thorough. Ruthless even in their methodical ways.

They look for her. People just like her. Lanterns swinging with their confident steps, they move from block to block, batons and firearms out and ready.

Coleena creeps from corner to corner. Heart beating quickly, muscles on fire and twitching with regret. Like a little rat, she slinks from shadow to shadow. Each step is a cracking roar of thunder that will give her away. Sweat leaves a salty taste on her lips and her skin is sticky where it isn't burning with a heat worse than the inferno air of this city that refuses to cool.

Time passes through quicksand. Darkness does not fade, and the slow tick of the clock is lost to the chaos. How long is it taking for her to get down to the barracks? Stopping and waiting. Holding and then running. It's a game of cat and mouse, but there are far too many cats for her to get away with this. She can feel it.

Through windows, she can see families huddled inside their homes. Some sit around candles with arms wrapped around one another. Others have their windows entirely blocked and the only way to know they are even there is to watch as the patrols beat down on the doors. Angry voices bark into the night demanding answers and looking for fugitives that are hiding in each and every home.

This is a cleansing. Like Summers had said, a purge. The thought of the detective stops her for a moment, a block from where the barracks wait. Did he make it? She wishes she could have convinced them to come with her. Looking at the gate to the military compound, everything is quiet. The flag poles stand tall and straight at the entrance to the sanctuary, the fabric for which they all fight for barely moving with the non-existent breeze. A single guard, nothing more than a shadow at this distance, waits and watches.

She can see small lights flickering within the open flaps of tents. Men milling about as they wait for lights out. Even this close she can smell and taste the lingering scent of rations being cooked. Faint and barely above the smell of smoke weaving its way between the buildings of the city, her mouth dries at the thought of what comes next. What is she going to do? Will they believe her?

Of course, they will. Lieutenant Mason was the one who set her up with Summers. Does he know that the detective was part of Azhana United? She wants to think so, but the chances are slim. Mason is military enough for it not to matter. He wouldn't want this city to fall to ruin any more than her. If Roland is not lying about what is going on, Mason and the others will be there to help him.

Taking a deep breath, she waits until the nearest patrol

fades into the distance. The light of their lantern barely a star in the darkness of the next street as she steps out from behind a rusted and decrepit dumpster and begins a slow jog to the fence. She isn't within a hundred yards before the soldier snaps to attention, his rifle swinging from his back to his hands as he waits.

"Hold," the man commands. "These premises are off limits to citizens."

Coleena slows to a strong walk, her shoulders back and stiff regardless of the pain. Steadying her breath, she holds her head up high, but does not stop her approach.

"I am here to talk with Lieutenant Major Mason. My name is Captain Coleena Armigera, and I am requesting shelter within the grounds of the Azhanian Joint Military Command."

The soldier is young. He looks her over as she gets closer, his eyes narrowing. She can see him taking stock of her disheveled appearance, torn t-shirt and pants covered in the gods know what. With a slow and deliberate move of her hand she pushes back the hair plastered to her face and stops an arm's length away. His rifle stays in his hands, but he does not threaten her with it. She can see him chewing on the thoughts as his narrow jaw and smooth cheeks work back and forth.

"We are not to have any visitors this late at night, Captain," the man says.

Judging by the few pins on his jacket the man is barely a grade above private. Coleena nods. She has to do this correctly.

"I understand that... private?"

"Corporal Vassallos, ma'am," the guard answers.

"Corporal Vassallos," Coleena starts. "I understand you are following orders. As I mentioned, my name is Captain

Coleena Armigera and I am here to see Lieutenant Mason. I am stationed within this city by direct order of General Whittaker. Under normal circumstances I would agree that we must follow given orders, but as you can see this city is under distress. I request an audience with your C.O. immediately and you are welcome to accompany me all the way to his front door."

Conviction and confidence waver on the young soldier's face as he looks off into the distance. Small specks of light reflect off dark irises as the fires continue to burn in the distance.

"Understood, Captain. Wait...wait just one moment as I get an escort to bring you directly to the Lieutenant Major."

"Make it happen, Corporal," Coleena says.

She stands and waits. The young man goes back to the gate where he left his radio tucked behind the small pile of sandbags. Turning she watches as the little specs of light move up and down the streets, distant stars weaving in and out of the darkness between the buildings. None of them approach the military gates. Parliament isn't that dumb, yet.

"Captain. Your escort will be here momentarily. They will take you directly to Lieutenant Mason. It appears they were already waiting for you," Vassallos says.

Now that is a surprise.

"What makes you say that, Corporal," Coleena asks.

A feeling of dread washes through her like cold water, but she stamps it away. She is safe. This is somewhere these monsters can't touch her.

"They said Petty Officer Tul was already there and waiting. He will be here in no more than a few moments."

Like clockwork, she can already see a dark figure working its way down the path from the center of the compound. Stalking his way through the shadows like a predator, she watches the officer pass by others, all of them standing at attention or turning from their route to avoid him entirely.

Corporal Vassallos snaps a salute as Tul arrives. He gets little more than a grunt, Coleena occupying all the older soldier's attention.

"Are you alone?" Tul asks.

She looks around at all the empty space behind her, this night already wearing too thin on her nerves.

"Do you see anyone else with me, Tul?" Coleena snaps.

The Corporal takes a step back at the physical slap of the words, but the Petty Officer is not deterred.

"Strange night out there, Captain," Tul replies, his narrowed eyes sweeping the darkness beyond. "I wouldn't want anything to happen to any of your companions if there was a way to stop it."

Coleena can feel her cheeks go red with anger, a flash of pain igniting behind the bandages of her face as the threat against Summers is clear. Maybe she is wrong. Could these people also be within the military ranks? No, it's not possible. Plus, there is no going back. She made this decision and now needs to see it through.

"I'm alone, Tul. But as you so graciously mentioned, this city is in turmoil. I need to see Mason and I need to see him now."

The man nods his head but does not say another word. With a swift turn he begins the trek back to the center of the protected barracks. Vassallos keeps his mouth shut as they pass, but he snaps another salute that again is not returned.

Walking in silence, Coleena can see the army men and women as they try to relax within their tents. All of it is a show. Cook fires sit and smolder. The smell of cooking rations turns quickly to the stench of burning meat and boiled gravy so thick it's probably tar. Eyes do not turn her way for more than a moment before shifting toward the lights burning within the city. Words are spoken in whispered hushes and there are far more sitting around fires than she can see resting within the tents. Almost all of them are still in their uniforms. Boots are laced and belts haven't even been loosened.

"Is there a reason we aren't out there trying to stop this, Tul?" Coleena questions.

"Stop what?" the officer returns but does not look at her.

"Look out there. There is fighting in the streets. They are sweeping from home to home, pulling out anyone they can accuse of treason, and doing who knows what to them."

Coleena fights the urge to spin the man around and demand he march right out there and stop this himself. If only it was that easy.

"Orders, Captain," Tul responds.

"From whom?" Coleena demands.

The officer does not answer. Sliding from shadow to shadow, the man is definitely a predator as he moves. Darkness envelopes him like it is his home. Silence follows him and Coleena fights the natural urge to let the distance between them grow.

"I asked you a question, Petty Officer Tul," Coleena starts again. "You are going to answer me, or I will report..."

"We are here," he says with a quick glance back her way.

The man is correct. So concerned with finding out more about what is going on, she didn't even realize how quickly they had covered the distance. Front door still shut, she watches as Tul makes his way up the steps and wraps twice in loud succession. Above his head the tiny sign shakes and cracks against the outer wall.

If any words pass between him and the inside, she

cannot hear them, but within a quick moment the dangerous man turns the knob and opens the door. Words that are lost to the night are spoken, and he waves her to him.

The smell of vanilla is stronger than she remembers. It's as if the man bathes in the stuff and Coleena coughs entering into the candlelit darkness within. Her lungs burn and the bones along her spine pop with the violent release of air, but she refuses to be cowered. Stiffening, she waits just within the door until she gets a proper summons.

"Captain Armigera!" Mason bellows within the small enclosure of the building. "It is so good to see you. Please, come in and find yourself a seat."

With a small nod and a narrowed glance at Tul, who finds his way into his corner, Coleena moves to the table in front of where the Lieutenant sits. Candles and paper are scattered across the unbalanced top and dark rings stain the first pages of each pile. A napkin is tucked into the collar of the man's shirt, stained with something still fresh enough to drip.

"Tell me you know what is going on out there, Lieutenant," Coleena demands.

Mason sucks on the tip of his finger before wiping it across the napkin he leaves hanging from his neck.

"Are we talking about the circumstances of this evening or whatever it is the General has sent you here to discover?"

Coleena works her jaw back and forth, the words wanting to spew from her mouth more venom than sugar.

"I'm talking about right now, this very fucking moment!"

The big man puts his hands down on the crumpling couch and shoots a small smile toward the shadow waiting and watching from the corner.

"You seem a bit excited there, Captain. None of this

involves you. This is a city police action. We are the army. Unless we are called in directly, then we have no reason to step outside of these fences. Have you received any direct orders to assist in any way, Officer Tul?" Silence hangs like a knife and Mason turns back to her. "You see? Our hands are tied. I understand your concern, Captain. I can see it in the eyes of every man and woman out there. We want to help. Whatever madness has taken this city is threatening to find its way in here every day. Can't you see we are helpless in these matters?"

Coleena throws her hands into the air and walks a tight circle in the small room. She wants to shove the candles down in one big sweep, but this is too important to lose her cool.

"What I see is an entire battalion of men and women standing and watching as the citizens of this city are killed on their very own streets. The dragon is here, Lieutenant. Within these very fucking walls. Orders or not we can't sit here with our thumbs up our asses."

"The dragon?" Mason says as he taps one pudgy finger on his first chin. "Do you have evidence that the monster has made its way here? Anything other than rumor and the hysterical cries of people lost to the madness of poverty and drugs?"

Coleena grips the top of the chair in front of her, her knuckles swelling as she tries to strangle the life out of it. Taking one hand she rips the bandage off the side of her face, the tape tearing her skin in one smooth motion.

"This, Lieutenant. A minion of the dragon did this to my face right here in Parliament City. It tried to kill me in the back alleys and when that failed it tried blowing me up with a bomb that decimated an entire street in the lower quarter of the city."

"Apparently it failed in its mission," Mason says before taking the napkin out from the collar of his shirt. "Never realized the dragon was changing tactics and bombing us now. Other than your word and a very sorry looking injury, do you have anything else? The dragon and any of its minions are beyond the resources of this city's government, police, and local forces. This is military jurisdiction you are speaking of and if you have proof then maybe we have all that we need to make this our problem regardless of what they may want."

The smile on the man's face is sinister as the story of what he is thinking passes behind his beady eyes, but Coleena cannot wait to try to figure it out.

"I have nothing else. Those damn politicians threw me out the moment I tried to tell them. Said something about instigating panic and lying about the existence of the damn beast. They are behind something, Lieutenant. I'm telling you there is something very bad going on here," she answers.

"We can agree on that, Captain," Mason says. "Politicians are never to be trusted. But...no evidence does not help us. What about Detective Summers? What are his thoughts on all of this?"

Regardless of the pain, Coleena stiffens and steps away from the table.

"Summers. Yes, he was there both times, but he's hurt. He broke me out of jail and went off with..."

"Wait, you were in jail? Again?" Mason asks while sliding himself to the side of the couch so he can stand up.

"Long story, Lieutenant. But Summers is hurt. Badly. We got out of the jail and I tried to convince them to come with me, but they wouldn't have any of it. I know where to find them though. He can tell you everything. With both his testimony and mine, we'll have enough to give us the right to stop this madness. General Whittaker can help handle the rest. We have to hurry though, Summers is in bad shape."

Mason, with a grunt, pushes himself to his feet. Several globs of whatever sauce it was he was eating make it to his shirt, but he does not notice.

"You say you know where they are?"

Coleena nods an affirmative. The Lieutenant turns to Tul who melts away from the shadowed corner. "Go grab a handful of men. Arm them but keep it quiet. We are going to get our Detective friend and see what he knows. If what the Captain is saying is correct, then we may have a dragon to fight tonight."

Without a word Tul is out the door and gone.

"So, Captain. Can I offer you a drink while we wait?"

No, she does not want a drink. She doesn't even want to stay long enough to get a few men, but this will have to do. This is the help she came for. Once they have Summers' word on everything that has happened since her arrival, there will be no reason not to step in. She looks out into the lights burning deep within the city.

Hold on Summers, help is on the way...

17

———

Six soldiers dressed in their military blacks and avenging red slashes. Two officers, one with his button dress blacks and metals polished to a shine above his heart, and the other in a uniform of solid darkness. Tul, his persona already darker than the pits of hell, is even worse now that he is geared for combat. And there is no other way to describe the way he is. All shadows and no curves. There is no telling how many weapons he has on him, other than the rifle he carries over his shoulder. It does not take many years in a combat zone to know he is someone she wants to avoid, especially at night. Deep set and cold eyes. Hands flexing before casually brushing against sealed pouches on his belt. This man is ready for war.

She on the other hand looks disheveled as ever. Mason had enough courtesy to allow to at least wash her face and before giving her a cotton shirt of gray more commonly worn by recruits. Of course, this one is clearly two sizes too big as it balloons out from where it tucks in beneath her belt. Between that and all her bandages and scares, there is

160

no way she doesn't look the mess she hardly recognized in the mirror before they headed out from the compound.

None of this compares to what is going on in the city around them.

Parliament City is ablaze with fires and fighting. An hour of nothing and wasted time passed before they left the barracks and in those lost moments the chaos of the night has practically become rebellion. They can see fires burning across most of the eastern side of the city. Dark smoke rolls like a mist through the streets and there are screams echoing from all corners within the four walls.

Quietly and without any type of escort, they make their way up Congress Street. Lieutenant Mason and Tul keep to the lead while the six soldiers Tul handpicked remain to the rear. Rifles slung over shoulders so they can be at the ready in the blink of an eye, they fan out and keep her in the center. Part of her wants to believe it is to make sure none of the patrols stop them and try to arrest her. Mason assured her that even if they did, she was under his jurisdiction and their authority held no weight with him. She appreciated the try but looking at how the men stay out of her reach no matter where they turn, deep inside a voice says it feels more like a cage. A moving, breathing, living cage that she isn't willing to fight her way out of.

They make steady progress as the sight of the police department fades in the distance. The front was still clear, but with a quick glance as they passed by, she could see two more silhouettes behind the front doors. Apparently, they wouldn't be making that mistake more than once. Turning off Congress Street, Tul takes the lead as they move from alley to crossroad and through the darker parts of the city as they separate themselves from the inner districts. Here she can see the garbage and refuse begin to pile where the carnage and destruction from previous attacks did not reach.

Which was worse?

Live a greater life of existence but with the possibility of being blown up or killed by enemies you did not see coming, or to live and die fighting for everything you have. Food is scarce here, not as bad as Beggar's Town, but the signs for places to eat are becoming further and further apart, many of them looking like they haven't been in service for a very long time. Broken doors. Boarded glass windows and graffiti covering everything.

"Is he sure he knows where he is going?" Coleena asks.

Buildings begin to take on a different shape here. More round, less wood. Rocks with deep cracks make walls that are made smooth with the ultimate chisel of time. Broken terracotta shingles lay in millions of pieces at their feet and the sloping roofs over their heads are in a bad need of repair where holes and bowing can be seen even at night. A little city lost out of time. She can hear flowing water in the distance, not a thunder, but a constant growl. The smell of thick smoke thins as the air cools against her skin, but where the stench of burning city fades it is quickly replaced with the sickening taste of sewage that saturates everything. Rot and mildew are unwelcome bed partners here. Where the rocks are scrapped clean with the passing of time, she can see bits of mold and other growth filling in the corners. Weeds of various sizes growing between the cracks and crevices. She pulls the collar of her new shirt tighter around her neck.

"There isn't a hole in this city that Tul doesn't know about, Captain," Mason answers with the confidence of a man speaking about his prize-winning dog. "He's like a ghost. He sees and hears everything. Once you told us the name of the establishment we were looking for, he knew exactly where we were going."

"Makes me feel a whole lot better," Coleena says. Mason shoots her a big grin, his teeth sparkling in the fire light leading their way. Turning away she regards the shadows with a hesitant look. They are watching her; she can feel their eyes every time she turns away. Just out of her line of sight. "We have much further to go?"

Tul disappears around a corner, not a single look back as the wraith leads the way. Mason puts a pudgy finger up to his lips before following. Coleena looks at the other men around her and all of them are stone faced and following orders. She does not like this one bit but has no other choice. Stepping around the corner leads her into a darkened alley. All black and suffocating, she inches her way to the two starkly different figures waiting at the end. Tul's lean figure remains agile and ready as he stands on the balls of his feet. Knees bent and fluid at his hips, he's ready to pounce should the need arise. Mason and his bulbous shape leans against the stone wall, one ankle crossed in front of the other like he is waiting for the boy he's been picking on to come by for a good scare.

Coleena slides up beside them, neither bothering to look her way.

"Is this it?" she whispers.

Not sure why she did, in the chaos enveloping the city, there wouldn't be anyone to hear her for miles if they were lucky.

"Yep, right over there," Mason says with a point of his pinkie finger. His pointer works its way across the inside of his mouth, digging at something she can't see. "Have to wait here though."

"Why is that?" Coleena asks.

Hell's Toilet.

Could barely be named more appropriately. Refuse and other indistinguishable objects lay scattered in front of the plank-board building. Unlike everything else in this part of the city, this place sticks out like a sore thumb. Built into a recess of its own, she can see where it backs itself against the wall, the towering presence of dark stone looming overhead. Even during the day, she would think this place was stuck in permanent shadow. Then there is the smell. Where before it was a nuisance, here on this street it is straight assault. Her eyes water, and she wants to cough but swallows it back. There is almost a green miasma in the air as it works its way down the street, the slight fog meandering and taking its own time as it moves further along its path.

"Patrol not too far away," Tul answers, his beak of a nose doing all the pointing while the Lieutenant keeps working at whatever is lodged between his teeth.

Sneaking a look around the corner, she sees why they are hesitating. A squad of eight figures materialize in the distance. The fog of stink, smoke, and cloud slowly reveals their movements as they work their way down the street. Two lanterns swaying back and forth, she can see the edges of the men behind. Barrels of rifles sit over shoulders and helmets round the tops of their heads. Even from this distance she can see their wall guard uniforms and the added Parliamentary security. The police wouldn't be dressed like they are going to war. Her heart skips a beat as the little fire in her stomach flares to life again.

This is not a search party. More like an extermination squad if they were to ask her.

"What are we going to do?" she asks.

Other than her, they shouldn't have a problem even if they are caught out in the open. These are soldiers from the army, curfew has little effect on them as long as they are on official duty. Lieutenant Mason's presence alone should see to their safety, regardless of her being there.

Something still doesn't feel right.

"Keep quiet," Tul warns with a hand up.

The men behind shift their feet and gear as they wait, his signal telling them to get ready. She looks at Mason who does nothing but shrug. Coming down the street, the patrol does not stop at any of the buildings with lights in their windows or spare a glance at those boarded shut. They do not hesitate or bother looking into the darkness of passing alleys. With clear determination they move down the middle of the street. Lanterns lighting the way, they make their way until they near Hell's Toilet. There they stop, form two, three-man lines and let those with the lanterns approach the doors.

"No," Coleena starts. "We can't let them go inside. If they find Summers, he's a dead man. How do they know he is even here?"

"Doesn't matter," Mason says. "They beat us to it but doesn't mean we aren't out of options." He pats Tul on the back of the shoulder and gives him a nod of his chin. "Best get to it."

Tul doesn't say a word before turning to the men at their rear. "You all know the drill. Let's keep this quiet."

Coleena has nothing to say as all seven of the men strip off their weapons, remove their uniform shirts, and stow everything neatly into piles against the wall. Other than the dark pants and uniform boots, they would probably pass for regular men in this type of night if six well fit individuals all went jogging in the middle of a riot in similar t-shirts and are led by a lanky older gentleman who could make babies cry.

Mason shrugs again as she turns toward the patrol awaiting their orders.

Without a word they slide from the darkness of the alley and into the street. Loud knocks rock the door to the building, a sign with missing letters proudly proclaiming 'H Toil' slapping against the wall. No one answers the door and the men make it almost to the middle of the street before the guards at their rear notice the group approaching them.

"Halt! Hands where I can see them!" one of the guards demands.

Tul does as he's ordered with his hands but keeps his forward movement. The six other soldiers behind him do the same and mimic him like independent shadows. They fan ever so slightly out creating a slowly ensnaring box that the men with rifles probably don't see.

"We mean you no harm, sir," Tul says, his voice as deep as the grave. Finally noticing the other six, two of the guards step to the side, their lines of sight finally taking in the trap closing in around them. The two with the lanterns turn away from the door and take the couple of steps down to the road.

"All citizens are to be off the streets. Parliamentary Order," one of them barks.

With a shrug, Tul turns their attention to him. Coleena doesn't like this. There may be seven of them, but the others all have rifles, though most of them shake with nerves she can see from here. A rifle in an untrained hand is no less dangerous than anywhere else at that close of a range.

"My friends and I were thirsty. Never got a chance to stock up before the streets were cleared and since nothing ever really happens down here, we thought we'd step out to get something. As you can see, we aren't armed and to be honest, I voted for these snobby pricks in the last election," Tul says.

"It doesn't matter who you voted for, asshole. Orders are--," the nearest man with a lantern starts.

He never finishes as Tul's raised elbow crashes into his nose. Head snapping back, the soldier is a blur of movement as his shoulder meets the man's chest in one fluid movement. The six soldiers behind the falling one turn with the attack, their eyes focusing on Tul and away from the other men for just a moment. All of it is a mistake. One. Bloody. Mistake as Coleena can't breathe fast enough to follow the carnage. Ripping the lantern from the man toppling backward, Tul lets it shatter into an oily fireball across the face of another of the victims, his screams a high-pitched wail as the flames spread across his head and chest.

No bullets fire as the six-armed guards scream in their own agony. Knives cut vicious arcs across necks and leave gaping holes in bellies as the guards drop. Those who struggle are cut down before whatever strength they have left builds enough to fight back. It is only moments and seven of them are dead, only one man still alive albeit with a shattered nose.

"Man is a real piece of work sometimes, isn't he?" Mason asks before stepping out onto the street.

Coleena wants to scream. Her mouth is dry. She has seen men and monsters killed, but these are Azhanian citizens. There is no way to tell if they were just following orders or if they had any part of this. With practiced precision, the men begin to remove the bodies before Mason or herself even reach the site of the battle.

"What in the seven hells do you think you are doing?" she is able to demand.

Tul gives her a hardened look, his eyes narrowed and a

small drip of blood wiggling from the tip of his nose. He turns to Mason who shrugs before going back to the cleanup work.

"You said that the dragon is here in this city. According to you our only proof is in the mind of a man inside this building. This is a military operation, Captain. You as well as I know that in matters of world security, we have authority over everyone. Plus, what else were we going to do? Politely ask them to leave?" Mason answers.

He has almost no look to give the man sprawled on his back, blood seeping between fingers as he waits between them all. Eyes wide, fear reflecting in the way he waits by their boots, all fight has fled from him as if it was never there.

"Rules of engagement, Lieutenant. These are not enemy combatants. You cannot just simply kill them at will," Coleena says as she bends down to check on the injured Parliamentary guard.

The red stain on his white undershirt is bright in the firelight, his fingers neatly trimmed and without a single scar.

"Not us, Captain. WE did this," Mason adds for emphasis. "You will not forget your part in all of this. You brought the matter of the dragon to my doorstep. You are the one assigned here by the General, and just in time to see an all-out riot start between these well-guarded walls. There is no going back. You as well as I swore an oath to destroy the dragon and see our world returned to the way we once knew it. If it is here, we will do whatever it takes to see it done," Mason says before pulling on her shoulder until she is standing beside him. "And by whatever, I mean WHATEVER."

He nods to Tul. Without a word, the soldier, now more

like assassin, grabs the fallen man's prone body and begins to drag it across the pavement. Words of protest start to scream out but a quick punch to the jaw puts his skull into the ground hard enough to silence any other words.

Coleena watches as his boots refuse to fight as they drag him around the corner.

"We can't," she starts.

Mason gently touches her chin with one hand and turns it slowly to him.

"It is for the good of this city and the world, Captain. How about you and I go inside, and we find Summers. All of this will be over as soon as we can find him and get this whole thing straightened out. You'll be the savior of the city, I promise."

As if a spell holds her quiet, she cannot say anything. She looks back at the small trail of scattered stones and dirt left by the heel of the man's boots. There are no more screams. No mercy as she knows the deed is being done. Out of mind and body, she lets Mason lead her into Hell's Toilet.

18

———————

This is definitely the latrine that everyone is so scared of.

Hot and stuffy to the point of suffocation. There is hardly any room to move or breathe once they pass through the door. Heavy candle smoke fills the air, a mix of sweat and stale alcohol creating a horrible aftertaste. A thunderous grinding threatens to overtake the sound of voices filling the open seating area of the bar. More than a dozen circular tables, old and put together with random cuts of wood, are situated like someone shot gunned them into place. Random and in no order that she can see. The louder the nuisance in the background grows, the more people yell to be heard.

Like an engine struggling to turn its gears, Coleena can feel the rotation of giant turbines beneath her feet. A small humming that works its way up her bones and does not help with the pain lingering within every joint of her body. The hydro-electric plant of the city located beneath the building where it juts into the massive wall does not care if it bothers her or not. Like the river itself, it will continue to move regardless of what she thinks. Huge pipes, large enough to fit a person into them run along the back walls, green and colored with their age. The building itself built right around the working mechanisms of the energy plant.

How convenient. Gritting her teeth, she tries to let the pounding fade into the back of her mind where it belongs.

"Welcome to Hell's Toilet," Mason says.

Once the door slams shut, the sound of talk and drunken desperation comes to a screeching halt. A coin could drop inside the room and it would shatter the world if it wasn't for the constant thrumming of the engines. Several dozen sets of eyes regard them as they stand by the entrance. Bearded faces, tired eyes, and scars telling of one too many fights judge them from all of at least thirty men and women sitting in the room. Mason's crisp uniform stands out like a stain on a white shirt.

All the tables have drinking glasses of some sort, either empty or full on their worn wooden surfaces, though beneath the smell of alcohol, refuse, and the cramped quarters, Coleena can almost make out the smallest taste of grease in the air. Roasted chicken. Oh, what she would do for a taste of roasted chicken again.

No one moves their way as they stand and wait.

"Best we get this show on the road," Mason says and with a wide smile he finds his way to the bar.

The closest customers, men dressed in ash covered shirts and dark overalls, slide away as the soldier finds his seat. They smell like a bath hasn't happened in over a month, and she can almost see a shadow of their stink still sitting in the stools they once occupied. Inside she prays that the drinks are far better tasting than what the people are leaving her mouth.

Giving as many of them a quick glance as she can, she

finds herself on a stool beside the lieutenant, a dozen set of eyes burning into the skin of her back. The surface of the serving table is sticky and there is grime worked into the film as she rests her arms across the top of the bar.

"I do not see him anywhere," she says. "Do you think they brought him somewhere else?"

Mason points a finger at the woman behind the bar and bends it slowly and as seductively as he can toward himself. His smile grows though she returns a strong upside-down reflection.

"Why don't we just find out?" he says as the bartender steps up to them. "What's the best drink you go here, my fine-looking lady?"

She is a stout one if Coleena is to be any kind of judge. Wide shoulders, thick as tree branch arms corded into layers of muscle that flex with every movement, and a set of bear paws turning white as she strangles the poor glass between her grip. Dark hair sits in a ponytail behind her head, braided into a rope that reaches the middle of her back. Not exactly the greatest idea should a fight break out but judging by the long jagged white scar up her left arm and the healed cuts around each of her knuckles, this woman knows how to keep the establishment running in peaceful order.

"Bar is closed," the woman says.

She continues to wipe her towel around the inside of the glass as her eyes trail away to all the men and women situated around the room. Everyone's glares turn as the door opens and Tul enters with his men quickly behind him. Back in their uniforms, their weapons have returned to their shoulders, though it doesn't seem to matter if they are held or just hanging loose. Tables slide and chairs fall as everyone in the room finds a way to scatter to the nearest wall.

The whole room takes a collective breath. As if they were scared to put out the last remaining fire in the world, no one breathes or moves. Tul spares them only the quickest of looks before returning to Mason who waves his hand down to the floor. With a nod, the men split equally around the door and stand watch over the room and the poor souls stuck with them.

"We are not here to cause trouble," Coleena says as she turns back to the bartender. "What is your name?"

The woman looks at her before turning back to the six-armed men guarding her exit.

"I told you, the bar is closed," she answers, her hands shaking, the towel no longer cleaning the inside of the empty cup.

"This is not...," Mason starts and Coleena quickly puts her hand on his shoulder.

No way she is going to let these men lead the way. She can still see the look on that guard's face before they dragged him around the corner. Who knows what Tul will do to all these people if he is forced to get involved?

"Your name, honey. Let's just start with your name," Coleena says, her eyes locking with the woman.

"Isidora," she says, her voice breaking.

"Do you recognize these men, Isidora?" Coleena asks bending forward over the bar to speak with a softer voice.

The woman nods, a small movement as her voice fails her.

"Good, then you will know that they are military. We are not part of the chaos tearing apart so many parts of the city. We are different. We've come to see you tonight because we have a friend who was brought here. Several hours ago. You couldn't have missed him; he was badly hurt."

Her eyes are like little squirrels and her lower lip quivers. She puts down the glass.

"Look, we don't want any trouble with the military. You fight against the dragon and many of the men and women you see in this room have experience doing just that. Having served our time, we just want to get back to living what lives we can in this world. Is that too much to ask?"

Coleena smiles. Spinning on her chair she regards the men and women of the room differently. All of them have hollowed looks. Dark eyes and hair seeing more gray than color. Though there is nervousness in their appearance, very few show outright fear. They have faced death. They have fought it and lived to see another day.

"No, it is not, and it is no less than you deserve. We want the same thing, Isidora, but we can't do that unless we find our friend. He would have come in with a big woman, her name was Narin."

Isidora looks from her to Mason who does nothing but give her a big smile. He leans against the bar as if this was his favorite place to drink and gives no notice to the men and women on either side of the room.

"I... I don't know any woman..." she starts.

"So, you decided to come looking for us," Narin says, her growl too familiar to mistake even beneath the loud thunder of the turbines. "Is this the help you went looking for?"

The big woman steps out from a door in the back of the room by the massive pipes. A corner full of shadow and dust, Coleena hadn't even noticed it was there until the older woman's appearance. Looking past her, she does not see Summers. Where is he?

"This is Lieutenant Major Mason. He is stationed down

within the barracks. That over there is Petty Officer Tul and his men. We need to speak to Summers. Where is the detective?" Coleena asks, sliding off her stool to look the woman in the eyes.

"I think I've seen you around, Lieutenant. You've been here since the migration, am I correct?" Narin asks.

Stepping to the side of Coleena, the big woman waits for Mason to move as well, her husky bulk more dominating than the soldier's round girth.

"Glad to hear I made such an impression," Mason says. "As the captain here so eloquently introduced me already, would I have the pleasure of your name, ma'am?"

"The name is Narin," she answers.

"Well, Narin. It is a pleasure meeting you," Mason says with the slightest of bows. "But as you can see outside these doors, it is of dire importance that we speak with our friend, Detective Summers. Would you be able to help us locate him? I was told he has some important information that I must hear."

Narin turns away from Mason and gives Coleena a good hard look. Turning back to the lieutenant, she lets her gaze settle like a rock in the river on Mason before moving on to the seven men standing beside the door, her face hardening but her eyes giving away the exhaustion behind them. Running her hand through her graying hair, she sighs and takes a few steps back toward the private door she entered through.

"Look, army girl. I told you when we got out that I didn't trust you. I wasn't lying, but that detective friend of yours spoke highly of you on our long walk over here."

"So, Summers is alive?" Coleena cuts in.

Narin nods her head.

"Yes, he's alive. For now. He is not here though. I told you to come looking for me because this is somewhere I could use to prove if you were trustworthy or not. Looking at these men, I'd say that the jury is still out, but Roland is a good man and I owe him one from way back. Come back in a few days and once he is fully recovered, we can all talk," Narin says.

Coleena steps up to where the woman now draws closer to her exit. Mason and the rest do not bother following.

"We don't have a few days. You see what is going on out there. This whole city will tear itself apart if we wait that long. If I could just speak with Summers. All I need is for him to back up my story and these men will have the authority to step in and end all of this before anyone else gets hurt. They just need to speak with him," Coleena pleads.

Narin turns back to the soldiers waiting, any sign of impatience in stances buried beneath years of training.

"This is a lot bigger than you think, army girl. You may have all the best intentions in the world, but you are far above your level here. Come back in a few days. If Summers is up to it, I'll let him decide if it's OK to show you where he is," Narin answers.

Before Coleena can answer, the door to Hell's Toilet explodes open, the force knocking the closest man down to the wood floor, shards covering his uniform and blood beginning to trickle between the fingers gripping the side of his head. The men and women waiting against the wall break their silence with a few shouts and complaints, but they quiet at the entrance of a man in robes darker than the night outside.

"Yes, I would like to say that there really isn't much time to wait," a voice says that Coleena does not recognize.

Before anyone can move, a stream of men push their

way in, rifles at the ready, and full body-armor covering their black uniforms. Tul's men react as quickly as they can but that leaves rifles pointed in all directions and men's voices yelling and screaming threats of guaranteed death. Stepping back toward Narin, Coleena watches as everyone moves to position themselves in a room too small for half of them.

"Now, everyone, stand down!" Mason barks, his shoulders back and the smile on his face more than a mile away from where it used to be.

Some heads turn his way, but no one follows his orders. Rifles remain aimed and itchy trigger fingers flex as less than an inch separates everyone in this room from an apocalypse of their own making.

"I don't think that is going to happen, officer?" the stranger asks.

Sharp lips form into a small smirk as a glimmer of violence sparkles in the man's dark eyes. Pale skin makes him look like a ghost beneath the dark hair he wears long as it flows over both sides of his face, thick curls bunching over his narrow shoulders. His dark robes and hooded cowl give him a priestly appearance. If priests regularly walked with a dozen armed soldiers within arm's reach that is.

There is no fear in his face and his long and lanky body is too relaxed for a situation where everyone sits on a knife's edge.

Coleena feels a warm hand grip tightly onto her elbow. With the smallest amount of pressure, it pulls her back toward the shadows at the back of the room.

"I am Lieutenant Major Mason of the Azhanian Armed Forces. I am here performing an investigation into allegations of outside interference within the city limits and under jurisdiction by civil code...," Mason begins while wiping his hair back into order with a smooth motion of his hand.

"There has been no outside interference within any operations of this city, Lieutenant Mason. I can assure you of that. I would advise you to take your men and quietly find your way back to the barracks. There have been no orders giving you precedence to disobey the curfew ordered by Parliament, but in a show of good faith, my men will allow you undisturbed passage."

Mason looks to Tul who has eyes only for the priestly man in dark robes. He does not spare her any glance as he straightens up the collar of his shirt and the medals on his chest.

"That is a gracious offer, my good man. May I have your name so that I can put it in my official report when I return to the barracks?" Mason asks.

The tiny sneer on the man's face curls into a more lopsided smile, his eyes narrowing like a viper.

"No, you may not, Lieutenant. Be assured that I have been sent here by Parliament itself and that any report you submit will have to include the eight dead men tucked neatly into the shadows of this building. I would think it best we all forget you ever went out this evening."

She can see the folds of Mason's necks flex as he turns to the Petty Officer who still does nothing, the darkness surrounding Tul growing into a threatening mass.

"Well, then. I think there is no good reason for any violence this evening. My men and I will be returning to the barracks as you mentioned and maybe in a few days, this city will see some order returned to the populace," Mason says, his voice steady and firm.

The stranger nods but no one moves.

"Your move, Lieutenant. Have your men stand down and

head on out. We will not follow as our business is with the patrons of this establishment."

"Agreed," Mason says and with a hitching of his belt begins to move toward the door. "Men and women, you heard the man."

He sends a quick glance to Coleena as the others begin to slowly lower their rifles, none of them too eager to back down. The grip on her arm tightens into a vice before she can shift her weight more than half a step.

"The Captain here will be staying with us, Lieutenant," the dark robed man says. "Under Parliamentary orders she is to be arrested and charged with felony civil disobedience. Furthermore, if she instigates any kind of resistance, methods up to and including lethal force has been approved."

"What?" Coleena blurts out.

The man smiles and Mason stops moving. Officer Tul is a shadow that melts behind the big Lieutenant and the tug on her arm is almost enough to pull her from her feet.

"Hold on just one minute," Mason starts.

His words do not finish as the sound of metal releasing pressure, like a train blowing off steam, erupts into the center of the bar. Pipes groan as water shoots in a tidal wave across the whole of the room, the shock enough to punch Coleena forward as the force washes across the floor. Candles extinguish and the room begins to flood in an instant as everything falls into darkness.

Screams from the patrons come in small bursts over the torrent of water and the sudden bursts of gunfire. Coleena can barely get her bearings as the pounding wave of water beats on her back, cracking the bones of her spine as she struggles to reach her knees. A firm grip grabs her arm and pulls her toward the source of the flood, the pounding of the power turbines growing.

"Follow me!" Narin shouts, her words barely audible over the hurricane of confusion.

A few more gunshots ring out, but everything is behind them as Narin leads her through the door she had entered from. Water follows them in but quickly gets swallowed by drains located on the floor. Above, rusty green pipes shudder with the flow of liquid pushing against their sealing joints and the entire building sounds ready to fall into itself. The walls bow in the middle and narrow the width of the hallway as they stumble forward. Puddles line the floor, and she can hear the water chasing them faster than their forward movement.

"Where...are we...going?" Coleena demands, her words coughed out and wet.

Her over-sized shirt hangs heavy from her body as she crawls forward, joints aching, her hands wet and cold with stiffness. With a solid heave, Narin pulls her to her feet. The world temporarily spins as she orients herself.

"If you want to get out of here alive, follow me," Narin says without further explanation.

Wood creaks beneath their wet feet as they race through the back compartment of Hell's Toilet. The smell of refuse here is sulfur thinned by the damp humidity of running water. Pipes drip into rippling puddles as they move deeper, going down steps, and along empty halls. The sound of the engines churning along with the river is deafening and Coleena can feel her ears begin to pop.

"There is no way out of here!" Coleena shouts, her teeth chattering.

The air is a dozen degrees colder down here where everything is soaked to the core. The walls, the ceiling, even the floorboards beneath their boots drip with moisture. Green mold grows everywhere, and the walls close in on them like a cave, their passage lit by individual bulbs flickering along the damp, empty tunnel.

"Not into the city there isn't," Narin says and with a shove of her shoulder she opens a rusted old door that creaks with every inch.

Pulled from an old hanger, Coleena can still see the outline of the numbers once painted onto the barrier, the decay of time and oxidation having eaten most of it away.

"What do you mean not into the city? Where are we going?" Coleena asks following the woman into the room.

Narin stops at a metal hatch, something that looks like it belongs more at the top of an old tank than it does against the floor of a bar.

"Look, do you want to survive or not?"

Coleena looks into the woman's eyes. They are hard but there is fear deep within there. Something she hasn't seen up until this point.

"Of course, but what is going on? Who were those men?"

Narin shakes her head and with a grunt pulls on the hatch until the wheel begins to turn. Flakes of rust and bits of moss fall to the floor as it slowly turns. Stepping forward, Coleena grabs a handful and helps pull until the movement eases and the hatch lifts away.

"There is no time. I can explain later," Narin says. She looks back at the door they entered through and somewhere in the distance they can hear the sound of boots pounding on the floor. "Can you swim?"

Coleena can't find the words to answer. The marching in the hall is now clearly the sound of trained men, and they are coming fast.

"Can you swim?" Narin shouts before shoving her toward

the opening. "Get your ass down there. When you reach the end, hold your breath and jump."

There is no more arguing. Taking a deep breath, Coleena does as she is told. Stepping into the hatch, there is a metal ladder that is as cold as ice against her skin. As quickly as her aching body and freezing hands will allow, she descends into the tunnel below. With little more than enough time to clear her fingers, Narin follows and pulls the hatch shut from the inside, cutting off the light from above and shutting them into the darkness.

Teeth chattering. Heart pounding. Coleena does as she is told until her feet find that the ladder ends far quicker than she could have ever imagined. With a silent prayer to any gods that may be listening, she jumps into the unknown.

19

Freezing cold.

Darkness everywhere.

No air.

Impossible to know which way is up.

Coleena struggles to keep her bearings as the river tosses her around like a leaf. Left and right, under and over. There is no telling which is which. The raging water is as loud as thunder and her world is one storm after another.

Lungs burn. Her knee smashes off something hard. A rock? The ground? Pain is a glaring red light flashing before her eyes as she grows weak. Arms are heavy. Her skull aches and feels like it is splitting into two pieces. This is it, her death. Washed down the sewer pipes like a piece of trash. What a life. What a fitting end to such a failure and a mess.

Iron wraps around her wrist and yanks her hard. Shoulder joint pops, and she does not have the strength to fight. Head breaking the surface of the water, air forces its way into her lungs after water spews from her mouth. Gritty and salty, her stomach heaves and more spews from her mouth before she goes back under.

Dark black hair bobs above the water as she resurfaces. Pulling her toward the shore, she lets the small ball of floating hair tug her along. Shadowed masses line the beach where bulbous monsters hang low over the ripples of raging water. Arms of spindly bones and long fingers are so close she can almost touch them. She wants to reach out to those fingers. Take hold and feel something solid again, even if it's the warming embrace of a monster. Another yank on her arm sends pain tearing through her chest and solid earth finds its way beneath her knees at first and then her feet.

Straining to stand, she half staggers, more crawls out of the water and onto the shore. Water drips from her like the rain, and she collapses into the muddy sand and rocks. Little jagged points slice into the side of her face that isn't burned and it has never felt better. Taking a deep breath, she coughs, and more liquid evacuates from deep inside her gut. How much could she have possibly swallowed? Sand finds its way into her mouth, and she gags out even more water. Her lungs convulse and she wants to puke again.

She digs into her shirt, hands shaking uncontrollably, she finds the dog tags wrapped tightly against the flesh of her neck. She squeezes them for reassurance and takes a deep shuttering breath.

Her shoulders hurt. Her stomach is one big knot and her legs have no strength. Rolling onto her back she stares up at the sky. Pitch black behind the lights of the fires within the city. The moon lost somewhere in the nightmare of the night. The giant wall is a mass of darkness that is impenetrable and towers over her and everything else. The rolling thunder of the river continues less than an arm's length beyond where she lays. Small vibrations echo through the earth. A low growl that moves with the mass of water.

Never in her life has she felt so relieved to be here, alive and soaked to the bone. A deep breath feels good and she closes her eyes.

"Get up, army girl," Narin's voice calls out.

Coleena tries to wave her away, the movement more like the flopping of a landlocked fish.

"It won't take them long to find where we are. If any of them are adventurous they may even follow us out. We need to get into the cover of the trees."

Groaning, Coleena shifts onto her side and catches the image of Narin getting to her feet. Broad shoulders and thick legs power the older woman's body as it shakes the water off in short movements.

"There is no way," Coleena starts to say before looking out on the water, waiting to see several heads pop up from beneath the raging surface.

"I wouldn't count on it with those assholes," Narin says.

Not wanting to disagree, Coleena digs into the ground with her hands, the stones cutting at her palms, and pushes herself up. Every joint in her body pops with angry complaints, and she feels a hundred years older than she is. Bending and flexing at the hip does little to release the pressure.

"Where are we going to go?" Coleena asks.

Narin doesn't answer but instead pushes ahead. Long confident strides have her into the darkness between the monsters. Shadows of trees turned into empty husks. Branches and twigs brittle and broken. Coleena struggles to keep up. The heat of the night settles in quickly the further they get away from the river. Refreshing air cooled by the rushing water is replaced with the humid stickiness of the burned plains. Broken limbs devoid of leaves and life have never forgotten what they lost so many years ago and now they take their revenge. Small cuts. Angry slaps. The cracking and snapping beneath their feet is nothing to the biting pain as another slap across the face opens a cut across Coleena's face.

Time passes and the water soaking her to the bone is replaced with the clinging hands of sweat. Her skin burns and her feet feel the hard edges of every stone, the tripping points of every root, and the distance of every step. Her heart races and yet Narin does not seem to slow even in the slightest.

"Can we take a break?" Coleena calls out.

She does not wait. Letting her legs give way, she falls to the forest floor, old brittle leaves and sticks breaking beneath her weight. She closes her eyes and the world continues to spin. Leaning against the nearest tree trunk, she takes a deep breath and feels the heat radiating from her body.

"Not much for hiking, are you, army girl?" Narin asks before dropping down beside her.

Muscles cramp and Coleena tries to work the knots free as she takes deep breaths to slow her heart. For the first time she takes notice of the graying of sky in the east and the sound of birds singing the first songs of the day. A welcoming sign she hasn't known in a long time.

"I've marched from here, following the length of the Niarana river, all the way to Zacele. Not long ago I would hardly have broken a sweat," Coleena answers.

Putting her chin on her knees helps with the tightening of her back, the coolness of her wet shirt helping relieve the pain.

"What happened?" Narin asks handing over a small hand-sized fruit.

Not recognizing it, she looks at the older woman's face but there is no malice there. She isn't even looking at her. Taking a bite, the juices are tart but her stomach growls and enjoys ever last bite.

"My last deployment. Damn Gorgoth got me in the back," Coleena answers pulling up the big shirt to expose the puckered skin stretching itself along her spine.

Little fires burn along the scarring, and she can feel the woman's eyes as they examine the damage and the extent of how much she has lost.

"Hurt like a bitch I bet," Narin says.

"You could say that. Lost everything I ever knew because of this. Fighting was my whole life. Everything I was born to do. Now what am I?"

Narin doesn't answer right away. They sit quietly and watch as the sky to the east turns from gray to a warm orange and yellow. There is no sign of pursuit and the heat promises to get worse with every passing minute.

"You're still a captain in the army, aren't you?" Narin finally says.

Coleena gives a quick chuckle.

"By title only. Part of me still believes the General only assigned me here out of pity. I'm a born fighter, Narin. Not a detective like Summers or anything else. Since the moment I got here I've caused nothing but trouble for myself and have learned little else."

With a big grunt Narin pushes herself to her feet. The effort the first sign of fatigue breaking the big woman's stone exterior.

"If fighting is something you are good at then you've definitely come to the correct place. Get back to your feet. We've got a good distance still to cover."

She does not wait as Coleena turns to see her moving

deeper into the woods. Within a few strides she is into the thinning shadows of the forest and gone. Refusing to be left behind, popping joints or not, Coleena gets to her feet and finds a way to follow.

20

———

By mid-day, the dead husks of forest begin to thin. Gaps open where tracks of small animals stir the dusty surface beneath their feet and bits of green begins to sprout through all the browns and yellow. The sky is a bright blue through outstretched branches, the sun so bright the world has never been clearer. With a deep breath, Coleena lets the warmth and fresh air sink deep into her body.

Birds sing and if she doesn't glance back, she may even forget that the city walls would still be within sight if the forest was not there. The creaking of wood, song-like in its symphony carries through the land. More welcoming and pleasant than if she was in a dream. Wiping away the sweat covering her forehead and ringing a good handful out of her hair, she steps up beside Narin, the woman leaning against a maple struggling to survive. Leaves turning orange, but with a little green still showing, they give a little shade for them both to stand in.

"How much further do we have to go?" Coleena asks.

Narin keeps her eyes on the horizon. Ground slowly

sloping downward, it is much easier to see what they face should they continue in this direction. From where they stand the canopy of the forest continues endlessly for miles as it encircles long bits of grasslands. Bits of green and other colors decorate the approaching landscape and the Niarana River snakes its way through all of it, a deep cut through the darkness of the forest.

Such a drastic difference to the walled fortress of Parliament City. Where dirt and ash, stone and wood dominate, here life is trying to claw its way back. Wilderness and diversity. A clean feel. The world returning to the way it should be.

"We'll be to the first outpost by sundown. After that, we'll see," Narin says.

Her answer is cryptic. Coleena looks out to the trek ahead. Once part of Azhana's largest wildlife reserve, now it truly has returned to what the gods had intended it to be. Humans have had no time to encroach upon its beauty and resources in the twenty-five years since the beginning of the dragon's reign. Taking another breath, the feeling and taste of the beauty is intoxicating. Finally, something in this world worth fighting for.

"Lead on then," Coleena says, regardless of the argument quickly put up by the soles of her feet.

Turning toward her, Narin nods before taking the first steps down the slope. At a steady pace they move from the shelter of the forest and out into the open grasslands. Bits and pieces of open space exposed to the bright sun and clouds before being quickly swallowed again by the returning hands of Mother Nature.

Coleena lets her hands run across the thigh-high grass. Like velvet, it glides across the skin of her palms.

"You get out here much?" Coleena asks. "I mean, before they shut down the wall."

Narin does not turn back. Her hands do not touch or explore the field they pass through. Shoulders back, pace strong and firm, the woman is on a mission, and she will not be delayed.

"Maybe once a year. Too dangerous to do this too often. If we do make it obvious Parliament will find out and follow. We try to memorize the path and then never use it again."

Coleena gives a quick glance back the way they have come. There hasn't been any sign of pursuit, yet that doesn't give her any feeling of assurance.

"So, what is Azhana United? How big are we talking?" Coleena asks.

Narin chuckles.

"It is exactly everything you have been lea to believe and it is also not."

"What? That makes no sense," Coleena responds.

"Yes, and there is too much to explain without showing you. What I will tell you is there is enough of us to know what is going on here. Men and women dedicated to the survival of the human species and in particular, the central government of what we call home. For years we have stayed in the shadows, watching over the changes in the attitudes of the people. At first everyone was glad to have survived. Some even had the gall to try and fight back against the monsters and you see where that led everyone. Then something changed. It wasn't sudden or a surprise in the middle of the night, more like one of those lingering colds. You know, the ones that start as a small sniffle, or a scratch at the back of your throat."

"Definitely," Coleena says.

"Real lingering bastard. That's how it happened. People

started worrying more about themselves and the country. The army was quietly pushed as far out of their mind as it could be. Rumors of a military coup and the strangest theories of why so many men and women were never seen again after leaving to go fight."

"Come on, you're joking. What did people think? Men and women would leave, then what? We'd experiment on them or something?"

Narin stops. Looking up at the sky, her eyes are closed and beads of sweat slide down the edges of her tightening face.

"Something like that. All kinds of things. Didn't really help when those who came back refused to speak of the horrors they saw. Many felt abandoned by the whole thing. The army used them up. People who didn't have the balls or ability to fight with them didn't believe in any of it. Became really easy to call it a big hoax and act like it never happened."

There is nothing to say. The reality of the whole argument was like a punch to the gut. Without another word, Narin turns and continues as the field hardens beneath their feet, and they reenter the darkened canopy of the forest.

"If you are so dedicated to fighting the dragon then why don't you join the Army? We could always use more soldiers and with enough strong fighters we could make a push to the damn beast itself."

Narin shakes her head.

"I'm a little passed my prime, army girl. Plus, I do enough here. Someone has to keep Parliament on their toes until we figure this shit out. The whole city would be in chaos if we didn't keep our hand in the cookie jar."

The shadows grow long as time turns, and they quickly

begin to move back uphill. The trees grow thicker with foliage and some with needles begin to take the place of the colorful leaves giving life to the dead world. A sweet smell of sticky sap fills in the gaps. A fresh sent. One that helps fight the weariness after miles of hiking.

Squirrels and other rodents dart from tree to tree as they pass by. Birds, like shadows, fly through low branches, their passage giving rise to the feeling of life within this world.

"Azhana United wasn't the one who planted the bombs was it?" Coleena asks.

Boots kicking dirt up into the air, Narin spins and the anger on her face is hot enough to set the trees next to her on fire. Eyes glaring, fists balled, Coleena stops where she is, hands up protectively.

"We may be spending our resources keeping tabs on whatever has gotten its talons into those fools on Congress Street, but we sure as well would never attack our own. Like it or not, we are their only protection. Keep that straight, army girl."

"Look, I'm trying to figure things out just as much as you are. I'm new at this. I've barely been in the city for a week and look where it has gotten me. Out here in the middle of the first forest I've seen in years, running for my life with a woman who won't even tell me where we are going!"

Narin shakes her head and continues on, refusing to slow.

"You may have spent your life fighting and dying in the trenches with the monsters that demon spits out, but the shadow it casts reaches far beyond the battlefields the army has chosen to die on. Out here, we play a different game. Politics. Men and women with ambitions far beyond their station and many of them are willing to do whatever it takes to get what they want. Even if that means signing a death warrant for every man, woman, and child in the entire world." Narin says, no struggle evident in her body as she continues to push forward.

Coleena, every joint in her body aching, struggles to keep up as her legs burn and her heart pounds blood through her ears. The endless climb seems to have no end. The darkness beneath the forest ceiling is closing in on them, the shades of green and orange become gray and black as time continues its endless pursuit. The snapping of twigs and moans of trees shifting in the late afternoon begins to follow them, uncomfortably close.

"And you mean what by that? What are they planning? If you already suspect something, why haven't you done anything? Parliament City is practically in anarchy, yet you stay out here, hiding," Coleena says.

"I wouldn't call it hiding," Narin responds as she pulls up, hands on hips and overlooking a dip in the land that leads down to the Niarana river.

The water is far calmer here. Like a sheen of glass, the reflection of the fading sun, a ball of orange and warmth across the western sky, shimmers in the slow-moving water. A single wooden pier cuts into the calm flow, small white caps splashing against the pilings. Hardly used, the boards are whitewashed from the sun and bow with age and saturation. Tied and bobbing in the water sits a flat raft, more or less logs tied together to form enough surface for a maximum of four people with straps of leather holding it all together. Swaying in the soft current, their chariot awaits. Narin points her chin at the waiting vessel, and they make their way out of the trees and down toward the river.

Coleena watches the shadows as they continue. The long grass of the field bends and breaks beneath her heavy boots. Nothing moves or follows. The sound of birds calling goodnight and the buzz of grass-beetles fills the early evening with a peaceful melody that brings exhaustion out to the open. Eyes heavy, body weary, they slip quietly onto the pier. Boots echo with every step though none of it is loud enough to break the soothing melody of the early evening.

"Where we going to take this?" Coleena asks while Narin makes her way to the end of the pier.

The sound of the moving water beneath her feet is rhythmic and doesn't help with the need to rest. Shoulders heavy, she finds a way to lean against one of the pilings, the stiffness of her joints making a sudden and terrifying comeback.

"You'll see. From here there are few who know where we are going," Narin answers.

Squatting down she checks the ropes holding the raft in place. Releasing the loop securing the vessel to the first piling, with practiced ease she spins it around the second and pulls it tight.

"Aren't we supposed to be releasing those, not securing them?" Coleena asks.

The words are barely out before the brush beyond the reach of the dock explodes with movement. Dirt and grass lift up into the air, tarps blended in with camouflage roll back and figures take shape as the familiar click of rifles jump start the fire within Coleena's belly.

"What the fuck is going on here?" she demands, a small turn revealing the four guns pointed at the back of her head.

Garbed in dark clothing, helmets and paint covering their faces, Coleena cannot see if they are men or women. None of them wear the uniform of the army or of anything stationed within Parliament City. They close in on her slowly, weapons held steady. Her knees bend, hands sweating, she watches as they being to surround her.

"I wouldn't think of doing anything stupid, army girl," Narin says.

She approaches slowly from behind. Hands up and open she shrugs as Coleena eyes her every movement, the fire in her blood heating every inch of her face.

"Then explain yourself. You get me out of the city, walk me a dozen miles into the wilderness, to what? You could have just left me to die back with the others," Coleena says.

Narin nods and two of the dark strangers lower their weapons.

"As I mentioned, only a few know the location of where we are going. I don't trust you, army girl. But Roland asked me to watch over you and that is what I plan to do. Doesn't mean I have to like it or that I need to show you the secret that keeps those of us in Azhana United alive. You are coming with us, army girl, like it or not. Now keep your mouth shut and do as you are told."

Coleena doesn't like this a bit. Grinding her teeth, she fights the urge to back away as the four-armed soldiers approach. One of them pulls a large canvas bag from a pack strapped around the waist. Sighing, she does nothing to resist them. There is nothing she can do. She is out of options. Feeling them tie the bottom loosely around her neck, her world goes black, and she waits for the next surprise to make itself known.

21

The ride is smoother than she thought it would be. After securing bindings to her wrists and forcing them behind her back, they loaded her onto the raft and at least two others joined her and Narin. Their body weight shifting the poor vessel, forcing Coleena to bite back the fear they were going to dump her over the edge. It's not like she could have done anything anyway. Hands bound; she would be an even worse swimmer than she is already. Sitting and trying to shift with the movements of the raft, the passage of water beneath her and time's slow progression is soothing regardless of what she feels.

In the darkness of the hood, her eyes go heavy, and she knows she has fallen asleep several times. The air above the river is cool as they pass along with the current. She can't smell the water anymore now that the overwhelming stench of potato and root vegetables surrounds her. Couldn't they have used something a bit cleaner to do the job? Her stomach growls and part of her wishes she could bite her way right through the sack.

Small splashes of water find their way onto her exposed

skin and the cold touch is a relief against the dry air of the waning day.

She has no way to tell how far they have traveled. Below she can feel the current begin to pick up, the small rocking of the boat shifting her position and forcing her to struggle to stay seated upright. Little has been said between her captors. A few instructions here. Nothing to point out a direction or landmark she could possibly use if there was a chance for her to break free. Stewing silently, her anger burns with warm embers just waiting to ignite.

"Not much further, army girl," Narin says.

The first words they have spoken since this tragic turn of events. Coleena cocks her head to the side, maybe if she stays quiet the other one will think she can't hear.

"Don't even give me that look. I don't need to see your face to know what you are thinking. That is nothing more than a potato sack so you can hear me perfectly fine. Sure as well didn't hold back your snoring when you fell asleep."

"I was not snoring!" Coleena barks at her.

Narin and the others chuckle. The first reaction she has gotten out of any of them since they left.

"Could have fooled us but think of it this way. We are doing you a favor. If what we have to show you doesn't suit your needs, there will be less reason to kill you. Wouldn't be hard to toss you in the river and let you drown, now would it?" Narin asks.

Coleena shifts her seat.

"You could just trust me. How am I going to get this through your thick skull? We are on the same side. Detective Summers wouldn't be vouching for me if we weren't. You seem to trust him a hell of a lot more than me, and he asked you to watch out for me. Or does that courtesy only extend within the walls of Parliament City?"

"Me and the detective go way back. He's gotten me out of a few sticky situations, and I owe him a lot. Him speaking up for you goes a long way, especially with those you will soon meet, but I'm just not that trusting, army girl. Plus, everyone makes a mistake after a while. It would be his first, but it's not impossible. I'll give it to you, you've got spunk, but when we are talking life or death here, there is never a time to be sorry."

A loud creaking gives little warning as the raft jerks with a sudden stop. Losing her balance, Coleena can do nothing to stop her forward momentum and the sudden change tips her over onto her face. A flash of light passes over her blocked vision and a new pain erupts within her head. Growling, she rolls until she finds herself back up, sitting on her ass.

"Sorry about that," Narin apologizes.

"Go fuck yourself," Coleena mutters.

"Still have that fight in you, that's a good sign," Narin says, her voice drawing closer as the raft continues to shake. "Here, let me see if I can help you up."

Big strong hands grab onto Coleena's arm at the shoulder and pull her to her feet. The ropes loosen around her wrist and fall away. She can feel Narin's large presence next to her without actually being able to see her.

"Going to keep that on you for a few more moments. We are here, army girl. Home sweet home until we figure out what the hell is going on in Parliament City."

With gentle nudges and small directions, Narin leads Coleena off the raft and up a few steps. A new pier. She can feel the wooden planks creak and bend beneath her feet and the rush of water below is easy to hear with swift splashes and the sound of water dripping.

"Can we finally take this off?" Coleena asks.

The bindings are loose, but it doesn't stop the irritation bothering the skin of her neck. Narin hesitates and then with a gentle nudge gets them moving forward. Stepping carefully, Coleena tries to see anything she can through or beneath the mask.

The air is warmer than it was over the river, but not enough for it to be morning yet. Small bits of light pass beneath the seal of the sack, yet the feeling that it is still clearly dark is evident. Oil and pitch burn nearby. The smell of torches filtering in with the stale air as they keep moving.

"A little longer," Narin says.

"I really doubt I could find my way back from here," Coleena argues. "Even if you just let me go, I'd be lucky to get a mile from this place without getting lost."

Narin chuckles.

"Now there is something I know you aren't lying about, but orders are orders."

"Orders from who? I'm getting real fucking tired of all these secrets. Where is Summers? If he spoke so highly of me, why would I be treated like this still," Coleena demands.

The hard dirt path beneath their feet turns to wooden boards as Narin leads them up a set of two steps. Their passing echoes into the night and a dog barks in the distance. The sizzling of fire is not too far off to her right, like a big candle flickering in the night air. A door opens with hinges that are in bad need of grease and Coleena is led in. The room is stuffy. She can practically feel the walls closing in around her with the staleness and warmth beginning to suffocate her. Narin's grip on her arm tightens as she forces her to sit down, a thin mattress not enough to stop the pain of the boards beneath from hurting her pelvis and spine.

"Here we go. You'll wait here until we come and get you," Narin says.

The bindings around her neck fall away with a quick twist and the light of a few burning candles is enough to force her to squint. Standing back and straight, Narin is a wall of darkness as Coleena tries to adjust her vision and puts a hand on her ace for shade.

"Don't expect me to say thank you," Coleena says.

"I wouldn't expect it. Get some rest, army girl. Someone will come and see you in the morning."

"Yeah, good luck with that," Coleena says before turning away.

The large woman shrugs her shoulders and heads out the door. A heavy lock clicks shut, and she is alone. Eyes adjusting to the dim light of two candles, the walls of the room begin to expand as the shadows keep their distance. Rectangular in shape, the cell isn't too small. She could get up and walk around if she wanted to, but stubbornness tells her it's better to remain seated. A small bowl of water sits by the bed and the rest of the room is empty other than a single chair waiting in the far corner. Like an old rocking chair, it sits alone and waiting for a grandma or grandpa to settle in and tell her a story. With a huff she scoots back on the bed and rests her back against the plank-board wall.

What is she going to do?

Detective Summers has to be here somewhere. How long would he make her wait? Still recovering from his injuries, it doesn't surprise her that he'd only be awake during the day, but what is with all the secrecy? Where is she?

A loud click of the lock knocks her mind out of the thousand questions running off like a machine gun without any answers. Slowly the door slides open with the light of another candle pushing its way in. Coleena rocks forward and finds her way to her feet. It has to be Summers. Legs aching and feet feeling like they are about to crack in half, she waits.

"Still awake I see," an old man's voice says.

White hair cascading down a long narrow face, he is a bright light within the gloom between the empty walls. A white beard, peppered with small amounts of black, forks its way from his chin down past his chest and his face is a roadwork of lines. Able hands hold the candle steady, and he moves with a walk that defies the age of his appearance. Clean gray robes drag over the floor with each of his steps and the thin rope keeping everything shut ties neatly over a narrow waist.

Beyond his sudden arrival and the stark contrast of his bright white appearance, Coleena takes a step back as he turns to look at her. His eyes, thoughtful and full of a strength she can read immediately, are as green as the sky is blue. The depth within those jewels belittles anything she has ever seen. She is trapped beneath their gaze. He could draw a knife stab her right through the heart, and she'd never resist him. Ensnared with magical bonds, no one in this world could escape that look. She doesn't even try to speak.

"Ah, not exactly what I expected, but definitely worth the effort," the old man says.

Without reason, Coleena begins to wipe at the dirt of her clothes and runs gentle hands at the scars and bandages still clinging to her body. For the first time in as long as she can remember, her appearance takes on an importance like it never has before. Ashamed of the damage so many years of fighting has done to her body, she shifts away from his judging look. As if reading her mind, he waves her concern away without a single word.

Turning to the chair in the far corner, his gaze breaks, and she can feel the chains holding her in place release. Staggering from the effort of just moving, Coleena slips back until she flops down and sits on the bed.

"Who are you? Where am I?" she asks, her voice strained and broken.

"I am many things to many people, my child," the old man says. "To some I am grandfather. Others consider me wise and worth speaking to when the time suits them. While there are a few who see me as nothing more than a nuisance."

"What should I consider you?" Coleena asks, her strength slowly returning as he pulls the chair forward until it is right before her.

Sandals gliding smoothly over the boarded floor, he neither grunts nor groans as he sits himself within the rocker. No signs of age or pain pass through his features as he settles himself comfortably. Placing a single finger over his lips, he puts the candle down by his feet before rocking back a few times.

"I would hope one day you would consider me a friend. Until then, you can simply call me Phydel. For where you are, my daughter," Phydel says, "you are in a village within the Azhanian Reservation Gorge. A place where the Niarana river reaches its deepest point within the wilderness reserve. Well hidden from the men and women who search for us, yet still close enough to keep an eye on everything that happens within the walls of the city fortress."

"So, this is where Azhana United hides?" Coleena asks.

"Not exactly hiding, but yes, except for those we still

have stationed within the walls of the city, this would be where our main strength remains."

Coleena leans back, her arms over her chest as she looks at the door. It would take her nothing to push past this man and get through. Even if he seems more capable than his apparent age, she would be on her feet before he gets out of that large chair. Looking back at him, the thought of flight passes like a breeze escaping through a gap in the room's walls.

"I'm not sure if anyone has told you, but Parliament City lost control of itself not more than two nights ago. Guards and Parliamentary forces were sweeping the streets looking for anyone and everyone associated with Azhana United. Anyone you still have there is no longer safe," Coleena says.

The man nods before pulling out a little canteen from the inside of his robes. Untwisting the cap, he takes a small sip before offering the drink to her. Hesitating for a moment, she accepts the offer, now suddenly realizing how thirsty she is.

Liquid fire burns the inside of her mouth and throat. A heat like nothing she has ever felt melts its way through her gut and with a slight cough she feels it make its way through her body. The substance has a calming effect. Muscles loosen. Her joints release and the itching and burning of the wounds to her face, arms, and back begin to fade. Taking a deep breath, she settles into a more comfortable position against the wall.

"Terrible situation up there. Part of me wonders if any of them are even still alive," Phydel says.

"Still alive?" Coleena questions. "You hardly seem worried if all you are doing is sitting here and waiting for news."

The old man nods before rocking back and clasping his hands together in front of his chin.

"You've been to war, my child," he starts. "There are risks to every action and in this case, we would risk more than the lives of a few to do anything until we are ready. Why lose the war just to win the battle?"

Now it is time for Coleena to chuckle.

"So, you consider this a war? Fighting against the damn dragon is a war, old man. I'm not even sure what this is. All I know is if someone doesn't do something about it, a lot more people are going to die along the way."

A smile stretches across the man's face and his beard lifts an inch or two. The rocking of the chair lifts the thinnest hair in tiny wisps as he waits to respond.

"Oh, my dear child, many people are going to die before this is finished. That I can sadly promise you. Of course, how many will be determined by the choices of a select few. Isn't it such a sad thing that the outcome of so many lives can be determined by others? Makes you reconsider the whole idea of freedom of choice, doesn't it?"

Is this man crazy? Letting her head rock back, her eyes settle on the roof. Shadows dance through the beams and cobwebs which swing in the smoky air.

"You're talking in riddles, old man. Whoever these people are better make a choice soon. A lot of good civilians are going to die if no one does anything. The dragon has, I'm not even sure what to call them, things within the city walls and if we don't stop them, everyone is at risk."

Phydel closes his eyes and keeps his rhythmic rocking going, slow and steady.

"We call them Dragon-Touched. Half-breeds are more like it. Men and women who've given themselves to the subversion of the dragon's magic. Much stronger than your average man, but more conniving than the animalistic ones it likes to use on the battlefield. They are a dangerous group, and here in Parliament City, I'm afraid it gets even worse. I can't be certain but I'm pretty sure it has sent his general. A strong move on its part. Not one I would have made so early in the game, but the beast senses a weakness. Cut the head off the snake and the whole-body dies."

"You're not making any sense. How do you know all of this?" Coleena demands, the strength in her legs returning so that she can stand up and look down at him. "We've got people who claim they don't even think the monster is real and you are here talking like you've been studying the damn thing since before it founds its way into this world. Where is Summers? I need to speak with the man so we can get all of this cleared up."

Phydel clears his throat and nods his head with a small smile. Shifting his weight, he slides out of the chair with little effort and glides across the floor until he is between her and the door.

"You seem tired, my child. There are so many questions that you want answered that I could not possibly start to touch them all this evening. Lay on the bed and rest your head. You will need the strength of a good night's sleep. We can speak more in the morning. I assure you that Detective Summers is well, and I will see if he is available to speak with you when you wake up."

Coleena goes to protest, but all that comes out is a yawn. It has been a long and hard road to get this far, but sleep can wait. She wants her answers now.

"Wait, I'm...not really...," she begins as the yawning continues. "Look, I'm...not...sure...."

She can't finish the words. Legs laden with lead, eyes dropping, she lets the gentleman lead her to the bed where she lays down. His smile is genuine, and those eyes steel away any hope of resistance. Sitting on the edge, he pats her on the shoulder before running his fingers across the scabs and scars spread across the side of her face.

"Rest my child. Everything will be clearer in the morning," he says.

The candles begin to fade in the distance as she watches him leave. Deep inside she can hear her voice scream for him to stay, but the warmth running through her body is like a freshly knitted blanket. Wrapped in its loving embrace, she lets the sleep take her away.

22

———

Not exactly the most comfortable of beds, but it beats sleeping on the floor. Eyes stiff, head pounding, Coleena stretches and wipes away the drool dripping from her mouth.

Warm air fills the small hut. Nothing too bad, relaxing and just on this side of comfortable. Small streams of light break in through the gap at the bottom of the door, and she can see that the candles are little more than puddles of hardened wax. Her body is far less stiff than she can ever remember it being. Joints don't pop. Muscles don't stiffen, and with a quick stretch she turns and lets her bare feet down onto the floor. When did she take off her boots?

Even the floorboards are warm to the touch. A soothing wave of heat lifts through her feet into her legs. Flexing her toes, she feels good. Moving her jaw around, she lets her vision adjust as the sound of children yelling filters in from outside.

Joyful screams. Full of happiness and dreams. Some are right outside her door; others are in the distance. A constant bang of metal vibrates from further away. Something like an old blacksmith, but she hasn't seen one of those outside of a storybook. Rhythmic and regular. The bell like quality of metal on metal.

There are even birds singing into the morning air. Beautiful songs that dance and put peace in one's heart. She can't even remember the last time she felt that.

Rubbing her hands over her face to finishing waking up from what feels like the best sleep she has had in years; she stops as they reach her cheek.

The scabs are gone. Rippled skin flexes beneath her touch, but there is no pain. Looking around at least proves that nothing has changed. There is no mirror, only the rocking chair that found its way back into the corner. Her stomach rumbles, and she is forced to wait until someone comes to check on her. What is she going to do? How long are they going to keep her in this room?

As if reading her thoughts, the heavy lock on the outside of the door clicks and the door slides open. The hinges cry out in pain, and she grimaces as it pops in her ears, the sound too harsh for the quiet tranquility of this morning.

"I thought you could use some breakfast," Summers' familiar voice says.

The detective takes a step around the open door and it takes everything she has not to jump up and wrap her arms around him. Or she might punch him square in the nose as she isn't sure just yet where her feelings lay.

"Where the hell have you been?" she demands, her eyes falling on the plate of eggs and flat bread delicately balanced in his hand.

Leaning on his cane, he gives her a big smile, his dark eyes shining as he waves her over with a shift of his head.

"Come outside. Eat where the sun can warm up those

bones of yours," he says, turning and heading back the way he had come in.

Following him out, she has no words to say. It's like she's been transported out of her time and into a different world. Log houses sit nestled between giant Oaks and Maples, their leaves turning mesmerizing colors for as far as she can see. The canopy of the forest blocks any view of the village from above the trees and the smell of cook fires mingles with the fresh scent of life within the wilderness. A wonderful and clean feeling. Like rushing water, there is a crispness that tickles her skin and sends shivers through her body.

Children run down the main path bisecting everything she sees, their faces full of smiles and wonderment. Their clothes are a mismatch of colors and styles. All of them look hand sewn and fit them in generally odd ways. The younger looking ones have stuff that is far too big, and those having a few years under their belt are better suited for the material if it isn't a tad short. None of them have holes. Patches where some may have been at one time, but these are not poor children. They have plenty. Living out here in the forest, they are still miles ahead of those she saw in the city.

Then there is the surrounding rock. Sheer cliffs of solid earth, dark and sharp pointing out into the clear sky. They are in a bowl, surrounded on three sides. A valley of some sort protecting them and giving them shelter from the elements and enemies. It is hard to take all of this in.

Some children stop and glance at her, their voices quieting. She has piqued their curiosity, but quickly they turn back to whatever game it is they are playing. Their smiles never disappearing before disregarding her entirely and moving on.

"How can this be?" she asks.

Summers slides a foldout chair behind her, damn thing

even still has a "property of P.C.P.D." stamped on it. She takes a seat before scooping up her first bite of eggs. Milky with a hint of salt, her stomach roars, and she can't get it down fast enough. Pulling one for himself, he sits down beside her, his cane a balance to lean on between his feet. The man is correct though. The feeling of the sun on her skin is wonderful. She sighs and lets her head roll back for a moment, the food she wolfed down working its way down to her belly.

"Many of us have been outside the city a long time. We do our best to keep it a secret from as many within as we can. Not too long ago we learned the hard way that in the hands of the wrong person, our way of life can be considered a threat," Summers answers.

"Wait? What do you mean? How can this be a threat?" Coleena gets out between shovels of more food.

Feeling stuffed or not, she is not going to let any of it go. The detective laughs, one that lets him lean back and put his head against the wall of the house she was locked into.

"Do you see any guards? Any police? People don't understand what they can't control. That has been the problem with Parliament since after the time of the great migration. It has never been a case of doing what is right for people. Instead, they have used their positions to consolidate power and make sure the line between those who have and those who do not is clearly drawn. People thrive when they know the rules and the boundaries. Mother nature is our only boundary out here. We take care of the land around us and it takes care of us. Some people do not understand that. Call us outsiders or worse, anarchists."

"But what about the dragon? We all surely can't live like this," Coleena says with a wave of the empty plate.

Summers takes it from her with a smile before putting it down on the ground beside him.

"No, sadly you are correct. This works because we are small, mobile, and resilient. If we were much larger it would be easier to spot us. Both from within the city and by those monsters looking to destroy everything within their path. The last time we tried to expand, Parliament sent enough spies in that half our community revolted and burned the village to the ground. We relocated here within the gorge and have kept a tight seal on who comes and goes. Even greater control on who knows about it where we can."

Coleena looks at everything she can see. Men and women work their way from building to building. Some carry wood, others hold bundles of clothes. Small game like rabbits and pheasants hang from wooden eaves, freshly caught with buckets of blood still collecting as the carcasses wait to be prepped. Beneath the shadows the world is not too hot. A comfortable warmth that keeps them all safe and happy. But what about the other dangers?

Looking closer she sees signs of weapons on everyone, including some larger children. A few have small pistols and a man or two carry rifles over their shoulders. Many more have small intricate knives strapped within cloth belts with blades that reflect like silver mirrors.

All of it is so intertwined with the way they are she hardly noticed at first. No one is brandishing anything. It feels like the weapons are nothing more than tools they are forced to carry, like a shovel or ax.

"So, this is your big plan? Live out here like hermits. Hide your spies in the city and do what? Did you really ever plan to stop the chaos? Does your oath to the people of Parliament City stop once you find yourself outside those stone walls?"

All jovial softness and the curves of Summers' face wash away before the hard lines and dark circles she remembers reappear. He looks off into the shadows of the trees surrounding the village before taking a deep breath.

"None of us have forgotten the people within those walls. They are our friends and our families. We watch over what we can and do what is needed when we have the chance. I'm afraid things may have gotten a bit passed us now, with what you saw and all."

Almost aging before her eyes, he leans forward and drops his face into the palms of his hands, shaking and wiping away at the sadness breaking its way through.

"What I saw? You were there. You fought right alongside me. The dragon has found its way into the city, and they are doing nothing about it. We can't sit here in the forest and do nothing," Coleena says.

Summers sits back, hands behind his head, he gazes out into the distance.

"You are correct. For the most part. I did fight beside you, though I did not see the same things you did," he answers.

"Did not see?" Coleena rages. "Do you think I did this to myself?"

Standing up, she knocks the chair to the ground with a crash of metal and forces her way in front of him. Putting her hand on her cheek, the fire in her falters for a moment as her hand passes over the rippled, relatively smooth skin, the heat of the moment making her forget. The detective puts up his hands, palms out, as if to ward her off.

"Oh, I don't deny what you said you fought. I saw the burns on your face and the molten rock on the ground beside you. I know firsthand the smell of your face cooking under that fire. I'm just saying I didn't see the man or thing you fought. It could have been a full-on demon for what I know."

"Your Phydel seems to think differently," Coleena says before giving the chair a swift kick and leaning against the railing of the porch. "He seems to think he knows a lot and the only one who believes me around here."

"Well, Phydel is kind of a character in these parts. Most would call him an elder, while the rest call him crazy, though I would disagree he is the only one who believes you."

"Seems perfectly sane to me. Other than that drink of his. Damn stuff almost ate right through my gut," Coleena says before rubbing her stomach to send the message home.

"Oh yeah, his one touch miracle cure. He's a real big stickler that anyone who is sick should drink it. Child or not. Stomachaches, headaches, even a twisted ankle or two and there he is with that canteen of his. Damn stuff works too. As long as you can get it down. Even helped me out a bit."

Coleena turns back to Summers. He's rubbing the area below his ribs and the side of his abdomen. She tries to chuckle.

"How are you doing anyway? In all of this I forgot to even ask."

Looking away from his injuries he shrugs.

"I've been better. Took a deep gash in that explosion. Shards of wood and a few panes of glass got me. Had to cover myself up to get into the cells to find you. Real stroke of luck that it didn't take me longer. Would have bled out if it did. In the struggle the pillow full of gauze I was using slipped and soaked through. Narin got me stable before having them sneak me out of the city. The people here did the rest."

"They didn't flush you down the drain, did they?" Coleena asks with a small smile.

With a shake of his head he smiles back.

"No. Parliament doesn't have the city locked up as well as they think. We leave that method for emergencies only. I heard you had to take a little swim yourself. I'm glad you made it," Summers says.

"So am I. You think old Phydel could have done this?" she asks, her hand rubbing the side of her face again.

Summers takes a good hard look at her. His dark eyes stare into hers and for a moment she doesn't want to let them go. Taking in his appearance, she sees the small amounts of gray beginning to work their way through his hair, the thickest spots along his sideburns. He is a lot more handsome than she gave him credit for. The way his hard edges frame his narrow cheeks and solid cut chin. For a brief moment she doesn't even realize he isn't sitting in front of her anymore.

"Heal your face? Never known a drink to be able to do that, but with Phydel, you never really know. As for your other questions; we may call this our home, but all of Azhana are our people. If Parliament City falls, the rest of the world as we know it will fall. It is only a matter of time," Summers says before waving her to follow him. He steps off the porch, the heavy lean into his cane more evident than it was back in the city. "Follow me and I'll show you a few things."

Walking out onto the dirt path, it is easy to keep up as they make their way through the small village. Everyone they pass has a bright smile on their face, lines of hard work etched into sun-browned skin, and a quick wave of hello to the detective before they move along.

"Does everyone know you here?" Coleena asks as they near the blacksmith she could hear in the distance.

A large furnace glows red, and she can feel the heat before they ever reach the front table. Set up similar to a booth at the flea market she remembers visiting with her mother back before Obrathe burned to the ground, two burly men work the hot fire and smoldering black smoke of the furnace. Oxidized air tickles the inside of her nose with its bitter smell and the soot of the fires cover everything. Heavy hammer crashing onto heated metal, she can feel the vibrations in her bones long before she can lean on the polished surface of the presentation table.

Knives sit displayed openly and without anyone watching their presence. Even blades as long as a sword hang from small hooks hammered into wooden pilings keeping a roof over the two men's bodies. Black dust covers both of them where sweat hasn't soaked through to the skin beneath. Large shoulders, burly arms, and legs like tree trunks work the heated metal without ever realizing they are there.

"We are a small group in relation to the city. Having spent so many years together we are going on our second generation," Summers says as a little girl with a bright brown ponytail turns the corner of the blacksmith before disappearing down the main path. A small puppy yips as it chases her, its tiny paws stirring up a cloud of dust. "It's really not hard to become known around here."

"I can see that, but what are you planning?" Coleena asks with a wave at the two men still working before the fire. "You can't possibly believe storming the walls with these is going to do anything."

To make her point Coleena lifts up one of the knives. The hilt is made of a polished oak, deep brown and like velvet beneath her fingers. Small metal inlays create patters along the grain of the wood and the blade itself is a mirror shining back at her face.

She can see the markings along her cheek. Tiny white lines, almost unnoticeable beneath her tanned skin. Her blue eyes reflect in the high-noon sun, and she takes notice of the weight as she lets it roll from one side of her palm to the other.

"This can't be," she whispers to herself.

There is almost nothing to it. Even the small amount of wood in the hilt would weight more than what it does in her hand. Looking over at Summers he is nothing but a smile.

"Real astonishing thing isn't it?" he asks.

"How?" she stumbles with before turning back to all the other weapons on display. "This would break the first time you go to use it."

"Go ahead and try."

Wanting to make the man regret his words, in a quick motion she reverses her grip on the blade and drives it down into the table. Expecting it to bend or chip, there are no words as the tip cuts deep into the wood. Lodging itself almost an inch beneath the surface, she lets go and watches it rest without moving, handle waiting in the air.

"Fine piece of craftsman ship isn't it?" a big burly voice asks.

Both of the blacksmiths have turned around, their eyes on her and Roland. Her breath catches in her throat as the two big men stare at them with gigantic smiles. Twins! They are identical down to the bushy mustaches and the wild look of their brown eyes. Rosy red cheeks shine with a thick layer of sweat and even their stance is the same as they lumber up to the table and cross their arms over barrel chests of black hair sticking out from beneath their soaked cotton shirts of gray, white, and ash.

"Did...did you make this?" she questions.

As if their smiles couldn't get any bigger, the one closest slaps the other on the back of the shoulder.

"Of course, we did, young lady. My brother Grimar here is the only man in the village willing to wake up in the morning early enough to start the fire. Takes hours to get it to the perfect temperature," the blacksmith says.

"And my brother Gils here is the only man with enough hot air inside of him to keep the coals burning until long after the sun goes down!" Grimar boasts with a slap of his big hand on his brother's shoulder. "Would you like to keep that one?"

Coleena looks over at Roland who shrugs his shoulders.

"I... I'm not sure. What kind of payment do you want for it?" Coleena asks, a quick patting of her pockets showing off that she doesn't have a coin to her name.

"For a pretty woman like yourself," Gils starts, "we would be honored if you would take it with you for free. Not many blacksmiths in this world can say their goods are carried around this world by someone as stunning as you are."

There is no stopping the blushing of her cheeks as she looks at the two men, their eyes wild and smiles as genuine as she has ever seen them. Taking a look at the knife, its blade driven deep into the wood, she considers what taking the gift would mean.

"Please, let me help," Grimar says.

Without even the slightest of effort, the man's gigantic hand wraps the hilt and pull it free. Turning it, he hands it to her handle first.

"Thank, thank you very much," she says.

"You two can go back to what you were doing," Roland

says. "The lady has a lot more important matters worth her attention than spending her time with the likes of you two knuckleheads."

Putting his hand onto the small of her back he begins to lead her away from the little shop.

"No problem, boss. Anything you say," both men answer with matching laughs.

"Why did they call you boss?" Coleena asks, the blade turning in her hand and the mirror reflection refusing to let her gaze go.

"Those two are some of the most skilled men we have. Too bad they probably have a total of ten brain cells between the both of them, but you can't deny their craftsmanship."

Letting the small knife bounce from one hand to the other, Coleena stops as they reach the end of the path where the forest begins with a line of low brush and a brief wall full of pine. To their left is a building not much unlike the rest, tucked in beside a large oak, she would hardly have known it was there other than the two men seated out at the front. Both watch them, their eyes narrowed and lips tight and in a straight line. Rifles leaning against the front wall, they wear green cargo pants that end at black army boots. Rather similar to the last time she was asked to enter a protected room. She doesn't go a step further.

"You still haven't answered my question. What are you all planning to do? These knives may be the best I've ever held, but Parliament has a practical army and the dragon has demons."

Roland sighs and looks at the two silent men.

"Is he in there?" he asks. Both men nod but do not say a word. At least they aren't statues. "Come inside, and we'll explain it to you."

Summers extends his arm to the door. Soft candlelight flickers behind a single window, and she can see no movement from where she stands.

"No more games, Summers. We don't have time to waste and I want answers. I gave up a lot trying to reach you and it better be worth it."

With a somber face he looks her in the eye.

"Please follow me. There is a lot you need to understand."

Following his footsteps, he leads her into the building.

23

There is a whole lot of something going on around here, and she is not getting half of it. The log cabin is ablaze with light, maps of Azhana tacked to the walls, corners hanging and torn. A table with papers spread into a dozen different piles sits abandoned in the corner, an empty plate of crumbs and hardened cream sitting precariously along the edge. At least this place has a couch, worn in the center from too much sleeping, it finds itself warming in front of a fireplace. A mop of white hair shines above the flat cushions as it rocks back and forth, the soft sound of snoring filling the room.

Following Summers in, the two men outside are quick to shut the door as she passes through the entrance, no hesitation in closing it with a loud thud. With a startle, the figure on the couch jolts upright, a cough and a shake turning him around.

"Oh, there you two are," Phydel says.

His bright green eyes show no signs of sleeping, and he drinks them both in, a small devilish smile spreading over his wrinkled skin.

"I see you've made yourself at home," Summers says. Leading her to the table, a quick swipe of his arm clears a spot right in front of a vacant chair which he quickly positions so she can sit. "Can I get you anything to drink? We have a great source of spring water near the entrance to the valley and it tastes a hell of a lot better than what you get in the city."

"Yes, thank you," Coleena answers.

The detective nods his head, his smile returning as he makes his way to a back room, the shadows receding as a match is struck and a candle lights up.

"I'm glad to see that a good night's rest has done wonders for your injuries," Phydel says, stretching his arms and legs as he slides across the cloth couch, crossing his legs casually as he drapes one arm over the edge.

Nothing marks the man's bright white robes. Not a stain, or blemish. Even beneath the warm light of the fireplace and a dozen candles, he lights up the room.

"Yes, I feel almost like my old self. What is in that drink of yours?" Coleena asks letting the warm sweet smell of the wood smoke sink deep into body.

The old man puts a finger up to the side of his nose.

"Now that is one of those, if I give you the answer, I'd have to kill you questions," he answers without the smallest of grin. "What would Azhana do without you after that?"

She doesn't know how to respond. The look on his face suddenly serious and the tone of his voice deathly cold.

"I think the world would do just fine, with me or without me," she says.

His smile returns, the sparkle in his eye the reflection of a million devious plots.

"Don't be so quick to misjudge your contribution to this world, Ms. Armigera. Others who have been dragon-touched like yourself seldom last longer than a few days. You on the other hand seem to have a knack for surviving, wouldn't you say?"

Her heart skips a beat, a cold wash of dread washing down her spine like a cold shower.

"Dragon-touched? What do you mean by that?" she asks.

Phydel slides deeper into the couch, his finger returning to the side of his nose.

"Here we go," Summers says while putting her drink down beside her. A clay chalice of crystal-clear water. "Did I miss something?"

Coleena looks at him before returning to Phydel.

"Yeah, Phydel was..."

"Just mentioning how remarkable it is how quickly she has made a recovery," Phydel cuts in. "My tonic does perform miracles every now and then, doesn't it, detective?"

Roland chuckles and finds a seat in a rickety old lawn chair opposite hers.

"It sure does, but sadly that is not why we are here, and you know that old man."

Phydel rolls his eyes.

"All work, never any play. One of the biggest reasons I'm so fond of you, detective."

Summers takes a sip of his cup.

"You ever going to let me in on the other reasons?"

"Another one of those answers I cannot share," the old man answers with a wink toward Coleena and a touch of his nose.

"OK, enough with the small talk," Coleena cuts in, tired of going nowhere. "What are we going to do about Parliament City? I've been here almost a full day now and all we keep doing is going in circles. Do you two have a plan or is it just to distract me long enough that the fires burning within the city go out themselves, and you hope I don't notice."

Her cup rattles the small table like a gavel and both men eye each other, unspoken words passing in that hard glance before they turn to her.

"Yes, Coleena, I think it is time we opened up. Do you want to start, old man?" Summers asks.

Phydel nods and with the grace of a cat he pushes away from the couch to step before the warm fireplace.

"How much of what we spoke about before your nice rest do you remember, Ms. Armigera?"

"You mean when you all blindfolded me and boated me half-way across the country?"

"Protocols, I swear," Roland says, his voice a whisper.

"You spoke of hybrids within the city, half man and half dragon spawn. You fought one yourself and survived," Phydel says.

"Yes, but barely. Do you know more about them? Where are they from? How can this be? When did they get into the city?" Coleena starts shooting off.

With one hand the man stops her, his gaze turning long and hard to the flames flickering inches from his robes.

"There are so many answers to your questions that it would take a lifetime to explain them all. I will tell you what I know and with that we must do the best that we can," Phydel says before turning back to her. "As we all know, the greatest threat to all of mankind is the dragons that spawned twenty-five years ago. With them a magic was unleashed upon our world. A form that lets objects, where once there was no life, rage across the land killing at will."

"The rock demons," Summers says and Phydel nods in agreement.

"Wait, you said dragons?" Coleena asks, her look passing between both men.

"A story for another time, my dear," Phydel responds. "Let me finish before we get too far ahead. Research leads us to believe that these monsters did not just appear out of nowhere. Neither were they sent by the gods to punish us as some devout morons like to believe. They are the manifestation of a summoning ritual crafted and performed by a deranged sect of worshipers who believed they were bringing a god into the world. We can obviously see that they failed miserably."

"The general told me this. Her father made records of it before he died in Obrathe. The sect, they had a symbol like the one you described to me," Coleena says looking at Summers.

Reaching into a small box beneath the table, the detective pulls out a sheet of paper showing the symbol he described to her previously. A rising dragon over a crescent moon breathing flames.

"We have found many of these throughout the city," Summers says. "At first we brought them straight to Parliament. The initial reaction was swift as they ordered investigations and searches to comb the entire city. Then after the election, even after the attacks started, their interest started to wane. By the end they even started saying that we were the ones posting these around the city. Azhana United was the culprit behind these and the attacks."

"Then who is behind this, and how did you both find out about this?" Coleena asks. "This is information that has been under lock and key with the army for the last twenty-five years. You are just a detective and a..."

Phydel smiles at her.

"An old man? Your general, though she is a strong

woman, has a lot to learn. Not everyone died back in Obrathe or the other cities we lost. The military was also not the only ones looking into the little hornet's nest these crazy fools were stirring up before the big day. A lot of good people with very important information were lost from this world."

"So, you hid this information away? You didn't feel it should be brought up before now?"

Getting out of her chair, Coleena begins to pace around the room. She can see the shadows around the front of the house begin to lengthen as the day races itself across the span of time.

"Not exactly like anyone asked," Phydel says.

Coleena spins on him.

"Asked?"

Phydel shrugs.

"Anyways, what would you have all done with the information? Your general seems to have had it already and nothing happened. More lives were thrown at the monsters and more dead were buried beneath the ground. Plus, we have more urgent matters at hand than who knew what and when," Phydel says with a sweep of his arm toward the couch. She doesn't want to sit; she'd rather burn off all of her anger but a sudden weight presses down on her shoulders making it more of a good idea than she thought. Flopping on the couch she waits for him to continue, an anger building deep within her. "As I mentioned, this magic of theirs turns things like stone into living, breathing things. Well, it can do a lot more than that. Many of those insolent fools who wasted their lives bringing these beasts into this world thankfully lost everything in the destruction. It wasn't until years later that we realized there was a community of them that survived. Cowering in the wastes trying to avoid reaping the fruits of their labor, it seems that some of them have turned back to their lizard masters and found a new purpose in life."

"They've become demons," Coleena says.

Phydel tilts his head to the side, a question flashing behind his eyes before he shakes his head no.

"I wouldn't call them demons. You proved that when you ripped the ear off of one with your teeth." She shoots an angry glare at Summers who can do nothing but shrug. "Men are men and the monsters here are stone, Ms. Armigera. Had the thing you fought been a being of pure magic and hatred you would have broken your teeth and probably died right there on the street. Here, I'm afraid we are fighting against something far worse."

"Dragon-touched. When we first talked you called them Dragon-touched," Coleena adds.

"Yes, half-breeds. Men and women with the brains of a human but the power of those magic infused monsters. Enemies of the worst kind and an abomination upon the green surface of this world. Cunning. Angry. Certain of their superiority. In some cases, even able to blend in with the normal populace like you and I. Instead of rushing in to kill like those you fight out on the front lines, they work their own kind of magic on the minds of the people. Turning them against one another, or worse, making them believe the dragon isn't such a bad thing. Monsters in their own way," Phydel continues with a growl forming in his throat.

"So, what do we do? How do we help those who are still in the city?" Coleena asks.

"This is where the good detective and I disagree," Phydel answers before turning to Roland who sits forward, a heavy lean on his cane.

"We go back in and see how much damage is done. If our

strength within the walls still stands, we will try to convince Parliament of what is going on. They still believe that Azhana United is the ones behind this. We will convince them otherwise," Summers says.

"I think we are a bit beyond that, detective," Coleena says.

"And I would have to agree," Phydel adds.

Standing herself up, the old man slides in beside her, his figure more imposing that she remembers it being. Half a head taller than she is, his robes are filled out and what is beneath does not look like a man of many years.

"You were pretty out of it after that last attack happened. Parliament swept the entire city or is still in the process of doing it. Men dressed in uniforms that I do not recognize came looking for Azhana United and from what I am thinking they were not taking prisoners. Very little leads me to believe Parliament is going to be swayed in any way."

"Then what do you suggest?" Roland asks.

"We go in heavy-handed. Cut the head right off the snake," Phydel cuts in.

Taking a step away, Coleena stares at the man in white. His eyes, the bright green within carrying a dangerous reflection of the fire.

"I need to get a message to General Whittaker. She is the only one with enough resources to help straighten all of this out. With the evidence that she has matched with what you have, Parliament will have to believe us and turn its back on whatever crazy ideas it has about Azhana United. The real danger is already on the streets. If anyone can help, she can," Coleena says.

Phydel shakes his head at both of them before turning back to the flames in the fireplace.

"Neither of you understand what we are facing here.

This isn't just a riot and government set on calling itself king. The monster is here. Right at your door. These men, these monsters won't stop until the streets are running red with the blood of every man and woman within those walls. There is no amount of persuasion that is going to stop them. They understand only one thing," Phydel says, his voice growing cold and distant.

"I understand plenty," Coleena answers. "I've fought these things since the day I was rescued from the burning streets of Obrathe. No one knows what it is to face death every day like I have. We do not have the resources or ability to take the entire city. For the gods' sake, Phydel. Most of us are doing nothing but carrying these damn knives. Plus, what are we going to do after we take it? Set ourselves up as King and Queen?"

A smile crosses Phydel's face as his eyes bounce between her and the detective. When she doesn't return the same look, he shakes his head.

"You haven't even bothered telling her, have you, detective?" Phydel asks, his fists buried into his hips, eyes glaring at Summers.

"I...it didn't really come up in conversation, yet," Roland answers.

"Tell me what?"

"Show her detective," Phydel says throwing his hands up in the air in disgust.

Roland sighs. Shuffling from his chair, he finds a stained cardboard box in the back corner buried under dozens of papers and scatters them on the floor. With a grunt he drags himself back to the table and drops it on the surface. The middle bowing beneath the weight.

"Do you recognize one of these, Coleena?" Roland asks lifting off the top of the filing box.

Making her way over she can see whatever it is absorbs the light around. A blackness as dark as a moonless night filling the inside. Her heart skips a beat as she gets a clear look at the inside. The round curvature of the top, two deep cut inlets over a wide jawline. Beneath, teeth chiseled into needles and as long as her fingers cut into the bottom of its prison.

"That's...that's a Gorgoth skull. Where did you get one of those?" Coleena asks.

"A lot of us here are military veterans. Inevitably, someone dragged the damn thing back with them. With enough promises and a few swapped coins, I got a hold of it."

"But what does this have to do with anything? We've been talking about half-breeds, not full on Gorgoths," Coleena questions.

"Hand me your knife," Summers says holding out his hand.

She looks back at Phydel who has turned away from the fire to watch what they are doing. Removing the blade from her pocket she hands the weapon over.

"Those things are as hard as steel. Bullets barely do anything when they are alive. Once they fall it's like firing into a...," her words cut off.

Sinking in, the edge of the knife cuts its way right through the volcanic rock. Inches into the black stone the resistance stops the decent and Roland lets go. Like the table, the blade does not move or sway, the bright reflection burning away the darkness within the box.

"Those two blacksmiths of ours are better than they think," Phydel says sliding up beside her. "Of course, they may have had a little help, but a fine job for two former cattle ranchers, isn't it?"

"Not possible. That isn't possible," Coleena stammers.

"We aren't exactly advocating running at the things with a little pot sticker like this in your hand, Captain, but the men and women of Azhana United can't be underestimated. The danger to Parliament City is far greater than anyone wants to believe," Phydel warns.

"You say that old man, but at the moment we need to handle what is in front of us, not what the future holds," Summers says before turning back to her. "Your suggestion is a good one, Coleena, but I think it holds too many hopes in the general."

Backing away from the table and the impaled skull, Coleena looks at both men.

"I don't care what you think. The general will do what she needs to do. Parliament City cannot fall to anarchy or the dragon. She is our best option," Coleena argues.

"Just think. How many men and women do you think she can pull from the front line. The men and women working for the dragon know that we can't afford to thin the battle lines any more than they already are. Creating a distraction here forces us to decide, lose the city or lose the front. Why else do you think the General sent you, Coleena? Think. Haven't I been asking you that same question since the day I met you?" Roland asks.

He steps around the table and approaches her, one hand leaning on his cane and the other extended to her. She stares at the skin, rough and calloused after years of hard work defending the people of Azhana. Turning her own over, she stares into the scars and lines running the course of her palm. All the fighting. So much blood.

What are they going to do?

Looking up into Roland's eyes there is so much there.

Too many questions, yet there is a softness. He will let her decide. But what can they do? Time is running out.

Phydel is a mirror of the fire she used to have. If they had asked when she was nothing but another soldier, her answer would always be to charge into the fight. She sees those flames in his sea of green. A fire burning deep within an endless well. With a sigh and a deep breath, she lets her shoulders relax, the movement for once sending no pain down her spine.

"We'll go into the city, Roland. If we can do it your way, we will. If not, we are finding the Lieutenant and getting word to the general. I can only hope that we aren't too late," she answers.

Summers nods his head, a look of gratitude spoken without words from his flat lips. Phydel turns away, no argument or complaint passing his lips, his gaze back on the fire.

24

———

I t still took more than a day to get ready. Every minute an excruciating wait that dragged at Coleena's mind and soul. Narin and a few of the others within the village were dispatched to prepare for their travels back into the city. Regardless of what it felt like coming to the hidden sanctuary, via river the return would be just over a half day.

The sun bright and having broken the tree line no more than an hour ago, everyone moves as if there is no difference between today and the next. Children who are not working with parents around houses and in gardens still run the streets where it is warm and a nice breeze keeps everything comfortable. Coleena stiffens in the newly gifted clothes. Thick material. Scratchy against the lumps of scars and sharp edges of her body, but it is the closest thing she has felt to her old uniform since the day she fell in combat. A mix of green and browns, it fits oddly perfect and the knife the two blacksmiths gave her fits so well within a hidden boot sheath, she almost forgets it is there.

Taking a deep breath, she lets the sweet taste of the fall morning reach deep into her lungs. This may be the last time she sees or feels this. Once they are back in the city, who knows when they'll come back out. Worst yet, if they'll ever come back out. Parliament could do anything once they are found. Summers is still certain that they'll listen, a full confession and layout of the evidence is certain to sway their opinion. She wishes she had his convictions. Already she works on the plans of what to do when it all goes sour.

Lieutenant Mason and Tul should still be in the barracks. Regardless of what happened during the purge, those politicians would have one hell of a time expelling the entire army from the city. Even if they tried there hasn't been enough time to get it done. General Whittaker would have to be involved and that would be a good thing. Which to her makes it even more unlikely.

A mob of kids, some of them hardly five-years-old at her best guess, chase each other around the corner of the house they moved her back to. Same empty bed. Same lonely rocking chair. At least this time they didn't lock the door.

The children's laughter and smiles fade in the distance as the shadows of the trees swallow them up.

"Beautiful isn't it?" Phydel asks, his presence as sudden as the wind.

Catching her breath, Coleena turns and looks at the old man. There is no emotion on his long and wrinkled face. He has said nothing about their refusal to agree to his plans since they made their decisions over a day ago. Such an enigma for one who would have nothing to do with any of it. Safe within the confines of this village, the old man is so urgent to see his method followed.

"The children?" Coleena asks. Phydel nods with a little smirk of a grin working its way within the wrinkles of his face. "Kids are great as long as they are someone else's."

"Never thought of having your own?" he asks, taking a

step around her to look around the corner which the group had just passed.

"I'm a soldier, Phydel. We don't have the pleasure of such things. Even those of us who survive long enough for the possibility. Give someone something to worry about, a reason to want to return home, and they'll be too distracted to do what needs to be done. I've seen many men and women hesitate at the wrong moment with the fear of what they are losing in their eyes. It never ends well," Coleena says watching a family walk down the street hand in hand.

Father, mother, and a young girl in between the two. Her long blond hair flutters in the wind as she skips to keep up with their longer steps. On the count of three they lift her up, and she giggles as she kicks her feet. Little sandals going at the speed of a child's legs. Not a care in the world. Happy just to be with and paid attention to by the most important people in her short life.

A little hole opens up deep within Coleena's heart. Like a sinking feeling, it drags her down. Hands going cold and chest feeling heavy.

"Lost your own parents, didn't you?" Phydel asks.

Coleena gives her head the smallest of shakes and the feeling goes away. She turns back to him.

"We've all lost family, old man. There isn't a person in this world not affected by the dragon. I'm no different than anyone here."

Leaning up against the building, he crosses his arms over his chest. The long robes, still perfect in every way, balloon ever so slightly with a pass of the wind. He looks her over, those green eyes of his searching for something, but she isn't sure what.

"You are different, Coleena. There is no doubt about that. This plan is folly and you know it. The city will be lost unless the people are prepared. Summers is a good man, not a perfect one, but usually worthy of the trust we give him. In this I fear he is stepping beyond his abilities. You know what we fight here, Captain. Politics and evidence mean little when rock meets flesh. You would be the first to know this."

"What are you trying to say? You know something, don't you, Phydel? What aren't you telling us?" Coleena questions.

The old man puts his finger up beside his nose.

"A tidal wave is coming, Captain. The walls can only hold so much back, and we both know the dragon's reach is far. We must be prepared," Phydel says before turning away and looking up the road toward Summers' house.

"If there is more to this, we need to know, now, Phydel," Coleena demands.

"Ah! There he is, looking better than ever," the old man says stepping out onto the hardened dirt path.

Detective Summers gives a small wave, the lean in his walk less evident today than it was previously. Small cotton hat back on his head, and long coat looking freshly washed and sewn back together resting over his shoulder, he looks like nothing has happened. He could be coming back from a needed vacation if no one knew any better. Even the dark circles beneath his eyes have faded and there is the returned color of his cheeks as the sun continues to warm up.

"Thanks, old man," Summers responds. "I see you are looking fit to be a soldier today, Coleena."

Turning away from Phydel, she finds she can't keep the small blush from her cheeks.

"Feels better to be back in my old skin," she says pulling at the unique uniform.

"I see you still haven't lost those," Summers says pointing at her neck.

Tracing his look with her fingers she feels the chain of

her dog tags poking out from beneath the collar of her shirt. With a quick shift she tucks them back in.

"That is something you never..." Phydel begins to say reaching a hand toward her.

"Are we ready to go, detective?" Coleena cuts him off.

With a nod and as deep a bow his leg will allow, Summers sweeps his arm out.

"Ladies first. Word reached me that Narin and the others returned no less than ten minutes ago. She says that everything is set for us to get back within the walls. We must hurry though."

"Thanks for all the advice, Phydel," Coleena says as she steps around him. "When we get back, we are going to have a personal talk on all these secrets you've been hiding. I'm an army girl. I know a thing or two about killing in the name of a secret. You remember that until we get back."

With one finger she taps the side of her nose and the old man dips his head, emerald green eyes flickering in the warm sunlight.

"What was all that about?" Summers asks once they are out of earshot.

"I've got a sick feeling that we are playing into a game and that man holds more of the chips than we do," Coleena answers.

Moving through the little village, she can hear the river before she can see it. The sound of rushing water, the air itself takes on a slight chill as the shadows grow longer with the forest closing in around the docks. Two men, the same that watched the front of Summers' house, wait along the pier. Rifles held at the ready on their shoulders, their uniforms match hers. Less unique than she thought earlier, they blend in with the background and could easily be lost if they weren't statues waiting beside the river. They remain stone-faced at their approach. Narin on the other hand sits on a piling, twiddling away at a small piece of wood between her hands. A little anthill sized pile of shavings building between her boots.

"Took you two long enough," Narin says wiping away a few stray pieces clinging to her pants.

Dressed in a white t-shirt, sleeves rolled up to her shoulders, and canvas pants, she looks the part of average blue-collar Parliament City worker. Still a little gray around the edges though with arms that ripple when she moves the tiny blade between her hands.

"Not as fast as I once was, Narin," Summers says.

The big woman chuckles.

"You never were fast, detective. With those two left feet of yours or in that thing you call a brain. She ready for this?" Narin asks with a point of her chin toward Coleena.

"Let's hope we all are ready," Roland answers. "If not, we may have more problems on our hands than we bargained for."

With a shrug of her shoulders, Narin leads them to a similar raft to the one they used to transport her here. Wood beams tied together with crude leather straps, now that she gets a good look at it, her confidence on its ability to transport them isn't so strong.

"I'm a better swimmer than I proved to be last time, but you're telling me we don't have anything better than this?" Coleena asks.

Summers, with cautious steps, braces himself with an arm on the pier as he steps onto the raft. Water splashes up and soaks his pants up half his shin until he waddles to the middle of craft.

"See, nothing to worry about," he says as everything struggles to settle with his uneven balancing.

"If we could, we'd get a real boat, army girl, but we have to be quiet about this. The city is locked up pretty tight and our window of opportunity is pretty small. If even a single set of eyes catches us, we are done. You could walk if you want, it would probably take you maybe two to three days if the wolves didn't get you," Narin says.

Coleena mocks a laugh before stepping down onto the raft, the shaking and uneasiness quickly sending ripples through her stomach. Knees growing weak, she stumbles and slips as one of her boots slides out and dips into the water. Spilling forward, the whole craft begins to spin and Summer's arms catching her is the only thing that prevents her and him from dumping into the river.

"Whoa, watch your step," Roland says as he helps her settler herself.

"Sorry about that," Coleena says, shifting her weight away and straightening up her uniform.

"Of course she is," Narin says, her large frame nimbly finding its way onto their little vessel. Without a word the other two men make their way on and cast them off into the flow of the river. "If you two want to make yourselves comfortable. This is going to be a bumpy ride and a lot of miracles have to happen between now and the wall if we are going to make it in."

Coleena looks at the four joining her on the journey down the river. There are no more happy faces. All hard lines and looks of determination. Sun high in the sky, air cool as it rushes over the water, they have nowhere else to go but forward.

25

The walls even at this distance are impenetrable and harsh with their gaze. Miles of black stone reaching high into the sky. No gaps. Smooth and unclimbable all the way around. An unscalable cliff on a mountain with no mercy.

Dark stacks of smoke rise into the early evening air. No sound of fighting or gunfire echoes into the night. That is at least one good sign.

Long poles pushing at the riverbed, the two guards strain against the current of the river. Slowly their raft makes its way to the shore, shadows growing darker and the forest here a graveyard compared to where they came from.

Brittle grass, long dried and dead cracks beneath their boots as they begin to file off. Worried glances watch the top of wall, no movement and no sounds of alarm. All is good for the moment.

"I hope you two can get your land legs fast enough," Narin says before accepting one end of the rope to pull the raft out of the water.

With a heave, her and the two guards work until the raft

is out of the water. Some dry grass here, broken sticks there and it is hard to see even while standing next to it.

"What are we looking at, Narin?" Summers asks.

He glances at the wall again, little more than a hundred yards between them and the city. Darkness shrouds the top stones, a thick haze that could hide anything and anyone. Coleena coughs as they wait for Narin to clean herself up. Enough sticks and dirt cling to her she may as well have been sleeping on the ground.

"Around the south side, the moment the sun dips beneath the horizon, our window will open," Narin answers.

Without waiting, she waves them forward and makes her way through the scrub brush and empty husks of the dead forest. Taking up positions on both sides, both guards ask no questions with their rifles at the ready. Coleena and Summers quickly step in behind, the detective moving as fast as his gimp leg will allow.

"What kind of window? Last time I knew there were no openings in this wall other than the front gate," Coleena says.

Narin looks back at her, eyes as hard as stones before turning back to their path.

"If we can't go through, we'll go over," Summers whispers to her as he steps up, his shoulders rubbing hers.

"Over? You've got to be joking," Coleena replies.

"Quiet you two, we are almost there," Narin demands.

Watching the forest recede from the city, the open ground between them and the wall is a hundred feet of killing ground. The beginning of the night is almost here, a strange mist rolling around the wall like a moat. A chill in the air sends a shiver down Coleena's spine.

"Now what?" Coleena asks, Summers shuffling in beside her.

Between deep breaths, Narin gives her that same hard stare.

"We wait. Down here it's dark as fuck but up there they should soon be seeing the last bits of the sun. Then if...," the big woman says.

On queue the sound of wood and chain cracks against the rock as a thick snake curls it way down the back of the wall.

"A ladder?" Coleena asks.

There are no other words. They were actually going to try and climb a fucking ladder up the side of the wall. She stares at the older woman.

"Did you expect a magical door to open. Yes, a fucking ladder, now get your ass moving," Narin demands.

Without another word, their three escorts bolt from the cover of the brush and forest to cross the wide-open space. Their boots are like thunder on the hard soil, tiny puffs of dust picking up around them. Darkness falling completely around them, the ladder is a flicker of movement against a wall of black.

"Summers, you up first. Army girl, you stay right on his ass. We have maybe ten minutes. Be prepared for whatever when you get up there. I can't guarantee anything," Narin orders.

"You've done well, Narin," Roland says.

She nods while handing him the chain. Thin wooden rungs spin between thumb thick chains as the man makes his way up the first few steps. Everything creaks. Even the sound of the city inside is not enough against the racket this thing is making. Grabbing the first rung immediately after Summers moves his foot, Coleena follows right behind.

"Ah!" a man's voice screams.

It is not a sound of pain. Full of fear and the realization

of death, the voice is cut with the rush of wind and the echo of an empty night. They do not see him fall, but the sound of bone and flesh cracking open upon impact is wet and sloppy.

Coleena stops all climbing as the world goes silent. Her heart stops, the fire in her belly igniting as she looks down. Little more than a half-dozen feet separate her and the woman who brought them here, the look of fear clearly visible in those eyes.

"Go, now!" she screams.

Flashlights kick on across the open field illuminating the wall and the ladder they are using to climb. Both guards turn, rifles level they fire without a second thought. Pops of gunfire fill the gap between and Coleena does not stop to think.

Letting go of the wooden bar, she lets herself drop, pain rippling through her legs as the ground rushes to meet her. Rolling to keep her momentum, rock explodes behind her as a bullet slams into the wall above her right shoulder.

Lead hits a wet sack as blood erupts from the back of the guard nearest her. Two more bursts rip from his body before he falls, rifle dropping next to his lifeless corpse. Another scream tears into the night as the sound of a body taking a heavy fall shakes the ground. Never hesitating, Coleena grabs the rifle, crouching beside the dead man's prone form, she squeezes off three rounds.

A light explodes with the sound of screams. Rolling to her left, angry bees speed past her head before exploding on the rock behind her. The rifle goes empty as two more rounds eject, hitting the target just below one of the lights. More screams confirm the target is down as she reverses her roll.

"Frag out!" one of the attackers screams.

Grabbing the guard's corpse, Coleena rolls it on top of her, the sound of metal hitting and rolling away from the wall too close. The explosion brightens the world like a mid-day sun and rock and stone rain to the ground.

Dust and dirt fill the air, a choking mess as Coleena scrambles to get out from beneath what remains of her human shield. Tugging on his belt she finds the small compartments holding his ammunition.

One magazine falls and she slides it in. The world rings and everything is pitch black except for the dull beams of gray cutting through the cloud. Sighting down her rifle, there are too many. They would get her before she could take them all.

What is she going to do?

Heart calming, time seems to slow as they approach. A flanking semi-circle, these soldiers are trained. Yes, that feels correct. They have to be soldiers.

Dirt shuffles off to her right. A dark figure moves, rising to their knees. Lights flash as the barrel ejects a string of rounds. Pops echo in return, the bullets tearing through the poor soul's body.

Coleena does not think. Turning back to the enemy she squeezes back on the trigger, her own rifle answering in kind. Another light drops. She rolls.

Bullets slam into the ground and the wall behind her. She fires another round. Continuing her roll, the world spins, and she stops firing.

They are chasing her. Rock explodes behind her, always a step behind.

There is no other movement in the cloud of dust. Is she the only one left?

Everything stops. The lights click off one by one and the

world falls into darkness. Holding her breath, Coleena tries to let the thunder of her heart quiet down.

Silence.

Pure unadulterated silence. Empty of all life, she waits. There is nothing.

They know she can't go anywhere. She is trapped. Even if they have to wait until sunrise, there will be no escape.

"There you are," a deep voice growls.

Coleena can only get her arm pulled back against her chest before the boot connects with the side of her ribs. Pain ruptures all along her side and the air in her lungs ejects with a mist of spit and salty blood. Letting the momentum carry her, she rolls, and another stomp is a graze against the side of her shoulder.

The joint pops and flopping onto her back she raises her rifle and fires. Light erupts and the bullet shatters through the man's leg. He drops to one knee, and she changes course to close the small distance between them.

More gunfire goes off. Rocks shatter and several rip through the man's chest. He spits blood, the knife in his hand dropping. Scrambling, Coleena crawls behind his prone body.

Lights kick back on. All of them are aimed in her direction. Only half the circle remains. They begin closing in. Heart pounding and out of breath, she prepares for her last stand.

They cannot take her like this. There will be no getting out alive. They'll bury her so far beneath that jail there will be no getting back out.

A dark figure comes to life along the wall. Broad shouldered it rises from the thick mist and none of the approaching soldiers take notice. Coleena watches as it turns and throws something into the air, a heave that creates a sharp thwack as it lands in between the approaching men.

Light and sound tears into the night as the ground erupts into a volcanic blast. Screams are cut short as the earth beneath her body shakes and Coleena covers her head. World spinning for a second time, she tries to look out into the killing field.

Two lights remain, but they are pointed in the wrong direction. One does not move, the other inching its way back and forth as the shadow carrying it crawls away from the carnage.

Loud thumps shake the ground, Coleena wipes at her eyes as the shadow lumbers its way in her direction. Pulling her rifle free of the dead soldier's body and newly planted debris, she lines up the killing end as the monster gets closer.

"Get your ass up, army girl," Narin demands.

A dark substance coats the side of her head, and there is a clear limp as she favors her right side. Thick, wet hands grab onto Coleena's arm and pull her from the embrace of the dirt and mud.

Knees wobbly, she struggles to remain upright.

"What...what the fuck is going on?" Coleena chokes out between gasps of air, smoke, and ruin.

"Fucking hell is what is going on. We need to get the hell out of here," Narin answers.

Throwing Coleena's arm over her shoulder, the big woman nearly lifts her from the ground in the effort of getting as far away as they can.

"Roland. We can't leave him behind," Coleena says.

Tugging on Narin's shoulder is like trying to dislodge a stone from the wall with her bare hands. And it proves to be just as effective.

"Summers will have to fend for himself if he's alive. Man took a big spill before all hell broke loose. It won't matter if we don't get out of here alive," Narin answers.

Coleena knows she is correct, but it still isn't right. The cold grip of dread takes a piece of her heart as they make their way back toward the forest. She wants to go back and find him. If he is still alive, they have to try. She has never been one to leave a man behind.

Wood shards explode to their right as they hit the first line of trees. Turning back, pivoting on her strong leg, Coleena fires off several rounds. The figure approaching from the ruin of the field screams and drops.

Pulling on her, Narin turns her back into the forest. The darkness swallows them whole. How the large woman knows where to go there is no way to tell. Coleena's boots catch on everything and their passage is a train wrecking its way through.

Blood leaks from a thousand cuts, each stinging as they struggle on. The older woman's breathing is shallow as they push to keep moving.

"Where are we going to go?" Coleena asks, the strength returning to her legs.

Still leaning against the big woman, she tries to take as much of her own weight as she can.

"The...the river," Narin coughs out.

Wet and thick, the sound rattles in her chest and the thick wetness coating the woman's shirt is easy to feel.

"You are hurt, Narin. We need to stop for a moment," Coleena pleads.

The sound of the river is just beyond the wall of black in front of them. Narin stumbles and they both tumble forward. Thin needles of broken brush poke and cut as they hit the ground. Coleena rolls onto her butt before shifting back onto her knees. Narin is sprawled on the ground beside her, her bulk pressing against her.

"Grab the raft and get out of here. Find a way to clear the city and get as far away as you can," Narin says through wet slurs.

"On your feet, soldier," Coleena demands.

Gun shots erupt further back in the forest, the sound of bullets shattering into dead husks are close. They are searching. They don't know where they are just yet.

"Don't waste your breath, army girl," Narin whispers back.

A stick snaps close by, a shattering of the emptiness closing in on them.

Coleena spins and aims her rifle at nothing. There is no one there. Even if there was, she could not find them. Heart pounding, head throbbing, she lowers her weapon and grabs onto the other woman's shoulder. Pinching her fingers as tight as she can, she pulls.

"We have to move."

Groaning lightly, Narin slowly rolls onto her side and then tumbles onto all fours. Coleena hooks her hand under a shoulder and pulls. Body shaking, coughs wracking her body, Narin trembles as she steadies herself on her feet.

"It isn't much further," Narin whispers.

More falling than leading, they crash through the remaining brush. Cool air slaps them in the face as the river opens up before them. Small amounts of light shines from above, the dark water full of white caps over rapids on its way through.

"The raft, we have to get the raft," Coleena says as she tries to steady Narin.

"Would you be looking for this?" a man's voice asks.

A lantern bursts into life as the small riverbank ignites

with light. Eyes squinting, Coleena watches as two men step away from where they hid the raft.

Her chest seizes as the lantern draws a clear picture of their faces. The soldier moving in from the back she does not recognize, but the other.

Petty Officer Tul.

Tall, lanky features hang loose. Eyes narrowed, he looks calm, but she knows he is ready to strike. A pistol sits loosely in his palm.

"Go fuck yourself, traitor," Narin barks.

Coleena lets the big woman lean up against her, the weight of her bulk immense and enough to almost tip her over.

"You are the two trying to sneak your way into the city. Probably planning another attack," Tul mocks.

"That isn't true, and you know it," Coleena yells back.

"Doesn't matter what is true or not. All that matters in the end is what we say. We have the power here, not you."

Narin leans more of her weight against her. Bracing her legs, Coleena struggles just to stay standing.

"The dragon will never win, you scum. Not as long as we still breathe," Narin says.

Arm extending in a flash, light flickers as the knife flies through the air. Tul does not miss the movement as he ducks to the side, arm coming up. His partner is not as fortunate as the blade cuts through uniform, vest, and breastbone as it buries itself below his neck.

Four shots ring out and the world begins to tumble as Coleena begins to fall backward. Narin's weight, all of it falls into her as those hard eyes squint through the pain. Trying to catch herself, Coleena steps back and her boot finds rushing water as another shot arches the big woman's back.

"Go!" she says, blood spraying with the words.

Foot slipping, Coleena stumbles into the water. Ice cold, the current drags her down and under the surface as it carries her away. Lungs burning, body aching, she cannot get the look of Tul's face from her mind as she fights to get out of the water.

The river is as cold as the depths of hell. Knives of ice cut at the skin, a thousand deadly scratches and a few that slice to the core. Up is down, down is up. Darkness is everything. Breath burns, chokes the lungs, and fills the belly.

Coleena can no longer feel her limbs. They are nothing but dead weight, like rocks tied to a rope wrapped around her body. She tries to kick to the surface, but which way is the surface?

Her head breaks free and she gasps for air. Water full of silt fills her mouth, and she coughs out what little oxygen she got in. The current tugs her back down. Her boots scrape the bottom, concrete jostling her legs, and she feels a pop within her knee. She tries to push away but fire erupts through the limb that should be her leg.

The world spins. Her mind races. Everything aches. Heart pounding louder than grenades, she kicks and sends her head back above the surface of the raging river. Cold, misty air slaps her in the face.

She gasps. Flailing with her arms, she tries to stay afloat.

Pain and the sound of bones crunching sends a flash of lightening across her vision as her shoulder slams into a rock or a fallen tree. She isn't sure which. All she knows is the world is cartwheeling again.

Opening her mouth brings another flood of water and filth to fill her throat. She can't cough. More water. Everything burns until she goes numb. Arms will not move. Legs fell off ages ago. Everything is so dark.

She wants to breathe. Muscles spasm and her lungs ache. There is no holding back. Chest heaving, she draws in through her nose.

Burning.

Fire.

Vomit.

Her entire body turns into a cramp that rips her in two. The solid world slams into the back of her head. Light flashes one more time and then there is only darkness.

EVERY BONE IN HER BODY IS BROKEN. TINY SHIVERS RIPPLE through her skin and it hurts more than anything in her life. She tries to open her eyes. Even her lids are cold and frozen shut.

Her lungs burn, but at least she is breathing. Salt and dirt fills her mouth. Sticky and full of grit. Moving is painful. Muscles pinch and tear. Joints pop. The raging thunder of the river is a barrel rolling downhill within her ears.

A cough wracks her body, and she involuntarily rolls to her side. Water and bile vomit from her belly. The taste is acidic and her stomach rolls tighter with nothing left to expel. Curling into a ball, she waits for it all to go away.

Tears fall and time passes. Hours crawl away but isn't

sure if that is reality or a horrible dream locked within her mind. Her skin is cold and clammy. Light filters in through her closed eyes but there isn't any strength left to open them. Birds sing in the distance.

A sad song. Full of pain and anger. Others screech and there is no wind. Only the smell of the rotten river and her vomit piled next to her face.

Unconsciousness takes her. The warmth of the day brings her awake. Skin begins to burn but shivers still control her body. Is she dying? Taking a deep breath, she isn't so sure. Rolling her eyes into the back of her head, she is able to force them open.

Light burns and it takes everything she can muster to throw her arm over her face. There is no going back. She cannot turn the world away. It has found her and now she must face it.

Slowly, carefully, she looks back up at the sky. A pretty blue. Peaceful in its everything. Not a cloud in the sky. The sound of buzzing rattles in the distance. Heat rubs at her skin and shifting her head she sees the dead remains of the trees that stretch over the river. Lifeless and forgotten, their useless arms drape over the current with a thousand brittle knives.

Where is she?

Dust and dirt give color to everything. A scorched brown and burned out black. Sitting up, the world spins. Her stomach heaves but she can hold it back.

The horizon stretches forever. Waves of heat rising and blending the world into a mosaic lacking all definition. Rocks and scrub brush bake beneath the high sun. Running her hands over her chest and body, she is still whole.

Face scrunching into a knot, she finds where her shoulder slammed into something. It hurts, the joint popping at the movement. Her ribs ache, but maybe if she is lucky, they aren't broken. Wiggling her toes, they still move within her boots. Thick and hard, the polished black is gray and inside she can feel the cold wetness of the water soaked into the wool like material.

Taking another deep breath to slow the world from spinning, she rocks onto her side and gets to her knees. Darkness clouds her vision, and she waits for it to clear. Lips are chapped and her throat goes dry as she pushes away from the ground.

Her belly cramps, but her weight shifts, and she reaches the balls of her feet. Knees shaking, a grunt of air forces its way out but the heel of her boots hit solid earth. Arms out for balance, she watches the land around her slip into focus.

She is down river.

Way too far down river.

The city is not within sight. It would take miles to do that. Her mind races and the sharp pain within feels like her skull is about to split.

Where does she go?

Looking up at the sun, it is past mid-day. Racing across the sky, the flaming ball of scorching heat heads to the west. Branches snap and birds take off into the air. Dark figures with wings that carry them away.

No food. No idea how far she has to go or what she is going to do when she gets there. Coleena, one boot in front of the other, follows the river back the way she came.

MILES STRETCH AND PASS BENEATH HER BOOTS. THE SOAKING wetness of her clothes dries and is quickly replaced with the dripping salt of her sweat. Thick material chafes in all the wrong places and with the bottom of her eyes she watches as the dog tags bounce across her chest with every step.

The world is an endless death trap. A carcass of a bloated sheep boils and bubbles as she passes. The sun is almost to the horizon, a ball of fire racing across the horizon with flames of red and gold.

In the distance there is a tiny spec. Black and no larger than a grain of sand on her finger. Parliament City. This world's newest asshole.

Somewhere deep in her mind, she wants to watch the sky. Dreams within dreams wait for the shadow of the dragon to fly overhead. Darkening the world below, she wants to chase it as it soars with reckless abandon toward those stone walls. Fire belching from its open maw, she'd watch as it all burned.

Like she did twenty-five years ago.

Her steps slow and the dust settles around her feet. Skin stretches and the burns are already warm, but she stands and stares at that little black spec. Twenty-five years ago she did this exact same thing.

A little girl standing beside her parents. Her home burning to the ground. There was nothing she could do. The dog tags flip between her fingers, the metal still cold to her touch.

This time it is different. She is no longer that little girl. Her tiny fire, the one lit so many years ago begins to smolder within her belly. As long as she is still alive, the dragon will not win.

With a renewed vigor, the tiny speck begins to grow in the distance. The sun dips below the horizon behind her and the darkness of that wall looms before her.

People come into view as the caravan of those fighting to get within those protective walls now stretches several miles.

Little camps burning dry wood with families sitting beside them fan out from the clogged road that leads to the front gate. The smell of refuse and filth sweeps the land and Coleena moves away from the river and toward the unmoving train.

Staying to the outskirts, her muscles ache and the pain in her head makes her stomach swim, but she cannot stop. Voices carry through the empty night. Thousands of them. An endless, off-key song of the desperate and homeless.

Like a shade she keeps to the shadows. There is no telling what those out here would do seeing a woman dressed like a soldier walking within their midst regardless of the dirt and torn pieces. If Parliament has any sentries this far out, things could be even worse.

What is she going to do when she gets to the wall?

They'll probably be looking for her. Or they assume she is dead, which she should be. The look on Narin's face as they tumbled into the river. Tul's hard glare as he called them traitors and it was his gun that killed the woman who saved her life.

Balling her fists, Coleena fights through the exhaustion as she moves past the first layers of the desperate people. Some of them have tents. Patchworks of cloth that are hardly held together with twine and prayers. Most are not that lucky. Bed rolls used as pillows, their sleeping bodies curl around tiny burned out fires with empty discarded tin cans crushed beside them.

Paying close attention to those still moving within the crowd, she does not notice the man coming from the side of the river. Hands jostling with the front of his pants, his head finds her shoulder and damn near knocks her over in the process.

"Hey, watch it!" the man says.

He's still too busy fighting with the fly of his pants as she straightens back up. About her height, she can see he's been out here too long. Even in the thickening darkness she can make out his gaunt cheeks and tired eyes. Poor bastard probably hasn't eaten a good meal in weeks.

No chance to regret the decision, Coleena drives her fist into the soft spot right below the man's chest. Air that smells and tastes like rotten eggs ejects from his lungs, and he doubles over.

Taking his weight onto her shoulder, she shifts until his ear is next to her lips.

"Sorry about this, but I need this more than you do at the moment," she says.

Grabbing his shoulders, she drives her knee square into his nose. His knees give out, and he falls backward with a loud thud. Blood begins to pool on his face, but he gives no resistance as she begins to pull his long coat off.

Slipping it over her shoulders, it drapes and hangs from her, but it does the job. Looking down at his prostrate form, she wonders what he was like before all of this. How much did he lose when this world fell to shit?

Having no more time for this, she pulls the opening to the jacket tight across her body, and she steps out into the crowd. Picking her way around tiny families with their kids sleeping in the dirt, thin and malnourished individuals digging through belongings that may or not be theirs, she makes her way to the center of the road.

Wagons, carts, anything that will help move one's belongings crowd the hard-packed path. There are no animals to help pull the things along. If there were any, they would be dead already from starvation or having been used to stave off the starvation of their owners. Of the working vehicles still left in this world, the military has confiscated them all.

Making steady progress, she weaves in and out between the shadows. Those few who stop to watch her pass don't have time to ask questions before she is gone. The night grows longer, and the front gate of the city turns its watchful eye toward her.

Thick.

Solid.

There will be no way to get through it.

The pileup in front of the city has worsened since she was here a little over a week ago. Grown easily tenfold, the crowd stands or sits shoulder to shoulder. Men, women, and children. Cries and arguments are everywhere.

Her mind stops and her heart skips a beat as she steps her way through a crowd that smells like too much alcohol and far less bathing water. Words of riot and revolt are clear between the angry banter, and she wonders if there is anyway those out here will realize it is no better inside than it is out here.

Up near the front, she finds something she does not expect. Amidst the wreckage of a tipped wagon, wooden axle splintered and pointed to the sky in a sword-like thrust, is an army surplus van. Truck bed stripped and empty, the engine sits idle as it waits before the giant doors.

What is that doing here?

Coleena looks around and no one is paying attention to her. Slowly she slides between shoulders and around the backs of people. Like a shadow she passes by without notice. Reaching the truck, she lets a hand slide up against the metal sides. Cool to the touch, she closes her eyes and for a brief moment she lets a feeling of relief wash over her.

Finally, a break in all of this. The General must have heard about the purge.

Moving toward the driver side, she keeps her eyes on the mirror, hoping whoever is inside will be someone she recognizes.

Reaching the door, there is no one there. Empty. At least smart, whomever brought it here took the keys with them, but where are they?

"What do you mean I can't go in? Your dumb ass sent a message for me to come all the way out here and now you are saying I can't enter?" a gruff angry voice protests.

Turning to the wall, there is a cluster of guards in front of the gate and it appears one individual has all of their attention. Maybe up there she can find an answer or two without being noticed.

"Parliamentary Order...," the gate guard begins to say.

"I don't give a dragon's shit about any Parliamentary Order. Who the fuck do you think sent the message to General Whittaker? On their orders I was forced to drive this piece of shit through sand and storm to come here. I do not care if you tell me the pickup spot is out here," the man with all of their attention says.

It's the old man who drove her to Meclav. Still gruff as he was when she last saw him, all tens years are out on display now. Fists balled. Skin turning red from more than the heat, the guards keeping him back stay a safe distance away, his temperament giving them good reason to.

"Orders are orders. The only message I am to relay to you is that your package should be out here and under no circumstances are you to enter the city. You are more than welcome to wait until morning to turn your vehicle around and return to the General, but you will not be going any further," the guard answers.

"Package. What sorry shit for a mother birthed you into this fucking world. Package. She is a soldier and a hell of a lot better than your sorry lot," the man says.

A few of the guards stiffen their shoulders and shift the rifles held across their body, but with a wave of his arm, the old man waves them off and turns back toward the truck.

Coleena, pulling the coat tighter around her shoulders, slips into the shadows beside the truck. The ground practically trembles as her savior stomps his way toward her, dust lifting up into the air and fire burning the tracks he leaves in his wake.

"Fucking Dragon shit, piss ants," he mutters to himself.

"Hey, soldier, any chance I can catch a lift with you back to wherever you came from? Has to be a hell of a lot better than standing out here waiting to die in this shit hole," Coleena asks from around the corner of the truck, her voice as hoarse as she can make it.

"Fuck off," he doesn't have to fake the grumble in his voice. "This whole world is dying, and this place is no worse than anywhere else."

Opening the driver side door, he gets nothing more than a foot up onto the step before she slides out from behind her concealment.

"What would you say if I could get the package you were looking for?" Coleena asks, her head tilted to the ground to keep it in the shadows.

"Then I'd say you've got thirty seconds to show me where you've put it, because a soldier's body is not something to be fucked with. Not unless you want to find my boot buried so far up your ass that you'll be tasting rubber for the rest of your short existence."

Slowly looking up and pulling back the fabric of her hood, Coleena looks the gruff old man in the face.

"I'm dead, am I?" she asks.

His eyes widen, but only for a split-second. With a very subtle but quick glance around, he steps closer until he needs only to whisper for her to hear.

"By the gods, what the fuck is going on around here?" he asks. "We got word there had been an incident involving a riot and in the chaos, you had been murdered. The General is all but ready to march the whole fucking army here to settle the score. I was sent to retrieve your body, which by the way, those pricks told me was waiting out here for me to pick up like an overdue grocery bag. Set of low life little pukes. Who the fuck boxes up a Captain's body and sticks it outside the damn gates to the city?"

She can see his fists turning white again in the light of campfires as he strangles the air between them.

"It appears the rumor of my death is rather exaggerated. Though, this is news even to me," she says. "Did they tell you if they caught the person who did it?"

He nods and begins to dig into his pockets.

"Part of me didn't want to believe them. Said it was some traitor they found within the ranks of their own police department. A detective if I remember correctly. Didn't really read too much past their sorry excuse for what happened to you."

"Summers? Let me see that," Coleena demands.

Snatching the document from his hands, she smooths it against the side of the truck bed to work out the wrinkles. On a formal paper, the story unfolds about her untimely demise at the hands of the dangerous faction Azhana United and its ringleader Detective Roland Summers. A more than twenty-year veteran, he is the mastermind behind the attacks on Parliament City and because of her courageous work, the man was forced to eliminate her before it was too late.

"Real piece of poetic license they have there, isn't it?"

"Good fiction reading I'd say," Coleena responds. "Says here that Summers is to be executed by hanging over the wall?"

"Yep, that's what those pencil dicks confirmed for me. I demanded that they let me talk to the bastard first, but they said I could ask all the questions I want from this side as he hangs. I'm not going to get much from a corpse, even if he had any information, and I sure as hell wasn't going to stand here and wait two days to watch."

Shoving the paper back into the man's chest, Coleena takes a quick glance at the wall to make sure no one has noticed her presence yet.

"Two days? Fuck! I need you to do something for me," she hesitates before snapping her fingers.

"Fiddler. Those who know me call me that," he says.

The corner of his lips curl into a look that says there is more to the story she does not have time to ask about.

"OK, Fiddler, get back to General Whittaker and tell her to rally up as many as she can and begin that march here. Parliament City is in a lot more trouble than anyone wants to admit, and she is the only person with the resources to get this shit straightened up."

"Won't be too hard," Fiddler says. "Something is going on all over the place. The front line has moved. Damn dragon and its minions stopped attacking hardly two days after you left. We can't find hide nor tail of the bastards. She'll have an entire battalion here within the week."

"Front lines shifted? How can that be?"

The wrinkly old soldier shrugs his shoulders.

"You tell me. It's like the damn bastards just up and disappeared."

Heart pounding and looking up at the wall, Coleena's throat goes as dry as the dirt beneath her boots. Gigantic and as smooth as ice, how long can the ingenuity of man actually last against the magic of a monster?

"Get back to the General as fast as possible, Fiddler. Tell her to send everyone. Even the fucking janitors if she has to. Spare no one. March the whole fucking army if she can," Coleena says.

"You can tell her that yourself, Captain," Fiddler says with very little conviction. "Come with me and you can explain everything once we get back to base."

"No time. Tell her to march everyone. The dragon is here. If she doesn't bring the hammer down on this city, we'll lose it," Coleena says slipping the cowl back over her head.

"The dragon, here?" he asks, one eyebrow lifting and eyes narrowing.

"No time to explain. Turn this damn truck around and do as I ask. They may want you to believe I'm dead, but I'm as far away from the grave as I can be. Now go get them or there won't be any Parliament City left when you get back," Coleena says, slipping back behind the truck.

"And what are you going to be doing, Captain?" he asks, following her slightly into the shadows.

"That detective needs me. They aren't lying about Azhana United. He is one of them, but they aren't the bad guys. Without them this city will fall. Plus, I owe him my life. Now, stop asking questions and go. I've got a man to rescue."

Without another word, Coleena pulls her coat tighter and disappears into the darkness of the night.

How do you break into a walled city sealed up like a fortress? Miles of the poor and desperate camped outside, besieging the more fortunate as the doors remain locked and impenetrable.

Scaling the wall is an option, but she has tried that already. The remains of that failed attempt still fresh in her mind and the sound of the unfortunate soul tossed from the top still echoing into the night. Talking to the guards, explaining the urgency of the matter could work, but staring out at the tidal wave of beggars with their own concerns and worry proves that has less chance than the front gates creaking open and Parliament itself asking for forgiveness as they walk by.

No, the city is impenetrable. At least by a single person. Dark stone, smooth as glass staring back at her, there is little else she can do but return the glare tenfold. The sound of children and adults crying, empty bellies and sickness running rampant among those still stuck out here in the dirt.

Daytime is still hours away, the sky and its nothingness

absorbing everything, even the lights of tiny campfires and torches with the oil hissing as it burns. The smell of the people is the worst of it all. Hundreds of unwashed bodies. The old, the young, and everyone in between. Through hundreds of yards of dead forest, not a one attempts to take care of their basic human needs in fear of losing their space, a tiny hope that they may reach their destination before it is too late.

Leaning up against the rough bark of a long dead oak, Coleena watches the guards as they stare blank-eyed at those they cannot help. Part of her wonders if they care. Are they simply following orders or is there something else to their separation of heart and duty? She suspects the former but fears the later. How do you save an entire city full of people who do not know or understand the consequences of letting so many of your fellow men and women die?

She shakes her head to clear up the cobwebs catching every bad thought that makes its presence known. There is no time to waste. She must act now or the city and worse could be lost.

Taking a quick glance to the west, the horizon is nothing but a wall of the darkest black velvet. A haze of heat bending the image in its relentless pursuit of draining them all of what little they have to keep them alive.

Going back to the guards, she has to attempt something. Even if it gets her killed, she would have at least tried. The faintest of ideas is better than nothing.

Removing the long coat, she hides it in a heap beneath the thick rat's nest of brittle branches and twigs that marks the beginning of the tree line. Looking down at her shirt, stained and torn from previous flights, she takes a firm grip on the collar and pulls until it begins to rip. At first the fabric resists, but like a skin, once it starts the separation and tearing is easy to continue.

She stops as the opening reaches the middle of her breasts. Grabbing a chunk of the bottom, she helps a small slit extend itself until it reaches above her navel. Lifting a set of twigs from the pile scattered beside her feet and reaching for unknown miles, she grits her teeth and rakes it across the skin of her belly.

Fire lances itself across her mid-section. Not to be deterred, gripping it tightly she slaps herself in the chest, a thousand needles injecting a venomous hatred in her skin. Unable to stop herself, she lets out a small yelp of pain as the sharp edges cut tiny lines beneath her chin.

Looking down at herself, she looks like shit. New spots of blood soak into her shirt and her pants could stand on their own if she wasn't wearing them. Running her hands through her hair, she does what she can to mess it all up. This has to convince them, or there won't be any other options.

Stepping out from the forest, a small flash of light catches her eyes. Not wanting to draw attention to herself yet, she waits for it to return.

It happens again, but this time it wasn't from the fires within the wasted caravan. Glancing down at herself, another reflection catches her eyes.

The dog tags.

Completely forgotten, they would have given her away immediately. Removing them and stuffing them into her pocket, she moves slowly around the outer edges of the waiting line. A pronounced limp in her step, she keeps her eyes down and sniffs at the air. Burning the inside of her nose, her eyes water out of necessity more than the act.

Eyes turn and watch her from those gathered in hopes of

reaching safety, yet none of them stop to help. Coming around the front, she sees the man-door that she is looking for. A single guard waits with his attention out on the collected masses.

No one else is close enough for her to draw their attention. As it has been for days, all other soldiers are congregated to this hour's newest demands and pleas at the main gates. Four armed guards holding back a flood of the needy and desperate. She can feel the tension in the air. As thick as fog, the men and women on the wall are strife with it. Tense muscles, nervous glances. Hopefully just enough for what she needs.

"Help me, sir," Coleena coughs out.

Keeping her head down, she runs her hand across the small stretch of blood stinging the flesh of her chest as if it was a struggle to speak with her ruined neck. Reaching the man guarding the door, she lifts her hand up to her cheek and feels it wet the side of her face.

"Stop right there," the guard orders.

Older, gruff, and with a dark set to his eyes, he makes Summers look young with the graying of his temples and hair beneath his issued cap. The growing potbelly beneath his uniform speaks volumes of the lack of rigorous physical demands of his job.

"Please," Coleena chokes out again. "My sister and me. We stepped out into the forest, for privacy, so I could help her clean up some personal matters. They followed us, sir. You must help me. My sister needs help."

She does her best to squeeze out as many tears as she can muster. Digging deep, the images of her home burning back when she was a child helps build the lump in her throat.

"Go find someone else to help. Don't you see I'm busy?" the man says before shifting his stance.

His eyes dart all around him, never stopping on the gathered masses before the gates but rather to the other guards waiting and watching.

"Those who did this are out there. I can't go to any of them. They'll think I can point them out. They'll kill me!"

She lets a little hysteria slip into her voice. Heart racing, she steps closer. If she can't convince him...

"Bugger off. I don't have time for this shit," he growls.

Looking up where he stands, Coleena wipes up at a tear on her face and lets her hands trace the edge of her cheek before falling to the marks on her chest. His eyes follow and linger as she makes sure that a nail catches a piece of her shirt's fabric.

"Please," she begs again. "My sister is younger than I am. She doesn't understand what just happened. I'm not strong enough to help her. If you could spare just a few moments. Bring her out here where someone can look at her. I'm the older one. I've been around the block a few times."

She lets the words hang in the air between them.

Biting her lower lip, she watches the man's second chin pull itself tight. Eyes going brighter, he looks over at the crowd still building by the front gate. Not a single one of them looks this way. The citizens look angry and lost, the soldiers bored with their rifles keeping everyone a safe distance away.

"You said she is not too far in? Small girl, correct?" the man asks.

Never said she was a small one, just smaller, but who is she to point that out. Assholes always find ways to stick on a detail that means more to them.

Coleena nods her head, the most appreciative look she can muster spreading across her face.

"Please, hurry. I promise this won't take long. You'll be a hero," she says.

"Doubt that shit," he answers.

"To me you will be," she says with a smile.

His shoulders stiffen and his back straightens as he takes one last look at the others. Still nothing. Positioning his rifle further up his shoulder, he nods toward the forest.

"Lead the way. We have a little sister to rescue."

Coleena, exaggerated limp aside, turns and heads for the darkest corner she can find.

———

NOT EXACTLY THE SMARTEST OF MEN, BUT THAT FIT HER NEEDS perfectly. Twigs and leaves cracking and splitting beneath their boots, the darkness grows as they leave the wall and the besieging army behind. All noise other than the beating of their own hearts and the passing of their own feet fads into a low hum in the background. The deathly hollows of the forest swallowing them and wrapping them in its cold yet humid embrace.

"I thought you said she wasn't that far into the forest?" the man asks.

She can hear him begin to puff between breaths already. Not turning toward him, she continues forward. Tiny pin pricks of light make their way through the dead husks, and they begin to reach the very limits of what they can see before they stumble into total darkness.

"Not much further," Coleena answers. "Can't you hear her crying?"

"Fuck no I can't!" the man says, the fire in his voice rising.

"We better be damn close or I'm gonna drag us both back and toss you into the cells."

"She's right around this corner. I think I can see her," Coleena says and with a little skip turns the corner around a thick trunk broken and split high above her head.

Much to her surprise, the man is less than half a step behind, his large mass practically knocking her over.

"Where is she?" he demands.

Thinking on her feet, Coleena begins to examine the ground, scuffing what she can with the toe of her boot.

"I'm...I'm not sure. She was right here," she says through as many sobs as she can force through her throat. "Do you...do you think they came back for her?"

A vice-like grip wraps itself around the back of her neck and more strength than she thought he had in him thrusts her against the solid trunk. Cracks and bits break away as the pain sends tiny spasms down the muscles along her spine.

"You have ten seconds to explain what the fuck is going on here," he growls.

His face is inches from hers, and she can smell today's rations on his breath. Stale cheese and hot processed meat. A small amount of alcohol lingers, and it burns the back of her throat.

"Nothing is going on. I told you my sister needs help. She was..."

He slaps her across the face, and she drops to one knee. Shifting his rifle to remind her he still has it; he yanks her back up with one hand under her shoulder.

"I don't give a shit about your sister," he says, his eyes dropping low again. "Even if she exists or not. You dragged me out into this fucking shit hole and I'm going to get something out of this. If they find me away from that door, it's gonna be my ass on report and I expect your ass better be worth it."

"Don't hurt me, sir," Coleena starts. She traces a finger down her neck and like a tiny cat toy, his eyes follow. "I swear I was only looking for help."

He licks his lips as she takes a half step forward. His bulk begins to push against her as his gaze moves lower, and she slowly lifts her other hand up into the greasy locks of hair beneath his cap.

She can practically taste him already. All sweat and cheap beer. His pulse is practically racing through his shirt as he goes to drop his rifle to the side. Taking a firmer grip on the back of his head, the smile on his face takes on a more sinister look.

"So, you like it rough," he purrs as he wraps his arms around her to pull her practically inside of him.

Using the momentum, she wrenches his head forward at the same moment she drops her chin down onto her chest. Nose meets the top of her skull and the fat man staggers backward. Lights flash before her eyes and the world spins, but only momentarily.

"What the fuck," the guard yells through bloody hands as he tries to stop the flow.

"Sorry about that. Don't know my own strength sometimes," Coleena says as she moves to close the distance between them.

He swings with a wild punch that easily sails over her head, and she counters with a blow to his midsection. Air and blood spurt out and across her face as he curls into himself. Without a chance to react, the man leans into her and lets his weight tumble them both down to the ground.

Sticks and stones cut deep gouges into her back as his full weight crushes into her. Air punched out; she feels his thick hands grip onto her shoulders as he goes to lift himself up.

"You are going to pay for this," he gets out between gritting teeth.

Letting go of one hand, he lets his weight and hand slap her across the face. Red and white lights flash across her version and the taste of blood begins to warm the inside of her mouth.

"You are beginning to make me regret this less and less," she cuts back before spitting in his face.

Rearing back, he lets go of her shoulder again for another slap but this time she is ready. Swinging with her open hand she swats him across the ear as hard as she can. The man's eyes go wide for a quick moment as his grip loosens. Curling to her side she slashes back with her hand into the center of his throat.

She feels a small crunch beneath the blow, and he rocks backward, breath coming in short little coughs. Cheeks going red, he tries to scoot himself across the ground, anything to create distance between him and her.

Picking herself off the ground, she wipes at the broken leaves and debris that sticks to her clothes and skin. Taking a hand, she runs the corner of her mouth across her sleeve to remove the small trickle of blood as she keeps up with him, his momentum stopping as he finds a nice big stump to slide into.

"I was going to try and make this easy on you," she says. "But I no longer have any doubts. You are one of them."

"What are you talking about? You stupid bitch," the man coughs out with thick streams of saliva and blood stretching from his lower lip. "You are going to pay for this. I swear."

Coleena picks up a branch from the brush. A big fat one that takes her entire hand to wrap around. His eyes widen as they go from the weapon she holds and back to the look in her eye.

"Someone is going to pay for this. This many can't suffer without anyone being punished," she says back. Lifting the branch over her shoulder, she smiles. "Too bad for you, it won't be me."

Blood, teeth, and splintered wood flies as the man's head cracks to the side, and he slumps to the ground. A large gash opens across his cheek and for the tiniest moment she wonders if she has killed him, but then the feeling passes. Second chin moving with the smallest of breaths, he is still alive. When he finally comes back around, he'll have the largest headache he has ever had in his life.

She couldn't care any less.

Throwing the branch on the ground, she begins to pull his boots off and then the rest of his clothes. Most of them are too large for her. He is the same height, but where she is large and muscular for a woman, he was round and lazy for a man. Wide at the gut, she pulls his belt to the point where she has to force the hook to create a new hole just to keep it held up.

These don't have to be perfect. She only needs to get inside the door and to the other side. If none of them pay much attention they won't be able to see the large difference between her and him. If they do, well...

Slinging his rifle over her shoulder, she works her hands through his pockets. A small ring of keys and a crunched pack of cigarettes. Not a single coin to the bastard. Looking at his slumped body, a small fire of anger ignites in her belly.

What would he have done to someone else had it not been her?

The rifle feels heavy across her back, but she shrugs it

away. No way of knowing and no time to stop and figure it out. Turning back the way they had come, she does not bother to try to move or hide him. She only needs to reach that door.

Walking through the forest, the lights of the caravan and the wall grow brighter with every step. The smell of bodily waste and rotting food grows thicker as the shadows grow. The sky remains a black void and the heat of a thousand bodies is a fog as she reaches the end of the tree line. Thick and soupy, it almost staggers her at the thought of having to cross the distance back to the doorway without anyone noticing.

Guards still patrol the walkways above. Helmeted heads making their way from one battlement to the next. Before the front gate, the crowd has grown. Men and women's voices can be heard breaking over one another. Several of the guards have taken a step back and now keep their eyes on the bunch directly in front of them instead of the unmoving masses stretching for miles.

Coleena watches for a few moments. Even several of the men and women at the top of the barricades watch the confrontation folding out beneath them. Taking a deep breath, she leaves the dark confines of the tree line and begins the long walk back to the door.

No one notices her lone figure move across the field. Uniform too many sizes too big, her pants begin to slip, and she's forced to grab her belt buckle to keep them up as she slips into a small jog.

"Hey, what are you doing?" a man's voice barks at her.

Coleena stiffens as she slows to a casual walk. Hitching the rifle further up her shoulder, she tugs on her pants to keep them from falling.

"Needed to hit the head," she growls back with the deepest voice she can grumble.

It's a man who walked around the corner some hundred feet from where she is. Sparing a glance, she has less than fifty feet to her destination. Not waiting, she begins to walk again.

"You can't be leaving your post without reporting, soldier!" the man barks again.

He's in no hurry as he slowly sheds the distance between them.

An anger flares to life within her. Turning enough that she can see him with the corner of her eyes, this piece of shit is no soldier. Dressed like any of the other guards, black uniforms and lacking any slashes across the breast, he is Parliament trained. On any other day, he'd have no right to call her or anyone soldier.

"Tell that to those assholes up at the gate. I can't hold my shit all night," she growls again with a flick of her head toward the crowd so close to hysteria.

The man shifts his gaze to the mob still growing beside the steel doors. Not waiting she finishes the remaining walk to her temporary post.

"See to it you never do that again, soldier. I'll have you on report if I catch even a word of you or anyone leaving their post. We are at war with these savages," the man says as he walks by.

He doesn't take his eyes off the unruly protest. She waits until he is little more than the shadow of a man she'd rather put a bullet through before making her way into the city. Turning the handle, the door is locked. Fishing out the keys, it takes little more than a few tries to find the correct one.

More shouts and screams fill the void over the hum of desperation and despair as the handle turns and the entrance waits for her to walk through. A gunshot rings through the night and the screams turn into a panic.

Having no time to waste, she does not look back. Stepping in, she shuts the door behind her and lets the darkness within swallow her whole.

28

─────────

Darkness broken by small humming light bulbs. A dozen feet between each, they flicker with unreliable electricity, and the stuffiness of a closed in space squeezes her tightly. She can taste it in her mouth. The stale air, bitter and unbroken. Tiny fingers tickle the little hairs on her skin, and she can hear people ready to jump out at her with every step.

A thousand dark corners. Rumbling piping and echoing stone floors. Water drips somewhere off in the distance and the rifle in her hand feels like a child's toy. Nerves shaking her hands, she checks to see if there is a round in the chamber. Copper reflecting in the dim flicker of the incandescent lighting, the tiniest spark of reassurance dampens the edginess as she moves her way through the emptiness.

If anyone spots her there will be no way to talk her way out of it. Clothes hanging from her like old skin, the pants drag beneath her boots and scratch across the stone floor creating a wet dragging sound that follows her like a shadow.

Heart thumping in her ears, she follows the route she

remembers from a week prior. Mostly straight, the access tunnels are narrow, and she'll be up shit's creek without a paddle if anyone comes from the other side.

More gunfire erupts from deep within the wall. Boots pound above in shadows she cannot see beyond. Her heart aches for the people. Don't these monsters care about them in any way?

There has to be a way to end this. The dragon is coming. If they do not stand together, this city will fall and then the whole world will follow. Smothering the thoughts in her mind, she continues forward.

Pipes continue to rattle before turning as the narrow tunnel ends and a hallway made of wood paneling leads to her left and her right.

No way forward.

Which way was it?

No time to waste, she turns right and follows it. Lights become more numerous as papers and other signs begin to fill the walls. Duty rosters. Sign-up sheets. Memos from Parliament itself are tacked and stuck with adhesive up and down the hall. Some have tiny bits of graffiti written on them. One even says Parliament can go suck a dick and it brings a little smile to her face.

At least they all can't be bad.

Relaxing the fingers strangling the grip of her rifle, she edges forward, the vibration of the city's life making its way through the floor and up into her legs. She is getting close. The other side of the wall is coming up soon.

Flapping lazily a strip of paper catches her eye, the words pulling her attention. She grabs it and presses it back against the wall. Parliamentary Order 247-U7, Captain Coleena Armigera of the Azhanian Armed forces, wanted Dead or Alive. Found with evidence proving connection to the deadly bombing of the Parliament City Central Bank. The suspect is to be considered armed and dangerous. Do not approach without proper assistance and if required, deadly force is permitted.

They don't hold back, do they?

She rips the paper off the wall. The photo they have of her is from when they locked her up after the bombing of Mama Filiz's place. Darkened eyes and a thousand scratches make her look like someone else. A monster with danger and hatred hidden behind those eyes. Doesn't help the damn thing is in black and white and makes everyone look that way.

Squeezing the paper between her fingers, she goes to crumple it into the smallest piece of trash she can create when she hears a door slam somewhere close behind her.

"Hey, you! Have any idea what the fuck is going on out there?" a man's voice asks.

He's half asleep, the words dragged out into a partial yawn. She doesn't look back his way.

"Not sure," she growls hoping it will work again. "I was on my way through to switch shifts when it all started."

"Something wrong with your throat? Need to lay off those cigarettes a little," he says, his voice practically against the back of her ear. "What's that you got in your hand?"

He takes it from her before she can stop him. Short and a bit scrawny, his cap is tilted, and he scratches at the thick brown hair beneath. Uniform wrinkled and buttons shifted one up with the lonely one hanging below his belt, he looks more like he fell out of bed than woke up on his own.

"Real piece of work, this one," he continues. "Saw her arrive myself. Not sure how they go saying she had anything to do with the bombing as she didn't get here till after, but you never know what those pencil pushers up there can dig up. Makes you stop and ask yourself sometimes."

Looking up from the wrinkled paper, his eyes take a moment to register as they draw even with her own. The world goes silent and still as they stand there waiting for the other to do something.

"Don't," she starts, and he doesn't listen.

Reaching for something around the back of his pants, she drives the butt-end of her rifle into his midsection, and he stumbles back against the wall. Hand coming free, it's a pistol, and she crashes into him, shoulder first.

Air with the force of a grunt escapes his lips as she wraps one hand around his wrist, and she digs her boots into the stone floor to force her shoulder deeper in to his gut.

"Listen to me," she says, her voice heavy with strain. "I'm not guilty of anything other than being in the wrong place at the wrong time. Parliament is the one behind all of this. You have to..."

Her boot slips out as the wet pants slide across the floor, and she tumbles to the ground. Weight no longer against him, he shifts forward but catches his own boot against her leg and spills himself across her. Weapons rattling to the floor, Coleena rolls forward to get back to her feet when a fist catches her square across the corner of her jaw.

A bright light flashes across her eyes, and she hits the wall with a thud. Shaking her head, she keeps it looking down to the floor and throws her entire body in the man's direction. Arms and legs kick as she rolls into him, both of them crashing into the other wall.

Teeth bared and snapping, the man fights like a tenacious little devil and it takes everything she has to keep him from regaining the upper position. Elbows hit soft spots.

Knees punch bone and grind as they both scratch their way over the floor.

"Why are you doing this?" the man asks through gritted teeth. "You swore and oath."

Coleena gets a clearing and cracks her head into the side of his jaw. Pain erupts in her skull, the need to vomit filling her mouth with bile, but his eyes roll backward enough to lose his grip on her.

"I'm trying to tell you, I had nothing to do with any of this. The General sent me," she says, crawling away until she reaches her rifle. "My orders come directly from her. Parliament is the one with problems here, not me."

The guard shakes his head, his eyes squeezing tight as he knocks out the cobwebs in his mind. Blood drips from his lips in thin lines before he spits a wide wad of it on the floor.

"Doesn't matter. All politicians are corrupt in one way or another, but as the men and women who swore an oath to this city, we must follow orders," he says in return.

Taking a deep breath, Coleena slides against the opposite wall from where he kneels on the floor. Her head aches and she is tired. Fingers swollen, her arms and legs feel like lead bricks.

"I am following orders. Everyone inside and outside of these walls are in danger and if we don't do something about it there will be no orders left to follow. Parliament is broken. Let me walk out of here and you won't see me again," she says, the barrel of the rifle settling its aim at the man's chest.

His eyes follow the movement. Wide and unblinking, she can see them dilate even more as he runs through his options.

"Orders are orders," he says, his voice dropping to a whisper.

"Don't do it," she pleads. "You'd make one hell of a soldier. This is stupid and you know it."

She doesn't want to squeeze. He's more than a body's length away from where his pistol rests against the wall, and she couldn't miss even if her eyes were closed.

"By Parliament...," he starts.

Not going for his weapon as she thought he would, the guard shifts forward and dives toward her, hands out to push away the rifle in case she fires.

He's too slow. Even in her beaten and battered state, the distance is too great. A cold wash races down her spine as the bullet rips through the man's chest and splatters the wall behind him.

His weight does not fall on her at first. He stops mid-distance and tries to take in a breath that is all wheezing and full of liquid. Skin going pale, he looks her in the eyes. Ears ringing, she doesn't even remember hearing the eruption, but there is no doubt everyone from here to the front gate heard its loud recoil.

Mouth opening, teeth wet and red with blood, the man tries to say something. Hot air with the stench of iron leaks from his mouth, and he topples into her. Like a baby, he slides, and his head stops upon the crook of her shoulder.

"I'm... I'm sorry," she whispers.

He tries to take another breath and his body shivers with the attempt. Dark red pools begin to form against her legs and his belly where he is curled up against her.

Moments pass and he stops moving. The life leaking from his chest ceases and there is no strength left to keep him propped against her. Sliding out from beneath, she gently lets him rest against the floor. His glassy eyes follow her. So many questions burrowing into her with that glare.

Her heart races and inside her stomach, where the fire should be burning, all she can feel is the cold misery of hardened stone.

"I'm sorry. You should have let me go," she whispers before closing his eyes and leaving two trails of blood over his lids with her fingers.

Fingerprints pressed into his skin she knows she is responsible for this. A man is dead at her feet. If only he had been a soldier and not a guard. He would have made a good one.

A door slams in the distance, and she can hear the sound of boots on rock floor. Looking back the way she had come, the pounding begins to draw closer with every second.

Grabbing the pistol from the ground, she tucks it into her belt and spares one last glance at the corpse. With a shake of her head, she turns and runs into the darkness.

THE DOOR WAITS FOR HER. CLOSED TO THE OUTSIDE WORLD. Darkness a veil between her and the world she must return to. Tiny streams of light, sickly and weak work their way through tiny gaps between floor and the inches of solid steel.

Pipes rattle and the sound of water dripping in the distance, the air is thick and wet with its taste. Her pursuers have not caught up. Their voices and their boots pounding the solid rock does not echo here.

A crypt built into the thick stone wall. Full of shadows and secrets, she wonders if it will be enough in the end.

Sweat coats her hands as she holds the rifle, the vibrations from its recoil still echoing through her bones.

Why did he have to fight?

If he had listened to her, he'd still be alive. None of them had to die. At least not by her hand. The dragon was coming and that was enough. She isn't even sure they have enough to stop it with all the people locked within this cage, let alone if they lose themselves one by fighting over nothing.

Reaching for the door it is cold to her touch. The ice-cold caress of death. Twisting the nob lets out a horrific screech that cuts the silence like broken glass. Her heart skips a beat, waiting for what she knows is coming.

A shout.

Then the recognizable piling on of men fighting to be first in line to get her.

Here they come.

But they don't.

Opening the door hits her in the face with a slap of ash and heat. Sucking the air and moisture right out of her lungs, she forces herself to take a deep breath to steady herself and the muscles in her stomach pinch with the effort.

The sound of the chase draws closer. Metal and rubber clang against the wall, and she slams the door closed behind her. Grabbing the keys still in her pocket, she tries the same one that let her in, and it doesn't fit. Voices punch through the thick steel.

They are too close.

Rifle lifted, she jams it between the handle and the railing of the steps down. It will no longer turn. Pushing her weight onto it begins to bow the weapon, and she lets go.

Good enough.

Heading down the stairs, the city looks like it is still asleep. A thick fog of smoke and ash fills the streets and the few lights that there are scatter and fade through the haze. A quiet fear hangs between the buildings. From the wall she can see almost no one on the streets. The only movement are patrols of the same Parliamentary guards she must avoid.

Ducking away from the steps, she does not follow the well-worn path that leads to the entrance to the city. Her clothes are soaked in blood. Some of it that asshole sitting in the forest with the world's worst headache. Most of it that poor bastard.

The look in his eyes glares back at her, his questioning burned into the back of her mind. Finding a good spot behind a stacked pallet of supply crates, she strips the bloodied guards uniform off and straightens her clothes beneath. From here on out, there will be little chance of tricking anyone.

But where does she go?

The barracks are an option, but what about Tul? That smile of his as he called them traitors. Narin's eyes as she took the bullets meant for her before they both fell into the river.

Not her best option but it's a start. Just because the Petty Officer is involved with this mess doesn't mean Lieutenant Mason is.

A loud crack hits the door up on the wall. Frame shakes and her rifle bows with the effort of the guards inside. Decision made or not, she leaves the safety of her concealment and as calmly as her body will allow she walks away like nothing is happening.

The men's shouts from inside can be heard from a hundred feet away. She does not dare to glance back, afraid it will give her away. Moving with purpose, she follows the path they brought her along a week ago.

Being forced to stay out of the city as much as possible, she catches a glimpse of the barracks fairly quickly. The army's flags lay limp on posts where they have been tied at half-mast. Tiny smoke fires lifting in slow streams and the smell of cooking meat is thick.

Who died?

Stepping out from the thinning shadows of the morning, the military compound comes into view and in one fluid motion she reverses course and quickly slides back into the space between vacant buildings. A line of men form a semi-circle around the front of the fence line. All of them dressing in the solid black uniforms of Parliament.

They do not look at the soldiers within the perimeter, their solid stone faces looking out at anything and anyone who approaches.

"Shit," she swears to herself.

There is no way she'll get in now. Somehow they must know she is still alive. Figuring she would try to make her way to those within the barracks, they have blocked it all off. Plan two it is then.

Hell's Toilet.

Unless they are truly unlucky, all of Azhana United hasn't been caught and maybe she can find a few trustworthy people there. That is of course assuming the place still stands. Checking that the pistol tucked into her belt is still secure, she steps out onto the street, all intention to avoid the barracks with a wide birth until she can make her way to Congress St.

"There she is!" an alarm is sounded.

Bullets slam into the stone wall inches behind her head.

The guards, six in total round the corner at the end of the road.

Running as fast as she can, Coleena makes it for the alley across the street. Legs already burning, more shots send shards of stone into the air as the sound of buzzing bees and explosions echo into the morning air.

Turning and racing without a second thought to where she is going, Coleena twists herself between trash and other junk thrown between buildings. Grabbing what she can, she pushes it down as she passes, anything to block their way.

She can hear them closing in on all sides. Angry orders are barked and the words echo off stone walls and empty buildings. Drops of sweat burn her eyes and her lungs are on fire. Taking the next corner too quickly, she slams into an empty street cart and parts, trinkets, and her body topple to the ground.

Heaving for air, she struggles back to her feet, knees shaking and the world spinning. A loud pop pierces the air as pain and the force of a hammer slam into her shoulder, and she spirals back to the ground.

Instinct and training has her pistol out and two shots return in the direction down the street. The dark figure arches backward before falling to the ground, rifle clattering to the pavement. Jumping over the dilapidated cart, she is back on the street and running.

Bullets slam into the next building as she turns the corner and heads down a secondary alley. The smell of refuse and bodily waste sucks the air right out of her lungs, but she keeps going. At the end there is a brick wall with paths leading both right and left.

She decides left. Turning, her boots slip on brown sludge and with all her momentum carrying her, she slams into the barricade with enough force to rattle her teeth.

Knees buckling on impact, she hits the ground as two of the bricks explode inches from her head.

Raising her weapon she returns another short burst and the figure at the end of the alley ducks behind a rusted steel dumpster.

"She's over here!" the man screams.

Growling, she shoves herself from the ground and fires another shot at the dumpster. The bullet tears through the weakened metal and the man does not return any of his own shots as she bolts down the alley.

Jumping over boxes and weaving between the broken remains of fallen walls, her heart pounds in her chest as she slides to a halt.

Another brick wall. Looking left and right, there is no where else to go. Turning around, a dark figure steps around the corner, and she fires without thinking. Shadow disappearing, the guard hides and her mind is made up.

With a leap, her hands catch the top of the wall and the sharp edges of the cut stone dig into her skin as she pulls herself up. Muscles cramp and her shoulder is on fire as blood leaks out freely.

Explosions of gunfire echo as she rolls onto the top, the red wall erupting into dust and tiny shards cutting into the skin of her face and arms. No ability to hesitate, she lets her weight drop her off the other side, hoping against the likelihood the fall could kill her.

Boxes like wet paper crumble and the squishy splatter of rotting vegetables cover her as she hits them half-way down. The sweet taste of mold fills her mouth as the stench circles her mind. Hitting the ground with a thud she is still alive.

Heart pounding and the world spinning in her eyes, she struggles to get to her feet. For a moment there is no strength in her legs, and she sways until she hits the brick wall again. Vomit erupts from her stomach and the pistol in her hand drops.

Darkness closes in around her eyes. More than the early morning shadows, consciousness begins to slip away. Taking a deep breath, she fills her lungs with the gas of the rotten waste, and she takes a step forward. The inside of her mind begins to split and the world tilts to the left and spills her against the building.

The voices of the men chasing her reach the brick wall. She wants to scream but her throat is shut. Words die before reaching her tongue, and she rests herself against the stone of the empty structure.

They have her. At least she doesn't have to run anymore. If she is lucky they'll make her execution quick, and she won't be here when the dragon arrives. Her eyes are heavy and she lets them close.

A vision that has haunted her all her life comes back to the front of her mind. Fire everywhere. The screams as thousands upon thousands died to the burning slaughter of a monster.

This is it. She has tried her best. Taking a deep breath she waits. The shifting of equipment as more men arrive signals the moment she has been waiting for. They will scale the wall and take her.

Opening her hands and spreading her arms, she waits. A thick hand clamps its way over her face. Her eyes open as her mind freezes, and she is yanked backward. Gravity pulls and throws her to the ground.

A golden doorway sits illuminated in the darkness. Standing in the shadows, a figure grabs the door and shuts it quickly and quietly. Locks set themselves and the room falls deathly silent except for the sound of her breathing, her heart, and the slow calmness of whoever is in the room with her.

"Who...who are you?" she whispers.

"Ssh," a familiar voice says.

The voices of the guards falling over the wall and helping those with them fill the space outside. She can see them in her head, fully armored and looking for her as she sits just on the other side of the door.

The handle rattles and the frame shakes as they try to force their way in. There is no movement. No give as the tugging takes on a fevered urgency.

"Come on, she has to have gone this way," a man's voice barks.

Boots echo down the alley as her pursuers move on. In moments the sound they make is a fading memory as she sits in the darkness, her shoulder throbbing and the rest of her feeling torn to pieces.

"Who are you?" she asks again, her voice cracking with pain.

There is a shifting as her savior moves though she cannot see them. The sound of metal scrapping across the floor fills the room until it stops right in front of where she sits, her back against what feels like a wall.

A match is struck and the sizzle of the phosphorus fills the room with a quick flash of light that burns her eyes. Adjusting quickly, she watches as the end of a candle is lit and brought up to the back of a chair where a man sits straddling the back.

Wide shoulders and a wider gut watch as she begins regain her composure. Dark uniform with a matching dress shirt decorated with gleaming metals wait as her mind freezes. Big smile waiting with the smallest hint of vanilla, she does not know what to say.

Sitting in the chair waits Lieutenant Mason. Black eye,

swollen lower lip, and a bandage that is an angry red as blood seeps through the fabric, he looks her up and down where she sits.

"Nice to finally catch up to you, Captain. We have a lot to talk about."

29

The tunnels beneath the buildings are cramped and wet. The smell of mold and waste thick in the air. Water and soft dirt splash beneath their boots and the taste fills Coleena's mouth and throat, making it hard to breathe.

They move in silence, Mason's candle their only light. Beneath the darkness and empty blanket of the crypt someone once called home, a flat board panel had been cut through the floor leading to the tunnels that link building to building beneath the original structures of Parliament City. Before it grew to the behemoth that it is now. Swelled beyond its rock boundaries.

"Where are we going?" Coleena demands.

Her shoulder still throbs, a pulsing pressure running down the bone of her arm. Heart beating faster as they walk their way down one silent corridor before entering the next. She can feel the warmth and pain run down her arm as it seeps through the bandage tied tightly against her body.

"Always so full of questions, Captain," Mason returns. He does not look her way as they stop at a cross section, this new area of the underground growing shorter and forcing them both to crouch. "Haven't you learned that putting your nose into areas it doesn't belong has gotten you into nothing but trouble since you arrived?"

Coleena sighs and lets herself rest as she leans up against the damp wall. She watches as his eyes study both passageways, in the darkness neither of them distinguishable from the other.

"You make it sound like things would be better off if I was never assigned to this," she says. He cocks his head and turns toward her ever so slightly with a tiny uplifting of his lips. "Is that why you sent Tul after me?"

The man's face drops like a rock and the smile is buried so far beneath the hard line on his face there may be no chance for it to ever come back.

"Petty Officer Tul is both a disappointment and a tragic mistake. I trusted that man with countless assignments and immeasurable information. I had no idea he would do what he has done." Mason wipes his hand on his pants, a frantic movement as if there is a film he can't get off. "A monster maybe, but I at least thought he was loyal. No, Captain, Tul's actions outside these city walls were done without my knowledge. I look back at it now and I wonder how many things he has been involved with regardless of my intentions or knowledge."

Coleena isn't sure she trusts him, but what option does she have?

"Do you have any idea where we are going?" she asks, the strength in her legs draining and the sweat on her face stinging the shit out of the tiny scrapes all across her body.

"These damn tunnels are as old as time. We found them before the great migration. Many thought I should have reported them to Parliament, but I'm no fool. The army needs its secrets, and this one is mine. Had to demote a bastard or two to keep it that way."

"And this helps us how?"

Lifting his nose, he takes a couple big whiffs of the air.

"Smells worse down that way," Mason says with a nod of his head to the left. "Best we head for drier ground."

Without waiting for a response, holding the candle high, he winks at her one more time and pushes forward. Taking a deep breath, she steps away from the wall to follow. She doesn't know what the man is talking about. Everything stinks like a sewer except for that candle which again reeks of vanilla. Holding back her gag reflex, she falls in step behind him.

Time passes slowly as the tunnels turn left and right. The lieutenant seems less confused with this path as he does not hesitate further. Candle burning down, the streams of melted wax drip over the big man's hands and down onto the floor. How much time have they lost down here?

"We'll stop here for a few moments," Mason says as they reach a new intersection.

The air is much drier and sand and gravel crunches beneath their feet as they stop to rest. Sweet beads freely on both of their heads and the pain in her shoulder is now a numbing that forces her to flex her hand to ensure that it is still there.

"What part of the city are we under now?" Coleena asks as Mason ducks into a small opening within the wall, his large girth barely fitting between the rock opening and into the dark room beyond.

"If my calculations are correct, and undoubtedly they are, we are somewhere within the vicinity of Poor Town," Mason answers, his voice echoing within the shadow and off of the old rock. Squeezing himself back out into the tunnel, he has a fresh candle in his hand and a dry rag that looks to have been white at one time. A thick layer of gray dust covers it. "Here take this. Wipe some of that sweat off and take a breather. Once we get back topside, who knows what we are going to see."

Wearily, she takes the offering and dabs at the sweat and filth covering her face. The cloth is gritty against her skin and pulling it away, the gray dust is now black as mud. He gives her a tiny wink with those eyes of his before turning back to the path ahead. Gritting her teeth, she wipes the rag through her wet hair before watching as large droplets fall to her boots.

It is far warmer down here than she realizes.

"What do you know about, Summers?" she asks. "Are they going to actually execute him?"

Mason checks the candle and then the watch on his wrist. Hitching up his pants, he turns to look at her, the look on his face worn and tired.

"That is a bad hand for Summers. He was a good man, very reliable," Mason answers. "Yes, I do believe they will execute him."

"But he didn't have anything to do with those bombings. Anyone with a brain would know that," Coleena says, her throat dry and her mind now going a mile a minute.

Mason gives her a small chuckle.

"No one ever said politicians had brains. No, Captain, I think we are both aware that Parliament is no longer working with the best intentions of the people on their mind. If they did, they would be promoting Detective Summers for everything he has done."

"What do you mean 'what he has done'?" Coleena asks, grabbing the man by the shoulder.

His expression changes to one of curiosity, his eyes looking over her as if she had just appeared out of nowhere.

"You really aren't any good at this detective thing, are you, Captain?" He shakes his head and that smile returns, a mischievous look. "I figured even someone with your skills would pick up on it better than this. You disappoint me, Captain."

Balling her fist, Coleena lets her shoulders, aching or not, widen with a threat.

"Just spit it out, Lieutenant. We do not have all day."

He looks at his watch and then back down the two passageways.

"No, Captain, we do not. That you are correct. As for enlightening you, Parliament is not going to hang Summers because of the bombs. As you so clearly expressed it is obvious to anyone that he is not involved, and it would threaten losing the entire police force if they killed him under such a lie. No, my dear woman, Summers did not set the bombs. He does lead the one thing that those airtight assholes up Congress Street have yet to get a single handle on. The biggest thorn in their side since the day they were even established."

Coleena's gut tightens as if she was punched, and she finds a way to lean against the wall.

"Azhana United," she whispers. "He's their leader?"

"Really need to get you into some off-duty training, Captain. I knew you wouldn't know right away, but his involvement was the entire reason I put you two together," Mason adds. "After your little escape through the proverbial crapper, I thought you would have had it all figured out."

"So, if Summers is their leader, where do you fit in all of this?"

Mason puts a finger up to his nose and winks to her.

"All in good time, Captain. Even with your slow senses, you will know everything you need to know, all in good time. Now, follow me. We don't have much further to go."

Without another word, Mason, candle in hand, turns into the right tunnel and leads the way. Miles pass beneath their feet as they turn through a dozen different channels. Coleena tries to keep it straight, but after more than a dozen switchbacks, she can no longer tell how they even got there.

This part of the underground system is different from where they found their way in. More openings pop up between intersections and within each, she catches glimpses of ladders cut into the rock walls. A dozen or more, all of them passed without a simple glance by Mason as they work their way down.

Feet aching, neck stiff from crouching, and muscles burning, Coleena can barely continue as Mason finally pulls up before stepping into a side alcove. With a strike of another match, he lights three more candles, all of them still smelling like fucking vanilla. The stench cuts through the stagnant and dry air, Coleena's lungs burning and throat cracked and begging for water.

"Here we go, my dear," Mason says with a smile from ear to ear. "Our ticket out of here."

Coleena follows him in. There is a ladder cut into the ancient stone, thick metal rungs covered in dust and cobwebs.

"You sure about this? We could be outside the city for all I know," she says.

"There are very few of those passages, and we keep them locked tight. Can't afford for anyone to know that there is a way into the city that does not include through or over those walls, now could we?"

Anger flairs in Coleena's stomach, but she bites it back

as the big man widens his smile and begins to climb. Metal creaking, dust and dirt falling all around, the Lieutenant makes his way to the top, thick arms and hands pressing on the board locking them off from the surface.

"S.s. should be just a little more," he grunts.

Debris spills all around them as he thrusts the paneling open, a wave of cooler air sucking into the room and putting out two of the candles. Coleena backs away, her eyes watering from the silt as Mason coughs and pulls his way up.

Darkness swallows him as his bulk disappears over the edge. Silence leaves her in the room, the opening to the building above a chamber of shadows and secrets.

"Everything OK up there?" she asks.

Mason's big hand sticks down and waves her up.

Slowly, Coleena takes the last remaining candle and holding it in her aching hand, she begins to pull her way up the ladder. Bones popping and muscles cramping, she makes it one slow step at a time.

"You know, Mason," she begins to say as her head reaches the opening, "if it wasn't for you finding us a way out of here, I'd be darn tempted to throw this fucking candle right in your face."

The Lieutenant does not answer as she turns and with a turn waves the candle in front of her. Sitting against a bracing pole, legs spread and extended, Mason looks at her, a fresh new line of blood trickling down from his left ear.

Coleena goes to yell and drop herself down, but the sharp prick of a blade against the side of her neck stops her movement.

"Now, how about we be a good little soldier and keep those lips of yours shut," Tul's voice whispers. The words are quiet, unrushed, and without emotion. "Give me the candle and you can come over here and join your traitor friend Lieutenant Mason."

Coleena tries to turn and look at Tul's dark figure but the man lets the edge of his weapon run its course over her skin as she does so. A searing pain inches its way across her neck and up her cheek.

"I wouldn't do that if I were you. There are more than enough people in this city willing to see you dead, traitor. No reason to make this messier than it needs to be," he says.

Turning back to Mason, Coleena puts the candle onto the floor before struggling to get a good enough grip to finish pulling herself up. Arms shaking, she grunts as her body slides its way out of the tunnel. The tiny fire running its course through her neck ignites, and she bites away the pain.

"So, you are working with the dragon now, Tul? Is that it?" she asks.

In the candlelight she sees the tiniest of movement in his eyebrow but it disappears with the flickering of the tiny flame.

"No one works with that beast. I heard about your little fantasies about men and women in league with evil itself. No wonder the senators marked you as mentally unstable. Now, go sit by this worthless bag of wind who has proven himself to be no more use than the traitors you have bedded yourself with," Tul says, a wave of the knife showing her there will be no allowance for hesitation.

"Always thought better of you, old man," Mason says, his voice cut and out of breath. He doesn't move and the smile on his face seems almost too much for him to manage. "Working with the enemy. We have been together since the beginning. When did you switch, you owe me at least that."?

The twist in Tul's look is hideous as all his features take

on a dangerous air. Muscles tense, his body working their way into hard and sharp edges. The shadows enveloping him as his eyes turn into daggers, the dark insides cutting the air between them.

"Switch sides? You putrid, fat, waste of a human being. I have been loyal to Azhana and Parliament since they day I was born. You are the one who is the traitor. I have been forced to stand by your side and watch as you bend and all but break the rules and regulations based on your whim," Tul spits. The smile on Mason's face grows just a little bit wider. "Keeping military secrets. Working with men and women strongly considered to be enemies of the state. Don't you think I haven't been watching and documenting everything you have done since we arrived in this city? Parliament knows of you, Lieutenant, and they have ordered me to treat you no different from our Captain here."

Tul turns to her, the look on his face solid as stone and the tip of the knife not wavering even the slightest. Coleena takes a large swallow of the dry air and shifts her ankle, the weight of the hidden knife heavy against the bone where the boot is tied tight.

"Captain Armigera has been doing nothing but following the orders she has been given. Those sniveling idiots on Congress Street have all of their panties in a bunch over nothing, Tul," Mason says, the dangerous man's attention back to him. "She has vital information that they need to be made aware of and if we delay her any longer it will be of dire consequence for any and everyone within these city walls."

"Keep your trap shut," Tul barks, his nerves rattling for the first time. "I have heard what she has to say, and I wonder how she'll explain the death of a private within the wall guard itself. A death by her own hands. A man expecting a child any day now. I bet she didn't even know."

Coleena practically feels her heart stop. That can't be true. It can't be. She won't let it. The feeling of her blood draining itself from her face is water washing through her veins and settling in the deepest parts of her soul. This man is a liar. A traitor who killed Narin and is helping those who want this city destroyed. None of this can be true. But what if it is?

"You are a liar, you son-of-a-bitch," Coleena swears at him.

The corner of the man's lips form a slight hook.

"Am I? About which part? The fact that you killed a man while forcing your way into the city? Or that the man you killed is a five-year veteran of the wall guard, just recently promoted, who struggles to stay awake on duty because his wife is suffering from final trimester pains so bad he sleeps maybe one to two hours a night?"

Coleena has nothing to say. The look on that tired man's eyes as he practically stumbled out of the room flashes before her eyes. Catching a much-needed nap. That is why she had never noticed him until he was practically on top of her. He must have sneaked away to catch a rest, and she found him by accident.

The tiny fire in her belly struggles to flare. It is her fault he is dead. A picture of a woman, nine-months pregnant walks its way across the darkened room. She can see into those eyes, tears sparkling at the edges, knowing what she did to her husband.

"You monster. I did not mean to kill him. I was just trying to get into the city to warn people. I wish it could...," she says.

"What you wish and what you did are two different

things, traitor," Tul says in return. Like a cat stalking its prey, the tall lanky man begins to walk a semi-circle around where her and Mason sit, his legs always a step out of their reach. "But the man's wife will have to live with the fact that her husband's killer found justice quickly and assuredly. Now, get your ass up!"

Tul reaches down and hooks her by the shoulder with one long hand. Even his fingers are thick knives that drive between her bones as he takes his grip. She refuses to call out in pain, her eyes locked on his as she gets to her feet. There will be no satisfying his blood-lust with fear or begging. Balling her fist, she is ready to go down fighting if she has to.

"Tul, you incompetent idiot," Mason says as he shifts his weight to look at them directly. "Hasn't years in the military, particularly by my side taught you anything?"

Anger flares behind the big man's eyes. Wrenching his grip deeper into her shoulder, she is unable to hold back the tiny yelp as her bones pop beneath his unrelenting hold. The knife in his hand points its deadly edge at the throat of the large officer sitting, the look on Mason's face as relaxed as she remembers it being back in his little shack of an office.

With a swipe of his hand, the Lieutenant wipes away the blood dripping from his cheek and then cleans his hand off with the edge of his dress shirt.

"I haven't forgotten a damn thing, you fat pig. I remember every little transgression, every disobedient order, and absolutely everybody we've had to bury over the last twenty years," Tul barks back.

The smile on Mason's face grows an inch longer.

"But I'm not talking about any of that, my good man. Where are your manners? Don't you remember the military code that demands senior officers must always go first!"

In one fluid motion, the Lieutenant kicks his leg out, heel first, but Tul is too quick. His long legs, bent and ready to strike, move out of the way as Mason's boot comes forward, the thick rubber not intended for his strikes exactly who he meant to hit. Pain ruptures through the back of Coleena's leg and it buckles beneath her own weight and waning strength. Unable to hold herself, she tumbles and both her and Tul come crashing down to the ground at Mason's feet.

"Never underestimate a soldier of the Azhanian army, you fucking little ingrate," Mason growls as he rolls forward until he is on top of Tul.

A meaty fist comes crashing down on top of the man's angular face and the sound of bone and cartilage cracking fills the room. Scrambling, Coleena flexes her leg, the immediate pain subsiding as the muscles begin to work out the temporary numbness from the blow that buckled her.

"You. Would. Trade. Everything I have ever taught you," Mason continues as he pummels fist after fist into Tul's face. Blood and darkness begin to spread from the man's broken features, yet he does little to fight back. Out of breath, Mason leans back, bloody fists on his lap. "I gave you every-thing. Time, training, every secret I ever knew."

Coleena sees it before Mason ever has a chance. Like a wire trap ready to spring, Tul's arm and knife is up and into the Lieutenant's ribs before she can ever get a word out. The look on Mason's face as his eyes widen, the whites dim, and his lips move but no words come out.

"You fat fuck," Tul hisses, his lips broken and draining blood and spit in equal measures. "I have endured your shit from the moment we met. For years I have dreamed of cutting your damn throat, and for all of this, the best I get is leaving your fat corpse here in an empty hole to rot."

Twisting the knife, Coleena hears the tiny gasp escape Mason's lips as Tul pushes the dying man off of his legs. She rocks forward, her hand slipping to her boot as she watches the killer crawl up beside the officer, a large pool of dark blood forming where the knife yanks out.

"You always were a bastard, Tul," Mason chokes out, blood bubbling between his lips.

"A bastard I may be, but I'm still alive," Tul answers, the bloody knife working its way over to start its deadly work from the left side of Mason's neck.

"Not if I have anything to say about it," Coleena says, driving her own knife into Tul's side.

It is beyond explanation how easy the blade cuts into the man's skin. She has fought with knives before, watched as metal bends and chips while working its way through stone and magma. Knife shinning even in the candlelight, the tip pierces the man's body and slides in like butter.

Tul grunts as the weapon buries itself hilt deep. Turning, he looks her in the eye, those dark beads of hatred scoring into her mind.

"Stupid, bitch," he grunts.

Light flashes before her eyes as the slap rocks her head to the side and sends her sprawling across the floor. Dust kicks up into the air and the bones of her back crack as she hits the wood planks, the air in her lungs ejecting.

Rolling her head to the side, she watches Tul's dark figure shift itself until it is no longer seated on top of the dying officer. Large streams of blood pour from the wound in his side, the hole empty where the knife still sits in her hand.

"You fucking piece of shit," Tul says. "Don't know when

to quit, do you? Well, it all ends here, Captain. The gods are my witness, you will not walk out of this room."

Coleena tries to crawl backward, her whole-body aching and the dark menace quickly closing the distance between them.

A grunt escapes the man's lips as his knee buckles. Mason's bulky form lumbers up like a shadow and falls down on top of the lanky killer, and they both crash to the ground.

"Go, Coleena," Mason pleads, blood draining from his lips and his face whiter than bone. "I'll hold him as long as I can. Find Summers. He'll know what to do."

She watches as the big officer drives his forehead into the back of Tul's head, the sound of bone cracking and wood splintering filling the room. Thin powerful arms working to get free, Mason's grip tightens as his body weight shifts.

"Go, now!" Mason pleads.

Unable to do anything else, Coleena crawls her way to the door. Fumbling with the lock, she throws back the bar holding it shut as the sounds of the struggle behind her take on a feral tone. Pulling and stepping out into the street, she leaves the two men behind.

30

A sea of bodies. Massing before the front steps of Parliament, the crowd ebbs and flows like the open ocean. Layer upon layer of people, all lined up before the chained gates of the government building.

The sun sits like an ornament on top of the wall, a glowing bulb stretching the shadows and making it damn near impossible to actually know how many remain between her and the place she needs to be. Armed guards, police, and others in dark featureless uniforms hold the citizens back.

Riot is in the air. Like a nerve waiting to twitch, the shouting is aimed at those who prevent them from moving forward and also those who stand anywhere within arm's length. She hears cries to 'hang the bastard', and others, 'where's the proof?'. Everything sits on a knife's edge as she watches from the shadows.

The tension and the heat are thick with the smell of ash and shit. A stench that coats the city like a blanket and this many people in one place at one time does not help. The men and women holding them back are angry. Deep frowns, eyes of little more than pinpricks that bore into the citizens directly in front of them. Coleena can feel the danger of the rifles they hold in their hand from here.

Twitchy fingers.

Easy triggers.

One bad move, and they'll have a bloodbath on their hands. Time passes and very little changes. No word from the politicians inside. Very little movement from either the onlookers waiting for the spectacle or those here to vent their frustration about these proceedings and life in general.

Signs now hang on every lamppost and building. Scraps of paper announcing the newly appointed curfew and the punishment for disobeying the Parliamentary Order 0945.3.

Up to two years in prison and a fine up to including all repossess able belongings. No wonder there are so many organized at once. The entire city is under siege by refugees outside their walls and by the government within. Coleena can feel enough anger for them all building up inside of her.

What is happening here?

She shakes her head and takes a look back down Congress Street. There has been no sign of Tul since her escape, though she knows it is only a matter of time. Lieu-tenant Mason was a good man. A big soldier, but he was not the killer that other bastard is. A simple knife wound won't be enough to stop him. Sliding her hand around the untucked part of her shirt along the rear of her pants, she feels the hilt of the knife resting against the small of her back.

Not exactly a rifle, but she won't go down without a fight. With one more glance at the fading sun, she steps out from within the concealing shadows of the alley and begins to inch her way into the rippling mass of bodies.

Very few take notice of her as she slides in between

them. Shoulder to shoulder, it is a tight squeeze pressing her way toward the front. Some turn and protest as she makes her way closer, her presence displacing their spot within the crowd. Night is approaching quickly, and she does not have time to waste. Many turn when they see the look of determination on her face. A glare that will send even the angriest of them back.

Summers is in there somewhere. When the sun goes down, they are to hang him for crimes he did not commit. No human in this world is going to stop her from doing what she needs to do.

Sweating, stinking, and feeling the hands of a thousand people still lingering over all parts of her body, Coleena finally reaches the front. Thick chain holds them back. Little different than a crime scene, armed police keep their eyes on the growing anger, rifles held to their chest.

What is she going to do?

A hidden knife will get her nowhere. If they recognize her, she would be out of luck. Scanning the faces of the officers, she sees little help reflected in their faces. Most would probably arrest everyone just to see this whole thing ended. The western horizon now little more than a blazing red mosaic of fire, everyone including her is liable to the new curfew.

Pushing and nudging her way left, maybe she can see a way that remains open within the sealed off area. It's a long shot, but better than a frontal assault by a knife wielding lunatic.

"It is time to return to your homes," a woman officer's voice begins to call out.

Coleena looks back to where she had recently been standing near the center of the crowd. Smaller than the others, Officer Payseur, stands between two burly officers as she issues the orders.

Men and women begin to protest. A uniform heave of the crowd moves the chains back a few inches. In a show of force, she can hear the collective chambering of rounds as all the uniforms step forward, their eyes narrowing and jaws tightening.

"Please, under Parliamentary Order...," Payseur begins again.

"Oh, fuck your orders, blue coat. We are here to demand that we speak with those senators ourselves. They serve the people. They do not get to sit up in their chairs and lay out new laws without even considering the starving and dying we are doing out here every day," a man calls back, his words quickly echoing by a hundred agreements.

"All citizens are to be within their homes when the sun drops below the horizon to the west. Parliament has requested...," Payseur continues only to be cutoff by more angry voices.

"Let us in!" becomes the chant taking on an urgency among the people.

Not joining in the building mayhem, Coleena keeps her head down as she pushes and steps her way toward the diminutive officer. Very few pay any attention to her. All of them far more concerned with the anger working its way toward them like a disease.

"Officer Payseur," Coleena says, half whisper half shout with all the noise of a thousand people behind her.

The younger officer pays her no mind. Broadening her shoulders, she steps up between her two guards.

"I will repeat myself one more time. By Parliamentary Order," she starts for a final time.

"Go tell the senators they can go fuck themselves if they aren't going to listen to us," the same man calls again.

At any other time, Coleena would be having the same thoughts she can read behind the eyes of the two-armed men before her. Cut the head off of the snake. Stop the lone instigator and the rest will slowly wither away.

Here, she knows it works to her advantage. She leans over the chain, not enough to draw attention, but enough to maybe be heard over the noise and static of everyone else.

"Officer Payseur, over here," Coleena says.

The woman's eyes, full of frustration and a little fear, drops down to Coleena within the crowd. She can't tell if there is a little spark of recognition or not, by the way those two little jewels quickly turn back to the men standing at her shoulders.

"What is our next move, officers?" she asks.

Coleena swears she sees a little smile form beneath the masked faces of both.

"Payseur, I need to speak to you," Coleena yells this time.

The officer's attention finally draws even with her own. That tiny moment is clear this time, and Coleena waves her to come closer.

Hesitation slows the woman's movements before a big hand falls on her shoulder.

"It's...it's all right," she says, and the hand falls away.

"Officer Payseur, do you remember me from the other day?" Coleena asks.

Payseur frowns, her gaze moving up and down Coleena's disheveled clothes and haggard appearance.

"You are that Army Captain who tried to save me during those riots. My memory is a little hazy of what happened, but I got good word that you did what you could to prevent them from killing me," she answers.

"Seems like someone around here is good at reports," Coleena says, her eyes scanning the men and women now approaching the chain line. "I need your help. I need to speak with the senators. I have important information..."

Payseur puts up her hand.

"As does everyone else. The senators are not seeing anyone at this time. Grievances can be filed when the clerk's office opens again in the morning."

Coleena sighs.

"This will not wait until the morning, you have to believe me. There is an impending attack on the city and if we don't prepare, we could lose everything!"

The woman's mouth opens and then closes. Her attention moves to the front lines that are now pressing forward as her fellow officers begin to shift riot shields onto their shoulders and the unmarked men in the back begin to prep their rifles.

"I am under orders, Captain. No one is...," she begins.

"Fuck your orders, officer," Coleena spits back. "Come with me. Listen to what I have to say. If the senators reject what I have to offer or refuse to listen, you can judge for yourself. I promise I won't leave your side and if it doesn't work to your satisfaction you can bring me right back out here. Even arrest me for refusing curfew if you want to."

A scuffle breaks out as the chains begin to fall and the armed guards start breaking the front lines. Payseur's head bobs as her two stand-in guards move forward and Coleena is forced to step back or be trampled.

"I...," she starts to stammer.

"Officer, we don't have the time. Innocent people are going to die if we don't act. You've seen how many wait outside these walls. What do you think will happen to them if we don't do something? Just a few minutes with the senators. Take me out back and shoot me if they deem me unreliable. It won't matter," Coleena pleads.

The large hand of one of the unidentifiable armored guards, gigantic even over her large shoulders, squeezes down and begins to push her back into the crowd. Coleena stares into the woman's eyes. So much confusion. Full out brawls scatter themselves as the guards and officers begin to use batons on anyone who is too slow.

Coleena pleas with silent breath.

"Wait!" Officer Payseur yells. Running forward, she grabs onto Coleena's hand and pulls her back. "This woman is with me."

The hand on her shoulder takes a tighter grip and it takes everything she has not to grab her knife and cut the fingers off.

"You heard the woman. Let me go," Coleena demands.

"It's all right," Payseur adds with both her hands up. "The senators are offering a big reward for this woman, and they will find it of particular importance that we give them that chance. Continue on, officers. All of these people are acting upon their own free will to defy Parliamentary Order 0945.3. Use all reasonable force in accordance to the law to ensure compliance."

Without a word, the big man, his face blackened to only reveal the whites of his eyes, nods and turns back to the crowd. Even standing where she is, Coleena can see the back rows beginning to thin. The smart ones know that the fight was lost long before it ever began. Up front, they are either too angry to care or too squished to find a better way out. Taking a deep breath, Coleena turns back to the young officer.

"Thank you," Coleena says. "I didn't think I was going to get a chance."

Metal cuffs slam onto her wrist that pinch and force her to yank her hand back. Without a strong grip, Payseur loses her handle on the cuffs but quickly gets them back, her one hand reaching to grab Coleena's other.

"Don't thank me," Payseur says. "I wasn't lying when I said the senators have made it quite clear that you are to be brought before them the moment you are found."

Growling, Coleena grabs the other woman's arm and slams the remaining cuff closed.

"I need to speak to the senators. You are coming with me, but I am not your prisoner. This city is in grave danger. Take me to them, but do not for a moment think that I will let them have me without a fight."

Payseur nods and turns toward Parliament's front doors.

THE STEPS ARE MORE CRACKED AND CHIPPED THAN SHE remembers. Practically aging before her eyes, the building seems to be slumped, tired and aching with the weight of its responsibility.

None of the guards who remain try to stop them as they pass through the front entrance. Warm stagnant air splashing them in the face as they enter, the darkness within sickening and hollow.

Their footsteps echo beneath the dome. A dreadful sound of rubber slapping on hard rock. Coleena looks up at the tapestries on the walls, their images darkened and forgotten. She does not feel the judgement that should be weighing down upon her. Those scales have already been tipped. Here there is treachery and lies. Right must be returned, the balance restored.

Payseur leads the way as they reach the end of the

central theater, the door to enter the senator's chambers shut and cold.

"Are they all in there?" Coleena asks?

The officer raps on the door three times. A bell rings in the distance.

"Arrangements have been made within Parliament to cater to the needs of our senators. Due to the instability of the city, our leaders have felt it best in a matter of their self-interest that they do not leave the building. Unless of course they are protected by armed guard," Payseur says, her eyes further taking in Coleena's look.

Turning back to the door, Coleena is sure to feel the pressure of her blade against the small of her back. Payseur. Far too trusting. A good woman, following orders, but not the most reliable under stress it seems.

"Let's hope they listen to me this time," Coleena whispers as the door slides open.

Harsh light burns her eyes, droplets of water running from the pain as she is pushed in. Payseur, still chained to her, is a step behind as the door slams shut. Two hazy black blobs materialize into armed guards, their faces masked like the riot control outside of the building. Two chairs sit waiting in the center as if they are permanent fixtures, and she feels, as the young officer presses up against her, the weight of this room's importance crushing her to the point of needing one of the chairs.

"Well, well, well, isn't it, Captain Armigera," Senator Reza says, her voice just as raspy and crackling with spite.

Coleena nods her head but does not say a word.

"What do we have the honor of listening to this evening," Senator Karagoz adds, his smile stretching beyond the steeple of his fingers.

All but two of the other senators are missing, their chairs

vacant and dark. A buzz fills the room from incandescent lights burning high above, the only place in the city with reliable power. Coleena waits to respond, her eyes following the shadows along the wall. Three hooded figures wait and remain unannounced.

"We must stop this fighting within the city, Senators," Coleena starts. "Open the doors and let all of the refugees in. The dragon marches upon our city walls. If they are left to themselves, they will be slaughtered to the man, woman, and child."

Reza pushes herself away from the semi-circle table, her arms crossing over her narrow chest.

"And you would know this how? Are you telling us that you have some special communication with this 'dragon' and it told you its plans?" the senator mocks.

Coleena shakes her head.

"No, ma'am. I spoke with the caravan that was to return me to General Whittaker, and they told me of the developments on the front line. The fighting has shifted. General Whittaker marches her forces this way as we speak. If the gods are willing, they will reach us before the demons do."

Senator Karagoz knocks his chair over, his bulk slamming against the table.

"You are here telling us the army marches upon our very gates? Who authorized this?" he screams. "We were correct. The General has full intention to overthrow this government and institute her own. This 'dragon' isn't coming. It's nothing but a ruse to warrant a coup. We must arm the walls!"

Coleena, gripping the chair with everything she has, throws it to the floor.

"Are you not listening to me? The army is not marching to take over the city. We will be lucky if it reaches us in time to stop the dragon and its demons from burning us all to ashes. We need to prepare, not stand here and worry about political careers."

Senator Reza shakes her head slowly, her hands coming down to rest upon the table.

"One day you will learn, Captain. Everything is politics. As for this 'dragon' coming to our city, we have it upon good order that you have been working with the traitor, a Detective Summers. Who, by evidence and confession, has been found guilty of treason and conspiracy to overthrow the Parliamentary Government."

"That is not true! Summers has done nothing but try to protect this city and the people within it!" Coleena spits back.

"Typical of an Azhana United sympathizer. You would say anything to see those you prefer in power, even to the point of causing mass hysteria about this dragon and its need to attack our fair city," Reza adds.

"Get this over with, Reza," Karagoz cuts in. "Hang her with the other bastard, and we can get back to governing like we should be."

The elder senator puts up a hand to silence the man. He narrows his eyes but does not say another word.

"Senators," Coleena starts. "I have fought the dragon and its forces for longer than I can think to count. I have shed blood and killed countless demons to keep the people of this city safe. No one here knows more about the habits of that monster and its minions than I do. We are in grave danger. You cannot simply wave this away."

Senator Reza does just that. Her fingers flutter like paper in the wind. With a quick nod to the hooded figures waiting in the shadows, she turns back to Coleena and Officer Payseur.

"We are doing just that, Captain. Parliament is not without its own resources and though you think very highly of yourself, we are certain what you speak of will not come to fruition."

Coleena, eyes narrowing, does her best to look within the darkness of those cowls. Who are these men? What kind of bullshit are they feeding these people?

"What does it hurt if we do what I suggest? The men, women, and children outside the walls are starving. You can't leave them to their deaths. Open the doors. If I'm wrong you've done nothing but show mercy for those in desperate need of help. How does showing grace and humility to the suffering not help you in the long run?" Coleena continues to plead.

"Silence!" Reza orders. "We do not have the resources to house, nor feed, every person in Azhana. They made the choice to travel here, unbidden and unwelcome. We will not be put out within our own city for the likes of them."

"Please, Senator," Officer Payseur adds in, her voice a tiny bird's whisper. "I know very little of the dangers that the captain speaks of, but I have seen firsthand the suffering of the people. Can we not offer something to aid them? Even if the dragon does not come, isn't it our responsibility to help the citizens we govern?"

Silence falls into the room like an executioner's blade and the two senators in their high positions glare at the officer. Like a child who has spoken out of turn, Coleena can feel the other woman shrink back beneath the intensity.

"Officer Payseur, is it?" Reza asks. The young woman nods her head. "You are clearly young and new to the position. I will forgive your insolence this once, as I see the Captain's influence has its ability to spread. If we had time, I would begin questioning about a certain missing Lieutenant Mason, but we are out of time. Guards, please see that this traitor is taken down to the cells for holding. Officer Payseur, we thank you for your help, and we hope that you may see yourself out."

"Let me see their faces!" Coleena demands, stepping forward. Both guards come forward to stop her but halt at the lift of Reza's hand. "If these are the men who provide you the information in which you convict and sentence me to death, I deserve to look my accusers in the eye."

"You deserve no such respect," Karagoz shouts. "A traitor and a murderer does not make requests of Parliament."

Balling her fists, Coleena does not look the man in the eye. Her stare is for Reza only. The old woman's face locked in a challenge that Coleena must win.

"I am a veteran of the Army. More rows of service medals reside on my chest than most see in an entire career. At the minimum I deserve to see their faces," Coleena returns.

Reza rubs her chin and then nods before turning to the other senator.

"Though I am inclined to agree with you, Senator, Captain Armigera does have a valid point. Her service to this country and its people are well documented. Tainted as it is now with her actions as of late, I will give her the right to see those who have given proof of her traitorous deeds."

"I object," Karagoz yells.

She waves him off and turns to the figure waiting directly behind her. All shadows and dark cloth, the man or woman makes no move, their body little more than shadow.

"Show the captain your face so that she may go to the grave with that image being the last that she sees," Reza orders.

With the slightest of shakes, the cowl moves but is not pulled away.

"Did you not hear me? I am ordering you to reveal who you are," the senator demands.

The shadow within the cowl shifts and there is no indication from the other two who remain near the walls. Coleena watches them all. There is something going on here. They do not want her to see their faces.

With a delay built of reluctance, the shadow lifts two gloved hands and slowly removes the thick black cloth. A woman of no shocking beauty looks back at her. With pasty white skin, her dark eyes drink in the light as her face remains emotionless, a thin line of lips regarding Coleena with a silent disregard.

She knows immediately she has never seen this woman. There isn't even the slightest bit of recognition, but something is not correct. The way she is covered. As if light hurts her. Coleena squints, trying to make sense of this woman who should know nothing about her.

"Are you satisfied? These men and women are under Parliament's jurisdiction and their information is beyond scrutiny," Reza says.

She nods and the pale woman moves to pull her cowl back over her head. That is when Coleena sees what does not feel right. Pulling the cloth back to loop over her head, a tiny bit of flesh reveals itself down within the recess of her robe. A flicker of orange light sparks within the shadows. Small scales pulling apart and the power within revealing itself.

"Dragon-touched!" Coleena screams and the room rushes into a flurry of movement.

The shadowed figures, stoic and impassive, drop into a slight crouch as their dark cowls take in the room. Senator Reza, aged and strangely agile through the appearance of fragility, stands and sweeps her arms to guard any intrusion toward her secret advisors.

The guards, still not certain what to do, lower their rifles and scan the room, their targets not revealing themselves.

"Take this woman into custody!" Reza orders, her voice allowing for no questions. Sharp and to the point, her words cut like a knife, and she points a crooked finger directly at Coleena's heart. "Gag her if you must, but I do not want to hear one more word about this dragon!"

Coleena can feel the guards' presence closing in on her. Any window of opportunity she has is rapidly closing and if she is going to do anything she must do it right now. Grabbing onto Officer Payseur's wrist, she yanks the woman hard and wraps her arm around her neck before squeezing their bodies tight against her chest. Grabbing the knife tucked away into her belt, she puts the edge dangerously over the woman's neck and presses down. With a tiny gasp, Payseur tries to pull away but gives up as Coleena squeezes tighter.

"Everyone back!" she screams and for a moment everyone stops. Not a muscle is moved. The guards stop mid-step, the senators frozen with looks of hatred in their eyes, only the three dragon-touched give off an aura of relaxed persona. "I am going to walk slowly out this door, and no one is going to stop me. One wrong move and I will slit this woman open from ear to ear."

A sense of calm sweeps over the senators' eyes, and they share a quick glance before turning back to her. Reza softly clasps her hands in front of her, a tiny smile spreading across her face.

"I do not believe you would harm such an innocent woman, Captain," she says. "Why don't you put the knife down, and we'll make this easier for you and the rest of us."

Coleena spits at the woman.

"You don't know what I'm willing to do to save the people of this city. The life of one person, or anybody in this room is worth less than the city as a whole," Coleena says in return, the image of that man within the wall quickly splashing itself like a bloodstain into the back of her mind.

"Somewhere deep in that disturbed mind of yours, Captain, I think you believe that. But oh well. Kill them both," Reza commands. "Not in here. The bloodstains would be hard to get rid of."

Shock hits Coleena like a fist to the gut. Payseur goes limp in her arms, the woman's whole body shaking with the realization of what the senator just ordered. Not willing to go without a fight, Coleena tugs on the woman, forcing her to spin and in one fluid moment she has her knife spinning through the air.

A flash of light catches the blade a moment before it embeds itself into the first guard's thigh, a high-pitched scream echoing in the room. Dragging the small woman, Coleena grabs the nearest empty chair and shoves it toward the second man, his rifle still aimed at the floor as the other topples to the ground, hands swelling with blood where the hilt protrudes from the meat of his leg.

The wooden back of the furniture slams into the man's weapon and arms as Coleena drags Payseur across the room. Reaching, she grabs the barrel before the man is able to regain his position and with a yank, she brings him forward enough to drive the crown of her head into his nose.

For the thousandth time, white light burns through her vision. A lightening streak of splitting pain follows as her knees grow weak. Toppling backward, the guard losses his grip on the rifle. No hesitation, she spins the weapon around and aims toward the dais where the senators are.

The problem is they are all gone. Dragon-touched and politician alike, the room is empty other than her, Payseur, and the two men sprawled on the floor.

"You got any more cuffs?" Coleena asks.

The officer does not answer, her face empty of blood and her milky eyes staring at the two men on the ground. A streak of blood grows beneath the one's leg. With a yank, she gets the young woman's attention.

"Uh? No, that set is all I have," Payseur answers.

Coleena grunts. Typical. For once something needs to go her way. She kicks the one holding his broken nose in the leg. Red bloodshot eyes stare back at her, pupils narrowed and hatred bleeding out faster than the blood seeping between his fingers.

"You have a set of cuffs on you?" she asks. The man shakes his head no. "Fuck, looks like these will have to do."

Coleena lifts up her wrist, dragging the other woman along with it.

"Take these off and put them on these two," Coleena demands.

Payseur hesitates, her eyes locked again on the blood spread across the floor. Coleena prods her in the belly with the barrel of the rifle. Eyes clearing, the officer's eyes go from the cuffs to the weapon pressed against her belly.

"OK, give me a moment," she answers.

Hands shaking and arms unsteady, she finds the tiny keys and with a click they fall away. Coleena grabs them and steps between the two fallen men.

"Don't think of following us. If you do, I won't hesitate to finish the job," she says. With a pinch the bindings close shut on both men's wrists. "I assume you are both good men. No matter what those lost souls say, I'm doing this to save the city and its people. Don't misunderstand what I am saying. You, nor I, are more important than what this place means to the people of Azhana. I will sacrifice whatever I need to so that the dragon will not have its way. Do you understand?"

Broken nose nods his head and the other keeps his attention on the knife sticking out of his leg. With a nod of her own, Coleena steps to the one bleeding all over the floor.

"I'll be taking this back just in case," she says.

Grabbing the man's dropped rifle with one hand and the hilt of the knife with the other, she yanks and the blade slides free with no resistance. Blood fountains out and the man screams, dropping his head back in agony.

"Might want to get that tied up."

Yanking Payseur by the arm, Coleena heads out the door and slams it shut behind her.

31

___

The domed center hall of Parliament sits empty, darkened in shadow and a relic of the past. Vacant, the structure feels more like a tomb than the living embodiment of the people's power and will to survive. Fighting and shouts, the anguish of the angry public cuts into the early evening air from outside. It appears the officers stationed and charged with crowd control are having a much harder time than they expected.

Coleena squeezes down on her young escort's arm.

"Look, I like you, Officer Payseur. You are a good woman and you've tried your best with the duty you swore to uphold. I can respect that," she says, her words short and to the point. "You heard what the senator said in there. She sentenced you to death just to shut me up. Everything is clearly wrong here, and we need to stop it. Do you understand?"

Payseur's eyes are locked on the door where they can still hear the screams of the bleeding man through the thick barrier. Coleena grabs the woman by the shoulder, squeezes until she gets a tiny yelp, and forces her to turn her eyes away and look at her. It takes a moment but the thought process clears in the young officer's eyes. She nods yes.

"Good, now take this," Coleena says handing the woman the extra rifle. "Do you have any idea where the cells are in this building?"

Payseur hesitates before turning to a closed door across the room. An unremarkable door, it sits alone in a dark corner with nothing but a small placard hanging on the wall beside it.

"I'm not certain, but I would guess they are downstairs," she says, her voice barely above a whisper.

"Come on then," Coleena says.

Pushing the woman in front of her, she takes up the rear as they cross the empty space, their passing accompanied only by the thoughts in their own minds. The fighting outside takes on a fevered pitch as the yelling and cursing grows louder. Inside these sacred walls their boots echo and no one pays them any mind, even the screaming man they left behind seems to fade into the distance.

Twisting the handle, the door swings easily as it opens to a stairwell that leads both up to higher floors and down to the lower levels. Pointing with her rifle, she lets Payseur take the lead, the dark gloom of the stairs filling in around them.

"You wouldn't happen to have a torch or maybe even a flashlight would you?" Coleena asks, her eyes struggling to adjust to the darkness.

Ghosts and demons dance within the shadows as they descend into the belly of Parliament. Cool air tickles their skin as the hard rock of the stairs is unforgiving against their feet, the walls dead and not caring for their needs.

"Hopefully they have working power down at the bottom floors like they do up above," Payseur says, both of them groping the wall to secure their steps.

A thousand slaps of feet against stone with rubber clapping and echoing in the empty chamber until they are finally able to reach the bottom. Abruptly and with no warning, their only acknowledgment that they have reached their destination is the shift in the air to a stagnant stench of dread and misery.

Nothing leaves this place. Coleena can feel it in her bones. The weight of all of this stone, the age, and the history. An iron door sits closed before them, small cracks of light coming from the seams and beckoning them to come through.

"Wouldn't happen to have a key would you?" Payseur asks, attempting to twist the handle and showing that it doesn't move.

Coleena sighs. She should have grabbed one of the guards keys. They probably had a way to get in. She looks at the officer and all she gets is a shrug for her effort.

There is a set of keys in her pocket, all she has left of the man she killed, but there should be no way those work. This isn't the wall, these are the seldom recognized cells held beneath the government building. Her best guess leaves it no more than a few dozen people in the entire city who know these even exist.

"Might as well try," Coleena says.

With a crack of her fist, she raps on the door several times, the sound loud and hollow in its echo. They both wait for what feels like forever before she tries again. What are the chances that someone is actually stationed inside?

"Was worth a try," Coleena says. "Looks like we'll have to..."

"State your business," a gruff voice calls from behind the door.

Coleena looks down at Payseur before screwing her

tongue up into the back of her throat and once again trying her best.

"We have another to join the traitor," Coleena growls, her voice as low as she can make it and scratching with every word.

"You don't have your keys?" the man on the inside asks, a hint of annoyance in his words.

"Had to pull this one on Senator Reza's demand. Didn't have time to check if I had them. You know what would happen if I didn't snap at that bitch's every word," Coleena lies.

A small chuckle from the other side.

"You sure are correct with that one. Step back a moment," the man orders.

Locks disengage and the handle turns as Coleena steps in front of Payseur, her hands behind her back and the rifle hidden from view. She does her best to keep the tiny officer pressed to her side enough the man inside will see her and not suspect anything. Slouching, she puts on the best angry and desperate look she can on her face, everything to sell this lie for as long as she can.

Light floods her eyes as the door pushes open, a crack at first and then enough to get an arm through.

"Let's see what you got," the guard says.

Coleena squints, fighting the urge to cover her eyes with the hands that are supposed to be bound behind her back. To her luck, Payseur does not say anything that would give them away.

"Not much to look at, is she?" the gruff old man asks.

Years of beard stretch from the man's chin, gray and thin it reaches the middle of his chest in a rats nest of little wisps and bits of dust and food that has not been combed away in years. He tilts his head toward Payseur, his eyes doing a one over on her as well. Coleena can smell the grease and the body stink leaking from the room.

A dungeon.

A cesspool where people are brought to be forgotten about.

How many lives have been lost down here?

She waits, her hand squeezing the grip of the rifle tighter as the time drags on. The old man chews on his lower lip, the wheels in his head working very slowly with gears that have not been oiled in ages.

"Well, let's get this show on the road. Time is a'wastin and from what I'm told, one of our guests is going to be putting on a show tonight," the old guard says.

He pushes the door open, a slow movement that grinds and slices like a knife through the silent air of the stairwell. Coleena cannot keep the smile off of her face as she swings the rifle around, the barrel coming up beneath the man's chest.

"Back away, old man," she orders. "I have no reason to harm you tonight, but do not think I won't if I have to."

He looks down at the weapon and then back up to her face, his features unchanging. Officer Payseur steps in beside her, and he does little more than give a tiny shrug.

"So be it. Who am I stop two pretty ladies," he says, no fear in his voice. "Most excitement I've seen down here in years. Take your pick, most of them aren't in any shape to walk out of here anyway."

The wave of a thin arm leads them down a row of cells at least a dozen long. Single bulbs flicker between every other one, their buzzing a droning that grates at the ears immediately. Coleena fights the urge to dig her palm into the side of her head already.

"Which one of these has Detective Summers?" she asks, her eyes watering.

The stink down here grows thicker the longer they are exposed to it. Death. Decay. Human waste and lost dreams. The walls are thick with it. Shadows are the only thing that makes a home down here. A place to lock monsters away and forget about the key.

"Center left," the man answers. "Not a talkative one, though from what I've gotten, he's different. Not much like the others."

Coleena does not wait for him to explain. Long strides cover the distance in a few steps.

"Why is that?" Officer Payseur asks.

"Most they bring down here are real hard asses. If they have any mind left to them that is," he responds, his tone of voice conversational and without much emotion. "Of course they all lose their mind after a while. From him, he seems rather bright. Friendly if you ask me. Doesn't really fit in a place like this, you know?"

Coleena looks into the cell. Darkened by the shadows cast from the simple bulbs, she can see a figure chained to the wall. Arms up and wide, it is difficult to see if it is actually Summers.

"Roland, is that you?" she asks, impossible to keep the hope out of her voice.

The figure's head begins to move. A shaking at first and then a slow lift. Even here she can see how gaunt and pale he has become.

"Coleena, is...is that you?" he asks, his voice hoarse and broken.

"Open these doors," she demands. "Is there any water down here?"

The guard nods. "I keep a barrel over in a small closet at

the end. They don't send much down here, but I do my best to spread it around as evenly as I can."

Walking past, he hands her a large ring of keys. Like a relic of an ancient past, they are all iron skeletons as heavy as the boots on her feet. Outside of a museum, she hasn't seen these ever in actual use.

"Which one is it?" she calls to the man.

He isn't anywhere to be seen, a single door at the end of the hall pulled open.

"Doesn't matter, you aren't getting any of those doors open," a female voice hisses.

Coleena turns, her rifle up and ready. Officer Payseur stands by the door, a cloaked figure behind her and a dark gloved hand wrapping around the back of her neck.

One of the advisors.

Dragon-touched.

"You thought your little antics up there would get you somewhere, didn't you? Stupid woman. Our master will...," the creature begins.

The sound of the bullet exploding from the gun is a bomb going off in the tight confines of the cell block. Ears go numb and pain rockets through brains as the shot rips through the cloak below the shadows where its neck should be.

Bright orange blood fountains into the air, a spray that hits wall and ceiling as they fall backward. Officer Payseur, legs giving away, falls forward. Three more shots ring out, the concussion reverberating through the wall as the enemy stumbles toward the door.

"Get Summers out of there!" Coleena demands.

She follows as her target goes to flee back up the stairwell. There will be no mercy. Burning magma smokes against the stone, small streams that smell of sulfur quickly filling in between the stench that coats everything between these walls.

Turning the corner, Coleena follows the running robes, the material billowing out in flight. She is hardly four steps up before the wall beside her head erupts in exploding rock. Bullets ping in the narrow corridor, shards and dust filling the air as she dives and lets her self roll back down to the bottom.

Body aching, she feels like a truck hit her and then backed up to finish the job. Biting back the pain, she crawls toward the dungeon, the door hanging open. A shot skims the back of her thigh as she tries to get away, a rupture of fire shooting through her leg.

Falling to her side, she spins and squeezes the trigger of her own rifle. Bullets fly out with no target, just the pure hope that they cover her retreat.

Hands grab her shoulder and pull her through the doorway. Slamming shut, she does not hear the crack against stone, her ears a thunderous ring that spins the world before her eyes. Locks are set into place, the old guard making sure each one is complete before turning back to her.

"Are...OK?" he asks, his voice a call from a hundred yards away though he stands at the bottom of her feet.

Coleena tries to shake her head, her heart pounding, and her leg bleeding across the floor.

"Is there another way out of here?" she asks, her teeth gnashing together to push back the pain.

The old man smiles. A devious look. One laced with a secret only he knows.

"Let's get you patched up," he says. Looking over at Payseur, "if that is the man you want, take those keys and get him out of there. It won't take them long to figure out how to get that door open."

A loud slam hits the iron barrier and the frame shakes. Pushing herself across the floor, Coleena bites down and yelps through the bile in her mouth as a dark stain stretches itself along her trail.

"This should do the trick," the man says. Pulling a long strip of fabric, he is merciless as he wraps it around the meat of her thigh and pulls it nice and tight. "Not gonna last forever, but it will get you out of here."

She fights the urge to roll her eyes into the back of her head. Her stomach heaves and a splitting crevasse works its way through her brain. Rolling her head toward the cells, she sees that Payseur has Summers lifted from beneath his shoulders. As frail as he has become, he still dwarfs the petite officer.

"Now, about that exit," Coleena says.

The guard winks and puts a finger up to the side of his nose.

"Thought they could lock an old man down here to take care of these poor bastards. Didn't think it would be a lifetime gig," he begins to chatter. Coleena bares her teeth, and he shakes his head before looking back at the door as it shakes with another good wack. "Just this way. There is always a second way out. This would be a trap if there wasn't. They sealed it off a dozen years ago, but they can't stop a stubborn old man. No they can't. Worked it free, stone by stone, nail by nail. I'm probably the only person in the world who knows it's still available."

With more strength than she imagined he had, the guard helps her off the ground, his arms solid iron and his shoulders made of bricks. Coleena leans against him, both sliding toward the small closet at the end of the row of cells.

"Even closed off the entire door. Made it into this storage room. Large enough for a water barrel and a poor old man to hang himself. Probably wished I'd actually do it," he says before spitting on the ground. "Goes to show them."

Running his gnarled fingers along the back wall of the little alcove, Coleena watches as dust and cobwebs fall away. There really is no other space in here. The barrel is an old whiskey style, charred marks stretching from the bottom. She isn't certain but it is hard to mistake the smell of alcohol still lingering in the background.

"Ah, got it," he says. A small latch presses in and the whole corner slides away, a gust of stagnant air rushing to meet them. "This is my little secret."

He taps his nose again as Payseur and Summers step through. The next crash against the dungeon door sends cracks thicker than her finger through the rock wall, chips falling down to the floor.

"You are coming with us, aren't you?" Coleena asks, the sudden realization that she is damning another good man to death hitting her like a punch to the gut.

"Hurry now with yourself. I'll just slow you down. Plus, someone has to stay and watch over these last souls. No matter how bad they were before they got down here," the old man answers.

Coleena takes a hard look at the darkened cages. None of them make any noise and the smell is too strong. He's probably the only living person down here. She nods her head.

"We'll lock the door behind us. Take care of yourself."

He smiles and then winks. Hoping on one leg, she finds the walls cool against her skin as she crosses the threshold into the hall beyond. Without a noise, the opening shuts behind her, and she bolts the half dozen locks keeping it shut.

"Good luck old man," she whispers.

Payseur and Summers wait at the end of a narrow hall, a single light bulb flickering between her and them. The detective looks stronger as he leans against the officer, his head no longer slumped against her shoulder.

Away from death's grip. Coleena takes a deep breath and hobbles her way down the passage, leg burning and shouts making its way through the thick stone behind her. No time to wait or regret what is done. Making it to her two companions, she does not hesitate.

Excruciating step after excruciating step, they leave the dungeons behind them. Now on to Plan B. Save Parliament City from itself.

32

———

Night is a full-blown blanket covering every street in the city with its dark embrace as they slide a rear door to Parliament open. The heat is stifling beneath the cloud covered sky. Darkness above them, shadows around them. Few lights cut through the void as they move gingerly across the street, the taste of dust and ash quick to fill their mouths.

"Where do we go from here?" Payseur asks.

She looks at Coleena, long dark streaks of filth running down her pale face and her breaths in short bursts from helping the detective climb out of that demon infested building.

"That's up to him," Coleena answers between large breaths of her own.

The pain in her leg throbs with every pulse of her heart. Cold sweat trickles down the back of her neck, old aches and pains returning to her body. She can feel her joints pop and for a moment she would kill for another taste of Phydel's magic remedy.

"One Church Chapel," Summers gets out, his voice hoarse and broken.

What color had returned to his face washed away with the exertion that it took to get him up those stairs. It felt like miles passed beneath their feet, though it couldn't have been more than a level or two.

"Not a good time to be praying," Coleena says with a grunt.

The strength in her leg is draining, and she can feel the blood seeping its way through her bandage.

"Not to the gods," Summers says weakly. "Our prayers will go out to someone who will actually answer."

Officer Payseur looks at Coleena and then shifts the man's weight back onto her body. Turning north they head into the streets, deserted where the fights between parliament forces and the citizens do not linger.

Shouts and fires deeper in, but yet out of sight. A city on the edge of a knife. Coleena can hear the riot from the other side of Parliament. Those men and women. They are not taking no for an answer. A warm spot opens in her heart. Maybe this city isn't dead after all.

Then the gun fire starts. A pop or two that could be anything, but then it begins to string. Short bursts turn into entire magazines worth.

The screams. Violent and terrifying. She stops and the flashes cutting through the night air are horrifying. The war front returning home.

What are they going to do?

Turning back, she catches up to Payseur and Summers. Sweat drips off of both of them like running water as they heave for breath in the heat of the night.

"We best get going," Coleena says. "Everything is about to

crumble into itself. We don't have any idea what those monsters in Parliament have planned."

Summers coughs and then straightens up, stopping their forward momentum.

"Yes, we do," he responds. "They made it loud and clear when they took me after the attack. They wanted Azhana United, but I'd die before I gave it up. They also know that killing me won't stop them either. With a loss of hope I thought I'd never say, reading between their words, I'm fairly certain the doom for us and the city itself is coming."

"What is that?" Officer Payseur asks, shifting so she can hold onto more of the detective's weight.

"The dragon's armies are coming, and they are going to open the gates," he says, his voice low and full of defeat.

"Walk them right in. Why in the fuck would they do that? It's those Dragon-touched, they've had this planned the whole time," Coleena says.

Disbelief.

Shock.

All of it hits her like a truck. She figured the politicians were willing to sell out the security of the city, the entire world if it meant securing their positions of power, but not like this. What do they think; the dragon is going to work with them like a new president or king?

Summers laughs, a wet sound from deep in his lungs.

"Those fools couldn't plan anything beyond their next dinner. You have to be correct, it's those advisors. They have some kind of hold on them. It's almost like they are different people when they are in the room," he says before slumping back into Payseur's arms.

"We need to hold them off as long as we can. General Whittaker is marching the army here as we speak. She'll be here within a week," Coleena says.

Summers shakes his head.

"Won't be soon enough. We need to get to the chapel."

"And what will you be doing there?" a deep, raspy voice asks.

Shadows shiver and slide across the street like a living liquid. A wave of nausea bites into the back of Coleena's throat. She knows who this is.

A predator in the night, they are lucky he didn't kill them outright. Petty Officer Tul. Stepping into the dim light of the street, he is the seven pits of hell risen. Blood seeps from open wounds in his forehead, over his left arm, and from the hole punched beneath his rib.

Violence burns bright in his eyes. Hatred of the purest sense. The knife in his hand, blood-red, waits in a steady hand.

"Let us go, Tul," Coleena says. "We have to stop them. They are going to get everyone killed."

The man shakes his head, a movement that shifts the darkness but not the fires burning within those two dark sockets. Short movements, like a cat stalking its prey, he slides to position himself where they cannot pass.

"The only people going to be killed tonight are the three traitors I see in front of me. Parliament and its leaders brought this country back from the brink of extinction. Do you think they would let it all be destroyed?" He coughs and it racks his whole body, the anger in his eyes flaring brighter. "The only thing threatening our world is you. Unable to understand your betters, you will do anything to see your-self in power."

"That is bullshit and you know it. Even Lieutenant Mason knew the truth and did what he could to stop you," Coleena says.

The soldier spits on the ground, a dark wad that splatters in front of their feet.

"Fat bastard was a traitor from the beginning. He got what he had coming and it was by the graces of Parliament that I even let him live as long as I did. Fucking mistake, but one I do not intend to make again," he says.

Not wanting anything more to do with this, Coleena turns her rifle toward him, the fire in her belly flaring. Searing pain bites into her shoulder as the knife that was in his hand cuts right through her shirt and deep into the flesh of her arm before she could even realize he threw it.

Screaming, she drops the weapon as she spins and falls to her knees, the rifle scattering across the gravel covering the road. Moving like a shadow, Tul is on them before they can react.

A grunt punches out of Payseur's mouth as she topples over, her knees buckling and dropping both her and Summers to the ground. Coleena grabs the end of the knife, a flash of red crossing her eyes as she grips and tries to yank it free.

The world spins with an explosion in her mind as Tul's fist slams into the side of her jaw. Blood fills her mouth, the taste of iron mixed with grit as she collides with the cracked pavement, an unhealthy meeting that rattles the teeth not already loosened.

"Let me help you with that," the murderer says.

Reaching down, he rolls her over, boot on her chest he rips out the knife. Blood bursts into the air and Coleena's scream is primal as it pierces the chaos of the night. A thousand knifes rip the back of her throat. Her lungs choke as they fill with blood, and he presses more of his boot into the center of her chest.

The pounding of her heart throbs in her ears and all she

can look at through the tears burning her eyes is the dark shadows cutting holes through the man's scarred face. No longer old and lanky, he's a monster and no expression other than hatred crosses his sharp features.

"I'm going to leave you for last," he says, his voice dropping to a whisper. "You put me through a lot and for that I'm going to enjoy this. Your friends will die first. I'll make them scream and you are going to watch."

Waving the knife in tiny circles above her face, she watches as droplets of her own blood drip from the sharp edge.

"Don't do this, Tul. You were a soldier once," she pleads.

He spits in her face.

"None of you know what it means to be a real soldier. After I'm finished with your accomplices over here, I'm going to take my time with you," he says, a tiny snarl crawling up his face. A look of disgust replacing the hatred. "You will beg for mercy when all of this is finished. Death will be your only way..."

His last words gurgle with bubbling blood as the explosion rocks his body. Blood strains his shirt darker, a pool spreading from the right side of his chest. Gritting his red teeth, he turns around toward the others, muscles taught through the pain and ready to strike.

Payseur is on her knees, rifle end smoking and hands shaking. Her eyes are wide, a look of disbelief painted across her features.

"You'll pay for this, you little bitch," Tul says.

The woman fires again and the soldier's body rocks back a step, his boots twisting with Coleena's legs before sending him to the ground. A gasp of breath finds its way through his throat already choking with blood as his body hits the pavement, the pain tearing through his body etching its way across his face. Scrambling to her feet, Coleena, arm bleeding profusely, takes the rifle away from Payseur.

"It didn't have to be this way, Tul," she says staring down at the dying man.

His laugh is short, rivers of blood draining from his lips.

"Fuck you, traitor. Nothing will stop what you have coming to you. In the end, you and all those like you will be punished for what you have done," he coughs out.

Coleena pulls the trigger one more time and Tul's body goes limp for the last time. Turning around, Payseur and Summers are back on their feet, one shaking from shock and the other from exhaustion.

"We need to keep moving," Summers says.

Taking a look down the street, the fires of the riots are beginning to chase them. The city is falling into chaos beyond a manageable point. Without a word, Coleena falls into step behind them as they disappear into the darkness, their nightmare still ahead of them.

THE PLAGUE THAT IS KILLING PARLIAMENT CITY IS SPREADING faster than they can move. Fights between armed patrols and the citizens are around practically every corner. Usually one sided, police and guards in armored riot gear pound men and women with batons and fists. The use of firearms seems to be limited to those closest to the Parliament building. At least so far.

Making their way more than six blocks to the north, the three of them stay within the shadow's deadly grasp as much as they can. Hiding in alleys to avoid foot patrols. Even angry mobs begin to follow them until they see the rifles split between Coleena and Payseur and the amount of blood being left in their wake.

Feeling dizzy, Coleena leans up against a light pole, the bulb burned out or the electricity is cut. It is hard to tell. As dark as their surroundings can be, they see the soft orange glow of the lights they are looking for around the corner and on the opposite side of the street.

One Church Chapel.

Bells ring on the hour, every hour. A soothing reminder that there can be some normalcy in this world. Tonight they are silent. A heavy blanket of mourning filling the air in a night of chaos and death.

"What is so important about this church, Summers?" Coleena asks, the words hard to get out.

She doesn't want to tell them, but her breath was lost a block ago and her heart races like rock rolling downhill. She needs to sit and close her eyes. There isn't much left for her to give.

"I know a man inside," the detective answers, his body looking almost as bad as hers. "He'll help us out and get word to those waiting for me."

"The church is part of Azhana United as well?" Officer Payseur asks wiping away the drenching sweat covering her face. A streak of blood makes its way across her forehead in a thick line. "You all are far more connected than anyone ever thought."

A small smile creases Roland's pained grimace.

"Everyone has a stake in the survival of this world, Officer. Would it surprise you that much if men and women of the cloth had a hand in keeping the people within this city safe? Not everyone truly believes we have anything to do with the violence of this city."

"I guess not," she responds, her eyes set on the road ahead. "The evidence is just so convincing."

"Open and shut case, isn't it," Coleena adds. "All perfectly tied together."

The petite detective looks over, her face aging so quickly beneath the exhaustion and the realities of their situation. Coleena can see it in her eyes. Like a curtain has been pulled back, the horror of what it will take to survive all of this is finally settling in.

"If you look at it like that, then I guess you are correct," Payseur answers. "Makes you doubt everything you've been told up till now, doesn't it?"

Roland gives her shoulder a little squeeze as he tries to straighten himself up.

"Don't blame yourself. Those in power do their damnedest to ensure that everyone has every reason to believe what they say. Knowledge is as much their enemy as the rifle or the blade. You've done the best you can with what you have been given. We wouldn't be here without your help," he says to her.

She looks down at the rifle within her grasp. Cold to the touch now, Coleena can see her eyes focusing on the barrel's end. Envisioning the tiny puffs of smoke that linger after the bullet ejects and hits its target.

"You did what you had to," she whispers, sliding up beside the woman. "He made his choices and with them came consequences."

"I'll have to live with mine as well," she says, the look on her face beginning to harden.

"Yes, you will. Never forget, it was him or us. Many good people have died because of actions associated with that man. Tonight, our only objective is to save as many as we can. We cannot possibly save them all," Coleena says.

"Spoken like a true soldier," Payseur responds, her shoulders cracking as she rolls them backward.

The world spins before Coleena's eyes before she can say another word forcing her to squeeze them shut. She shakes her head to straighten everything out.

"You OK?" Summers asks.

Clutching her shoulder, Coleena nods in return.

"We need to keep moving," she says, any other words becoming too much of a strain on her body.

Gripping tighter onto Payseur, Summers helps lead the way. Shuffling steps. Short, shallow breathing and a marathon of torture covering that final block.

Dry air. Crumbling road. Arm numb and soul drained. What would she do for a drink of water and a good night's rest? Gritting her teeth, Coleena stays with them, through sheer determination, she will not fall behind.

"Ah, fuck," Summers groans.

Falling to the side, both him and the smaller officer lean heavily against a brick building and slip back into the shadows blocking them from the street ahead. Coleena feels her heart skip a beat. Through everything they've been through in the past week, this is the first time she has heard him speak like this.

"What's going on?" Coleena asks, what concern she can put into her words drowning with exhaustion.

Slipping forward, she peers around the edge of the brick wall, the structure highly cracked and leaning. A line of armed guards. Four of them spread around the stone stairs leading up into the entrance of the church.

Black uniforms. No military insignia.

Parliament.

"What the fuck are they doing guarding the church?"

Coleena asks, bloodless forcing her to slide down against the building.

Every muscle in her body aches other than the ones gone numb. Throat dry, she knows she her tank is empty. There is nothing left to give. Even the darkness of the street night seems too thick. Her heart feels like a lead ball in her chest. A deep breath does nothing to ease the pain.

"I have no idea," Summers says. "There is no way they know about my man on the inside. They were always careful and are there only for an emergency like this."

"You planned for this?" Payseur asks.

Roland shrugs his shoulders. "You have to think of everything if you are going to be ready for the impossible. Who would have ever thought this city would be so close to falling? Plus, their only real duty is to get our message out. Nothing more."

Taking a deep breath, Coleena stiffens and pushes away from the building and up onto the balls of her feet. Knees weak, she wavers in her attempt to stand.

"Doesn't matter how they know. We need to get inside that building, and they are in the way. Any chance there is some secret entrance you know about?"

Summers shakes his head.

Looking at Payseur, she doesn't see any help coming from the petite officer. Checking her rifle, she has six shots left. Not going to help much in a fire fight.

"How many rounds you have left?" she asks.

Payseur looks at her weapon.

"Ten in the magazine, one in the chamber," she answers.

Not the best of odds, but it should get them inside. Taking a deep breath and biting back the pain, Coleena rolls her shoulders and reaches for the other rifle.

"The both of you need to get into that church. Give me what you have left and I'll draw them off. Once you have your opening, get moving. You'll have one chance at this," she instructs.

"But, they'll kill you," Officer Payseur says.

Roland is already shaking his head.

"We need you in this, Coleena. You may be good with that rifle, but I doubt you are going to kill all four of them with ten shots," he says.

Ejecting her magazine from her rifle, she puts it down on the ground and reaches for Payseur's who quickly pulls it back away.

"I don't intend on killing them. Draw their attention and then get them to chase me. Not very far in this condition, but enough to get you in those doors. Send your message, come find me after."

Coleena goes to grab the other weapon again but can't as it's kept out of her reach.

"That is a stupid idea and you know it," Summers adds.

"It's all we got, Roland," Coleena says. "Plus..."

Her words are cut off as Officer Payseur rips the magazine out of her hand.

"Plus, you two are the only ones who really know what in the hells is going on around here. You both also look like shit and can barely move. Even if you drew their attention, you'd make it what? A block, maybe two?"

Stuffing the ammunition into her pocket, the young woman checks her rifle again. Eyes hard, jaw set, she isn't shaking anymore.

"You don't have to do this," Coleena says.

She knows how the woman feels. Lost. Confused. Doesn't know who is right and how this whole thing had gone so wrong. The only thing she is certain of is she has to do something. Would have made a great soldier if she ever had the chance.

"This city is all I know, Captain. If it falls, I fall with it. You two seem to be the only ones doing anything about it, and if this is how I can help, I will. Anyway, I don't plan on getting caught, or killing any of them. You only need a few moments, correct?"

Coleena looks at Summers. They both look like death warmed over.

"A few moments, that's all," she lies.

Could take them minutes to clear the road and climb those steps. Probably longer than she has with sixteen shots.

"Good. Wait here until I get them running. Do not wait for me. I'll come find you," Payseur says.

Without saying anything, she steps up and wraps her arms around Coleena. The hug is a lot stronger than it should be. She feels the young woman take a deep breath.

"Thanks for everything, Captain. Not many have ever stood by my side like you have," she says.

Sweat or tears run down the side of the woman's face and Coleena feels the all too familiar sting in her own eyes. They both know the chances of this working. For either of them.

"Go, now. Time is running out," Coleena says.

The other woman nods, gives Roland a final look, and turns into the darkness. Retracing their steps, she is lost within moments.

Summers slides against the wall and lets himself lean against her good shoulder. He's warm, A feeling up until now she didn't realize she missed.

"Do you think she can do it?" he asks.

Coleena doesn't know what to say. Staring up into the darkness of the sky, she thinks about what she would be doing in her situation. Sneaking through the alley, she'd make her way to the next cross street. Set up and fire one or two rounds. Make sure they hit something close, enough to get them to look.

Exposing herself, she'd make a show of running. If her shots are worth it, all four will try to chase her down, especially if they see her as something they can quickly catch.

"Better than the two of us. Ol'weak in the knees and Ms. Bleeding from too many knife wounds," Coleena answers, the last coming out in a wet cough.

Her head is one splitting migraine, and she feels almost naked without the rifle. Flexing her good hand, she still feels the knife tucked into her belt. At least almost naked.

Time passes and she begins to worry. What happened to Payseur? Maybe she ran into trouble trying to find her way around. There is no way to tell how bad the riots are across the city. So many fires burn in the distance and pockets of trouble could be anywhere.

"Do you think..." Roland starts.

Pop!

Pop!

Both her and Summers jump to the corner, their eyes on the men guarding the church. Two lay on the ground crawling, one is crouched and other is behind a large block of concrete, waiting for another round of attack. No one moves.

The guards wait.

They wait.

Another round sends bits of rock into the air from the stone block above a guard's head. Then the shouts follow. The men return fire, and then they are off. All four of them.

Coleena grabs Summers under the shoulder with her

good arm, and they step out. She sees a dark figure racing down the street, rifle in hand, Payseur running for her life.

Dragging the detective with her, she splits her attention between the door ahead and the pursuit. The men are closer now that they have reached the end of the street. Without looking, the woman they chase turns left and disappears down another street.

Already running out of strength, she can see the silhouettes of the guards slow, almost creep to the street corner where Payseur turned.

"We have to get moving," Coleena says through gritted teeth. "She might have lost them already."

Summers grunts and begins to drag his bad leg faster. More gunfire erupts and then there are shouts. Coleena spares a look, and she sees all four of them round the corner in a hurry. Taking a deep breath, she mutters a few words under her heavy breathing.

"Take care of yourself, Officer. Don't let them catch you."

Six grueling steps later, they are at the entrance to the chapel. Pressing on the door, it slides open without any resistance. One good thing you can always count on. The church and its inability to protect itself.

The poor.

The sick.

The needy.

Looters.

Anyone can walk right in. This evening it is a gift from the gods. Inside, the smell of incense and the thick heat of smoke and bodies is as thick as oil in the air. Pews, lit by candles burning on all four walls, are filled to the max.

Coleena can't count how many people are inside. Half of them turn to stare at them, a mix of fear and desperation in so many of their eyes. Young and old, the collection could be a good percentage of the whole city for all she knows.

Sobs cut through the silence of the room, the closest backing away at the sight of her and Summers. She figures it's most likely her with the trail of blood she is leaving with every step.

"Who are we looking for?" she whispers.

Roland doesn't answer. His head sways from side to side and it's a miracle he is even walking.

"Roland!" she says, louder this time and with a good shake.

The man's eyes come open, and he looks around, almost surprised that they made it in.

"The priest," he says with a nod of his head toward the dais at the back of the room ready to burst at its seams.

Already the old man is heading toward them, his long white robes trailing across the floor and his arms extended. Hair growing in a semi-circle around the back of his head, the light brown locks are peppered with shades of white that extend past shoulders grown narrow and stooped. Warm brown eyes are opened wide with worry and his thin lips move but no words come out as he reaches them.

Hesitating, he doesn't say a word, but his gaze traces over both of them.

"We need help, Father," Coleena gets out.

The man nods, "I can see that. How about we get you both to the vestibule in the back."

People still shy away as they pass them down the carpeted aisle. Coleena tries to look them in the eye, but none of them will match hers for more than a moment.

A string of gunfire. More than one rifle at a time echoes from outside the building. Men, women, and children shout and many begin to cry again. The violence is drawing closer.

She can feel the vibrations working their way through the floor.

"Payseur," Coleena whispers.

Many in the audience are watching the entrance doors like she is. They are waiting for their death to walk in and end it all, though Coleena knows it will remain outside. Tiny tears burn the edges of her eyes. Her chest aches and the body she has been given begins to collapse.

Knees buckling, all the priest has a chance to do is catch Summers before she hits the ground and rolls onto her back. Another death at her hands. A life she could not protect.

How many more will die?

Her eyes trace the painted glass within the dome above. Dark images of saints and the demons they fight. She recognizes some of this. Deep inside she wonders what side she is on.

Shadows close in around her. Voices speak words she cannot make out for they are far too fast and a mile away. No strength remains in her arms or legs.

It doesn't matter. Payseur is dead and she is still alive. If there were any gods, how could any of this make any sense?

Vision blurry, eyes on fire, she watches the priest look down at her. He is saying something. She doesn't care.

All of this is lost. She is done.

33

———

The world spins yet the ceiling made of wood beams and open timber above is not so high. Nausea fills her stomach, pinching and turning, she wants to vomit but every piece of her body is on fire. Regardless of the warmth in the air and the burning of her skin, for some reason, she shivers with cold.

Tiny candles flicker with light along the wall, empty and white. The room is too simple for her, almost as empty as the interrogation room back at the jail. She tries to lift her head and a needle shoots its way through her brain. Taking a deep breath rattles the furthest reaches of her lungs and a cough fills her throat with phlegm.

Letting her head roll to the side, she can see the edge of the bed she lies on. Simple white sheets and a mattress hardly thick enough to keep her off the frame. A large red recliner, old, judging by the wear and tear of its edges, is occupied by Summers. Head fallen forward, chin resting on his chest, he sleeps beside a pile of papers and an open book.

Taking another deep breath, this one nice and slow, she

lets the taste of bile push itself away and her mouth fills with the sweet taste of roses and dust from the air. Looking up at the corner of the low rafters, there are cobwebs darkening the flat white color and the realization of what time it is finally hits her.

Sunlight gleams in the window, a singular domed cut in the wall with a barred opening. Birds sing outside, a feeling of normalcy in a world lost to chaos.

She tries to bolt out of the bed, but her body rejects that notion. Ripping pain pulses through every muscle in her body. Her vision swims. Heart racing, she lets herself lay back down.

For the moment it is only Summers and her. They must be safe. He wouldn't be sleeping if it wasn't. Turning her head to the side, she feels the bones within crack and a slight pressure release.

She takes a deep, slow breath.

"Roland, you OK?" she asks.

The man's head rocks to the side, and he coughs slightly. No one makes any noise from the other side of the single unpainted door leading into the room. Everything is quiet, only the birds outside the window making any kind of commotion.

"Roland, wake up," she demands, this time a little louder.

His dark eyes flutter. Shoulders rolling, he lifts his head and sits back. She can practically see parts of him awakening as muscles stiffen and the haze of rest washes from his face to quickly be dragged down by exhaustion once more.

"I see that you are awake," he says, his voice hoarse and cracked.

Rolling back until she is looking up at the ceiling, she takes another deep breath and lets it out slowly.

"Yes, but what is going on? Did we make it?" she asks.

He chuckles slightly.

"Alive, aren't we?" he returns.

Correct, but for how long? Trying to sit up, Coleena grits past the pain in her abdomen and forces everything into the darkest recesses of her mind until she is finally seated. Dizziness and nausea roar at her like angry lions, and she almost vomits on the floor, the ability to swallow it back barely enough.

"For the moment. Can we trust these people?" Coleena asks.

Looking around, there is no one else but them. Who are these people anyway? Roland lets his head roll back and forth before stretching his arms and both of his legs, including the bad one.

"Father Vallatoris has always supported Azhana United when he could. Plus, after getting you in here, he sent up the signal. Those watching for it are certain to have seen it by now," the detective says.

A momentary feeling of relief hits Coleena like a stranger. Something she has not felt in what feels like ages.

"This, signal, what is it?" she asks.

"You ever seen the single torch that burns at the top of the chapel? The one for our world's unity and strength?" he asks.

Coleena isn't a devout church member, but she has seen it before. Can't really miss it on all the flags.

"Yeah, what about it?" she returns.

Pushing away from the chair, Summers finds his way to his feet, the big red chair a good sturdy cane for him to use.

"Seems like it may have turned green last night. One of the acolytes must have accidentally put in the wrong fuel. Damn thing could probably be seen for miles."

Coleena damn near rolls over laughing, but it hurts too much to try.

"The wrong, fuel? It's that fucking easy? Now what? The torch is glowing green, so we just sit here and wait?"

Summers nods his head, a small smile forming on the edges of his lips.

"The troops will be on the march. Probably already in the city," he says.

What troops? General Whittaker is at least a week away with the fastest of divisions. No way she could be here already.

"Troops?" she asks.

The detective says nothing but his smile grows larger. Limping his way over to the door, he hits it with a gentle knock. Nothing happens for a moment, but then the nob turns and it is eased open a few inches. She can see a figure beyond standing, but the shadows do not allow her to make anything out.

"Tell Father that we are awake. He will probably want to come see us," Roland whispers to whomever is beyond the portal that keeps her here. He goes to turn away but stops. "Oh, if there is any food available, we'd really appreciate anything that can be spared."

The words whispered back are muffled enough she cannot hear them. Letting the door close behind him, Summers turns back to her.

"What was all that about?" she asks.

"Father Vallatoris may be a trusted friend, but we do not know what kind of eyes Parliament or its new helpers have. No one other than those who saw us come in last night know we ever stepped into this place. If we are lucky, none of them recognized either of us and have no idea that we did not leave once we were seen by the clergy. Very few are allowed in this part of the chapel, and those who are, will be loyal to our cause. The father would see to that."

Coleena nods her head to agree, but deep down she isn't sure she can trust anyone other than the two people occupying this room. Her stomach growls and pinches at the thought of breakfast or any food being brought to them. She doesn't even remember the last time she ate.

"Wouldn't be possible that they are going to bring us some eggs and bacon is it?" she asks, a vain attempt at feeling better about their situation.

Roland grins at her, a little brightness returning to his eyes before he lets himself slip back into the chair.

"The priests of this world are pious men, Coleena. They have little and ask for less. Probably be more like some prime rib and a side of oysters fished directly from the Southern Ocean."

Coleena grabs onto the pillow sitting next to her and goes to throw it at him, but the pinching in her shoulder stops her dead in her tracks. Putting it back down, she bites back the chuckle that tried in a vain attempt to help her feel good.

"Could probably use another swig of Old Man Phydel's elixir, couldn't you?" Summers asks.

Coleena lets her head roll back and the bones pop again.

"You and me both," she says back. "What troops are you talking about? Who is actually looking for that green flame of yours?"

Summers lets himself get settled back into his chair, a stern look wiping away any liveliness that had reappeared.

"The people of Azhana United. Our signal is only to be used if the city is under ultimate distress. It can only burn once and then all able-bodied people will march into the city to help shore up the defenses against whatever is causing the problem until help arrives," Summers answers.

Coleena's mind tries to spin a thousand miles a minute and it hurts. Even thinking beyond basic bodily functions is too much. She closes her eyes, balling her hands into fists, she presses them into her eye sockets and grinds them home.

"You are telling me the entire village is going to march here? Then what? Knock on the front gate?," she asks, hardly trying to hide the skepticism from her words. "The dragon's army is making its way here. We have these dragon-touched here within our midst and Parliament is working with them hand in hand. Are you telling me your last ditch effort to save this city is a village of men and women with knives and sticks coming to take over the city and defend it?"

She doesn't know if she should laugh or cry. Probably both at the same time if she could manage it. Roland goes to answer her, but she puts up a hand to stop any words vomiting from his mouth. There is only so much she can take and this has tipped the scales.

They need to hold out until the General gets here. A week, tops. If they are lucky the dragon's army will have to circle around and the straight line of General Whittaker will get them here first. All she needs to do is keep her head down and hope that no word of her survival will leak from this church. Of course the chances of that happening are slim to fucking nil, but it's all she has.

"You make it sound so much worse than it is," Summers cuts in beyond her protests. "Rest a little. We will hear word of their arrival within the next day or so and then you'll see."

"I'll see? How the fuck are they even...," she starts but is cut off by a slight knocking on the door.

Opening slowly, the smell of warmed oats and ale waters

her mouth and spins her mind into a circle. Her legs go weak and for the first time she notices a slight tremble in her hand.

"Did someone order breakfast?" a voice she recognizes asks.

In all of his white robed glory, Phydel steps into the room, a tray filled with steaming clay bowls balanced over one gnarled hand.

"How?" Coleena goes to ask.

"It is good to see you, old man," Summers says, the grin on his face returned.

Mind locked in solid stone, Coleena watches the old arthritic hand pass some of the food to Summers before turning to her. His deep emerald eyes fix on her, and she has no words, no thoughts, she is lucky she is even breathing.

"Don't be so shocked to see me," he says. Stepping closer, he hands her a hot bowl, the steam smelling of sweat honey. "I told you cutting the head off the snake was the proper thing to do. Neither of you two children want to listen and so, daddy has come to help clean up the mess."

Coleena shakes her head, the ice breaking and a flood of thoughts running their way down to the tip of her tongue. It's an avalanche, and she can barely hold it in.

"You are in the city. How? Where is the rest of the village? What is going on here?" she stammers, her lips and tongue barely able to keep up.

"Take a deep breath and eat something," Summers says in between his own bites. "The old man here will tell you what he can if you will listen for a moment. Won't you, Phydel?"

White robes shifting, a long, swollen knuckled finger finds the side of his nose before turning back to her. For her and only her to see, he winks before clasping his hands across his stomach.

"Good words of advice, detective," Phydel starts. "Eat up, Captain, and I will fill you in on the specifics."

Coleena can do nothing more than nod and take a bite. Warmth floods her body with electricity and the pain flees in terror. Muscles relax and the pressure crushing her bones evaporates as the food finds its way down to her belly.

"A recipe I brought from home," Phydel says pulling out a chair tucked in the far corner. Opening his robe before tying it tighter across his chest, she sees that little canteen of his that holds his famous 'elixir'. Taking another bite sends a cooling shiver down her spine, and she loves every tingle on its way down. "As for your question, there are tunnels beneath this city. Do you know of these?"

She nods and then looks over at Summers.

"Lieutenant Mason found me when I got back into the city. Running away from the guards and other patrols, we found our way down there, and he led us through. That is when we ran into Petty Officer Tul. We exited the tunnels down in Poor Town."

"Ah, the Lieutenant. How is he? I'd like to fill him in on our current standing," Phydel says.

Coleena drops her spoon into the bowl, the urge and need to eat washing away with the darkness quickly filling the void.

"The tunnels were a trap. Tul has been working with Parliament for who knows how long. Mason fought him to get me enough time to get free and find Roland. I don't think he made it. We ran into Tul just before we made it to the chapel," Coleena answers.

A look of faraway thought crosses Phydel's face.

Pinching his pointed chin with his fingers, he looks over at Summers who nods his agreement.

"Not what I was hoping to hear, but what is done cannot be undone. The Lieutenant was a good man. Unique in his own way, but a good man. The vanilla business in this city will need a new patron if it is to survive," Phydel says.

"Old man," Roland cuts in.

"All right," a white knuckled hand waves at the detective. "Tul must have had some knowledge of the tunnels if he found you when you tried to escape in Poor Town. Obviously, his expertise was limited as he did not give away our biggest secret. Two entrances exist along the city walls, known to very few, and hidden to all but eyes who know what to look for. Once inside those tunnels, even an army could get itself within these walls."

Coleena pushes her empty bowl and now empty cup of warm ale away.

"Wait, are you telling me we could have gotten ourselves into the city through the tunnels and instead we tried to climb the wall?" she demands.

Phydel looks over at Roland whose face is solid stone, his dark eyes staring into hers.

"Yes. Those tunnels are a secret that only the top of Azhana United knows about and are sworn to secrecy. Limited in their uses, they are to be used if the green flame is lit, and only at that time," the detective answers.

"But Narin died trying to get us in. So did the others. I had to kill my way into this fucking city, and I could have just strolled in unnoticed?"

Muscles relaxed, Coleena pushes herself to her feet. Fists balled, she is ready to fight and doesn't care which of these two it is. Palms out, Phydel puts up both of his hands.

"What the detective here is forgetting to mention is that

the tunnels coming from outside of the wall, are one time use only. Once the seals are broken to allow entry, they collapse. They are to be used for the protection of this city, ONCE. Do you understand that, Captain?"

Of course, she does. It's all a load of bullshit, but she can't put the words to her frustration. Pacing the room, she wants to hit something, anything, but there is nothing of opportunity.

For the moment.

"So, what is our next step?" she asks. Looking at the two men, they stay silent but for glances between each other and all Summers can offer is a shrug. "You said you had this 'army' within the city walls now. You didn't march it all the way up here, break into the city effectively closing off any route of escape, to do nothing. Don't think for a moment I believe you are a man without a plan, Phydel."

The smile on the old white face is genuine, sneaky, and as wide as his cheekbones will allow. He taps the side of his nose with his finger.

"You are partially correct, Captain. I would never march all this way without a plan," he says pushing his way back to his feet. "The real answer is not a question for me, but for you two."

He wraps an arm around her shoulder, his long robe hugging her and pulling her close. She can feel the strength in his hold. Part of her wants to shove him away, but the tiny voice in the back of her head says it would be useless to try. He waves a welcoming arm to Roland as well but the detective gives nothing but a head shake. Sitting back and sipping his drink, he seems more than content to stay where he is.

"With me in this room I have the foremost scholar and warrior when it comes to fighting the dragon and its army. Also, sitting for his own comfort, is the proclaimed leader of the rebel army Azhana United. We have a city to defend, ladies and gentlemen. I think between your two active imaginations, we can figure out a way to stay alive for the next few days, don't you think?"

Coleena looks at Summers who still says nothing. One eyebrow is cocked at a weird angle as he watches the older man make his way toward the door. No words pass from his lips, only the soft slurping of the warm ale that she already downed.

A lack of words is not something that she suffers from though.

"Might sound good on paper or coming from these devious lips of yours, but it is easier said than done, Phydel," she says.

The man places his hands over his heart and stumbles back a few steps.

"You wound me, Captain. Where is your faith? We have known each other for what, several days now? That is a lifetime to some and yet you still doubt me?" His smile angles, and he looks like he's about to tell a secret. "You two finish your meals. Both of you will need all the strength you can get. I'll see you outside the chapel when you are ready. There is something I want to show you."

Without another word, Phydel makes an exit from the room and leaves the door shut behind him. Coleena looks at Summers. His eyes, locked on the wooden door, look distant and lost in thought.

"Has something to show us? Are you going to fill me in on any of this, Summers?" she asks.

Coming out of his trance, Roland's head shakes slightly before his gaze settles on her.

"Your guess is as good as mine. Man has always been sneaky in his ways, but he hasn't steered us wrong in the past. Do you remember that story of when we were betrayed, and Parliament almost destroyed us?"

Suddenly exhausted again, Coleena finds her way back to the bed she laid on and sits down. Outside the birds continue to sing and if it wasn't for their current conversation, she'd never know this city was in so much danger.

"Yeah, what about it? You told me that is when you and all the others found the valley within the gorge. Parliament hasn't been able to find you since."

Summers nods before finishing off his drink. He takes a deep breath and turns back to the closed entry.

"Phydel is the one that saved us. The people look to me for guidance and leadership, but that man's cunning ability to know things just before they happen is beyond reason. He had us post an extra sentry the night of the attack. We lost many, but it would have been worse had we not gotten those few extra moments," Roland says to her, the circles beneath his eyes darkening. "Then the gorge. It's like he already knew it was there. Helped us find it. Then it was his plans that built it the way it is, blending in with the woods and making it almost impossible to find us. He's an odd one if you ask me."

Coleena pushes herself back until she is sitting against the wall.

"So, we have an incoming army determined to kills us all. We have an unknown number of allies within the city walls, but no idea what that compares to the enemy already here. Help is half a week if not more away and our only knowledge comes from a crazy old man with a god-awful drink that warms you from your toes to the top of your head."

Closing her eyes, she is amazed how little her body aches. Tired as all the seven pits of hell, the pain and torture of the last few days seems to have been lifted from her shoulders. Only if the shit tasted better.

"He hasn't steered us wrong yet," Roland starts. "Best we figure out what he has to say and what he brought with him before we make any plans. We have the fight of our lives ahead of us. No reason to run in headfirst just to get ourselves killed."

Walking over to her, he extends a hand and pulls her to her feet. She looks into those dark eyes. A new warmth runs through her body. The life in his body is returning, a glow coming back to his skin. The shadow of a beard darkens the jawline grown sharp over the last week and for a moment she worries about how this will end for him when the monsters arrive.

He doesn't really understand what it will be like. None of them. The only ones with real combat experience have either been off the field for too long or are already dead. Wiping her hand onto the side of her leg, she wants to voice her concern. Let him know that for once he may be over his head, but the words find no purchase.

This is his fight as much as it is hers. She can't fight the small grin forming. Parliament City has become a mission for both of them.

Turning back to the door she says, "we best not keep him waiting too long. He doesn't seem like the patient type, and we still have to take over the defenses of the city if we are going to have any chance of this. Those senators aren't going to be any more willing to believe us just because we fought our way free."

Roland says nothing as he stands beside her. His presence helps remind her that there may still be a chance. As small as it may be, limp and all, together they will give it all they have.

34

The chapel, empty of all parishioners, echoes like a crypt. Lit by candles and piercing rays of light colored by the extravagant windows above, the chamber closes in on them as they pass through. Incense and dust fill the air. As if the people from the previous night never existed, Coleena and Summers could be the only humans to see the inside of this building for ages if she didn't know better.

"Parliament didn't come and take everyone, did they?" she asks.

The look on Summers' face says he is wondering the same thing.

"I'm not sure I can remember this place ever being this empty. If guards or anyone else came and cleared it out, we'd know. Father Vallatoris would have said something. Or at least Phydel," Roland answers.

Bright light, clear and vibrant, calls to them through the front door. The road outside has never been more in focus. A spotlight on a world hidden for so long beneath the shadow of the dragon which layers everything.

Too bad the heat hasn't gone away.

Breath and moisture wick away in equal measure as they exit the chapel. A blue sky, the prettiest she has seen in all of recent memory blankets the world, and she is forced to shade her eyes with a hand.

This can't be Parliament City. What happened to the hellhole and war zone they fought through last night?

"Almost seems like you are in a different place, doesn't it?" Phydel asks.

Coleena can't help but jump slightly as the old man somehow finds a way to sneak up on her. Even in the midday sun, bright and glaring, somehow Phydel finds a way to shine brighter. His long white robes may as well be on fire. Stepping back, she can't take standing next to him, her eyes watering.

"What the fuck is going on around here? What happened to all the fighting? There were guards and Parliamentary officers everywhere. Did they all just leave?" she asks.

Only the tip of the iceberg of what she needs to know, but Phydel listens, his eyes growing with all the answers he's just dying to set free.

"Too many questions and not enough time to answer them all. I think it would be best to show you," he says.

With a big sweep of his arm, he tries to wrap her in another embrace but this time she is ready. Stepping back, she bumps into Summers who finds a way to put both of his hands on her shoulders without falling over.

"Lead the way, old man. I am hot enough as it is out here. Those robes of yours will kill me," she says.

He taps his nose again.

"It's a fashion statement that grows on you. Wear it long

enough and you don't even seem to notice the heat anymore," he says.

Full of shit is what he is, she thinks to herself, but all she can do is glance at Summers. He winks at her. At least she isn't alone in the assessment of the man's shit level.

"Are you sure we are safe out here?" she asks.

Very few people are on the street. Stray dogs and cats can be seen in the desperate corners where trash has built up. Even the smell of refuse and ash seems to have washed away overnight. A city reborn. Suddenly, and without reason, everything is calm.

"Open your eyes, Captain. The battle is almost upon us. We can't have you blinded to such details as this," Phydel says not turning back to them as they head in a direction which will lead them back toward Parliament itself.

Large dome sitting dark and quiet, it sits and waits for their arrival. Watching their every step, the darkness between the crevices of its walls and roof hide so many secrets, she waits for the other shoe to drop.

A trap.

Hidden soldiers.

Something that will turn this sudden streak of luck into a living nightmare.

"Do you see them yet?" the old man inquires.

Taking a deep breath, Coleena bites back her retort. There are no more than one or two people per block. Average citizens judging by their clothes. Hand sewn. Patches made of mismatching material, and little else as they linger along the fronts of houses and city buildings.

Alert eyes follow them as they walk past. Some smile, at least one waves, but none of them approach. Standard city people. What else would she look for?

Then the glint of sunlight hits her so directly in the eye

it almost blinds her. Another flash knocks her back a step, and she puts up her hands in defense. Roland is right there, hands on her shoulders.

"What...what the fuck was that?" she asks.

Phydel chuckles.

"Misplaced blade sheath is my best guess," he says.

Blinking the water from her eyes, Coleena looks again and sees the long knife slid into the back of a young man's pants. Brighter than a mirror, he plays catch with a little girl who has one herself barely a quarter of its size in her little cloth belt.

Stopping, Coleena spins on her heals. One to two people per city block. Looking them over, she pays a little more attention. Clothing in similar repair regardless of the material. Able bodied and standing around doing nothing.

Another flash of light. More blades.

"These are Azhana United's people," she says.

Roland chuckles quietly.

"You really did it, old man. You actually pulled it off," Summer says.

Phydel walks with both his hands clasped behind his back. An air of satisfaction follows him like his shadow as his robes bellow out behind him somehow not picking up a spot of dirt.

"My part was the easiest of them all, Detective. What lays ahead is for you and the captain to decide," Phydel responds. "I will say that at least these conniving individuals made one part of it much easier than it had to be."

Rounding the corner of Parliament, Coleena isn't sure what to expect. Armed guards. Azhana United soldiers waiting and patrolling the grounds. Her heart and breath catch in her throat as the front entrance comes into view.

Six men, each of them armed with a rifle, flank the front

doors. They turn toward them momentarily before resuming their vigilant observation of Congress Street and the adjoining buildings. It is not them that stops her, it is what hangs above their heads.

Four lifeless bodies. The soft breeze sets them swaying as their heads tilt unnaturally to the side.

Senator Reza.

Senator Karagoz.

Two others who she can't even remember their names.

"You did this to them?" Coleena demands.

"Ha," Phydel responds. "If they were so lucky. Had I found them, there would be little that remains of their decrepit selves. No, Captain, we found them like this. Apparently, there was a huge skirmish before these very doors last night. Almost a dozen killed before those who remained lost their will to fight."

"Then who did this to the senators?" Roland asks.

Phydel shrugs his shoulders.

"My best guess says whomever they worked with no longer had a need for them. I would like to believe they did this to themselves when the fruition of their actions finally dawned on them, but I would rather be a realist. These self-indulgent assholes would have ridden out their decisions as far as it took them instead of admitting what they did. If only I had a chance to get my hands on them while they were still alive," Phydel says.

Coleena can't help but feel the same way. The bodies continue to swing, thick black cable wrapped around their throats and their faces purple and twisted in death.

"Cut them down," Coleena says. "We can't have people thinking they are trading one set of tyrants for another."

Summers nods his agreement and Phydel just stares at her. After a moment he nods as well and waves a man over.

Turning back to Summers she tilts her head so he can make his way closer, leaving the old man to get the guards moving.

"How much control do we think we have?" she asks. "This whole city is filled with thousands of people. We have no idea how long it will be before the dragon's army will get here, and what can we do in the meantime anyway?"

The detective shrugs, his eyes sweeping over the quiet streets.

"I'm not a general. Solving crimes is what I do, and looking at the condition of me, I'm not doing such a good job at it. Think about it Coleena, what would you do first? Do we know how much we can control what others do? No, we can't, but we have to work with what is in front of us," Summers answers.

Phydel, shinning bright like a star steps up and puts an arm around Roland's shoulders.

"Though I may not agree, the senators will be cut down as quickly as we can locate ladders long enough to do the job. So, Captain, what is our first course of action?" Phydel asks.

She looks both men in the eyes, neither of them flinching or showing any signs of doubt. This is really it. They are going to depend on her to lead this city. The little fire in her gut flares to life, yet she can feel the weight of the responsibility trying to pull it down deep.

Looking down empty streets, up at the clear sky, and into the deep shadows between buildings and alleys, Coleena lets the world around her sink in. If she tries, she can see faces of people looking back at her. As if they know she is the one that will lead them in the upcoming battle. Her throat goes dry, but she has been trained for this. The Army never leaves a soldier behind, and she isn't about to start now.

"Open the gates," she orders.

Phydel's eyes widen, his mouth opening ever so slightly with the drop of his jaw. A frozen look hits Summers but it quickly melts into a tiny look of satisfaction.

"You are going to bring in all the refugees," he says.

"Are you sure that is a good idea," Phydel asks. "That is a lot of people and the time it takes to get them in and situated will diminish what we have to prepare."

It is Coleena's turn to pat the old man on the shoulder. With a wink she taps the side of her nose.

"The Army barracks should have plenty of room for them. Whatever time it takes is better than having them slaughtered outside our walls. The moral would kill us faster than any of their claws or teeth," she says taking a few steps beyond where they stand and seeing the wall with her own eyes. "While that is happening, Phydel, you collect all the leaders of Azhana United you can other than Roland himself. Roland, find me anything that resembles a wall guard captain or Army officer. We need to know what kind of strength we have."

"If there are any still within the city, I will get them to you immediately," Summers says.

Phydel's eyes sparkle in the afternoon light, and he steps closer.

"Azhana United's strength runs deep within its people. I will bring you those you can trust. Use them wisely for the fight coming will test us all in ways we have never seen before," he says.

Coleena looks up at him, the fire inside of her warming her from toes to fingertips. She already knows this. He does not need to remind her.

"Duly noted, Phydel," she says. "Please find me these men and women. There will be no time for training or strategy. Shoring up the holes in the walls and setting our points of defense is our best option. The less time we spend here talking, the better. Can you do this for me?"

He nods to her, his lips curling slightly into a smile.

"You are the captain," he says. "We will follow you into hell and back. Let the world remember the choices we make in the coming hours."

With a wave of his hand, he turns and heads away. She watches him leave, his white robes spilling out behind him like a wedding dress. For the slightest of moments a thought hits her that she hasn't had in over a decade.

Unbidden and unwanted, the idea of marriage and children. At almost thirty-seven years old, she has never even taken a moment to consider this. Now, staring death directly in the face, she finds a soft spot opening within her mind.

Reaching into her shirt she finds the chain and dog tags that hang around her neck. The metal is warm to her touch, the stamped letters and numbers rubbing against the skin of her fingers.

Stamping the thoughts away like a dying fire, she buries them to the depths she may never be able to recover. Sentiment and fear of what she may lose will cost her and many others their lives. Being a soldier is all she has ever known and all she ever will. Taking a deep breath, she watches those of Azhana United patrol the streets and the guards before Parliament taking their damn sweet time cutting down the bodies of the senators.

She'd yell at them for being so slow and clumsy about it, but deep down she can't find the need. A part of her agrees with Phydel, they deserved their fate. Like it or not, it's one less problem she has to account for.

Walking toward the entrance of Parliament, she knows what she has to do. None of this will work without a plan, and she is the only one who can figure it out.

———

THE SHADOWS GROW LONG IN THE WEST, THE HORIZON BLOOD-red and filled with darkening clouds. Up on top of the walls the wind swirls as it howls, a growling of earth and air. There is moisture in the air.

Rain is coming.

A storm that will wash itself against these walls and take away the blood soaking along the hardened dirt and stone.

Coleena watches the last of the refugees line up to file into the open gates. Thousands have pushed their way through and into the city. The process has taken all day and not a minute too soon.

"We have found something that needs your attention, Captain," Gils says.

Standing beside her, arms behind his back and wearing a fine shirt of chain mail, the man is the statue of a god. Big and broad, he beams with life. As tall as she is, he still towers over her by a set of shoulders and head.

"What is it now?" she asks.

It has become a tiresome venture. Between officers fighting over rank, and citizens brawling about even the possibility of having to serve the city, there is the chaos of being forced to wait on a knife's edge for what is coming. She wanted to keep the impending attack a secret for as long as she could, but the cat was out of the bag almost as soon as the first refugee stepped within the gate. Two dozen guards currently herd everyone toward the barracks more in a manner of policing than ushering. The possibility of revolt is an almost certain outcome.

"If you would follow me, they say it would be better that you see this," Gils says.

Pressing her hand into the side of her head, Coleena nods and begins to follow the big man. Long legs cover ground even she can barely fathom and his boots echo like mortar rounds hitting stone. Other men and women manning the walls move out of his way without a second glance.

Phydel chose him and his brother well when bringing them to her. Their presence alone inspires those around them, either through fear or the fact that it looks like it would take a tank just to take them down. Standing beside the man even she feels just a little safer.

Nearing the stairs that lead to the tunnels within the wall, Coleena turns to take the first step when she stops herself. Gils doesn't head in that direction but instead toward the battlement at the end of the wall.

Towering an additional twenty feet above everything else, the domed tower sits in darkness and waits for their arrival.

"What is this all about?" she asks as they reach the entrance to the fortification.

Inside she can see the reflection of white cloth radiating like a star in the middle of the night. Phydel, his hands clasped in front of him, smiles from ear to ear.

"There she is, the Captain," he says. Opening his arms he welcomes her in.

In the center of the room is an ancient looking sixteen inch rotary cannon. Fifty caliber rounds she hasn't seen fired in ages. Dust and cobwebs cover the turning gears beneath and the thing looks like it hasn't seen repair since before she joined the army.

"What is all of this about, Phydel?" she asks. "Last time I knew these hadn't been fired since the World War. Not much use they are going to be for us."

The bastard taps his nose again.

"So little faith, Captain," Phydel says before stepping out of the way. Behind him is three stacks of crates, enough dust to bury someone beneath on top of them, but each marked with brands pointing out the ammunition stored within. "We found these in storage beneath Parliament. Hauling them up here was a bitch, but there is enough to keep both guns firing for at least the first few assaults."

Coleena turns around and looks toward the battlement at the far end of the wall. An identical cannon waits there, just as old and in just as much need of repair.

"Won't matter if neither of these weapons work. They haven't been used in over a quarter century. How can we be certain they won't blow the wall to pieces instead of actually firing into the demon lines?"

Gils puts a big paw down on her shoulder.

"We can make these work. Much simpler than setting the forges every morning. Before the monsters get here, these will be ready to fire," he says, his voice confident and full of joy.

She looks up into his bright eyes. Like a child trapped in a giant's body, she is glad they are on her side. With a big sigh she looks back to Phydel.

"Very well, get to work. A storm is coming and the rain and wind will not help you," she says. "Any other surprises you have for me?"

The old man smiles and steps around the big blacksmith. Stepping close, he leads her back out onto the wall and away from the battlements.

"We have rounded up all the leaders we can find within the non-Azhana United ranks of the men and women. They await your orders for what to do when the time comes," he says, his voice suddenly hushed and somber.

"If it comes to that I will address them," she answers back. "I leave it to you and Summers to keep them at their duties. There are no signs of the enemy yet so if the gods are willing, maybe this will all be for nothing."

Phydel steps in front of her, his bright emerald eyes flaring to life beneath the dimming of the early evening sunlight.

"We both know that is not true. There is no escaping fate, Captain. You are here for a reason, and deep down you know this. History will remember the rise or fall of this great city when the fires die out and the ashes finally reach the ground. Either mankind will find itself strong enough to weather this storm, or it will be washed away with the tide. Preparing for what we know is coming is all we can do," he says.

She knows he is correct, but exhaustion is finally settling into her bones. Her eyes burn, the lids heavy and dark. Sleep calls her name in the back of her mind, buried beneath the splitting pain and the thoughts of all the things she is forgetting.

Yawning, she puts a hand on the man's shoulder. It's warm and for a moment she can feel the aches and pains of everything wash away.

"Good advice from someone who once told me it was best to cut the head off the snake. I understand what you are doing here, Phydel, and your help can never be repaid. Summers and yourself are the only reason this city has a chance," she says, another yawn cutting its way in. "By the way, where is Roland?"

Phydel looks off toward the barracks, the last trailing lines of refugees inching their way toward the military encampment.

"He was helping the officers from the police force keep everything in order. Not much of a military man, he felt he was a better resource there than up on the wall."

Coleena nods her head, the darkness of the arriving night beginning to squeeze her tight.

"Smart man that, Summers," she says, sleep coming over her fast and furious. "Tell him I'd like to see him when he is finished. We have to go over the plans for patrols in the morning."

"What are you going to be doing?" Phydel asks.

She can barely keep her eyes open. Her body has taken so much she is surprised she is even on her feet.

"I'm going to catch what sleep I can. Once this attack starts, who knows when we'll get to rest," she answers. "That's assuming we are still alive."

Looking over at the canons, she shakes her head. How did they find the rounds for those? A part of her wants to let the small spark of hope ignite itself into a flame, but she has been here before. Hope is a dangerous thing if used unwisely.

Phydel keeps his eyes on her. He is such a strange old man. Nodding her head at him one more time, he taps his finger against his nose before she turns away.

Strange old man. With that thought, she descends back to the city level and heads toward the barracks. Rest will do her good. It will do all of them good.

They need a little good around here.

35

A storm is coming.

She can feel it in the air. Unnatural for this area or even the world. The wind whips with a cold bitter touch. The taste of water fills the air and the fires outside of Lieutenant Mason's old shack crackle and dance with the wind.

Large gusts rattle the roof, and she can hear pots and pans clang together. Any footsteps she hears outside are hurried as voices try to cut through the shrill cry.

Even Mother Nature knows what approaches them. Her hands are achy and her back feels like a thousand tiny knives are driving into her spine. She rolls her head and feels every bone pop, a small sensation of loosening before it all returns with a fury.

Lightning flashes across the dark sky. A jagged line of hatred and malice. Thunder rattles the wall, an explosion of power and the uncaring gods' might. Taking in a deep breath, she lets the stench of vanilla work its way into her lungs.

Calming.

Soothing.

Thinking back on the man's easy smile, the mischievous grin, and his last sacrifice, she can't help but remember him for what they lost as a people. Inside she hopes it was worth it. Tul got what he deserved, but should it still be her standing here?

Mason knew these walls, this city, and its people. She is a stranger to all of them. A single woman forced to lead them into the battle of their lives. She lifts her arm up to the window, the swaying light of fires and the lamp hanging outside her door brings out the white scars on her arm.

This fight, a battle where they will be out numbered, flanked, and fighting against an enemy with no mercy, will for most of them be their last. Of course, that is unless a miracle happens.

Coleena chuckles to herself. How things have changed since she was assigned this position. Miracles? When did she start believing in those?

No, the General will not be here in time to save them. She can feel it in her bones. The cries of the wind already carry the howls of the monsters coming to tear them all to pieces. Will the dragon itself make the flight all the way here?

Why not?

It burned down hundreds of cities in weeks twenty-five years ago. What is one more walled in fortress? Thousands of people lost in a blink of an eye. Humanities last bastion of hope.

Taking a deep breath she lets herself fall down onto the couch. A new gush of vanilla lifting into the air with a thin cloud of dust.

There is that word again. Hope. If only she could keep it within herself. Hands shaking, she leans back and closes her eyes, her fingers intertwined to stop the jitters as they press into the back of her skull.

Sleep will not be her friend this evening. Never has been on the eve of battle. Like a child before their birthday, she knows what is coming. Part of her wants it to be over and done with, the nightmare of the day far worse than any she could dream of.

The other half. That is what keeps her awake. A side of her that relishes in what is coming. Fighting these demons on a ground of her choosing. It's been too long since she watched them die at her feet. The sight of their blood fountaining into the air, and the languishing howls of their death throes.

What has she become?

She watches the ceiling. Shadows dancing and the small stains of smoke and ash from too many candles. Mason, what would you be doing at this time?

A knock on the door rattles the hinges and forces her out of her own mind. It is late in the night, who would be coming to report to her now?

Pushing away from the couch, her body groans as she makes her way to the door, a small voice of anger ready to rip into whomever is calling her this late. A second set of knocks rattle the door before she reaches it.

"Yes, yes. I'm almost there," she calls out, all the irritation she feels coming out with her words.

Pulling away the locks, she opens the entry enough to see who is on the other side. Summers. Cotton hat balled into his hands, he leans heavily against his new cane and his eyes are darkened as he watches the darkness above. Another flash of lightning burns across the sky, the boom of the thunder shaking the very ground with its approach.

"Summers, what are you doing here?" she questions.

He turns to her, a small tilt to his lips as he rolls the hat tighter in his hand.

"Phydel told me you asked for me to find you. Patrols and other reports before the sun rises," he answers, his face looking at her feet.

Coleena lets all the anger in her wash away, her muscles loosen, and she steps aside. He watches the floor like a child who just woke his mother.

"I forgot. Please come in. Forgive my anger. Waiting for the fight makes time drag and I'm not much for sitting around," she says. He chuckles as he makes his way over to the couch, sitting down with his leg extended. "How is it going out there?"

"Definitely not much for small talk," he says shifting himself to get more comfortable. She stands and watches as he does so. "Most of the force remains. A few deserters either lost in the rioting or in the chaos once they saw what happened to the senators. I have them working four man patrols all over the city. Six to a squad here closer to the refugees. A lot of scared people out there."

Coleena sighs and takes the chair across from him.

"As they should be. What do you think the chances are that General Whittaker will be here in time?"

Leaning back he lets his shoulders slump and his head roll.

"Shouldn't I be asking you that question?"

A sigh. He is correct.

"Probably, but humor me. Give me your opinion. What are our chances?" she asks.

Keeping his eyes on the ceiling, he sighs, "the chances that General Whittaker makes it here, I would say slim to none. Us against whatever shows up on the other side of that wall? That would depend on you."

"Me?"

She sits back on the chair, looking at the detective. The dark circle still under his eyes. The greasy hair that looks like it hasn't been combed in a week. When was the last time her hair was combed? Running a hand through her own greasy blond locks, she puts her elbows on the table.

"Yes, you. We have a small army here with no leader. You hope and dream for General Whittaker to arrive like a knight in shinning armor, yet the men and women within these walls look to you."

"They don't even know me," she says, standing back up. Her exhaustion washes away, the ridiculousness of the argument gasoline on the fire within her. "I'm just another soldier. These men and women of Azhana United know you and Phydel. You are their leader, not me."

"I might be their leader, but they are not the only ones here. The senators were not lucky enough to get rid of the soldiers stationed here before their untimely demise. Soldiers respect other soldiers. They will follow you and Azhana United will follow you," Summers says, getting up from the couch with a grunt and serious shaking within his knees.

"What makes you think they will? This is going to be a war, Summers. Do they have any idea what is going to happen? I'm a captain. They are a community of people built around the idea of standing against the status quo," she says, her voice cracking. "I am the status quo."

Summers steps up to her. She can feel his body heat against hers, his eyes looking deep in to hers. Those deep emerald eyes.

Her mind stops for a moment. Emerald?

"Your eyes," she asks, her hand reaching for his face. "I thought they were darker."

His skin is an inferno beneath her touch. Closing them tightly, he shakes his head as if knocking loose a few cobwebs that have found their way in. Looking back at her, his eyes are as deep and dark as she remembers them being.

"They are dark," he says, his voice low. "A reflection in the light. My mother always said they had a bit of green in them."

She smiles at the words. A vision of her own mother flashing before her eyes. Back to a time when things were so much simpler. Before that bastard of a dragon came and took it all away.

"There is still Azhana United. How can we trust that they will follow when the shit hits the fan?" she asks, stepping away to head back toward the couch.

Summers does not let go of her hand, his grip firm but soft. She stops and looks back at him.

"Because I will follow you," he says. "To the pits of the seven hells, I will not leave your side no matter what is thrown against these walls. If I am there, these men and women will follow you until the end. I promise you that."

He draws closer to her. Exhaustion flushes through her body but so does a warmth she has not felt in ages. She can feel him press-up against her, his dark eyes swallowing hers. Throat dry, she wants to pull away, tell him to go, so she can rest, but she can't make the words come.

"I'm not sure it is going to be enough, Roland," she says, her words barely a whisper.

A small smile creases the edges of his flat lips.

"It will have to be, Coleena. You are here for a reason. This is the purpose for which you were sent to this city. No one else. It had to be you," he says, his face inches from hers.

She can feel his breath on her lips. His heat and the taste of his last meal. Rations that do not make her skin crawl.

"What is going on?" she asks.

His smile grows larger, and he cups the side of her face with his hand.

"Something that should have happened awhile ago," he whispers and kisses her on the lips.

Lightening streaks across the sky lighting up the room and Coleena can feel every muscle in her body tense. What is happening? She can't be doing this. The battle could be lost as early as tomorrow. The demands and structure of her training throw every rejection she can think of at her, but deep inside she knows they won't win.

Wrapping her arms around his shoulders, she kisses him back. Pulling him closer, she can feel the warmth of her own body working its way all around.

"We can't," she says, out of breath and with no conviction.

He kisses her again and she doesn't resist.

"Tonight could be our last night," he says back. She can feel the beating of his heart through his uniform shirt. "This may be our last opportunity."

Running his hand through her hair, he leans toward the couch, and she lets him lead her there. Shifting their weight, he slips and lands with a bounce, her body settling on top of his.

Looking at her, he smiles and traces his fingers over the rippling lines of pink flesh across her cheek and the fire it sends through her body shivers the muscles around her spine.

Another flash of lightning and a thunderous cannon that shakes the roof of the building. Taking her own time, she lets the tip of her finger trace the scabbed line that cuts through his eyelid.

"We better make the best of it then," she says and kisses him again.

Outside the storm rages through the night. An onslaught of rain and wind that shakes apart unprotected tents and topples buildings weakened from weeks of bombs and attacks.

Soldiers bunker with civilians ready to fight should the enemy come to their gates. They face demons without remorse and a dragon bent on destruction. Parliament City sits within these walls. The fires of guards manning the walls through the elements refuse to be put out or away.

In the morning the sun will rise and with it the fate of their known world will be decided.

36

A cold morning.

An empty bed.

Coleena awakens, a chill in the air that makes every movement uncomfortable. The smell of wet and mud. Cook fires smoldering from soggy wood left behind by the rhythmic marching of boots.

Rolling onto her side, she puts her hand on the vacant pillow next to her head, the blanket disheveled and wrapped around her body. She lets her fingertips run across the smooth cover. No indentation. No stray hairs. As if he was never even there.

Resting on her back, she watches the lack of movement on the ceiling. Tiny cracks in the plasterboard and the endless circles of soot from burning candles. The old soldier needed them even here in the bedroom. The sheets and pillows still smell of vanilla. Damn Mason and his love for those things.

She pulls the sheet and blanket up to her neck. It is too cold for a day like this. Her bare skin prickles and she closes her eyes.

What did she let happen?

Knock!

"Captain!" Gils' voice yells from outside of the small building.

Deep and loud, the man damn near shakes the place like the rolling from last night's storm.

Reluctantly, Coleena slides to the edge of her bed. Feet hit the ice-cold floor, her naked body rippling with the sudden change in weather.

Another knock shakes the hinges and almost takes the entire door down.

"Hold on! I'll be there in a minute!" she yells back.

A mirror across from the bed gives her a great look at her face. Hair sprouting in a thousand directions, she looks like she has been partying for the good part of a decade and there is a distant look to her eyes. Like she is somehow watching herself from outside of her own body.

"Captain!" Gils yells again.

There is an urgency there, but somehow and for some reason he is trying to muffle it.

"Hold the fuck on!" she demands.

Fuck it! Wrapping a long robe around her body, she isn't even going to bother with her uniform. She can take care of that after she is done ripping this man to shreds. It doesn't matter if he towers over her.

The next set of whacks on the door send a crack splintering from the upper corner.

"What the fuck do you think you are doing?" Coleena demands throwing the door open. Gils stands in front of her, face ashen and his eyes darting from her to the wall. It looks like it barely registers to him what she is wearing. "Out with it."

"They are here, Captain," the blacksmith says.

"Who is here?" she questions.

If it was the dragon, they wouldn't be standing here like this. The wall would already be fighting, and they wouldn't have let her sleep. Couldn't have let her sleep.

"The...the demon," he says.

Coleena feels her heart skip a beat. This is not good if this man is already stumbling and the fighting hasn't even started yet. But why hasn't it? They don't normally wait or have any tactics at all. Throwing body after body, rock after tons of rock is what they do best.

"Get back on the wall!" she demands turning back into the little building. "I'll be right behind you."

She doesn't wait for his response. Aches and pains forgotten. Cold floor, chilly air, all of it pushed into the deep recesses of her mind. The fight is here. No room for indecision.

Throwing on her uniform, she doesn't bother with medals. Black battle pants, red slashed shirt tucked in and presentable. The others need to see her in control. They will fall if their own leaders begin to panic. Gils is already showing signs of that and it is something she'll have to take care of if she must.

A flash of silver catches her eyes as she ties her boots. Both dog tags slip out from her shirt and swing back and forth as they hang from her neck. She doesn't even remember putting them on. Taking them into her hand, she looks at them one final time.

Captain Coleena Armigera

Desert Spear

Azhana Army

Born 2246

Sergeant Brett Giles

Our Lord's First Battalion, Second Division

Knights of the Vanguard

Born 2223 -

Azhana Army

Regardless of the cold around her, the metal is warm to her touch. She knows every little curve, indentation, and letter punched into these. The dark stains on the one she has been carrying since she was a little girl burn beneath her fingertips.

A quick thought passes her mind, something she has not heard herself ask in a long time.

Will I have anyone to give these to when the time comes?

The gods do not answer her. More boots go running past the window, feet no longer marching as the time draws near. Stuffing the tags into her shirt, she puts her knife into the hidden slot within her boot, and she grabs her rifle.

Out the door, the city is in ordered chaos. More than a hundred men stand along the top of the walls, rifles at the ready, they do not look at what is behind them, their attention fully drawn to the world outside.

Behind the wall is what stops her in her tracks. Rows upon rows of men and women. Standing in perfect order, they wait behind the door, spears tucked within their arms and shields held over their shoulders.

"What the?" she begins.

"An amazing sight, isn't it?" Summers asks.

He slides in beside her, his outfit matching every single one of the Azhana United standing in front of her. Deep brown canvas pants and thick shirts of chain mail, he holds a spear like the others, though he leans on it for support.

"Where did they? Why?" Coleena begins.

"Our overachieving brothers worked day and night after we left the sanctuary. We don't have the training or the spare rifles that the army requires, but we have these," Summers begins. He puts his weight on his good leg and then brings the point of the weapon down so she can see it. "Figuring we weren't going to be any use unless they breach the wall, Phydel had them make something that would be better suited for combat here at the doors. Just like your knife, these will cut through them."

"But these are monsters we are talking about, Roland," Coleena says. "You aren't going to be able to just poke them with a stick no matter how sharp they are."

He nods though the small smile of pride on his face does not fade.

"We'll take care of that if it happens. Get up on the wall. Lead your men. If we are lucky, they won't be able to get past you and we'll stand here looking like idiots."

Coleena gives the entire group, hundreds strong one last look. The spears shinning in the early morning light. A stiff wind whistles down from the rocks on the walls and it forces her to wrap her arms tighter around her body.

"You see that you do that," she says.

He nods, and she turns away, her attention back to where the real fighting will happen. Soldiers make their way up and down the stairwell leading to the top. Those coming down move fast, their feet barely able to find the step below before gravity carries them forward. The soldiers going up carry the world on their soldiers, their lives and those who remain within these walls entirely dependent on how long they can survive.

Coleena walks away. She has no words for him. If the previous evening doesn't mean anything to him, she can't let it mean anything to her. If there is a tomorrow, maybe she'll find the time to tell him how much it doesn't mean anything to her.

"Hey, Captain," Summers calls to her.

Stopping, she doesn't turn toward him right away. When did he start calling her captain again? Turning, the man's eyes watch her before lowering themselves toward the ground.

"What is it, Summers?" she asks.

Gripping his spear tighter, he stiffens his back and brings his eyes up to hers.

"I wanted to apologize for last night. If I had a chance...," he starts.

She cuts him off with a raised hand.

"None of that matters now. We have bigger problems beyond these walls. Keep your apologies to yourself," she says back.

Without a word he nods and turns back to those of Azhana United who stand at the ready, spears held and shields waiting. She watches him go. Part of her expects him to fight back, but he doesn't, so she can't either.

Turning back to the wall, she makes her way to the stairs that will lead her to the top. Soldiers, young and too old part as she approaches. Mutterings of how many there are, how the world is ending, and all of this being a big mistake begin to hit her ears. Words she has heard before. None of this is new. Recruits and veterans alike are guilty of it. She'll have to find a way to squash it before the fighting starts.

Legs burning, chest tightening, she reaches the top. None of the soldiers turn to look at her. All of them are locked on the sight outside their protective walls. A flash of white moves and out from among the throng of mesmerized soldiers steps Phydel.

"There she is!" he calls. "Just the person we need."

At his disturbance, several of the men and woman turn and realize that she is there. Snapping to attention she can see the nerves pinching their hard faces. Soldiers, all of them. She isn't sure how much combat any of them have seen. A quick nod is all she can spare as she makes her way over to Phydel who waits at the part of the wall above the gates to the city.

"Miraculous sight, isn't it?" he asks as she steps up to the wall's edge.

There are no words for what stands before them. Hundreds of yards separate them from their enemy, but even at that distance the enormity of what they face hits home. Rows upon rows of monsters stare back at them. Their hatred and hunger for the flesh that hides behind these barricades of stone can be felt from even this far away.

The Banshees mix with the Gorgoths. Waves of moving rock that wait and watch. Her throat tightens as she lets her eyes settle over the sea of demons waiting for them. This isn't a simple battle. The dragon sent enough for an extermination. Even if they had enough strength to hold them off for a period of time, it would be futile in the end.

Any survivors lucky enough not to be killed in the fighting couldn't flee fast enough to escape this. General Whittaker, her whole army brought to the front, could probably only hold out for so long. Humankind is going to die right here against this old stone, its life's blood soaking into the dirt. Coleena can feel it deep inside.

The cold grip of death.

It latches onto her spine, shriveling up the strength and resilience that refuses to give up. The masses lined up against them ready to grind her into the dirt.

How can so few be forced to stand up against so many?

Coleena doesn't feel her hand begin to shake. Her eyes sweep the lines and there is no counting or planning. They will all come at once, a black tidal wave of rock that will knock everything down in one giant push. She breathes, and she can only find enough for a tiny breath, like the air from the world itself has been sucked away.

"The dragon is really pulling no punches today," Phydel says, his voice unbroken and unwavering.

She turns to look at him, his deep green eyes sparkling in the morning sun.

"Why doesn't it just come and do the job itself? A lot easier to fly here and melt the city to the ground than spend so many lives fighting a fortified position," she says in return, her attention back on the enemy.

Phydel chuckles.

"And you think lives mean anything to that beast, demon or human?" he asks. She regrets even letting the thought slip, but his smile doesn't waver, and he turns his own attention back to the demons. "Some would believe that the beast can't come here. That the only way it can fight us is to send its armies in hopes that it will be enough."

Coleena shakes her head.

"That's not possible. I've seen the damn thing. It has wings as wide as several city blocks. Something that big would require nothing at all to fly all the way out here."

"It's not like you or I, Captain. The beast is made of magic and the further it gets away from its source of power the weaker and more vulnerable it will become. Parliament City is as far east as you can get from its lair before running into the Halrood Mountains. Fire and brimstone do not rule there. No, Captain, I do not believe we have to worry about our lizard friend making the journey here. But," Phydel says, pointing to the mass of monsters waiting to attack. "We do have to worry about them. They have no qualms about how far away they must march."

Coleena sees what the old man points at. A single solitary figure walking its way toward the gates of Parliament

City. At first, it is some sort of hybrid between a Banshee and Gorgoth. Larger and broader than the first, but much smaller than the later. Drawing closer, she sees it's cloaked and wears its hood above its head.

Without any sign of slowing the figure casually closes the distance between them, time and urgency not to be seen upon its approach.

Men and women shuffle their feet. Whispers go up and down the line and Coleena can hear the gears of both mounted canons grind as they begin to target the nearing figure. Coleena puts up her hand to still the talking and hopefully stall anyone with an itchy trigger finger. She has no belief that this conversation will help avoid bloodshed, but she'll at least hear the person out.

"Stop where you can hear me," she demands with a shout as loud as she can make it. The cloaked shadow pauses. "Turn around now. There is no need for death here today."

It is the best she has. No one has ever spoken with these things. What does one say to a demon spawned by a dragon?

Moving slowly, the figure pulls back its hood. Shadows fall back, the head hairless and scarred with bright cracks in scaled skin of stone. Coleena looks down at the creature. Half human, half demon.

It is a woman. At least at one time it was a woman. No longer soft or curved, all hard edges, she looks at them.

"Open your gates. We know who you are, Captain Coleena of the Azhanian Army," the half-monster demands. "I can give you this offer. Throw open the city. Give its inhabitants to the dragon, and we will spare you. There are no other choices."

The fire inside of Coleena's belly flares to life, an inferno ready to engulf her in its hatred for this woman. She looks at the men and women standing next to her, all of them waiting for her next move. Turning back to the envoy, she rolls her shoulders.

"I will not open this city even to spare myself. You will die here on this field with the rest of your demon brethren" Coleena answers back.

"This is your one chance, Captain Coleena of the Azhanian Army. I will sweeten the deal. Our master knows of one other within your midst. They are of great power like yourself. If you open your doors, we shall spare both of your lives. Once we have cleared the city of the vermin residing within, you will march with us back to the sacred mountain. There you will bear witness to the great power that is our master."

Coleena has had enough. She turns to the men and the women standing beside her. There will be no negotiating with these monsters. Never thought there would be, but she owed it to all of these people for her to give it her best.

"Well, can't say we didn't warn them," Phydel says sliding in next to her.

She gives the old man a sideways glance. A lot of confidence for someone staring at total annihilation. Scanning the rest of those around her, their faces showing the fear deep within them, she realizes what she would do if she could have an army of men like Phydel. In the end this wouldn't be so hard.

Taking a deep breath, she draws what strength she can.

"Men and women. Soldiers of the Azhanian army and protectors of Parliament City. Before us stands the greatest army to ever march across this world. I will not lie to you. They are monsters. Demons pulled straight from the pits of the seven hells, and they are here to kill us all."

"In war as in life, there is no surrender. They have given us our choices so there is nothing left for us to do. For today, we are all soldiers. Today beneath this sun, I will stand by your side. Shoulder to shoulder, we will fight these monsters. We will fight them to the death. With our last breath, we will see these things, these spawns of a dragon that has taken everything from us driven back to the hell from which they came."

"Today, my fellow Azhanians. We are soldiers, and tomorrow we will still be alive, and they will be dust. Stand up today for what you believe in. Let us show them that humankind has not lost hope. Let us show them that they have stepped past a line that should have never been crossed!"

The soldiers erupt into a cheer that shakes the ground beneath her feet.

Boots stomping and weapons being readied, Coleena steps back to the wall's edge. More than a foot-thick stone sits between her and the ground below and with the fire in her blood, she has never felt stronger.

"What is your answer, Captain Coleena of the Azhanian Army?" the half-breed asks.

Coleena can feel the smile pulling at her lips. Palms sweating, eyes focused, she can hear a bird in the distance, its call a shrill song of the coming death. It won't be her death. Not today.

She says nothing. Turning, she looks to both cannons waiting within the battlements. A nod is all that she will give them. The soldiers along the top quiet as the gears begin to grind. Down below the monster waits.

Two explosions rock the stone walkways. Chips break away and the soldiers bend their knees to brace as the cannons fire. Fire, stone, magma, and dirt erupt into the sky.

The front lines of the demon army explode, mushroom clouds lifting high into the sky.

With a shriek, the monsters begin their charge. Thousands upon thousands of living rock rolling toward their walls. Coleena readies her rifle. Heart slowed. Hands calm.

She is home.

She is ready.

The battle has begun.

37

The battle to save Parliament City and humankind is as vicious as Coleena could have ever imagined in her darkest of nightmares. Waves upon waves of bullets tear into the lines of Banshees and Gorgoths as they charge the front wall.

Pools of magma cool in rippling tides of bright orange and fiery red. Dark rock shatters and turns to pebbles as it's trampled beneath the tearing claws of monsters ready to turn themselves to dust to get to the defenders.

Coleena fires three more rounds into a Gorgoth that reaches the gate. Half a dozen banshees lay cooling in puddles of their own blood around its feet, shattered and lifeless from being in its way. Even their brethren's lives mean so little to them. The projectiles punch through hardened skin and into the molten rock beneath. Glowing streams of orange fountain into the air and spray across the solid wood of the barricaded door. Tiny fires find hold upon the ancient beams but quickly extinguish beneath the onslaught of the Gorgoth falling forward, eyes going cold beneath the push of the thousands of demons waiting their turn.

"We are going to run out of ammunition, Captain," Gils says.

He holds his own rifle at the ready, a single round squeezes off before he picks up another target. The man is correct. After the first few moments of the battle, she was forced to call for a cease fire. Periodic waves of firing. Counts of ten between bursts of three. If they all remained trigger-happy, they'd be out of shells long before the enemy expended all of its lives.

Gils' cannon was the first to fall apart. Rounds firing, barrel glowing red, she is lucky the man is good at what he does. Noticing the problem, he stopped his assault before he blew himself up and brought the remaining shells to his brother manning the last cannon. Enemy still within range, he now fires at a more controlled pace, the deadly munitions tearing through the lines with each impact.

"Keep the soldiers in line," Coleena orders. "If we run empty there will be nothing between us and them but that gate."

Gils nods and moves his way across the wall. Big hand coming down on shoulders, the rate of fire from the defenders continues to slow even beyond the ten heartbeats. Those that continue to fire concentrate on anything that approaches or has reached the front gate. All others can wait their turn.

Attempts to scale the walls have failed in all attempts. Rocks carved and mortared into perfectly flat surfaces, claws of magma and stone do nothing and it is better than ice beneath their grip.

"We always have the men and women waiting below," Phydel says.

Somehow in all the chaos and smoke, he is still a picture perfect symbol in white. Hair frazzled, green eyes practically aflame in the late afternoon light, the old man slides in beside her.

"You mean those down there with pot stickers and knives?" she asks.

Phydel gives her a look. Eyebrow raised, he reminds her of a parent who can't believe what their child just said.

"Don't underestimate the determination of those willing and waiting to give their lives for the cause of humankind," he says.

Coleena sighs, the thunder of gunfire turns into more of a background rattle that melts her aching brain into a splitting migraine.

"I never said I doubted their determination, old man," she returns. "But look what we face. Our weapons do so little against such hatred. Even if they can help, what do we expect them to do?"

Both of them walk to the edge and look down. A cloud of dust, shattered rock, and the heat of cooling magma layers itself across the front of the city like a skin. Scanning the battleground, it is a sea of stone bodies moving in undulating waves that crash upon their only remaining protection.

"They are here to support you, Captain. If you ask them to fight, they will. If you order them to die for you, they will," he says.

She looks at him then. His words barely registering beyond the pounding cadence keeping the monsters at bay.

"And what makes you think I want them to die for me? No one here should die for me."

Phydel's eyes take her in, their depth drowning her better than the chocking smoke of spent gunpowder.

"But here they do," he says. "At some point this battle will turn. Deep down you know that. Keeping these things from the wall will only work for so long. Once they find a way through, it will depend on their combined strength and your leadership if this city is to survive."

Turning away from the battle on the ground, Coleena looks over the city. Shadows grow long and darkness settles itself between the surrounding embrace of the dark stone that keeps them alive. Fires burn throughout the streets, bonfires set to keep areas of the city visible should somehow everything turn into chaos.

"Let us pray that never happens, Phydel. These walls will hold. Our soldiers will do what they need to do," she says more to herself than to him.

A horn blows in the distance. Deep and booming, the echoes are enough to shake deep within her bones and Coleena rushes to the edge overlooking the invaders. She can't believe what she sees. Like the tide itself, their enemy begins to pull back. In tiny waves their push against the outer defenses begins to lesson.

Gils works his way up the line. All soot and sweat, the man is streaked from head to toe. Shoulder caked black with oil and gunpowder, his eyes never leave the killing field beyond. Without a word, a wave of his hand stops the weapons that continue the attack into the retreating lines.

"Phydel, you ever seen them retreat?" Coleena asks.

For once the old man is speechless. Just what she thought. She hasn't either.

"Soldiers, hold your fire!" Coleena demands of those who have yet to catch the message.

The last of the banshees scatter, their high-pitched screeches cutting into the early evening air. They watch them go, without order and beyond chaotic. A Gorgoth tears into banshees who get too close. Heads and limbs ripped off before being scattered across the torn ground.

Sulfur and smoke settles itself within the tiny breeze. Humid and thick, it is little relief as the soldiers watch the monsters mass at a distance just out of range of the cannon.

"This day is ours!" Coleena screams.

The men and women stationed along the wall cheer and their voices are echoed by those below. The big blacksmith grabs her arm and lifts it high above her head.

"Let's hear it for the Captain!" his bellowing voice echoes into the coming night.

The ground shakes with the pounding of boots and the slamming of spear on shield. Coleena can do nothing but smile as the chaos of war begins to settle. Yes, they did win this day, but it is not over. As those around her cheer, she eyes the black sea of monsters waiting. They will come again and it may not be as easy next time.

A big sweaty arm wraps itself across her shoulder and without warning she is pulled toward the stairs down into the city.

"First round is on me tonight, Captain," Gils says.

He smells of sweat and grease. She can already feel it across the skin of her face, but there are still too many important things to do. A night watch. Shifts of rotating soldiers. Hand coming up to the big man's chest, she stops him.

"We still have plenty to do," she starts.

"Preparations for the night watch will be made, Captain," Phydel cuts in. "You have given us a victory today, and we cannot let that out of our sight. Follow Gils and get some rest. I will put everything into its rightful place with new sets of eyes and fresh weapons. Once my work is complete here, I will join you down below."

Coleena looks at the old man. He doesn't look tired at all. Actually, he looks more awake, even slightly younger beneath the red light of the dying sun and the rise of an early moon.

"My mother always said one cannot pass up good advice, Captain. If my ears do not deceive me, then this crazy old fool is speaking some of the best I've heard in a long time," Gils says.

His brother, red-faced and covered in black soot from head to toe, comes up and joins them. "We have some drinking to do, brother. Let's take the captain down with us and celebrate."

A big smile reveals a mouth full of teeth coated with the same spent powder tattooing his skin. Coleena looks over the men and women of the wall. They all watch her. Eyes darkened, skin pulled tight, they have all witnessed a nightmare today and have lived to see another day. That is what matters.

"All right, you talked me into it," she concedes. "One drink and then everyone is to get some rest. We have no idea when they'll come back, and we must be ready."

No one disagrees, and they begin the long procession down the stairwell. Wood creaks and the shadows of the night within the city begin their dance beneath the fires that welcome them home with open arms.

Spear tips and chain mail armor glint like grounded stars as those of Azhana United wait in an ordered mob around the bottom of the wall. Cheers and shouts surround her as they reach the ground.

She doesn't know what to say. Their numbers have swollen. Men and women of the rebel faction now intermix with those who wear no uniform at all. Thick work shirts, sturdy pants, and worn boots dress those who hold knives and bats. Wooden broom handles chiseled into points mingle with the demon killing spears as citizens of the city come to join the fight.

Looking over the gathering, faces of hundreds, if not a thousand, watch her every move. She looks for Summers. He must be somewhere, but she does not see him. Better off that way, she guesses. They were able to hold them off like they had hoped. His men and women, as brave as they are, were not able to help.

"Well done up there, Captain," a familiar voice whispers from behind her ear.

A shiver runs down Coleena's spine, but she does her best not to show it. Turning, Summers stands behind her, a genuine smile on his face, and a sparkle in his dark eyes.

"We gave them more than they could handle today," she says pulling away. He lifts a hand toward her shoulder but quickly drops it noticing the distance between them. "The men and women here will be ready when the battle starts again. You can rest assured that we will stand vigil while yourself and others get the rest they need," Roland offers.

She nods.

"Phydel is already taking care of the watch from above. You may keep those down here you believe necessary, but let them rest as well. We won't know until it's too late if they will be needed at a moment's notice."

Roland says nothing, his mouth opening and closing without a word. A big hand slams down on his shoulder, his weakened knee giving slightly beneath the added pressure.

"The Captain here is showing you how a real soldier celebrates such a victory, Gils says, his voice bellowing across the courtyard behind the gate. "For we have much to celebrate. We showed those monsters that we will not be pushed around. They will die upon our gates. They will not step one hellish claw within these walls as long as a single man or women of this city breathes."

The cheers through the soldiers and citizens is deafening. Coleena looks hard into Summers' eyes. Dark and uncertain.

It is true. Today was a hell of a victory. Hardly one that they should forget, but she has seen small battles like these turn in the blink of an eye. The gains of one day erased by the mistakes of the next. The big blacksmith in turn grabs her by the shoulder and begins to lead them back to the barracks.

"So what should we drink first?" he asks. "Something to put a fire in our bellies and help keep the horrors of this day deep into the back of our minds until the sun rises tomorrow."

Turning slightly, Coleena watches the dark figures of the soldiers manning the wall. Shadows masking everyone in the fire light as patrols work their way around the stone barrier.

Tomorrow. Could they really be lucky enough that the monsters wait to lick their wounds? A small tug pulls her back toward their destination while a tight ball begins to find its way deep into her gut.

"You should have seen the look on that monster's eyes as the Captain signaled for the cannons," Gils says, his words loud and heavy with alcohol. "I guarantee the first two rounds took out a hundred. Ripped them right from the ground and sent them flying back to hell!"

The laughter in the mess hall shakes the tent as the gathered soldiers cheer. Fabric ripples in the night breeze, the sour smell of beer and smoke filling the air as bodies push in to be close to one another.

Fires burn on posts at each corner and there are no servers this night. Men and women help themselves to kegs that have been tapped and the fear and darkness behind their eyes slips behind a drunken haze. Coleena sips at her own. Nursing the same drink since the moment they arrived, she watches over them all.

Let them get it out of their system. Nothing sobers a man like the cry of battle and though they may wake with a hangover, she hopes they will be ready when it comes.

"You did well up there today," Roland says, his hands wrapped tightly around his own glass.

He doesn't look any less haggard than he did before they reached the tent. Worry creases cut deep ravines through his forehead, his dark eyes watch more of the table than anything else. Much like her, she hasn't seen him get a second glass, let a lone actually sip from the one he has.

"Thanks," she replies. Taking a swig, the stuff is piss warm and a bit gritty. "The others did most of the work. I just kept them in line."

Summers runs a thumb over the rim of his glass, his eyes watching the small circles.

"Do you think we can hold out? At least until General Whittaker gets here?"

Taking a good hard look at the man, he is still the only one even thinking of the real dangers of this fight. Never one to let the moment wash him away, except maybe the other...

She pushes that thought away.

"Phydel tells me our stock of ammunition is higher than anyone gathered. It looks like Lieutenant Mason was a much smarter and cunning individual than we gave him credit for," she answers. "If the fighting keeps going the way it did today, we should have enough for several more days. That is plenty of time for Whittaker to get here."

"You are sure she is coming?"

This time she takes a deep swallow of her drink. The fire in her belly warming as it makes its way down. Without asking, someone pulls the glass from her hand and slides another in.

"As sure as I can be. There is no way to get any communication to her now that those monsters are here, and before that, only Parliament had that ability once Mason was removed. I guess we have to have hope somewhere if we are going to have it anywhere," she says.

Another swallow proves this glass is just as warm and gritty as the last.

"Speaking of those senators. Did anyone ever find those who did it?" Roland asks.

"Did what?"

"Hung them. They sure as well didn't tie themselves up there in the rafters," Summers answers.

Mind a little more cloudy than she wants it to be, Coleena tries to remember. Didn't she assign someone to...

Then it clicks. The one thing she forgot to do in the chaos of preparing for the assault. So many things to get in order.

Defensive lines.

Supplies.

Support for those who wouldn't be fighting.

But she forgot one important thing.

"Summers, we need to grab some of your best. Those half-breeds. I thought...," she can barely get the words out her mind is working too fast.

"What about them? Captain, what do you need?" Roland asks, both of them getting to their feet.

Those closest push away, their voices cutting as they realize something is happening. Others continue the party, cheers and demands for more beer cutting into the night.

"The half-breeds, Summers. They are leading this army, but there is more of them. The one I saw out on the field isn't the same from inside Parliament. Nor is it the bastard who attacked us in the alley," Coleena says as she pushes through the crowd, the air outside the tent just as sticky and warm as it is inside. "That means only one thing."

Roland steps up beside her, his cane returned and clacking against the stone walkway.

"What is it, Coleena?" he asks, both of them looking at the towering gates of Parliament city and the handheld torches marching across the top of the wall.

"They are still in here with us, Roland. Somewhere in this city, those half-breeds are waiting to strike," she says.

Across the city, the sharp report of gunfire begins to echo into the night. First a few rounds, then a slow build up that doesn't come from one wall but builds until it is coming from them all.

Coleena can feel her heart stop. The cold touch of death racing down her spine like ice. Gears grind over the shouts of men and women. Those still in the mess hall cheer as the sound of their demise continues to turn.

The bright tips of spears lower as the gates begin to open. Azhana United waits. Hundreds of men and women who refused to leave their posts stand between them and total annihilation as the walls of Parliament City begin to open and their end finally finds them.

Unarmed and waiting.

38

The darkness outside the city walls is a tidal wave waiting to come crashing in. With every agonizing inch, the barrier protecting the city from certain death spreads open and the inky void seeps its way in, the horrors outside fighting each other to be the first to spill through.

Shouts of alarm ring across the city as flashes of light pepper the night sky. Those fully disposed within the mess hall sober up and trip over themselves to get out onto the street, the sounds of war bringing them to their senses.

"What in the seven hells is going on?" Gils demands, his words full of anger and hate.

"To the walls! The gate has been breached!" Coleena orders.

She turns to Roland, his eyes wide but his face a stone façade of determination.

"What do you want me to do, Captain?" he asks, already beginning his journey to join the others of Azhana United.

"If any of them get in, hold them as long as you can. We

409

need to get those doors closed before the whole fucking underworld spills through."

Without a word he heads toward those preparing to fight anything that breaks its way through the widening gates. Shields of shinning iron and spears held at the ready, they wait.

Running past, Coleena can see their collective faces, hardened and determined. Young, old, it doesn't matter. They wait for their turn to defend the city. A part of her wants to stand at their side. Such tenacity. Bravery in the sight of pure destruction, but her charge is to prevent that destruction if she can.

Making her way to the entrance that has seen her into this city before, she throws open the door and enters the caverns within. Electricity flickers within the sparse lighting. A buzzing and crackling linger in the air as shadows fill in gaps between corners of walls and the pipes over her head. Water drips and the air is thick with humidity and the smell of blood.

Turning toward the gate, she knows the control room is a level up, built safely inside the center of the wall, there is only one way in and out. She left it heavily guarded. Two men at the stairs. Two at the door and three including the operator inside.

How could they have gotten them open?

Removing the revolver from her hip, she creeps down the hall, the last turn before the door to the stairwell a few steps ahead. A thick musky smell fills the air as the darkness blocks everything. Light bulbs shattered; the alcove is pure shadow.

Hands gripping tight, Coleena swings around the corner, pistol high and boot catching on something hard and heavy.

Her weight shifts, and she topples to the side, her shoulder hitting the wall as the rubber soles of her boots slip.

Blood is pooled in a thick dark mess. Spray coats the walls and the bodies of both men lay in tatters on the floor. Their weapons remain at their sides, the cold hard stairs of their eyes watching her with judgment and hatred.

Taking a deep breath, she opens the door slowly, a small creaking filling the dark void before her. Nothing attacks, not a single noise from within. Outside through the rock she can hear the shouts of soldiers and the vibration of weapons keeping the enemy at bay.

Monsters all around the city. In the darkness they must have surrounded and waited for their chance. The attack would have distracted them enough to get the gates open. Biting her lip, Coleena enters the stairwell and begins to slowly make her way up.

Metal steps sound an alarm with every step. There is no way whoever is up there will not know she is coming. But it doesn't matter. She can't see them anyway. There is no light up ahead. Darkness and an emptiness deeper than the pits of Hell sits in front of her, the weight of a million pounds of rock weighing on her shoulder with every step.

The stench of blood and death is king here. Blinded, her boot hits something that swings to the side before toppling itself down the stairs. Metal on metal, she could have thrown an iron pan down and made less noise.

Heart racing, throat dry, she reaches the top. A dead hand slaps the back of her leg as she presses against the body she didn't know was there. It takes everything she has not to put a bullet in the lifeless skull as she realizes it is one of the men she assigned to keep the control room safe. Blood still warm, Coleena pulls her hand away, no reason to check further. Whoever did this made sure they were thorough.

No mercy.

No survivors.

The door into the control room is closed. A solid barrier of nothingness with no way of knowing what waits for her on the inside. Cautiously, she reaches for the handle. Praying it isn't locked, she turns and the metal moves with her grip.

A small hope flickers in her gut. Methodical or not, they were careless to leave her an opening. Grip tightening around her weapon, she pushes the door open as slow as she can. She'll have a single shot at this. Take out whoever is inside and the close the gates. Trap whatever made it inside and hold the rest for as long as they can.

Holding her breath, she slides herself in. The gap between door and wall is big enough to fit her through but nothing more. Tiny lights of the control panels flicker, and a monitor sits at the end of the room cracked and sparking.

So much darkness. A body lays slumped on the desk of the controls, but there is no one else. Making her way across the room, she grabs the operator's chair and pulls them away.

Where is that closing control?

"I wouldn't waste my time trying to help if I were you?" a deep voice calls from the shadows.

Coleena spins, revolver out, she never gets a shot off before a sharp pain rips through her arm and sends the weapon flying. Clattering away in the darkness, a grip of iron wraps around her wrist, cracking bones before wrenching her arm behind her back.

"Such power, so much hatred," the voice hisses in her ear.

She can smell the sulfur on its breath, the feeling of stone beginning to grate against the skin of her arm. Trying to pull away, the monster tightens down on her wrist and her knees grow weak as the sheering of bones sends white-hot lances through her body.

"I'm going to kill you," she growls, the fire inside of her burning to let itself out.

"See, there it is. Can't you feel it? Our master knows what is inside of you. You are special in his eyes," the thing says before squeezing again and forcing her to her knees.

It steps around to look at her, all darkness in its cloak, the tiny cracks on its skin revealing the light of the magma beneath. Pulling back its hood she can see its missing ear and how much further the disease has spread across its face. He's barely recognizable as human with the amount of flaking stone stretching beyond one eye and engulfing his entire nose.

"You can tell your master that he is next," Coleena spits. "Once I'm finished with you and the thousands of your kind out there."

Lunching forward, she goes to strike him across the part of his face that still remains human. Not much of it left, she'll destroy whatever she can get a hold of. Her fist doesn't even make it halfway before his grip snaps around her neck, a vice that cuts off all air.

"Petty little thing. Such trivial responses. No wonder the master thinks so little of you vermin. Barely above animals," the monster says.

She tries to choke out a response. White flashes of stars form in her eyes against the backdrop of the shadowed room. Kicking and flailing with her arms, he keeps her far enough away that she is little more than a child. One that is slowly losing the feeling as her eyes struggle to stay open.

"Oh, wouldn't want you to die here, not now," he says dropping her to the floor. "Before I knew who you were it would have been acceptable to cut that beautiful heart of yours out. But now, no, the master would see me skinned alive. We can't have that, can we?"

Air rushes into Coleena's lungs as she gulps it down. Her stomach cramps and the world spins as the oxygen tries to work its way through her body.

"I... I will fucking kill you, you bastard," she croaks, her throat on fire. "You will never see your master again and the people of..."

He slaps her across the face, a blow that sends her sprawling to the floor. Her face slams against the side of the control desk for the main gate. Blood fills her mouth. The hot liquid is salty against her tongue, and she spits it on the floor. His steps are heavy against the stone, hundreds of pounds crushing down around her.

"No, you will watch as Parliament city and everyone within its walls are killed. We can start here, right at the gate," he says, his stone hand gripping the back of her shirt and pulling her back up.

She cannot resist him. Back on her feet, he drops her into the operator's chair, the corpse of the previous owner laying crumpled against the near wall. Green and flickering, the monitor shows the fighting on the other side of the screen.

Monsters pour through the door. Hundreds of them. Dark bodies burning red and orange with the magic of their master clogging the only way into the city. There in the fuzzy images, the screen cracked and spider webbing from corner to corner, she watches as Azhana United stands against the tide.

Men and women, shoulder to shoulder, they push back against the onslaught. Demon bodies blink out, their insides going cold as the spears slice through them like paper. The mad rush through the gate stalls, bodies crumbling beneath the jagged points of the killing weapons and the weighted claws of those rushing to get their first bites.

Defenders fall, their screams silent through the monitor, but the pain and anguish in their dying eyes easy to recognize. Where one perishes, another steps up. Those who fight with their lives for the city refuse to give ground. Coleena can feel the slow burn of defiance building in her heart. A tiny smile on her broken lips.

"Looks like your little plan isn't working so well," she says. "Enough of you die and you'll block the door yourselves with your corpses. Then what? Can't open a door made of stone."

The half-breed growls, grabs the back of her head, and slams it into the desk. The world around her goes white and red before it drops into nothingness. She does not feel anything when she hits the floor, but her eyes struggle to open as he lifts her up and shakes her until her bones begin to pop.

"It is only a matter of time before they punch through. There are too many of us. We can spare thousands; we will use tens of thousands if that is what it takes. This city will fall, and you will watch every last minute of it."

Coleena chuckles. He is right, there is nothing she can do. Her lower lip stings as the salt in her blood burns the broken skin, and she spits it in his face, the feeling of satisfaction giving her a little strength.

"The citizens of Azhana will never give up," she says, her legs unable to hold her weight as he lets her go.

Falling to her knees, she tries to move but there is no strength, and she lets herself shift until she is seated on her ankles. The fires beneath the man's skin flare an angry red, his eyes glaring coals that burn brighter than anything else in the room.

"You insolent little pest. I'm thinking I'll have to make an example of you. Master will not approve, but what he doesn't know won't kill him. You're a brave soldier. It was tragic to watch you fall from the top of the wall in all of the fighting."

Grabbing her again, Coleena does what she can to lean back and pull away from his grip. Shirt tearing, his claws rip gouges through her shoulder and chest as his hand comes away. A flash of silver brightens the surrounding darkness, her dog tags coming free to lay upon her chest.

"What are these?" he asks, his eyes narrowing on the silver chain.

He reaches forward, this time using his clawed finger to pull the medallions away from her skin without tearing it. On instinct, Coleena grabs the dog tags herself, the sudden need to stop him overwhelming and impossible to prevent.

"Do not touch..." she starts, her words full of conviction before all the world burns away in a bright white light full of pain and suffering.

THE PAIN IS GONE, NOTHING BUT SILENCE REMAINS IN HER mind.

Is this a dream?

Coleena is no longer inside Parliament City's walls. A hot breeze blows across her exposed back, the touch of tiny needles against her skin which radiates a heat of its own. Something is different.

Opening her eyes, she is kneeling in the dirt, blood, and caked mud spread across the earth. Her arms are burned beyond recognition. The skin peels back into large chunks that shrivel into black flakes.

There is no pain.

Reaching over, she goes to tear a piece away, the numbing feeling of her body too much to bear. A clawed finger taps at the skin the damaged skin. Shrieking, she pushes away from the ground.

Her hands.

They are gone.

She is...what have they done to her? Looking around, her mind races. She recognizes this place. The trees, the sky. This can't be true.

Obrathe.

Her home.

The roar of a thousand demons spins her around. Her body no longer resisting the forgotten pain and it moves with a power she has never felt.

The walls of Obrathe still stand. There are no burn marks, the rocks and mortar still strong. More of the monsters spill out into the open, their movements shaking the ground at her feet.

A dark shadow passes overhead, a shrill cry that cracks her ears and the monsters lined before her answer in kind. Trees sway as the dragon flaps its gigantic wings. Branches break, trunks split and moan.

Coleena takes another look at herself. Muscles of stone ripple, her clawed hands flex, and her skin breaks and hardens again. She is one of them, but how can this be?

Tiny bits of cloth hang from where they have caught

against her stone hide. She reaches down and tears a piece away. Military uniform. A shade of light brown with splatters of red drying into dark stains.

Those men. The ones that saved her. They wore uniforms just like these. How can this?

The monsters roar again and inside of her the fire ignites. Without thinking, she roars back and the first two rows of Banshees and Gorgoths step back.

Their faces of stone change. She can recognize that now. Doubt, confusion, even fear cracks the tiny surfaces as the monsters hesitate. The anger and guilt, twenty-five years of frustration built up within her boils over, and she roars again.

Several of the demons stumble and she has had enough. Claws digging into the ground, she charges at their front lines. For once in her life she can go one on one with these bastards. Kill her they may, but at last she will take as many out with her as she can.

Claws rip through stone like wet paper. Magma bursts into the air like tiny volcanoes as banshees split and die beneath her rage. Gorgoths fight back, their muscles and claws gripping onto her, but their hatred is nothing compared to everything that has built up inside her all of her life.

One grabs her arm, pulls it back and the stone muscles begin to split. Growling in pain and the hypnotic trance of chaos, Coleena spins and the stone heals as she drives her hand claws first into the monster's face. Bright orange liquid as thick as oil bursts out through the demon's head, streams of it pouring to the ground and cooling into brittle rock as the corpse goes cold and crumbles at her feet.

Two banshees jump onto her back, their tiny hands and claws scratching at her neck and eyes, but she grabs them both with hands that cover their entire heads. Squeezing, laughing, she feels their skulls begin to crack and the insides burst like a balloon as the bodies crumble.

Monsters back away, the devastation she has brought onto them forming a circle of death marked by broken gravestones of volcanic rock. She chases them until many flee back into the city, where they cower behind its protective walls. A few do not make it. Banshees burst and are thrown over the barrier in pieces while a Gorgoth sees itself put straight through the rock and splitting as it lands on the other side.

Power, rage, and unbridled anger flows through her like life. She can kill them all. Wherever her body hurts, it goes away in the quick moment it takes for the stone to cool. Her hand and claws flex. Gray ash of the dying beasts flakes away from the razor sharp tips at the end of her fingers.

Yes, she will kill them all. One by one she will slaughter them until this world is safe. Her revenge for an entire lifetime of fighting and scrambling to survive will be complete.

The roar of the one that brought all of this into being rattles the ground. She looks up at the sky. Its dark shadow spreads across the land, and she screams back in defiance.

No words, just the undeniable challenge of one monster against another.

The air spins in circles as the dragon comes lower. Coleena spreads her arms, muscles flexing and claws tapping as she waits. Her whole life has come down to this. Her against the monster that took this world from her.

No, she cannot shoot it down from the sky, but she can rip it limb from limb. The fury burning within her explodes with anticipation. Its long body comes into view as it drops beneath the clouds of ash and smoke that sits over Obrathe. Wings of stone scales bend and push at the world, the very air crackling with the magic the beast carries.

Coleena digs her heels into the ground. She will not give it a chance to attack. Pouncing at the first available moment, she will shred it until it is nothing more than the smoking ruin it has left her home.

Legs as thick as a truck touch the ground, feet with toes of solid boulders spread and crack the ground for several feet. A wall of dust lifts into the air like a cloud. Swiveling its head, the long snout and giant fangs drip with steaming magma as it turns toward her.

Red coals of fire watch her charge forward. There will be no quarter here. Launching herself with her new strength, her stone body lifts off the ground, and she finds a hold as her hand drives through scales and into the living stone along the side of the beast's head.

A shriek of pain and fire erupts from the demon's mouth. The nearest wall of Obrathe is consumed in seconds, the rock reduced to rubble, ash, and sizzling molten rock. Coleena tears her hand away and rakes at the monster's face.

Claws remove scales by the dozen as the creature shakes its head. Her mind goes a million miles a second as she beats into its hide, her glorious victory at hand.

Wings beating, the devil god springs from the ground, large hooks of stone from its wings racking its body in an attempt to dislodge her. Snarling, Coleena digs in deeper. Large streams of orange blood pour from the beast's face.

Jamming her fist in again, she grabs hold and rips another piece off, magma spraying across her body. The smell of sulfur is everywhere as the smoke envelopes them. If her eyes were still hers, they would tear, but pain and smoke mean nothing to her. Lost in her glory, she does not feel the claw hook into her back, one gigantic wing ripping her from the monster's face.

Before she can realize it, she is spiraling through the air, the burning remains of Obrathe spinning beneath her as the world of Azhana rushes up to meet her.

A new pain rips through her body as she splatters against the killing field. Her world spins and the inside of her mouth burns as orange blood pools inside and outside. Willing herself to move, she begins to climb to her feet. Large pockets of stone remain where she fell, her body falling apart faster than it can repair itself.

"You defy me!" a strange voice screams in her head.

Coleena grits her pointed teeth, the magma hardening and her eyes burning within her head with hatred and malice.

"I will deny you every day of my life. I will fight, tooth and nail, blood by bloody drop until the day I see you fall to the ground at my feet," she yells back, her own voice locked within the confines of her skull.

The dragon lands in front of her, large talons ripping gouges out of the earth. Heat radiates from the creature's body, waves of magic that melt and transform everything around it into molten rock and sulfuric gas.

Coleena squeezes her talons and roars in defiance. The monster roars back, its maw opening to reveal row upon row of dragon glass teeth and a throat full of fire.

"You will never have this world!" Coleena shouts, the words in her head and the growl of her inhuman body calling out as she stumbles forward with her best attempt at a charge.

A ball of fire swirls within the dragon's throat, its eyes burning bright as the magic bursts forward. Heat and pain sears Coleena's body, a pain like nothing she has ever felt before washes over her.

The one thing she hates the most stares at her, its demon head roaring with flames and magic watch as the flames consume her body. She will not give up. She can never give in. With one final effort Coleena lunges forward before the flames wash everything away.

39

The world of her reality flashes back with a cold hard fist. The light disappears, her eyes burned blind as the force of the magic sends her sprawling against the wall. The monster once holding her is thrown away as well, his half-breed body knocking a large chunk of the wall down with him.

Coleena tries to crawl and get to her feet, the pain and the fighting taking a toll on her body. The world spins as the tiny lights within the room come back into focus. She sees the dark figure opposite of her begin to move, a crawling motion that sounds like two rocks grating into one another.

Scrambling, she feels the floor with her hand, a desperate hope she might find her revolver or one of the dead dropped rifles discarded by the dead guards. A fist of stone grabs a chunk of her hair and pulls her to her feet. Head arched backward; she refuses to give the creature the satisfaction of hearing her squeal in pain.

"What was that?" it demands. "How did you show me those things?"

So, he could see it too.

Coleena looks into the bright red eyes that fill the man's sockets. Coals of fire burning so bright she has a hard time keeping the water building within her own from running down her cheeks. She spits in its face.

Gripping tighter, she can feel the hair and scalp ripping from her head. She cannot stop the gasp of pain as the warm feeling of blood begins to trickle down the back of her neck.

"You will tell me how you did that," the monster demands.

"I'd have you kill me first," Coleena chokes out, her words cut as he arches her head further back exposing the unprotected flesh of her neck.

"One way or the other, I will get what I want," the half-breed sneers.

Grabbing the dog tags with a clawed hand, it rips it from her body and this time there is no flash of light. He dangles them in front of her face. She watches as the small pieces of metal sway back and forth, dull and lifeless in the darkened control room.

He growls and throws them to the opposite wall. She watches them fly until they disappear beneath the shadows. Pulling her close, she can smell the sulfur of his breath as his mouth opens.

"If you will not tell me, my master will take it from you," he threatens. "His power is the greatest this world has ever known. He can get inside your head and there is nothing you can do to stop him. You will tell him your secrets. You will tell him everything."

Coleena smiles. Her mind clears as her eyes go from the hideous scars upon the half-breed's face to the place in the wall where her reminder of why they fight lays. They are only small pieces of punched metal. A gift from a dying man and the identification of what she does. Not who she is.

She turns back to the demon and her smile is genuine and full of promise. His face burns with the magma that pulses beneath.

"You can tell your master something for me," she says, her voice hardly more than a whisper. The half-breed squeezes harder and pulls her close enough that they are practically kissing, his head tilted to bring his remaining ear forward. "Tell him that I'm coming for him again, and this time, he won't stop me."

Sliding her hand from the top of her boot, the blade makes no sound as it clears the sheath and then plunges into the man's gut. Eyes going wide, he tries to push her away, but she takes a firm grip on his cloak and holds him close.

Ripping the weapon up, she feels the molten blood beneath begin to pour over her hand and wrist. The skin burns with its touch, but she refuses to let go. Tearing her way through his innards, she doesn't stop until she hits bone, and even then, she pushes in deeper. The smell of burning flesh fills the room.

Dark blood begins to spill from the half-breed's mouth. Not melted rock, the last bit of humanity still left in him leaking away as the knife twists and cuts through stone and tissue alike. The red coals of his eyes begin to dim. She watches as they cool, the shadows sinking in until there is nothing left but tiny pebbles.

Body lifeless beneath her, she tumbles until she lands against the desk of computer panels, pain pulsing through her arm and the sound of combat on the other side of the wall returning. She needs to shut the door, but how?

She does not want to look at her hand. Whatever is left

of it cannot be of any use. The green light of the monitor flickers and sparks. From the floor she can see the bodies still pressing forward through the open gate. Somehow the flood is still clogged and unable to move.

Grinding her teeth, Coleena rolls to her good side and shifts until she is on her knees in front of the keyboard cradling her hand against her chest. Nausea cramps in her stomach and with her good hand she pushes everything else on the desk to the floor.

Bodies lay everywhere the camera can see. Humans. Demons. Most indistinguishable beneath the carnage. Looking closer, she can see that one of the doors themselves has been all but ripped from its bearings. Wood splintered and burned, there will be no way of shutting them now.

The city is lost.

Eventually the numbers will be all that matters, and they will push through. There is only one thing left to do and that is to fight to the last man. Closing her eyes, pinching them shut as tight as she can, Coleena lifts and puts her devastated arm on the desk.

She has to see what is left. Can she even pick up a rifle? The pain begins to dull as she flexes her fingers, the nerves within dying. Tiny bit by tiny bit, her vision clears, and the green light of the screen reflects off the untouched blade held within her grasp.

Her hand and arm are not burned. The skin is tender as she moves it back and forth, but the monster's blood did not take a part of her with it. Skin swollen and red, she somehow still has every digit.

How can this be?

She shakes her head. It doesn't matter. All that matters is getting out there and doing what she can to help.

Steadying herself, she gets to her feet and stumbles

toward the door. Her legs are weak, muscles ache, head pounds, but she will not let it stop her. Hand on wall, she slides down the hallway. The sound of water dripping, the smell of blood and shit fills the passage. Down the stairs, over bodies gone cold and hard. She tries not to look at them.

The sound of the fighting grows louder the closer she gets to the doorway that will lead her out. What electricity helps light the tunnel flickers and struggles more as the world shakes beneath her feet. Screams and roars are so close now she can almost tell them apart. Gritting her teeth, she squeezes the knife in one hand and the rifle she picked up in the other.

One last fight.

One final battle.

If the dragon wants her, it'll have to come and get her. This city is for the people of Azhana. It will not fall as long as she is still breathing.

Finding the doorway out, she turns the handle and hits it with her shoulder. Hinges creak and the thunder of life and death hits her like a train. Dust and smoke fill the air. Bodies lay everywhere.

Human.

Monster.

Torn to shreds, she can barely tell them apart and thick black rivers of blood and cooling rock run between outstretched limbs and holes torn through the earth.

Taking the steps to the ground as fast as she can, the onslaught stops her in her tracks. The wall of Azhana United is holding a river ready to break its banks. Masses of black bodies, living stone built only for the destruction of the human race, push against the thin layer of men and women who still stand shoulder to shoulder.

Spears thrust forward, bright orange and fire red blood bursts as metal cuts through and the demons die. The weight of those that follow flexes and the line staggers back. Citizens, none of them soldiers, help push back, adding their own weight to the mess.

Like a bubble about to burst, the defenders try to plug the door. For a moment, Coleena tries to spot Summers.

Where is he?

It is a mess and total chaos. Impossible to spot him in a sea of bodies and corpses. Aiming her rifle, she fires off several rounds as she approaches. Bullets ping off and a few find purchase as they tear into the enemies' hard flesh. None of them bother to look her direction. Between spears cutting their way through them and bullets raining down from above, the kill zone comes from all sides and monsters have enough bodies to compensate.

Coleena can feel the ground move beneath her as the war machine of the dragon pushes with another burst. Her gun clicks and she does not have another magazine. Gripping the knife, she holds it in front of her, looking for a place to step in and do the only thing she knows to do.

A roar bursts from the back ranks of the enemy. So deep and low it sounds more like the wall coming down than anything that could have come from the throat of a living being. Even the demons pushing the front-line stagger and stop. A dark shadow looms forward through the gateway. Men and women from atop the wall scream but their words are lost to ears that can no longer hear anything but death and fighting.

A beast like nothing Coleena has ever seen before shoves its way through the mass. Well over ten feet tall, its shoulders crush banshees as it forces its way in between the gate walls. Creatures large and small try to get out of the way, but they are trapped.

A tidal wave created by the behemoth sends the demons forward and the wall of Azhana United falters. Caught between the struggle and the shock, she watches as three men at the center buckle beneath the press and fall. The valve opens and there is no stopping the current.

Spears cut through many as they press the new advantage, but the protection of the line is gone. Human screams begin to echo as claws rip into flesh and the new beast, a Gorgoth grown almost double in size, slams into anything and everyone in its path. Demons and humans alike die beneath its fury.

Coleena runs forward, knife in hand she jumps onto the back of the nearest Gorgoth. Her knife buries itself into the back of its skull. The rock parts like warm flesh. Bright orange blood spits out and this time burns the skin on her cheek, but she lets the pain bury itself deep inside of her mind.

Ripping, the blood and matter inside spill out and the hundreds of pounds of rock crumble beneath her. She goes down hard, a shock wave running its course through her body as the ground meets her. Mud, blood, and guts splatter across her burning face, and she rolls to the side.

A woman screams, her chest opened down to her navel as she falls. Spear and shield clatter to the ground.

Sharp hands cut into Coleena's shoulder. Claws rip through her uniform and shoulder until it hits the meat inside. Grabbing the shield, she rolls and thrusts it as hard as she can into the face of the banshee. Eyes of fire diminish for a split moment. Stunned, she rams her knife into its belly and rips to the side.

A thick stream of rock spews and falls onto the corpse of

the woman beside her. The stench of cooking meet fills her lungs, and she gags as she struggles to reach her knees. Another roar rumbles the ground behind her.

Gripping the fallen spear, Coleena turns and thrusts it as hard as she can. The silver point punches through the Gorgoth's chest, its mouth opening in a howl of agony before dropping to its knees.

She wrenches her weapon free as the dead rock tumbles, and she turns in time to catch another's swipe at her with extended talons. The wood of her spear snaps but not before she buries the spear head in its neck.

Anger flaring in its eyes, it swats her across the body and sends her rolling across the torn earth. Rocks cut into her skin. The blood and bowels of the men and women defending the city cover her body and her muscles scream for a break as she tries to get back to her feet.

Arms shake with every effort. She watches as the mass of enemies inches forward, the monstrous Gorgoth standing in their center. The smaller ones keep their distance.

Coleena makes it to one knee, a hand finding a broken spear next to her. Others back away slowly, some with shields and spear, others with makeshift weapons. Several of the citizens who came to fight turn and run. Banshees scream and give chase.

The defenders of the city are broken. Scattered in a line too shredded to close, they give ground. There is what she can describe as a smile on the massive monster's face. It is savoring this moment. The triumph they have been promised and fought all this way to collect.

Muscles made of jelly, Coleena gets to her feet. If she is going to die here, she will do it standing. Extending her arm, she holds the deadly end of the spear toward the heart of the one that has come to collect her.

"You will have to kill us all," she says, her arm shaking with fatigue.

The red fires of the demon's eyes brighten, tiny flames licking over brows of stone. It flexes its talons as long as her forearm and the beasts standing beside it shriek and gaggle with anticipation.

A whistle cuts through the air like a hot knife. Ear piercing, it turns heads as it grows louder. Coleena has heard this before. Her eyes widen, and she jumps to the side, her hands coming to cover her head as the world explodes into a fiery ball.

Rock and earth, shrapnel and body parts are obliterated in an instant. Dust and smoke fill the air. It is hard to breathe. Each breath chokes and tastes of ash. The ground vibrates with the aftershock.

Coleena can't hear anything other than a distant ringing in her ears. She gets to her knees, but the world is spinning, and she falls down again.

Bodies lay scattered everywhere. Humans and demons. Rocks covered in glowing magma stick out like tombstones and the defenders of Azhana who still live try to regain their footing.

Where the army of the dragon stood there is nothing more than a crater underneath a cloud of dust. Two more bombs go off. Both of them hit outside the wall sending mushroom clouds of black into the air. The hundreds still fighting to get inside the walls turn and face their new enemy.

Another shock wave rattles the ground as the central mass of demons erupts in a fiery blast. Coleena lets her head rest on the ground, her eyes on the sky.

Small specs of blue try to peek their way between clouds and smoke. Her eyes burn so much the tears run down her cheek like rain. The salt burns along the injuries to her face. Her body feels like it has been run over a million times, but she doesn't care.

Her hearing comes back slowly. Voices at a distance call for help. The screams of death and the pleas of those that think they can be saved. Gunshots rattle like drums from the walls and the advancing army surrounding the demons.

More eruptions as mortars and grenades rip into the lines. The howls and shrieks pollute the calmness of the afternoon sky and Coleena just watches it go by.

General Whittaker has made it. Parliament City is saved. A man comes up to her. She does not recognize him. He's asking if she is all right. She waves him off.

Her job here is complete. The city is saved. She will live to fight another day.

40

———

The smoke clears, the sky is bright, and the smell of ash and death fades into an all too recent memory. A warm breeze pushes its way through city streets carrying with it a feeling that tells of the changing of time.

Soldiers march through the streets. Armed guards on patrol. No one finds fault with their presence. Welcomed in, the Army gives those who lost everything the strength to know that the world will go on.

The dead are buried. The living care for those who are wounded and those who fought have stories they will carry with them for the rest of their days. Coleena watches the passing of time from the top of the wall. The gates of Parliament City are open and inviting as people from around Azhana continue to migrate to the home of those who fought back the dragon.

"You did one hell of a job here, Captain," General Whittaker says.

The woman steps up beside her, her ageless features firm and those eyes staring out at the battlefield still stripped bare and scarred. Coleena looks her over once before turning back to the world outside the city.

"I only did what I knew I had to do," Coleena responds. "You never sent me here to investigate the attacks, did you?"

The woman's face never cracks as she watches the sun begin to set in the west.

"There was always hope you would find the answer before it escalated to this. You are skilled beyond what you know, Captain, but yes, I needed you here should our worst dreams have come to reality."

Coleena turns toward her, the motion painful with every bone in her body cracking. Stitches itch all over her body and the tightness in her cheek makes it hard to speak.

"So, you knew the city was in danger. But still, you didn't tell anyone?" she asks.

The General takes a deep breath before turning toward her. Her eyes are cold and the scare on her face twitches.

"I warned those sniveling idiots a hundred times, and they ignored me every step of the way. I'm not sure when the dragon's agents started working on them, but I've been fighting the conspiracy that I want to rule all of Azhana for a long time. Never could get it through their thick skulls that my place is here on the battlefield. Like you, my only mission is to see that monster dead and buried."

Whittaker turns back to the horizon, the golden rays highlighting new lines of gray that have made their way into the woman's hair. Coleena follows her gaze, content to watch the passing of time as well.

"Well, I should be getting back to Parliament. Elections will need to be held once all the repairs in the city are complete. Government won't run by itself," Whittaker says. "Take all the time you need, Captain, but come find me when you feel ready for your next assignment."

Coleena goes to respond but the general is already walking away, her steps long and powerful. Realizing the woman is correct, she turns back to the world surrounding their city. Yes, she needs a break. These last couple of weeks have been hell and it will kill her if she doesn't stop. A good rest will do her some good.

"Haven't been hiding from me, have you?" Summers asks.

Turning her head, she sees him leave the stairwell opening to the top of the wall, his cane clicking on the stone beside him. A long set of stitches runs down the side of his face, zigzagging its way from eye to chin, and his skin has taken a poor pasty look, but the man is still alive.

"Why would I do that?" she asks, the urge to smile hard to keep back. She can't argue her relief when they pulled him from the rubble. Still alive, though not kicking as he would have probably preferred, and moderately OK. "There is still a lot of work to be done around here."

He steps up beside her, his body close but not enough to touch.

"Plenty of people here to do that. You saved this city, Coleena. Without you, we'd all be dead and who knows about the rest of the world," he says leaning heavily on his cane.

"And what about you? Are you going to stand there and act like you had nothing to do with Azhana United and the fact that they held the monsters back with their very lives when the gate opened?" she asks.

He shrugs.

"We do what we have to do. Azhana United is built to stand for this city and its people no matter who leads it. Long after I'm gone it will remain until this world is free of the dragon and its minions."

Coleena can smile to that. Reaching up, she takes the dog tags that they retrieved from the control room and watches the fading sunlight reflect off the smooth surfaces.

Azhana United.

Maybe not such a bad idea. The sound of construction fills the air, and they both stand there quietly as the day ends and the night begins its vigil.

"You know, we never did get to talk about that other night," Summers starts. "I found out so..."

She cuts him off with a finger to his lips. Moving in closer, she lets him put an arm around her shoulders and the feeling of him against her helps relax the aches and pains of her body.

"No need, Roland. All of that is behind us now. The world needs some time to recover and so do we. I have a lot to think about. We...have a lot to think about. Azhana has a rough future ahead of it. This didn't win us the war; it was only a single battle."

Roland squeezes her tight as he stands up a little straighter, his cane leaning against his leg.

"Do you still think we have a chance?" he asks.

She doesn't answer him. Looking at the moon high above and the twinkling of the first stars, she knows the answer. Deep down where she once asked that very question, the embers of doubt are cold and dead.

There will never be any second-guessing what humankind can do against these monsters. They will never give up. One day, no matter how long it takes, mankind will see these gods destroyed. They will watch as their magic is extinguished, and their corpses lay in smoke and ruin.

She hopes she'll be there when it happens. Her own boot resting on top of the dragon's head, but if not, she can rest assured it will happen.

One day. Somehow. The dragons will die.

EPILOGUE

The old man stops and turns, the climb slow but good for his ancient limbs. The air is fresh, clean, a turning of a new leaf. He watches the smoke rise into the air. Tiny little chimneys at this distance, limbs of black that stretch into the sky and disappear into a sea of blue.

Taking a deep breath, he feels good about himself. Another battle has been won, but the war is far from over. So much more to do before his job is complete.

He has confidence though. Some would say that wagering on the outcome of war is like counting your chickens before they hatch, but he has never been one for doing anything fairly. No, he knows where the golden ticket is hidden, and he has no desire to give it up.

Battles and wars. Death and decay. They are good at all of it. The walls of Parliament City still stand. Black as death, they circle and hold safe those within. A structure built by a people who refuse to die.

A smile creeps its way across his face. A wisp of hair

tickles his nose before he taps it and returns it to his head. Yes, this is the one thing they are truly superb at.

Survival.

Tenacity.

Like little roaches, you may kill millions, if not billions of them, but the fuckers refuse to go away. Down there a secret waits. His egg that will take generations to hatch. He takes another breath and the uneasiness that always builds when taking a risk comes back.

They may always find a way to live, but they also live on the edge of a knife. Go one way, and they will see the end of this journey. One he has set them upon. Slip the to the other, and they will cut their own throat.

A chill runs down his spine with the coming of the breeze. From the north, over the mountain a storm waits. The remnants of another choice. A darker choice.

That seed gone wrong still waits within the frozen soil. Not ready to let it mature, he bides his time. When the world is ready, the time to face those consequences will test them all.

Pulling his white jacket tighter around his body, he tries to see the outcome of what lays ahead. In the lands beyond those jagged teeth, a nightmare waits for them to awaken it from its slumber.

Sleep my little nightmare.

Your time is not here, yet.

He glances back to the city in the distance and the secrets that he has planted. Growing, they will either become a monster or the weapon they will need more than they know.

With a shrug of his shoulders he turns back to the mountains. A long walk, but he has the time. No rush. He will be here when they need him, and with his next step the wind howls. A brief roar that shakes the trees and rattles tiny pebbles down the hill.

Where the old man stood within the clearing nothing remains. Only footprints. Deep, large, and clawed. The roar echoes and in the distance, beyond the peaks, beyond the deserts and unknown plains, the call is answered.

The dark time of reckoning is coming.

ABOUT THE AUTHOR

William (Roh) Seymour is the author of Dark Fantasy which includes the titles Dark Choices, Merchant, and Pestilence. He lives with his family in southern Pennsylvania where he writes into the darkness of the night. You can find out more about him at his website.

www.worldsbyroh.com

ALSO BY WILLIAM J. SEYMOUR

Dark Choices

Merchant

Pestilence

Trail of Darkness

www.ingramcontent.com/pod-product-compliance
Lightning Source LLC
Chambersburg PA
CBHW030142200726
48285CB00004BC/1288